Sam North

Sam North is a Senior Lecturer in Screenwriting at the University of Portsmouth.

He devides his time between the UK and Canada. In Vancouver he actively participates in the Cold Reading series for writers and actors and Bolts of Fiction readings. He recently exhibited his 'Out of Season' travel photography at the IronWorks gallery Vancouver.

Sam is the founding editor of www.hackwriters.com an award winning writers' magazine and a member of the Writer's Guild of Great Britain.

Also by Sam North

(Fiction)
209 Thriller Road
Eeny Meeny Miny Mole * as Marcel d'Agneau
Ramapo
Going Indigo
Diamonds – The Rush of '72

(Radio Dramas)
The Devil's Dog
Final Accounts
Adventures with Randolph Stafford
Copycats
The War in Drab Nebula

(Screenplays)
The Pushover
Got it Bad

The Curse of the Nibelung – A Sherlock Holmes Mystery

Some reviews from the first edition:

"The triumphant return of Holmes and Watson."

Eric Hiscock – The Bookseller

"Chocolate will never seem quite the same again. With an irresistible, high-quality Goon-like zaniness, this dynamically paced thriller follows its own larger-than-life logic. Not to be missed."

Richard Pearce – Sunday Express

"Supremely enchanting..."

John Stonehouse – Books and Bookmen

"A splendid spoof, even better than the author's earlier parody of Le Carré, 'Eeny Meeny Miny Mole.'"

Francis Geoff – Sunday Telegraph

"Ingenious. So well crafted that the entertainment value is not in doubt. Others will certainly try to update Holmes and do far less well. Follow that, as they say."

Southern Evening Echo

The Curse of the Nibelung – A Sherlock Holmes Mystery

December 1939. Germany and Great Britain are in the fog of the phoney war. The First Sea Lord Winston Churchill knows that England is not ready for the fight, she could lose against the might of Germany. Four British spies have perished in strange circumstances in Nuremberg trying to discover the biggest secret of the Third Reich. Churchill turns to the only man he knows who can solve the mystery. But Sherlock Holmes is 83 now, Dr Watson even older. Are they still up to it? They must cross the Channel, pretending to be German sympathisers. If caught, England will disown them.

Holmes accepts the challenge; indeed he has been awaiting the call. They will solve the mystery, or die in the attempt. Two ancient men of England and one beautiful nurse enter enemy territory. Their loyalty will be tested, more than once, and there is no one they can trust. The secret of Nuremberg is more sinister than even Holmes could imagine; their chances of getting back alive very slim indeed.

———

This edition © Sam North 2005

ISBN 1-4116-3748-8
The right of Sam North to be identified as the author of this work has been asserted by him in accordance with the Copyright, Designs and Patents Act 1988.

———

Previous Edition British Library Cataloguing in Publication Data:
D'Agneau, Marcel – The Curse of the Nibelung I.
Title 823'.914 (F) PR6054.A32/ISBN 0 85140 561 4.

Foreword to the first edition, published in 1981

It is a tragedy that the full facts of Sherlock Holmes' last case have been kept from the British public for so long. For fifty years, a network of 'old boys' have sat on this story, claiming the events as untrue and preposterous. Winston Churchill himself, refused to release his personal diaries during his lifetime. It is only now, that the true story about this most daring adventure may be told.

From notes made at the time by Dr Watson (painfully done, considering his arthritis), and including certain private letters and diaries from the late Winston Churchill, I have reconstructed the events as they took place in the early months of the second world war. I have done my best to render the truth as near to the facts as possible. And it is with admiration and astonishment, given the great ages and physical condition of Lord Sherlock Holmes and Dr John Watson, that I relate their adventure against the Third Reich, undertaken by them with complete disregard for personal risk.

Foreword to the second edition, published in 2005

History often repeats itself. First as tragedy, then as farce. Almost before the ink dried on the first edition of *The Curse of the Nibelung* in 1981, containing as it did long surpressed details of Sherlock Holmes' final swansong, his bravest and most audacious case, events intervened yet again to bury this moment in UK history.

The publisher, who shall be nameless, after approaches from a certain 'éminence grise' took it upon himself to bury the book. The author was powerless to prevent this and indeed had to endure a further twenty-four years before the rights were obtained once again. Only death unlocked this volume.

Now, freed from chains, *The Curse of the Nibelung* is again available to anyone to read. 'Patience if often a way to defeat your most evil of enemies,' Sherlock Holmes would often declare, and it is true. I hope that you, the reader will find this book and guard it well from those who still do not wish its contents to be widely known. Defend the truth and you will live long enough to defeat your enemies.

Sam North – Southsea – August 2005.

The Curse of the Nibelung
A Sherlock Holmes Mystery
Sam North

Lulu Press

USA

www.lulu.com

The Baker Street Bunker

The afternoon fog, thick with sulphur, appeared laced into the very fabric of London town. The City lay in wait for a breeze, long needed these past three days. Figures stumbled through the streets with handkerchiefs clasped to their mouths, eyes stinging, cursing a winter that seemed to have lasted forever. In this December 1939 there was little to rejoice about; little to think about except the unfortunates in Poland, the bravery of the Finns and the fear that London could be next. Their only hope could be that the Germans would take one look at the fog and forget the whole thing; annex somewhere warmer, like Spain. General Franco was a natural friend, let Herr Hitler have Seville. South African oranges were just as good, the English could adapt to a different flavour marmalade, they were made of stern stuff, such hardships they could bear.

It was growing dark already, the gaslights were being lit (the new sodium lamps not having been installed in this corner of London just yet) not increasing forward vision one jot. This pea-souper was one of the worst in living memory, already accounting for some deaths in Stepney.

Gliding out of the gloom, a large black Humber Snipe Imperial swept down an usually quiet Baker Street, gingerly coming to a halt outside a smog-blackened residence not far from Mr Anderson's Tobacco shop, a favourite with those who felt Pall Mall too far to go for their favourite blend.

"A dozen Havanas, Calthorpe," a deep, baritone voice growled from the rear seat. "Make sure the things are well oiled. Get Anderson to roll them out for you, the last lot were a damned embarrassment to the whole industry."

"Yes sir." Calthorpe was not well disposed to this task. Fetching the First Lord of the Admiralty's cigars was a dangerous mission. The last two chauffeurs had made the foolish mistake of thinking any cigar would do and Calthorpe liked his job, at least it kept him out of the army. His patriotism was served well enough ferrying the 'old war horse' about London.

"Then wait for me Calthorpe, I shall be busy for a while."

"Sir," Calthorpe answered, never one for the excess word.

His charge waited until he had rounded the car and opened his door, then with the aid of the chauffeur's gloved hands, he eased himself out from the embrace of the Humber's leather seats and attained his full stoop on the pavement outside 221b Baker Street. His face flushed with the effort. He stood and contemplated the front door as damp fog encircled them.

"It's a long time since I've stood outside this door, Calthorpe. History will record this address as one of the most famous in all London, yet look, it is a ramshackle place, needs a lick of paint, I'll say."

"The address does seem familiar sir," began Calthorpe.

The First Lord shook his head at him. "Forget you ever saw it Calthorpe, you never saw this place. Now... the cigars man."

Calthorpe left his side and the large, rotund, balding man adjusted his heavy overcoat and ambled forward to the black painted door, up three clean, scrubbed steps from the pavement. The dense, yellow fog swirled around him, enveloping all, absorbing even the Humber, parked at the curbside. A pudgy hand lifted a cane and rapped on the door with some force, three times in all and he heard with satisfaction the echo resound along the hall inside. He cursed the damp, the weather, the war, the slowness of everything. He cursed Mrs Hudson, wondering why she took so long to answer his summons. Then recalled that she might be a bit long in the tooth by now – ninety odd if a day. If she was alive at all. He rapped again impatiently, wondering if Clemmie, his dear wife, had been entirely right in thinking that this sojourn to Baker Street would be a waste of time. It was too late, far too late, she had mused that morning to call in his old friends from the past, no matter how successful they had been in times now forgotten. How utterly reliable they had been then. There had to be a limit, a time when one was past one's best and heaven knows, they were not young in 1911 when he was first appointed First Lord of the Admiralty. Not young when Holmes first came out of retirement in 1917. Now here we were again, twenty-two years on and facing the same damn enemy. It was a time when all shoulders had to be shoved to the wheel, a moment in history when dictators on their tigers had found they dare not dismount. They were hungry and hungry tigers needed fresh meat. In his opinion England was to be that meat.

The door latch was freed from its rusty prison and the door opened an inch.

"Mrs Hudson?" The First Lord enquired, impatient with the recalcitrant door.

"Who is it?" A querulous old woman's voice demanded to know, "who calls at this hour?"

"It is I, Winston Leonard Spencer Churchill, come to call upon Lord Holmes, and the hour is before five o'clock woman!"

The door opened wide, a look of plain astonishment was fixed upon the aged and toothless visage of Mrs Hudson, herself dressed in black, a widow in mourning. Churchill was startled.

"He's not gone is he?" he asked, a measure of respect in his voice. "Not our Lord Holmes?"

Mrs Hudson shook her head, her hands clutched around her wildy beating heart, overcome to see Mr Churchill at her door again; it had been many a year since he had graced her steps.

"Come now, Mrs Hudson, I'm not as changed as all that, a little thinner, a little shorter but you yourself have plodded on; must be well up to pension age by now I should think."

Since Mrs Hudson was a mere eighty-nine years old, she was momentarily flattered and this was enough to bring her to her senses.

"Pray come in sir and leave the fog behind. The two gentlemen have not had visitors in a long time. Therein lies my surprise sir."

It had long been the opinion of Lord Holmes (confided not less than six months before, over a glass of hot cocoa) that his country had forgotten him and Dr Watson, yet here was the First Sealord to refute his words.

"Thought they'd been forgotten, eh?" Churchill asked, stepping into the musty, brown hallway, closing the door firmly behind him.

"Now there's a thing," allowing Mrs Hudson to remove his coat. "It would be a bitter day for England if Holmes and Watson were to be forgotten. The gentlemen are well, I trust?"

Mrs Hudson was glad the lights were dim and averted her face from her visitor, cursing herself for leaving her teeth in a jar by the sink. She did not take kindly to surprises anymore and the Lord knew there had been plenty in this house in the years Sherlock Holmes had resided upstairs in the first floor flat.

"The gentlemen don't get out as much as they used to sir. Now poor Sir John Watson's second wife upped and died, he came to live here, although Lord Holmes was reluctant, if you know what I mean sir. Likes his privacy. They fight like two schoolboys, they do sir, but they're still best of friends."

"I'm pleased to hear that Mrs Hudson, now if you'll be good enough to announce me."

Mrs Hudson looked at Mr Churchill then looked at the stairs, (none too well dusted) and sighed. "I must confess sir, that them stairs are not so much to my liking. It's perhaps all right for you, good sir, but my legs aren't what they were." She looked wistfully at the threadbare stair carpets. "I must warn you sir, their room is much changed, there has been a lot of banging about of late, I'm almost afraid to look myself."

Her guest understood, he himself was not well disposed to stairs. "Then I shall announce myself Mrs Hudson, I trust their hearts are sound."

"If their appetites are anything to go by sir, sound as a bell I'd declare."

"That is reassuring, most reassuring."

With that, the First Lord began to ascend the stairs, leaning heavily upon a much abused cane. As he approached the narrow landing at the top he fancied he could hear voices and, if he was not mistaken, the dull, muffled thud of bullets exploding against the far bedroom wall; but could his imagination be playing false with him? Sherlock had been forbade that eccentricity by the local magistrate more than once, if he recalled correctly. So many things had gone on in this house, so many strange people come and gone. Mrs Hudson had put up with a great deal, Holmes and his violin, his penchant for vile, chemical experiments that stunk the place out. Many a time an explosion or fire had broken out and occasioned the entire redecoration of the Hudson home; not that Holmes was careless and he paid Mrs Hudson enough, more than enough. Holmes could have bought several homes in Baker Street by now, but he had been an inquisitive man, never acquisitive.

"My dear Holmes," Churchill heard Watson remark. "I don't like knackwurst, liverwurst, or frankfurters and I never shall."

Holmes chuckled, a mean all-knowing chuckling, nothing diminished by his advancing years. "Nonsense Watson, my brother Mycroft swore by sausages. Ate four everyday."

"But dash it Holmes. The uniform, do I have to wear the uniform as well?"

Churchill's curiosity was aroused, he stood outside their door regaining his breath and rapped twice with his cane.

"The door, Watson, there's someone at the door."

This was no revelation to Watson, he had heard the knocking too, but nevertheless it was a shock for both men.

"Who can it be, Holmes?"

Holmes was already working on the problem.

"It must be someone Mrs Hudson knows well, Watson, else she would not let him up without giving notice. One understands, quite naturally, that it is a man, for a woman would never knock so hard with a cane; she would use a soft-gloved hand. I gather too, that it is a heavy man, for see how the floor dips below the door there. Turn up the lamp Watson"

Watson, already standing, shuffled to the centre of the room and pulled the long metal chain attached to the central lamp, bathing the room in its brightest green-white glow.

"Perhaps we should take a look, Holmes," Watson suggested, thinking it easier to solve this particular mystery of who was behind the door by use of their physical energy, as opposed to mental.

"The time is five o'clock Watson, yet note the man does not knock again, he knows we are awake and about. He must assume therefore we are adjusting ourselves to receive him."

"But is it safe Holmes? I mean, with all this?" Watson indicated the much changed room, the furniture all piled up at one end, all else as bare as the day the house was built, save for the new additions. Holmes looked up at the portrait of Herr Hitler above the mantle piece and nodded. "Perhaps it is a little bold of us to expose our room Watson, but how can we consider the thoughts and sensitivity of others if they aspire to surprise us without as much as sending a telegram or calling us on your telephone."

"Quite right Holmes, an insensitive man, one who is impatient furthermore."

Holmes struck his head in astonishment, turning to face the surprised Watson standing by his bed.

"Jove, Watson, that's it! You remain as indispensable as ever. An overweight, impatient, insensitive man who has the honour of knowing Mrs Hudson well enough to allow him to surprise us... it can be no other than the First Lord of the Admiralty. Come in Winston, come in." Holmes ordered.

Churchill smiled to himself. He had listened with great care outside the door and was mighty pleased that Holmes had lost none of his mental acumen. It was very reassuring. He turned the brass handle on the brown painted door and entered the humble chambers of Lord Sherlock Holmes.

Perhaps his first sense of euphoria abandoned him when he had the door open but a few inches and the very first thing he caught sight of was Sir John Watson standing beside a map of Bohemia-Moravia in full German General uniform. By the time the door was fully open and his extended frame was passing through the entrance, Churchill's open astonishment was apparent for all to see.

"Good evening, Winston, so interesting you could stop by," Holmes declared, brushing some of the dust off his blanket. "Forgive me if I don't get up, but I have had a cold these past few days and find that an afternoon nap does wonders for the recovery."

Churchill, one for the afternoon nap himself, quite understood, but although normally a man never at a loss for words, he was now speechless. Holmes and Watson were changed men. So old, so very old and white haired, and Watson did look a trifle ridiculous in that uniform. The picture of that damned corporal, Adolf Hitler, was a mistake he hoped, as was the other mass of German paraphernalia, books and unopened copies of Berlin newspapers. It contrived to remind Churchill of pictures he had seen of Hitler's study in the legendary Eagle's Nest. There was the air of the Bunker about the place, so changed from the former Victorian elegance he remembered from his last visit to Baker Street. Holmes himself was so thin, so criminally thin, it was almost painful to see him reduced so. Watson too, though obviously there remained something of the flesh upon him. Clemmie was right, though, they were past their best, no doubt about it. Could this be a wasted journey?

"No doubt you are surprised to find yourself in a little piece of Germany, Winston? Perhaps you'd like to find a place to rest your legs and Watson could administer a little schnapps."

Churchill held up his hands in protest. "No schnapps, Sherlock, a whisky would be in order and perhaps some sort of explanation is owed. I knew you were a fan of Wagner, Sherlock, but surely this is taking things too far? You are aware we are at war with Germany, I hope?"

But Holmes merely smirked, a poor imitation of his former all-knowing smirk. Watson busied himself with the Dewars, glad someone had arrived that could equal Sherlock's determination. He for one could not abide schnapps any way he tried it and if he ever saw another sausage he would be violently ill. Holmes and his obsessions were a blessing to mankind to be sure, but he noticed that his cold prevented him from donning *his* SS uniform. Never played fair, Holmes, never played fair.

Churchill received his drink gratefully, looking about his person for a cigar, only then remembering he had sent Calthorpe to Anderson's to get some.

"I perceive you are in need of a cigar, Winston. I believe Watson has something of the kind in his tuck box, behind the chest he brought back from India."

"I trust the cigars are little more recent than that Holmes," Churchill growled, not at all sure that he was not in some damn pantomime.

"Dash it Holmes," Watson protested, "I can't hide a thing from you." He made his way to the end of the room, clattering through the many hastily stored artefacts and assorted debris. "I shall be glad when this place is back to normal, I can tell you Mr Churchill, it's dashed awkward living under the Third Reich – dashed awkward. Unity Mitford sent us far too much stuff."

Holmes busied himself with his bedside gramophone, winding the thing up and forcing the distorted strains of Wagner on Parlophone to fill the room.

Churchill nodded sagely, he thought their living conditions odd, but in the years he had known Holmes, the man had never failed to surprise him, not once. He awaited the explanation with interest, if not impatience, not at all sure Wagner was a good idea at this moment in time. He had come to Baker Street a desperate man, he had no choice but to await Holmes' explanation. England was in grave peril, perhaps its final stand, nothing but desperation had led him to drive to Baker Street and seek out Lord Holmes and Sir John Watson, implore them to come to their country's aide. Yet now, as looked at them, Watson, in enemy uniform and shaking arthritic hands; Holmes with the 'flu', lying emaciated in his bed, the shock of white hair, wild and uncombed upon his head, he knew it had been a wasted journey. Time had dealt with them cruelly and its meanest streak of all, had made them senile. What else could all this Wagnerian homage to the Third Reich mean?

Holmes knew that his old friend was confused, but he stalled his explanations until Churchill was comfortable with his cigar and a glass of Dewars, the '24. Watson retired to his corner beside a map of Poland (sadly outmoded by recent tragic events).

Satisfied he had the attention of both men, he flung off his blanket, revealing himself fully dressed in his normal attire of frock coat, piped trousers, ruffled white shirt; a casually knotted cravat the only giveaway that Holmes was not entirely himself.

"I say Holmes, not fair what? Me in enemy uniform and you in civvies."

Churchill could see Watson was much put out. Holmes smiled wanly. "A simple expediency Watson. I had intended to don my uniform, but Mrs Hudson is having a little trouble with the buttons, ergo, I stand before you as an Englishman, is that not so Winston?"

"And I'm glad to say, a gentleman, Holmes, it's altogether too bad of everyone in the Commons to have abandoned the frock coat, no sense of tradition at all in Parliament these days, none at all."

"But to the explanation," Holmes returned, not wishing to be diverted once started. "Mr Churchill, you see before you two very worried men. That is to say, Watson and myself have long been concerned with developments in Europe. We have not been slack, despite our advancing years, which finds Watson arthritic and seriously depleted of weight; myself, wasted by years of a foolish addiction to morphine –" (he avoided mention of opium, knowing Winston didn't approve) "– which some claimed would kill me. But they reckoned not with the brain of Sherlock Holmes and his indomitable will to survive. I have followed the strictest of dietary regime and continue with exercises even to this very day, Winston – and now, at eighty-three years of age, you see before you an old body but a supple one. To be sure, slow, thin, ungainly, mere cladding around a mind, a mind as bright as a new pin sir, a brain still at the peak of its abilities, hampered only by a body, that despite all the tricks of the Indian mystics, has seen fit to betray me and decline into a mere shadow of its former self." He paused briefly.

"You find, Winston, not two old decrepit fools, but men ignored by their country in a time of need; men who saw a time would come, sooner or later, when that country would turn to them, reach out and grasp for men of experience, proven experience in matters criminal and politic. We, that is to say, I, with the aide of Watson here, decided some months ago, after the strangulation of Eastern Europe in fact, that we had to come to terms with Herr Hitler, grow to understand him and the German people and to do that we had to engineer the necessary, shall we say, mood?"

Holmes abruptly sat down, his legs obviously unsteady, not used to long bouts of standing.

"Watson and I constructed a replica of the Third Reich command post, taken from a drawing in an American magazine. We began to live a German life, absorb German thinking and thus hope to reach into the minds of those who would seek to control our destiny.

"Watson eats knackwurst, drinks schnapps and German lagers in great profusion and I observe. It is a curious fact that Watson has gained no weight in this enterprise.

"And thus we live, eat, think Germany and it is through this process Winston we perceive not only the strength of Herr Hitler's Socialist method, but the weakness too, not only of Germany, but of Europe as well. It is our deduction, Winston, England will see the Germans beating a path to our shores in the spring at the very earliest, but more likely after France is beaten, an easy victory that, for the French wear the Maginot line like a rabbit's foot. I see the jackboot in Sussex by July 1940. What say you?"

Winston put down his whisky and breathed a sigh of relief. With Holmes back in the picture, England might yet be saved.

"Yes, that is our conclusion too, Sherlock, I can only admire your method." He looked about the room impressed, the pieces all fitting together now. "A veritable think-tank Sherlock. We should have you in the Cabinet, there's none to touch you Holmes, or you Watson."

"And you should be Premier, Winston, we need strong hands on the tiller, nothing but a rubber band holding onto it now."

Winston could only nod in total agreement, his was the very same thought.

"By God, Holmes, you make me a happy man this day. England has found need of your services again and it gives me the greatest pleasure to be the one who calls you back to duty."

"It is no more than we expected."

"Indeed yes, Mr Churchill, the day Mr Chamberlain declared war, we began our exercises." Watson exclaimed, slapping his knees with obvious pleasure. "Holmes here said he expected a member of the Cabinet to call upon us, though it must be recorded that I'd given up hope. I did think we had been forgotten."

"I thought you'd retire to your bees," Churchill remarked to Holmes.

"My bees hibernate in winter, Mr Churchill, it is something man could learn a great deal from."

"Hibernation, Holmes?" Watson said brightly, "We've been hibernating for months now, I have to confess, there are times when it becomes, to be frank, a bore. There hasn't been a decent case to solve since Inspector Lestrade retired. The modern police force aren't interested in the analytical mind, everything is entrusted to dashing about in flash new Wolseys, detection is a thing of the past."

Churchill nodded in agreement. He had long been of the opinion that hibernation should be mandatory for all decent living gentlemen, as long as there was time to lay in sufficient quantities of brandy and cigars.

A rare silence entered the Baker Street bunker. Watson busied himself looking for a more comfortable seat. Holmes' eyes seems to glaze over momentarily as he ran his long, bony fingers through that ridiculous shock of white hair. Churchill, tired himself, was glad of the occasion to collect his thoughts, think of a way to present to the men the body of his request and observe the two men he had not seen for as many as fifteen years, at least.

Holmes was old, it was true, but that brain wasn't tired, he could see that now. Nevertheless, one couldn't ask a man of eighty-three, in the moonlight of his life, brilliant as he was, to re-enter the battlefield on behalf of the nation. It was asking too much, far too much. But who else could he turn to?

As for Watson, he looked cheerful enough, his eyes brighter than ever, as far as he could see. An admirable companion, and two men better suited to entrust the nation's secret he would never find. But there remained the doubt. Their fitness, and perhaps their death, would be his responsibility. Who in England would want the death of the world's most famous analytical mind on their conscience?

Holmes was the first to break the silence.

"With regard to your abrupt, but hardly unexpected visit, Winston, I think I can deduce what you have in mind for us."

"You can?" Churchill asked, always a little unnerved by Holmes' perceptive powers.

"The nation is up against the wall, we have no planes, hardly any guns, the appeasement boys have done Britain a great disservice, run the nation down to nothing. You, yourself, were jeered in August of 1933 for warning of the German peril. I, myself, witnessed the burning of the books in May of that year, being a guest of the Wagner society in Munich. It has been my own opinion that appeasement, a word I prefer to call by its French title, détente, was a deliberate attempt to ripen this country for a right wing dictatorship. Mosley's black shirts were but a warning of things to come. Now weakened by détente with an implacable enemy, we are launched into a war over the issue of Poland, a country in which the average Englishman has no interest and a country we could not defend, even if we tried. Which we did not. We should never have signed anything with Poland. It was sheer folly, plain emotional nonsense on Chamberlain's part and a country's leader cannot afford the price of such sentimentality."

"Hear, hear," Churchill intoned, pleased by Holmes' reasoning so far.

"As I understand it, the Russian-German non-aggression pact was a surprise for Whitehall?"

"Quite a shock," Winston confessed, "we'd been negotiating with Stalin right up to the last minute. The man's a swine Sherlock, first class swine."

"No doubt the Poles have also discovered that. But here we are, Winston, December '39 and the Finns are to be crushed by the overwhelming might of Russia and no doubt we shall lose Norway, possibly Sweden. All of Europe is threatened, France, the Low countries. Do we have the means to stop Herr Hitler? Could we launch an invasion of Germany? A pre-emptive attack co-ordinated with France?"

Churchill slowly shook his head.

"The sad truth is France is mislead and blind, Sherlock. She has not the will to fight, she lies like a dog waiting for her underbelly to be scratched, for she doesn't understand Herr Hitler has planned a fine kick between her ribs."

"So we have until July before we ourselves receive that kick?"

"Perhaps not so long."

"My word," Watson declared, wearing a worried frown. "My word."

"But we could be brought to our knees before that," Churchill reminded them. "The U-boats could cut off our supplies, the nation could starve before a bullet is fired."

Holmes nodded, he understood the problem well enough. "So in short, Winston, what can the modest services of both Dr Watson and myself do for our country in this hour of need, but endeavour to stay the hand of the executioner a while, whilst planes, tanks and men are prepared for the dark days ahead?"

Churchill nodded, furrowing his brow, grateful Holmes was so understanding.

"We need time Sherlock, we need to know those weaknesses, we need to turn the advantages to us, no easy task, no easy thing to ask of the Holmes-Watson team, but who else Sherlock? Who could I turn to?"

"My brother, Mycroft?" Holmes suggested.

Churchill sighed. "He was invaluable, but he never had your grit, never your instincts. He is sadly missed in Whitehall. His early retirement practically caused the slump. No one there to guide us when it was most needed. It was he who advised me against Sidney Street, in retrospect I should have listened."

"Indeed yes, but one learns by mistakes Winston. I have no doubt you learned your lesson."

Churchill flicked ash onto the bare floor, his eyes focussed on the dim past as he recalled the aftermath of that fateful day.

"So, Holmes," Watson interceded, "I think we can talk more pleasant matters than Sidney Street, or the British Gazette."

"Thank you Watson," Churchill muttered, re-lighting his cigar, "but I can take a rebuke or two, not to mention dish them out. Now gentlemen, so far you've been playing at the Boché, have you a taste for the real thing?"

Watson frowned again. "They are mad Mr Churchill, stark staring mad. It's all these sausages. You know what they do to the indigestion Mr Churchill, they don't call 'em bangers for nothing."

"Watson has not appreciated the finer points of this experiment, Winston. But I have been reading the stray wisps in the east wind, as is my fashion. I detect nothing more than a wish for world domination, slavery of the conquered and an almost childish wish to be loved."

"Loved?" Churchill and Watson cried out together, amazed.

"The German cannot see why he is not loved, he cannot see why the world hasn't flocked to their side to worship their Fuhrer. The German is the most unloved race in the world and quite simply, they cannot take it anymore. Unable to stir us to a spontaneous bondage, they will resort to rape and tie us to them that way. Love-hate, it is all the same to a German. This is why détente is no use against Herr Hitler, he craves affection, adulation, or utter contempt. He understands nothing between. There are those who see only what they want to see. I am of course referring to Mr Lindbergh, the aviator. To think the Atlantic hero would accept the Service Cross of the German Eagle from that fanatic Air Marshall Hermann Goring is beyond me. Lindbergh is as much your enemy Winston as Herr Hitler. He has great influence in America and if he should run for President, do not count on them coming in on our side this time."

"Holmes, you surpass yourself," Churchill decreed, holding out his glass for Watson to refill. A task Watson was most glad to comply with as he sat with an empty glass himself. Holmes, as usual, declined. "Indeed I have marked Lindbergh's cards. There are more than a few fellow travellers like him with influence. I am assured Roosevelt will run for a third term but there are those who want America to stay out of this one, at any cost. It is a problem, to be sure. I would not want to see Lindy as President." He sighed momentarily, contemplating this possible turn of events. "But to the matter in hand."

"Quite. Having defined their weakness, we need to progress," Holmes continued. "I was only saying to Watson the other day. We have to find out what it is that Herr Hitler considers his most treasured possession and when we do, we must take it from him. He is a child, a dangerous child, nothing but a jumped up corporal. It will make him mad, it will put him into a frenzy and then he will begin to make mistakes. We cannot defeat him militarily today, but we could make him mad. Perhaps that thing he treasures most is a bomb, something your friend Einstein was talking about, Watson. A correspondent of mine is worried about goings on in Norway and Denmark, rumours of a bomb so powerful it could destroy all of France in one go."

Churchill was deeply impressed. "Indeed, I have been advised that there is such a bomb planned. We have a department working on it Sherlock, we shall not require you to unravel those secrets. God knows how they make uranium explode, but a bomb that big? What use is a bomb you can never use?"

"A bomb that is all-powerful, Winston, he who makes it first and demonstrates its awesome power – wins."

Watson fidgeted in his seat. "Why Norway, Holmes?"

"Norsk Hydro, Watson, heavy water is manufactured there, the Boché need it for their experiments. Luckily for us that terrible bomb is still some two years away from completion, my informant tells me."

"A good assessment, Sherlock, I wish we had such accurate information as yourself, but it is the immediate threat that we are concerned with. I very much doubt we shall have two years at our present state of preparedness. As I've said before, our Government are decided only to be undecided, resolved to be irresolute, adamant for drift, all-powerful for impotence. Half the time I am persuaded Chamberlain and Lord Halifax are Germany's secret weapons, they don't need a bomb with them in charge. Quite simply put, Holmes, I want you and Watson to delay the war, keep it off our backs until we are good and ready for them."

"You have something in mind?" Holmes asked, his eyebrows arched in his customary fashion. "Would the mysterious disappearance of Sir Charles Hainsley be anything to do with it?"

Churchill started with obvious surprise. This was a closely guarded secret, impossible that Holmes should know. "There you go again Sherlock, you never fail to surprise me. It is indeed to do with Sir Charles, not to mention three other of our very best agents."

"Perhaps you would like to start at the beginning," Holmes suggested, fetching out his pipe to suck on, Watson having confiscated the last batch of tobacco. Churchill attempted to cross a leg, but thought better of it as the right leg failed to rise. He took a swig of his drink instead, rubbing his nose before settling back in his chair.

"In confidence gentlemen, I need not stress this of course. We got word from sources deep inside Germany, in Nürnberg, in fact. Indicating to us that there exists a man called Dr Otto Laubscher who has information for us that could be vital to the outcome of the war, a secret formula that could be the deciding factor about who wins or loses. This Dr Laubscher has actually worked with Herr Hitler, but in a secret capacity. However, it seems no one can get through to him. It's an enigma."

"Certainly to lose four of your best agents to him would indicate there is every likelihood they know you're trying. One can never underate the Boché." Holmes commented, already much interested. "This does not concern the bomb we talked of then?"

Churchill shook his head, "No, no bombs, something altogether more sophisticated we believe. We sent our best agents out and all of them were intercepted, never heard from again. Yet we know from a French connection that Dr Laubscher is still alive and working in Nürnberg," he lowered his voice suddenly to a more confidential tone, "and, under your hats gentlemen, I'm keen to get this secret formula before the Americans buy it from under our nose. We might have a bit of luck there, Dr Laubscher doesn't seem well disposed towards Americans."

"And Sir Charles was the last to go to Nürnberg?" Holmes asked, anxious to keep the story on a straight course.

"And he reached Nürnberg, for a postcard reached Paris only a week ago."

"Then he's only delayed," Holmes reported emphatically.

They could tell from Churchill's sad expression that this was not so.

"Afraid not, I received a cable this morning. Sir Charles was reported to have been run down by a tram, killed outright."

"This is monstrous," Watson declared, "were all four hit by trams? Did no one make contact with Dr Laubscher?"

"We do not know, Dr Watson. We do know Dr Laubscher is well guarded, an important man, a virtual prisoner in his own home."

"So you wish Dr Watson and I to penetrate the German defences and get this secret formula from Dr Laubscher. Will he require anything in return?"

"He has asked for nothing Holmes, save the freedom of the world from his country's oppressive hand. I wish there were more like him, but sad to say there are not."

"But to enter Germany?" Watson declared, "surely it is impossible?"

"An alibi lies close at hand, Watson. The January Wagnerian Memorial Concert in Nürnberg. What do you think of that, Holmes?"

"Jove, it just so happens I have an invitation," Holmes declared.

"No one alive is a greater fan, Holmes. All that remains is that you and Watson enter Germany openly, perhaps sympathetic to the German cause. It shall be concealed from the British public, who would not take kindly to you visiting the enemy."

"So, Watson and I must appear friendly, well disposed to the Third Reich." Holmes eyed Watson strangely. Watson drew back, he know what that look meant.

"Not more sausages, Holmes. I'd rather take a packed lunch."

Churchill and Holmes smiled at Watson.

"I should think we'll be gone longer than one day Watson. Come now, the German sausage is a very fine thing. I myself will be eating them alongside you."

"You must obtain the formula, decipher it if you can, Holmes. You were the only one I could think of to send who would be capable of judging on the spot whether we have something genuine, or not. You and Watson must retrieve, decipher and get it back to us. We have to have something that will enable us to sabotage their devilish plans. But don't delay, don't hold back. Every moment is a moment in Herr Hiltler's favour. Can you do it? There'll be no reward, no medals, it will be a secret between the two of us. We need time, Sherlock, planes and guns we can build, but time we cannot."

Holmes looked at Watson and with a familiar sardonic smile.

"Another case for your bottom draw Watson. This will prove to be our strangest case I think, we must find that chink in the enemy's armour."

"That's it entirely," Churchill enthused. "Operation Chink it is christened then." He stood up, not without considerable effort. "That concludes the business gentlemen. Now if you'd forward to me any particulars and requests for equipment and facilities you might need, use a telegram and Operation Chink as our code. I'll use the same."

"This is an honour," Holmes declared, struggling to his weary feet, the blood unable to keep pace and throwing him into a paroxysm of pain. "Damn and blast pins and needles. Watson, we've got to get the blood flowing better than this." Holmes suddenly remembered something and turned to his notepad to scribble an address which he thrust as Winston. "Watson and I have had this address under observation for some time. 50 Harrington Road in South Kensington. Former Admiral Volkoff is in residence there."

"The Russian Tea Room," Churchill recalled.

"Exactly. Something's afoot Winston. Those who are sympathisers to the Third Reich gather there and plot. You will take an interest whilst we are gone?"

Churchill pocketed the note. "Consider it done. It's a time of plots and plotting Sherlock. We shall out these vipers." He nodded. "Lord Holmes, Dr Watson, England is forever in your debt."

"Just the same," Watson declared, "we are grateful for action, is that not so Holmes?"

Holmes was too pre-occupied with the agony of pins and needles and he was forced to abandon attempts of civility and allow Watson to show Churchill to the door.

At the door Churchill stopped and looked back at Holmes. "I had my doubts about you both, but I am glad there's still the will to fight. England's greatest are dying like flies, Watson. Chief Inspector Lestrade's death last year was a blow to us all. Scotland Yard is still in shock I hear. Even criminals went easy on them a while, as a mark of respect."

"Yes sir... the great die, but Holmes and Watson survive."

Holmes sat down again, the pain subsiding. "I shall not mind if this is my last bow, it is enough to know it will be for England."

"Quite, Sherlock, quite."

And with that in mind, Winston Churchill vacated the Baker Street Bunker and putting all his weight on his silver topped cane, made his way downstairs where the ancient Mrs Hudson stood, teeth installed, ready with his overcoat.

"It is a cold night again sir."

"In December one expects cold nights Mrs Hudson. I have not lived this long not to understand that."

Mrs Hudson stood rebuked and mute as he fastened his heavy coat.

"But don't let me intimidate you Mrs Hudson, fetch your men some hot food, they are going to be rather hungrier tonight I fancy."

"I was about to send it up sir."

Churchill nodded. "Open the door woman, I'm about to be launched back into England and England must be readying my own supper."

Although Mrs Hudson had long thought her home in Baker Street was in London, England, she held her tongue.

"A tip from me, Mrs Hudson, find Lord Holmes a portrait of the King. I shouldn't like it known this house was the only one in England without one."

"But..." she began, but bit her tongue, thinking that tonight she would take supper upstairs herself, bad legs or no bad legs. It was time she inspected her rented rooms.

"Goodnight Mrs Hudson, perhaps we shall meet again in the new year."

"I hope so sir. God bless you sir and a very merry Christmas to you and your Ladywife."

Churchill donned his Homburg and walked towards the waiting Humber. "Calthorpe," he growled.

Calthorpe shot out from the shadows, flinging a lighted cigarette to the ground.

"Sir?"

"The club, Calthorpe, get me out of this infernal fog. There's supper to be had."

Upstairs, Holmes peered down from his gloomy windows and nodded to himself with some satisfaction. So the old warhorse needed them at last. Been pretty slow in coming to that conclusion, but at least he had come. He turned slowly, headed to the centre of the room and stared up at the portrait of Corporal Hitler.

"A secret Herr Hitler, you hold a secret in your grimy hands and I, Sherlock Holmes, intend to prise it from them, if it is the last thing I do." He stepped forward, lifted the portrait from the wall and reversed it. King George stared back at him and although it was quite obviously a trick of the light, it looked to him as though the King had winked at him.

"Gad sir, these eyes mustn't fail me now."

"Fail Holmes?" Watson asked sleepily, suddenly roused from an urgent nap on a chair by the door. "No sir, we can't fail. Sherlock Holmes never fails."

" 'Tis so Watson, but all this talk has made me damn hungry. Ring for our supper Watson, I cannot think for the sound of my rattling stomach."

Watson saw the King's portrait above the mantlepiece and smiled.

"The King Holmes, the King. I'll be damned if I'll eat another German sausage ever again. I want good old English food Holmes. Roast beef, roast pork, I'll not eat another sausage as long as England remains free."

"Brave words, Watson, but now it is up to us to keep England free. Are you up to it?"

"Upon my honour Holmes, I will serve my country to the last breath, just as I did in India, no need worry about that."

"Fighting talk, Watson, I'm glad to hear it, for we have quite a battle on our hands. Tomorrow we go to France. We have a too long played hosts to inertia. To search out that chink in Hitler's armour is our task."

"A woman, Holmes?"

"I fear not, Watson. Nothing so simple. Though perhaps a woman has a part to play in it."

"Never a man who hadn't," Watson declared.

"Excepting Oscar, Watson, don't forget Oscar."

"Of course, Oscar. Well I say it takes all sorts Holmes, all sorts."

"Time to get out of uniform Watson, it has served its purpose I feel."

"Never were words more gratefully received, Holmes."

Watson scurried away to his room and hunted out his evening suit. He had enough of the Third Reich already and the war was still only four months old!

2

To Heave and Heave Not

Holmes watched with some concern as their bath chairs (constructed from the highest quality bamboo, made by the finest craftsmen in England) were winched aboard HMS Mazarin, a naval vessel of the Minesweeper Patrol class, their transportation to France.

Churchill had been adamant. Lord Holmes and Watson had to have the very best protection against the German U-Boats, one could not entrust them to any lightcraft. They would land at Cherbourg and from there make their way by train to Paris. There was no intention to be discrete once on the continent. The plan was for Holmes and Watson to go to Paris and then make contact with officials in Nürnberg, to ask them for guaranteed safe passage to the Wagner memorial concert. It was thought Sherlock's reputation as a Wagnerite would sway the balance. Holmes was to declare that music was the language of peace. He had already cabled the German authorities in Nürnberg as to his wish to attend their celebration – reply Paris.

By doing things in the open, he hoped that he would gain acceptance over there and assuage fears that he might have come to meddle. His reputation was not easy to live down. Stealth would be impossible however, their age forbade it. Holmes hoped for the goodwill of the German people to show itself, for they had bought many copies of Sir John

Watson's prose accounts of the Holmes adventures, despite the unmasking of Von Bork in the last war (a devoted agent of the Kaiser).

No, the arrival of Lord Holmes and Sir John Watson in Herr Hitler's Third Reich was a flash of genius that even the PM (let into partial confidence) thought a masterstroke. He was thinking that if private citizens of the stature of Lord Holmes could be seen fraternising with the enemy (but never at home in the British papers) Hitler might construe that terms might yet be made for a treaty with London. Lull the German High Command into thinking there was popular support for peace, the spirit of appeasement was not yet quite dead. Anything that would give them time to prepare, rush up the defences.

Churchill, of course, never divulged the true purpose of his two proteges' visit. In fact, he roundly condemned their visit, talking in the club of traitors whose time was long passed, making sure that Hitler's spies knew that too. He wanted a big distance between himself and Holmes' activities, it was the only way of ensuring their innocence. The War Cabinet, influenced by Chamberlain's enthusiasm, sent a telegram to Holmes giving their support, asking him to send out feelers, explore every avenue of peace and compromise. Holmes ignored it, he had no intention of doing any such thing, he wished for nothing but a hard and well fought thrashing for the Germans. The PM did him an injustice.

Watson was surprised and hurt to receive an unpleasant telegram from the Zionists, deploring his association with that 'well known Fascist, Sherlock Holmes.' How had they known? It was very perturbing, but Holmes seemed to take it calmly enough. In actual fact, he seemed almost pleased. A telegram like that could only reinforce their position in Germany, he squared it away for German eyes to find it accidentally, should they wish to poke about his private papers. Waiting at the dockside, he had explained to Watson the subtle shades that this quest required of them.

"We must appear shocked that Germany would consider a war with their blood cousins, the English, Watson. The Duke of Windsor himself has sent me his best wishes, he is most concerned that Germany shouldn't be our enemy. His position is that the historic link between our two great countries should be preserved. I do believe he is none too well disposed towards the Zionists himself."

"I've heard, Holmes. His remarks concerning poor Winston have been less than flattering I'm told. Even suggested that Churchill should be confined to the Tower of London for the duration of the war."

"Did he, b'jove. We live in dangerous times, Watson. People have not yet adjusted to the climate of war. It takes a while to think of a country one trades with, holidays in, as an enemy. After all, we ourselves took in the Bremen air four years ago. You remarked on how much fun you'd had. How much more interesting Germany was now, since the Chancellor had rebuilt the economy."

"I did Holmes, I most certainly did. But I was intoxicated by the glorious sea air, the summer breezes. Bremen seemed to be a friendly place, hard to believe such friendly people should now be our enemy. "

"Quite, Watson, a friend today becomes an enemy tomorrow, such is life. The German has destroyed a way of life forever, Watson. There is no honour, to them it is a medieval conception. Believe me, if we do not defeat the Nazis, I should not care to live out the rest of my years under their influence."

"I'm with you there Holmes. The Germans can't even play cricket, how can you expect to rule the world if you cannot play cricket?"

"In a nutshell, Watson, in a nutshell."

The ship, the famed HMS Mazarin had left the cosy harbour of Folkestone and was already an hour out to sea at 01.00 hours and encountering severe, typical, channel weather, despite a weather report that predicted a clear run. The Met office and the BBC were short on accuracy this night.

It was moonless, but not motionless. The ship heaved and rocked with little dignity from side to side in the large swell. An icy wind cruised in from the Arctic and visibility was largely a matter of imagination.

The two new recruits to Britain's finest service had been disappointed to have missed the view of Folkestone's white cliffs bathed in moonlight. They had both been especially keen to see that particular view, but the weather had played foul, as usual. Now, not exactly at their best, considering the violence of the thrashing sea, they sat on deck, shivering, yet snug enough in their respective bath-chairs. Watson sat with a rug around his thin shoulders to shield them from the bitter December wind. They could have sat below in the officers' mess and partaken of some early Christmas cheer, but Holmes had declined, deciding that the sea air was a necessary prerequisite to expel the London fog, firmly embedded in their lungs.

"You have, I trust, remembered to fill your motor, Watson?" Holmes enquired, indicating the two horse-power velocette engine mounted on the prow of both bathchairs, a driving chain extending to the front wheel.

"Both engines, Holmes. I say, you're not thinking of taking a spin on deck are you, not in this weather?"

"No Watson, but I'm given to understand that we shall disembark some distance from the railway station and it is best to be prepared for such an event. Our baggage can be forwarded, but I'll be damned if we should have to walk if we can ride."

"I'm with you there Holmes. I'm with you there."

Holmes was looking up into the dim, blackened sky, not a star in sight. A fierce gust of wind blew along the deck, jolting the bathchairs, causing Watson some momentary anxiety as a giant wave hit the side and deluged them with a salty, freezing spray.

"Storm brewing Watson. Brakes on I think."

"Already secure, Holmes. I cannot drink my brandy without the safety of my brakes."

"Simple precaution, Watson, sensible as ever. I think I shall partake of a nip myself, then a smoke."

"As your physician, Holmes, I advise against smoking, it will only make you cough."

"I gave up taking your medical advice more than forty years ago Watson, but thank you all the same for your solicitude. You are right, of course, but when a man reaches the age of eighty-three, I believe he can endure one pipeful of tobacco without expiring."

Watson ignored him. No use arguing with Holmes. One might as well argue with an ox.

The ship heaved once again, and the sounds of great straining were heard on deck as the steel hull struggled against a greater force. An officer was sighted by Watson, strolling, or to be more accurate, staggering, on deck. It was Third Officer Thomas.

"Evening gentlemen. Advice from the captain, lash yourselves to the bulkheads, we're in for a rough night. My advice is to go below, some hot grog is being brewed."

"We'll stand fast officer, thank you all the same. However, when that hot grog is ready, I know Watson here wouldn't think it remiss if we were to imbibe a little."

The officer smiled, his concern for the two old codgers somewhat belayed by their interest in the grog. He and the other officers had been appalled to see England's most famous men shipped out to sea by HM Government. As bright as Sherlock Holmes was, there was little a man of over eighty could do to stop this war. It was a suicide mission, but he had to admire their spirit. The Boché wouldn't take England so easily if they knew there were brave men such as these standing on the beaches waiting for them.

21

"Just as you wish gentlemen, I'll send a steward with the grog as soon as it is prepared. Oh yes.." He stepped to one side and opened a nearby locker. "The captain advises the wearing of life jackets. He doesn't want to be the one to report to London that you were lost over the side. He'd spend the rest of his life on a Thames dredger, if he was lucky to get anything at all."

Both Holmes and Watson busied themselves a while putting on those cumbersome jackets, not really designed for wearing inside a bath-chair. Nevertheless, uncomfortable as they were, both men felt more secure as the sea continued to grow angrier and hungrier for English shipping.

"Lucky thing we have brakes, eh" Watson remarked to the officer. "But your point is taken, we will fasten ourselves to the ship. I trust the Boché are busy looking the other way tonight."

"The Mazarin runs pretty quietly sir and if it's of any comfort it's hard to get off a torpedo with any accuracy in a storm like this."

"We are much relieved to hear that. Most underhand method of war, don't you agree, officer?" Holmes stated, having difficulty with his knots.

"Yes sir, but there's no fair way to win a war nowadays."

"My brother Mycroft, swore in '14 that the battle of the Atlantic would be won by submarine. He was right, I fear, and the Germans seem to have the most, I hear."

"Well don't dwell on it Lord Holmes, we will be in Cherbourg before dawn. The Boché will miss us tonight, it's the captain's birthday tomorrow. He wouldn't miss it for the world, always a big party, you should stay for it, not one to miss. Always a stripper, or two, manages to get on board if we are in France. Don't know how, of course, against regulations." He winked and leered.

Watson laughed, thinking that a stripper was something he hadn't seen in a long while. Holmes was unmoved, as always, his blood as cold as the fish below them.

Holmes was pleased to hear the confidence in the young officer's voice. They watched him walk away, keeping to one side to avoid the tumult of water now pouring over the ship's sides, much to everyones' discomfort. The ship suddenly pitched into a big trough. There seemed to be a solid wall of sea ahead of them that miraculously did not submerge the entire ship.

"If I know the sea Watson, a trough such as that means trouble ahead."

"One doesn't need to know the sea, Holmes, my stomach senses trouble enough, you were right, no dinner was the best option."

"Of course, Watson. We have no sea-legs. Baker Street is no place to train for a night like this! I'm taking forty winks, wake me when the grog comes, I'll appreciate a sailor's potion."

However, the sea had other plans.

The captain of the Mazarin, Captain Terence Howard, was worried. Not least by his precious human cargo, but by the sudden switch in the weather. The force 6 gale was now a force 10 and rising. As far as he could see they were sailing right into one of the worst storms he had ever seen in the Channel, worse, on their present course they were now equidistanced from England and France. Le Havre would be their best course now, or to turn back, something he didn't like to do, knowing that Lord Holmes had a serious mission ahead of him.

In the light of this, Captain Howard made a few calculations and decided for Dieppe, it was positively the nearest, but bang in the middle of the storm's path.

"We could try turning for tail sir, running ahead of it," the first officer suggested, equally as worried.

"It's Hobson's choice Sullivan," the captain answered. "We run for cover and try to beat a path through the storm, or run like mad for Southampton and let the storm overtake us."

"Well sir, I'd take my chances with the British waves rather than the Frog's any day. But this girl will take any storm, I've been in worse off Scotland, far worse."

"This will go off the scale, Mr Sullivan. Look at the barometer. Damn thing thinks it is a speedometer. Quite frankly, I'm worried. I'd like to turn back."

"Your ship sir, your command." Sullivan was not about to upstage his captain, even if he was a two and a half stripe.

"Dieppe, Sullivan, full speed ahead and cancel galley duty, we are going to be knocked about a bit I fancy."

"Dieppe it is sir."

Which was the biggest mistake of Captain Howard's naval career.

It is perhaps one of the most unfortunate stories of the war, certainly one that can be told now with little amusement. For those that perished, and the bereaved, it is sad to record here the facts, long suppressed by Admiralty high-ups, that the HMS Mazarin, in difficulty, seeking shelter from a severe, destructive storm, was approached by a British submarine, freshly commissioned out of Barrow-in-Furness, one HMS Fortitude, and sunk that very December night in the Channel, the blame resting firmly with the vile German U-Boat. Commander Felix Mannion still denies to this day that his submarine was the guilty party; but the coincidence of his log book reporting the sinking of a German Minesweeper at 02.10 hours, eight miles out from Dieppe, and the sinking of HMS Mazarin at 02.15 hours eight miles outside Dieppe, with not one German vessel sunk and the drowning of the entire crew of the Mazarin, was too great a coincidence. To keep this episode quiet, Commander Mannion became Admiral Mannion and took charge of Simonstown, South Africa, ensuring the Third Reich did not get away with an easy passage around the Cape of Good Hope.

Holmes was the first to notice a change. He awoke with a start at just past 02.00 hours, sniffed the air and pronounced, "We've changed course, Watson. I can smell France, but it's not Cherbourg we are headed for."

"Indeed, Holmes. I had not noticed, but here, I kept a little grog warm for you," Watson replied, fishing below for the flask between his legs.

"Now that is a capital suggestion. I have to admit that I'm beginning to feel the cold, sleep may recharge the mind, but it lowers the temperature Watson. Grog will give me the illusion of warmth at least."

The sea was as foul as ever, if not worse and there were times when the roll on the ship was such that the sea practically lapped at their bath-chair wheels, a most disconcerting event for both men. But knowing this, neither would have exchanged positions for the warm officers' mess below. It looked to them as though the Mazarin would sink at the slightest excuse, neither wanted to be below if that was the case. Watson was a little queasy, but he decided he could take it. He didn't want to appear a ninny in front of Holmes, despite his greater age.

Singing could be heard below, the grog and expectations of Christmas contributing to a cheerful crew. Watson, cold as he was with the cruel sea lashing about them, enjoyed the songs.

"Our Gracie has given us some pretty tunes, Holmes," he commented.

"Simple tunes Watson, pleasing to some, but nothing of the texture of Wagner. The English popular song is quite empty."

Watson was not so well disposed towards Wagner himself, preferring Cole Porter.

"Does this night not remind you of Turner, Watson. Remember he had himself lashed to a mast and he rode out a storm, bringing every last detail to the canvas."

"No sunset," Watson pointed out, not a Turner fan, favouring William Morris or Whistler, himself

Even as the fateful word of Whistler, left Watson's lips, they both heard the two massive and shattering explosions, as the torpedoes hit the Mazarin, fore and aft.

"What the…" Watson cried out, taken by complete surprise.

"Torpedoes, Watson. The Boché are on to us. In this storm we will sink for certain. Unlash that rope from the bulwark, prepare for drastic action."

Holmes was right, of course, drastic action indeed. The ship sounded the alarm, sailors, officers, appeared from nowhere, dashing about the place, manning guns, depth charges, but Holmes knew it was to no avail, the ship was lost. No ship of this size could survive a blow fore and aft in a storm. It was already apparent that the ship was going down, tilting towards the water at an alarming rate on Holmes and Watson's starboard side, waves crashing over the ship, sending a torrent of icy water towards them in a constant battering wave.

"All is lost for the Mazarin," an officer yelled at them, running past for the lifeboats. A useless gesture for they would take too long to winch out and over, never mind load up with panicking men.

Watson had them loosened from the ship at last, and despite their brakes being full on, the two bath-chairs slid smartly to the rails with a resounding thump, jolting both men quite painfully. Some sailors ran by, reached for life jackets out of the locker, slipped them on at a run and with not so much as a yell, jumped overboard. Watson gasped.

"No word from the captain then," Holmes said quietly, obviously thinking that he might have time to inform them of what was happening.

"Abandon ship," someone was yelling through a loudhailer. "Get off while you can, take something that floats. God have mercy on you."

"I rather think the Mazarin is going down with great speed, Watson," Holmes pronounced. "The U-Boat has scored yet another victory, but it shall not have us, you can be sure of that, my dear fellow."

It was apparent to all that the engines had stopped, nothing would save the Mazarin; the dark, menacing sea stood in wait, jaws open. Holmes noted the pitch of the deck against the sea, heard the shouts and screams as men leapt for their lives. He made a decision.

"Brakes off, Watson, start engines."

Watson, ever ready to accept Holmes' command complied, tugging at the tightly wound rope that had to be pulled with some force to ignite the tiny velocette motor. Holmes did likewise. The engines were damp, sounded doubtful, but caught fire all the same, breaking into life with resounding blatts as they cleared their lungs.

Holmes understood sinking ships very well. One had to get away as fast as possible, or be dragged down with it. He remembered the Titanic. He had lost many friends on that fated voyage. How fortunate that he and Watson had been to turn that offer down to sail on her maiden voyage.

"Look for a break in the railings, Watson, we must cast off, abandon ship."

Indeed, even as they motored along the deck, Watson's college scarf trailing into the air behind him, they could see lifeboats being lowered into the water, not so very far from the deck by this time.

"This is a foul deed," Holmes called out to a passing officer, who stood astonished, yet afraid, as Holmes and Watson motored by, treating the sinking as if were no more serious than the Brighton Run.

"Here's the spot," Holmes decreed. Indeed, it was the spot, for Cook and his companions had arrived before them and were busy dividing bottles of rum between them as they struggled with their life jackets.

"Keep together, make for a lifeboat," someone yelled from up top. A flare shot up into the sky, the wind bearing it away from the area.

Watson found himself the recipient of a bottle of Lamb's Navy Rum and they both witnessed Cook, arm around two of his mates, lurch off the deck into the cold sea with something like 'Geronimo' on their lips.

"They won't last long in that," Holmes shouted, barely audible above the roar of the wind. "Watson, we must launch ourselves, heave to one-hundred yards from the ship." He produced two paddles from the interior of his bath-chair. "Here, fasten yourself in Watson, tight as you can, if, by chance, you should overturn, do as the red indians do in their kayaks, twizzle this paddle above your head and you'll turn right side up. Don't panic man, these bath-chairs are the best the Empire can offer, they'll float well enough in any weather. Thank God for inflatable seats."

"Holmes, you think of everything." Watson exclaimed.

"It's a fact Watson, now say your prayers for here we go."

Holmes engaged the clutch once more, did a grand circle to build up speed and with grim determination, he launched himself out into the sea. Watson, not making such a good job of it, followed suit, a bigger splash than Holmes, narrowly missing an officer swimming for his life.

"Keep that engine at full revs," Holmes shouted from some place in the dim, wild distance. "Keep the water out of it."

It was very well for Holmes to shout, but the sea was practically alive. It was so rough and the wind was making a determined effort to turn him over whilst he sought escape from the capsizing ship. Watson tried to turn and get the wind behind him, but that only took him back towards the ship, he had to steer right into the wind and pray that the velocette was up to it. As it was he had taken in water, much to his discomfort, but despite certain splutterings and occasional swampings, the engine kept on with a little frantic paddling on Watson's leeward side to help it along. Slowly but surely he began to move away from the dying Mazarin, as billowing smoke and steam suddenly jetted out into the water as the boilers were overcome down below.

It was fearfully cold and the night was full of yells, cries for help, men drowning in a most piteous manner.

Holmes was well clear, his mind sharp as a bell, in command of his not-quite sea going vessel. He was thinking that the Germans would pay for this, of that he was very sure. He passed by a lifeboat crammed with sailors, spluttering and desperate, an officer blowing a whistle to summons stragglers to him. There was an awed silence in the boat as first Holmes, then Watson puttered by. Some even crossed themselves, fearing it a portent of death.

Behind them, HMS Mazarin finally slid under, going by the stern in a most ungraceful manner to the bottom of the sea. Five minutes had passed from being torpedoed to her death. The captain went down with his lifeboat.

Watson caught sight of Holmes ahead of him and breathed a sigh of relief. Luckily Holmes had lit his pipe and a shower of sparks was visible every time the sea splattered him. Watson was so relieved to see Holmes that he celebrated with a tot of the Cook's rum, its warm glow setting fire to him, inspiring him with a new determination to paddle faster and catch Holmes up.

The velocettes roared on, the impellors on the half submerged drive chain pulling them on apace, the blistering hot metal sending enough warmth back to both men ensuring that whilst the engines were on, they would survive the below-freezing temperatures. It was rough out there, the bath-chairs were without stabilisers, something Watson had already decided to write to the manufacturers about and complain.

Holmes was growing concerned however. The bath-chairs, good as they were, were not water-tight. They would float all right, but they might run into trouble yet. The water was fearsomely cold. He worried about Watson. Neither of them could take the Channel waters for very long, let alone the giant rollers washing over their heads.

There was a shout. A boat loomed on his portside. A lifeboat, with only a few survivors in it.

"Ahoy there," a voice cried out, but at the same instant, a huge wave rolled between them and Holmes found himself surfing at an alarming speed in another direction. There was nothing he could do except hope he would be set down gently amongst the froth and phosphorus surging all around him.

He looked to starboard and suddenly was amazed to see Watson, practically aglow with phosphorus, riding the same crested wave, waving his paddle wildly in the air shouting, "Holmes, Holmes, I feel ill. Holmes save me, save me..." A huge fish lay across his chest, his scarf, all wet and stranded about his face gave him an almost comical look, but Holmes knew Watson was saved. The wave abruptly lost its power and set them both down in a trough of water that immediately became a crest once more and threw them together so that Holmes was able to secure Watson to his side with a piece of twine stolen from the bath-chair, itself

"Oh Holmes, Holmes, I thought I was a goner, a goner for sure."

"Nonsense Watson, you rode that wave like a professional." Holmes struggled with the knot on the twine. "My mittens are sodden Watson, a knot is a hard job on a night like this."

Watson was still reliving his experience on the wave. "Holmes," he breathed, offering the half empty bottle of rum to his saviour. "I thought I'd lost you for good Holmes. I didn't know whether I should set course for England or Iceland, no sense of direction without the stars. This is no sea-cruise, Holmes."

"No indeed, it would appear not Watson, but I am glad to see that you've found a new career as a deep sea fisherman. Grimsby would be proud of a cod that big."

Watson looked at the fish as if he had seen it for the very first time.

"However," Holmes continued, "I perceive from your breath that more than your fair share of a sailor's ration has disappeared down your throat, here help me with this twine, if you can."

Feeling guilty about the rum, Watson protested, "It was only out of sheer terror I drank, Holmes."

As Holmes took the cod and tossed it into the sea, the fish unable to believe its luck. Then he seized the rum.

"You don't need any more rum Watson, got to keep a clear head we've a rough night ahead."

Somewhat peeved to lose his fish and his rum, Watson began to sulk, asking only, "Are we saved, Holmes? That was a fearful disaster back there." It was dark, and although they were close, Holmes could not see Watson's face clearly, but he knew it was white with shock and fear.

"We are saved for now, good Watson, but will the dawn find us alive? This I cannot answer. That U-Boat might still be around and be bent upon finishing us off."

Watson now had something else to worry about. A damn U-Boat out to sink anything British, even bath-chairs, it was to be a bitter war, he could see that. He remembered his medical-school knowledge.

"We should last until dawn Holmes, but I fear our engines will not, we've already used a lot of fuel."

Holmes considered the velocettes. "Indeed we have, throttle back. Fortunately you did not drink all the rum. We can only hope it will keep these engines going for an hour more when the time comes.

Watson, let the engines idle, we must keep them going, the warmth will ensure our survival. Pray report how much water you've shipped so far."

"A good six inches Holmes, but I'm afraid to open up to bale out for fear of taking more in than I throw out. Judging from the activity down there, I could swear there are a couple more cod."

"Fiendish fish eh, Watson? Awkward what?" Holmes replied, pleased the darkness would hide his smile. Watson was fine, doing well for a man of eighty-seven, very well.

And there they floated, tossed from wave to wave, a strong wind, even stronger than before, if that was possible, adding speed to their uncertain ride. They felt battered, their bodies ached and even as they hoped things would get better a wave would bear down upon them and soak them through once again. Watson was afraid they would contract pneumonia from all this, but Holmes begged to differ considering that it was a virus and neither man was sick before the sinking. The worst he expected was a damn cold.

Not another sailor, not an officer, nor piece of wreckage did they see during the night. England seemed so far off, the world made of water, land some distant dream. Their drift was at a remarkable speed, the wind, the velocette and the current all combined to give them such a good run that Holmes remarked that they would soon be giving Mr Campbell some worries for his water speed record. "Wish we had a radio, Holmes. Could do with a touch of the Henry Hall's out here."

Holmes sighed. Watson was in decline to be sure. There had been a time when he would listen only to Tosca, or other fine fare of Covent Garden.

"This act of barbarism will not go unanswered Watson. We shall survive this and Herr Hitler will feel the mark of my revenge."

Watson could not see his long time companion, but he could hear the venom in his voice. He had not heard such venom in a long time. It was the mark of Holmes' quality as a man that his life had been devoted to crime and treason merely out of the best interests of justice. But this, this heretical act upon his person and the King's Navy was the straw that broke the donkey's back. He was glad not to be in Herr Hitler's position. It was one thing to have an interested enemy, but an implaccable one, bent upon revenge... Germany didn't stand a chance.

Just before dawn, land was sighted.

"Full throttle, Watson and get out your paddle," Holmes shouted as they neared the land mined beach. "Keep a straight course, watch out for land mines, you can't miss them. Pray to God for King George and our safe landing." So jubilant was he, that he failed to notice his pipe had set sail for France without him.

An astonished coastguard remarked later in the pub on how he saw two gentlemen in bath-chairs, motoring at full throttle out of the sea right through his minefield (laid only a week before) and out onto the seaward road; not stopping until they reached The Three Bears public house, where they discharged themselves of their vessels, trading four large cod for hot baths and a hearty breakfast.

Operation Chink had survived an attack, it could plan anew.

***

A telegram to Winston Churchill (now in the Brown's University Churchill collection) read:

charges to pay	**POST**		**OFFICE**	No.
RECEIVED	**TELEGRAM**			OFFICE STAMP

SLIGHT DELAY STOP COD MAKE POOR COMPANIONS DID THE
BOCHE KNOW WE WERE ABOARD STOP

REGRET LOSS OF LIFE PERHAPS A COMMERCIAL FLIGHT
WOULD BE THE ANSWER STOP

OP CHINK

STOP

It is recorded that Churchill immediately replied.

| charges to pay | **POST** | | **OFFICE** | No. |
| RECEIVED | **T E L E G R A M** | | | OFFICE STAMP |

ENGLAND GLAD YOU'RE SAFE STOP

AN ASSISTANT ASSIGNED TO YOU IMMEDIATELY STOP

LT SHAND WILL REPORT WITH FLIGHT DETAILS STOP

GOD SPEED ENGLAND WITH YOU STOP

3

A Brush with the Boché

"There are only two ways to dry a bath-chair, Watson," Holmes was saying over tea on the next afternoon. "This is positively the best way."

Looking up from their rough table laden with tea mugs, they observed their bath-chairs slowly twisting from the oak-timbered ceiling in the premises of Ambler and Brown, known the south-coast over for their finest smoked kippers.

"We are extremely fortunate to have beached in Hastings, Watson. On the whole coast of southern England, this is the only herring-curing establishment. Craster in Northumberland makes the best, as you know, but an Ambler and Brown kipper has slipped down the gullet of some of the finest throats in London."

Fascinated by the intricacies of bath-chair curing, both men steadied their gaze upon the wickerwork rotating in the careful blend of charcoal and secret aromatic ingredients known only to Ambler (not even Brown).

"I'd say the Hun will know we are coming now Holmes," Watson declared; a handkerchief to his nose.

"Why say you that?"

"Kippers, Holmes. They'll smell us a mile off."

Holmes shook his head. "It is only a herring that smells like a fish. This establishment has that odour, it is true, but a well suspended bath-chair, dunked in the salt water for twelve hours will smell like a rose when dry, Watson, take me at my word. Ambler and Brown are masters at the art. Our bath-chairs will be the envy of all bath-chair cognoscenti everywhere; there are few enough well-cured wicker modes of transport as it is."

"As you say, Holmes, but now, I've finished my tea, perhaps we could visit the hotel, or take a stroll by the sea?"

Holmes cast Watson an uncertain look. "The sea, Watson? I should have thought you would have had enough..."

"It's this infernal kipper smell, Holmes. I can't take it much longer." His voice quavered uncertainly.

Holmes saw that it was so and instantly stood up. "Come Watson, I'll walk with you to the sea. My apologies, I had quite forgotten your allergy to kippers."

"Think nothing of it, Holmes. I admire your ingenuity, as always. I had quite given up hope for our bath-chairs. Besides, the heat has driven out the chill. You were right, it is not only the bath-chairs that are cured, my lungs feel quite clear."

"It's an old fisherman's cure Watson."

Holmes steered Watson outside into the cold, crisp, wintry air and within a few minutes Watson was as good as new. A few callisthenics, a few minutes hard breathing filling their lungs and every last remnant of the smokehouse was expelled from their withered bodies, indeed both felt much better for it too, if a tad dizzy.

"You were quite right, Watson. A kipper is pleasant enough upon your breakfast plate, but overpowering anywhere else. Now what shall we do? This Lieutenant Shand is a devilishly long time in coming."

"I'm not complaining, Holmes. Our last adventure was quite taxing. I shall not readily take to a sea trip again."

"My sympathies are with you Watson. One wonders if any shipping is safe. Remember the Lusitania!"

There was a moment's silence as they recalled that momentous tragedy and its implications for America. Holmes wondered if Winston had a similar surprise for America? How long could they ignore this war and if they did, could they really live with a conquered Europe, cowed and bullied by one such as Adolf Hitler. How well would the master race concept sit in America's heartland? He thought not so well, but politics were not a matter of cold, logical analysis. The turn about in a politician's mind were meant to defy logic, all pretensions to sanity.

Watson purchased an evening paper, immediately turning to the local crime reports, a lifetime habit. Holmes had already consumed the London papers brought down by the Hastings early morning express, marking down the unsolved crimes list, trials in progress, as was his customary fashion. To watch him do it, one would think he was attempting The Times crossword puzzle. He would have the suspects filled in, the murder weapon unravelled, the culprit found, just by reading the reports. The famous Holmes correspondence with the Old Bailey had saved many an innocent from the gallows and sent many more villains to that quarter, who would have otherwise escaped to do more of their evil deeds.

This day was like any other, but with one difference. The crime was always in Europe or Scandinavia now and the perpetrator, Hitler's Nazi hordes: never before was such brutality recorded.

The publican of The Three Bears was waiting for them when they entered his establishment. "There's someone to see you, gentlemen," he said excitedly, but on no account would he reveal who it was. He directed them to the lounge bar, where a roaring log fire greeted them as they entered the cosy room; reflections from the flames appearing invitingly on all the walls. But neither man could feel the heat of the fire when their eyes fell upon the beautiful woman stood before it.

Petite, with a short dark mass of curly hair piled upon her head, an amazingly translucent pre-Raphaelite face quite free of any make-up, she was quite lovely, yet mysterious with penetrating green eyes. She was fine boned too, a creature refined, the like of which Holmes and Watson had not seen in a long time. She smiled at them, an enigmatic smile, her thin but elegant lips lighting up her face, so that she resembled a nymph or some such fetching creature out of a Burne-Jones setting.

"Lord Holmes, Dr Watson, are you they?" she asked, a note of nervousness in her voice, her eyes looking to Watson, for it was well known that he had the more sympathetic face.

"Why yes my dear" acknowledged Holmes, never one for the Ladies, but an admirer of beauty, nevertheless.

Watson was mesmerised; her ears were just like pixie's, he was bewitched, bewildered, his heart was pounding, this was the most exciting event in his life since he had met Daisy O'Brien, his last wife, * outside the Cafe Royal one momentous evening. Yet this snip of a girl could hardly be twenty and he, eighty-seven, was acting like a swooning swain.

His second, after Mary Morstan, Holmes' client in The Sign of the Four.

The girl took a step forward, extending her hand in a most formal manner. "Lieutenant Shand, gentlemen. Cornelia Shand – Special Services."

Holmes was astonished, astounded, quite flummoxed, possibly for the first time in living memory. Watson was anxious, over the moon, transported.

"I seem to have taken you both rather by surprise."

The silence that raged in that warm, flickering room was testimony to that fact. Holmes stifled a few well chosen expletives. They had sent a woman, a lightheaded, lightweight, (albeit beautiful) creature.

It was scandalous. Churchill must have gone off his head. The First Lord could not mean it. To send them a woman as an assistant was an insult and this one was a mere child from the look of her. It would not have surprised him if she was to tell him that she was still at school, let alone a Lieutenant in whatever Special Services were. Things had changed in the modern army, he could see that.

"I'm aware that you might be hostile to me, Lord Holmes," she turned to a nearby table and cooly poured out three glasses of Dewars for them all. In all Watson and Holmes' life, they could never remember being poured a drink by a female, the wrong side of the bar. "But," she continued, "I assure you that I will be most useful. I speak four languages. French, German, Polish and English. I can shoot straight, kill if I have to (though it seems most unlikely). I can swim, pour drinks and I am proficient in first-aid."

Watson felt that Holmes was being most unwelcome. "I think that you are splendid, my dear, quite utterly splendid."

Cornelia ignored Watson, it was quite obvious from the light bursting from his eyes that he had an instant shine upon her. It was Holmes she had to convince and she had been warned that it wouldn't be easy. Holmes was a renowned misogynist.

"What was your previous experience?" Holmes enquired. He was listening to the county inflections in her melodious voice, trying to place her background, her origins. He nervously sought out his pipe, noticing for the first time that it was missing and immediately suspecting its confiscation by Watson.

Cornelia was ready for questions, quite sure her answers would have effect upon that stubborn Holmes mind.

"I was mistress to Sir Oswald Partington, for two years."

This was devastating news to Watson, who could not believe an angel so young could have been anything but fresh out of finishing school. Holmes merely nodded, relaxing a little, understanding the situation immediately, though sceptical of her brazen answer.

"So it is politics that forces you upon us," he said. "Perhaps he wanted rid of you?" He suggested unkindly, suspicious of her, eyeing this young woman in a most intimate, yet clinical manner.

She did not flinch for a moment, a strong woman, obviously of independent spirit.

"You are a perceptive man, Lord Holmes. You are right. He has been promoted to the Inner-Cabinet and there's a chance he'll stay on when the reshuffle comes along in the new year. Either I went to Canada to join my cousin Rebecca, or I could serve my country assisting you."

She turned to Watson and smiled sweetly. "I have read every one of your accounts of Lord Holmes' cases, Dr Watson. I couldn't refuse, you'll find me indispensable. After Ozzie heard about your sinking in the Mazarin from Mr Churchill, he insisted that I should be the one who would look after you both, not that either one of you look as though you need looking after."

Holmes was thinking that two years of being an alleged mistress had silvered her tongue.

"Well just occasionally," Watson muttered bashfully, more than just a little excited at the prospect of being looked after by her fair hands.

"I shall have to think this over," Holmes decreed, reaching for his whisky. He drank it all down in one gulp, the only way to drink whisky in his opinion. He valued it as a palliative for shock, its medicinal value, no more; preferring a brandy and an ounce of shag anytime.

"I have your orders for tomorrow, Lord Holmes," Lieutenant Shand informed him. "Perhaps you'd like to go over them with me."

"I shall read them myself," Holmes told her testily, turning to Watson. "Watson, I'm going up to my room. Perhaps Miss Shand (Watson noticed the Miss) will amuse you whilst I read her orders."

Cornelia was co-operative about producing the thick envelope from behind her on the mantle. Watson reflected that she would have stood more chance with Holmes if she had come in a Lieutenant's uniform but, as it was, just being a woman was enough for Holmes. He would not be kind to her, not Holmes. The London instructions exchanged hands, young Cornelia still with a smile on her face, though the reality of it had died long ago.

"Watson, be on your guard now. Miss Shand and yourself must only discuss small talk. We cannot take her into our confidence until I have spoken with Winston Churchill on the telephone, as loathe as I am to use that instrument. I have had enough surprises this past twenty-four hours."

Watson nodded. "Certainly Holmes, just small talk," though his eyes were already dancing upon the fair Cornelia's lips as he agreed to this condition.

36

Cornelia Shand, mistress to the powerful, watched Holmes leave the room, a foul temper upon him, his shoulders stooped, signifying anger, the door slamming and causing a shower of soot to fall from the old chimney, fortunately being consumed by the fire almost instantaneously.

Watson turned to look at the newly closed door, thinking Holmes reaction to Lieutenant Shand most peculiar and very rude. He was hoping that the young lady would stay with them. Holmes could make one run about so and here was a pretty pair of legs that were willing and able. Holmes had to see reason, they were old men now. An assistant, even a pretty assistant was an asset, nothing more than a positive asset, not to mention all those languages; German being one he had been entirely unable to master, despite three months of sauerkraut and knackwurst.

"Another tot, Lord Watson?" Cornelia enquired, her voice somewhat crestfallen now that Holmes had stormed out of the room.

"No my dear, but come away from the fire and tell me more. Don't be frightened of Holmes. He runs like a jack-rabbit from women, never did say why, but something tells me that you could find your way into his difficult and yet expansive heart."

"Oh I hope so," she replied earnestly, sitting prettily beside Watson, taking up one of his large, wrinkled, pink hands. "I do so hope so."

Holmes sank upon his hard bed, buried his long, bony hands around his tired head and thought out the problem. He had never had a case where a woman was acting as his assistant and such a beautiful one too, it was absurd. Just what did Winston Churchill think he was doing? Had he forgotten the manner in which he worked? There was nothing about a woman mentioned before they sank in the Mazarin, did he think it made it easier? Quite preposterous.

There was a knock at his door.

"Enter," Holmes called out, his voice sounding more harsh than he intended.

The publican stood there, nervous, somewhat overawed by so great a man as Lord Holmes staying at his establishment (though to be sure he had already commissioned a plaque to commemorate the visit). He stood stooping under the low wooden ceiling, not built for giants of the twentieth century. "A letter Lord Holmes, hand delivered it was. The man's eating a pork pie downstairs in the saloon, done in he is, quite a ride down here by motorbike on a night like this."

Holmes glanced out of the leaded windows. The night had fallen and with it, the rain.

"Thank you, Mr Bartley," Holmes said, reaching for the rather fat and bulky letter, noting at once the Admiralty seal. "Be sure the man is well fed and watered, Mr Bartley, an Admiralty messenger is a vital resource to us now we are at war."

The publican nodded, "Anything you say sir. Will the young lady be joining you for supper? It is roast lamb tonight."

"We will be dining together," Holmes told him, "but in the lounge I think. The fire pleases Watson, he is still cold after his fishing trip."

"In the lounge it will be sir. I have told the regulars to rough it in the saloon tonight, though there's much amazement in the town, there's a lot who swore blind you was dead already, if you'll excuse me for mentioning it. The Major said that he thought you'd gone in 1927."

"Retirement is a kind of death, Mr Bartley."

Holmes turned away to his letter. The publican took his cue and departed.

The letter, opened with Holmes's silver knife, quickly revealed that it was from the First Lord, written in his own hand. Enclosed also were a large quantity of bank notes, both German and French.

> *Admiralty House*
> *December 18th, 1939.*
>
> *Sherlock,*
> *By now you will have met Lieutenant Shand and no doubt expressed some reservations to the whole affair. But the business of Whitehall is politic as you so very well know and I am not in charge of budgeting requirements. Sir Oswald Partington was most insistent upon foisting young Cornelia upon you. She has made a great impression upon him (a lot like the late fireball Mrs Lillie Langtry don't you think?) Unfortunately the Operation Chink budget is in his hands, a wretched affair, but he is a very private man. Our secret is safe. This money (to the value of £1,000) will enable you to cope with any surprises on the way. If you need more, get word to Siggy Rothschild in Paris, he will advance you all you need in German currency. Be at all times discrete my friend. An Englishman is no longer welcome in Europe.*
> *Lieutenant Shand is quite competent I believe, I have only met her once. But have no fear, she is well bred and from good county stock. It is my recollection that a closed door can be opened more easily by a pretty pair of legs and I am assured that her legs are the finest in all London. I am forced to accept this condition, Holmes.*

*There are reservations about your health and after the Mazarin episode
many questions are being asked about your presence on board. They
will get no answers. You have the skill, Sherlock, the girl has the
charm, a combination formidable against the Boché.
P.S. Destroy this letter immediately after reading.
W.C.

So that was it. Winston powerless, even as First Lord... things had to
change, it was essential for England that the man become PM. Perhaps then
he would not be bullied into pitting young girls against Nazis.

Well, if she was to come along, she had better be well behaved, better pull
her weight. One mistake and she would be sent packing. This was war, no
parlour game. It was like sending them out against the Boché with an
anchor around their necks. It was an insult, a brazen jibe at their dignity.

Holmes' thoughts ran on. An unhappy man, quite beside himself with a
seething anger, he was almost ready to call Winston or even the PM and tell
them to go instead, but loyalty to his country took precedence. It was the
more important thing by far. There was something he had missed too,
something his anger was blinding him to. He forced himself to calm down
and think more clearly, in the Holmes fashion, mourning the lack of his
pipe and tobacco, cursing his need for distraction to enable his mind to
concentrate. Tea was no adequate substitute.

By suppertime he was calm, not content, but calm, and having read the
instructions this Lieutenant Shand (so called) had brought down with her,
he felt better disposed towards attempting a civil evening, knowing that he
had another mystery to solve this night.

Watson was already at the table, enjoying Cornelia Shand's company no
end, quite bowled over by her grace and charm. "Holmes, Holmes, sit down,
a feast is promised us and that's a fact."

Cornelia, aware that Holmes was still hostile to her, just smiled as the
gaunt, long haired man sat down opposite her, the piercing blue eyes not at
all diminished by his age.

"What are our orders?" Watson asked, keenly.

"I haven't looked at the menu yet," Holmes replied with a twinkle in his eyes.

"No, the London orders," Watson protested. "You are really awkward
tonight Holmes. I really do think I shall let you smoke after all."

*The letter was given to Lord Watson to read. He did not destroy it and it now is
rumoured to be in the still sealed Bormann collection in Sao Paulo University library.*

Holmes noted that statement, he would take Watson up on that once he had replaced his pipe. "Our orders are quite explicit, Watson, but I'm sure Miss Shand," he gave her a quizzical look, "has already discussed them in great detail."

Watson smacked the table with triumph. "Not a word, Holmes, not a blessed word. I do believe that she does not know herself. We discussed her aunt, Mrs Lillie Langtry, quite a gal if you recall. Always had a yen for you, if you remember."

Holmes coloured. He remembered Mrs Langry well and her yapping dogs. The woman was more trouble to him than the entire Baskerville entourage. Nothing would dissuade her from the conviction that he was in love with her. It was a regular embarrassment to receive flowers from her every birthday (though if truth be known, he missed them now she was dead). But here was this name Langtry again, from Watson's lips as well as Winston's pen. Was it a coincidence? He rather thought not and the more sure he was of his suspicions about this Lieutenant Shand.

"We fly tomorrow at noon, Watson. From Folkestone to Paris. There we will stay at the Hotel Paix, near the Arc de Triomphe and meet our contact at a certain restaurant. A German official, or at least a man who acts for the Germans. They want to vet us before allowing us over the frontier. This was as a result of my telegram to Louis Le Villard, son of Francois, the French detective I have assisted from time to time in the past. Louis is no detective, but a diplomat with the French Foreign Office. I asked him to reply to the Admiralty direct, but with discretion. There are few men I can trust on the continent, but Louis is one. However, I think we should prepare for a French Christmas."

"Oh, Christmas in Paris, how romantic," Cornelia sighed, her soft, green eyes glinting in the reflection from the fire burning brightly and warm in the open grate.

"I find nothing romantic about waiting around for Nazis, Miss Shand," Holmes declared icily. Cornelia noticed that this was the second time Holmes had referred to her as Miss Shand, her rank obviously didn't pull weight with him.

"From Paris, assuming all goes well, we shall go by car or train to Nürnberg in time for the Wagner celebration."

"What shall I be?" Cornelia asked, enthusiastically, fingering a delicate emerald ring upon her dress finger. Noticing too, that Holmes was staring quite pointedly at that finger.

"I think a nurse would be proper," Watson suggested, "what say you Holmes?"

He nodded, abstracted. "Yes, our nurse. I think it most appropriate. Get yourself a uniform from the Hastings Service Suppliers, they should be able to accommodate you."

"A nurse? Couldn't I at least be a secretary or your publicity agent?"

A look of horror swept across Holmes' face. "Publicity? This is war Miss Shand. If you want to be a publicist, go to Hollywood, but with us, you will be a nurse. We are old, there's no denying it."

"I say, steady on Holmes," Watson interjected. Holmes ignored him.

"You are quite right Lord Holmes, a nurse is the most logical occupation for me. I'll attend to a uniform first thing in the morning." She seemed quite calm about it, throwing away her rank with the casual abandon of someone who had come by it easily, another key to the jigsaw Holmes was rapidly filling in.

He sat back in his chair and contemplated the fire. "Now tell me Miss Shand, Sir Charles Hainsley was a close friend of yours, was he not?"

Cornelia was more than just a little surprised. "How...?" She asked, unaware that Sir Charles had ever mentioned Lord Holmes, not even once.

"I observe, Miss Shand. I note your shoes are from Bond Street, I note your skirt and blouse are from Jaeger and that you have the garments most likely to be sported by the mistress of a rich man like Sir Oswald, or... his daughter."

"I am not his daughter." Cornelia informed him, gaining strength from that remark.

"No, indeed you are not, but equally true, you are not his mistress. He is a man of sixty-five. A man who is quiet, not outgoing, conservative, a man whose honour is old school. A mistress would be unthinkable for such a man, yet you could have been the mistress of the late and much lamented Sir Charles Hainsley, but even then, I have strong doubts for I believe there was a much stronger, more permanent relationship."

Cornelia was amazed, but kept her peace. She would not contribute one iota to this fabrication, fearing the worst and her undoing.

"The ring you wear," Holmes continued, watching her face very carefully, though he knew everything. "It is shaped in the famous Hainsley Crest. A Welsh family famous in northern Wales. If I know Sir Charles that ring was his mother's, the late Lady Frances Hainsley, a lady much admired in the late eighties."

Cornelia had to give in. She was indeed wearing Lady Frances' ring. Sir Charles had given it to her on the day she turned 14, she had never worn it until the news of his death, only then had it deigned to fit her.

"You brazenly say you were Sir Oswald's mistress, but I believe you to be Sir Charles' daughter, and that through influence, you prevailed upon Sir Oswald to allow you to join the investigation."

Cornelia was pleased. Pleased that Holmes was not so easily deceived as all the others. She had laughed with scorn when she had heard Lord Holmes, a man she considered long dead, would be the one to avenge her father's death, but now she had seen him in action, seen that he was truly a wily old fox, she understood the reason. This man was uncanny, his reputation entirely justified. It was a relief.

"So, it is Cornelia Hainsley," Watson said, "which would make you niece to Sir Oswald."

"You are quite right Watson," Holmes confirmed, "and that will explain how she was able to convince an otherwise sane man to agree to her accompanying us."

"I have to confirm all," Cornelia acquiesced, "you find me out. But I am amazed Lord Holmes, for not once do I recall your name being mentioned in my house, except in passing reference to your adventures in the newspapers or old Strand Magazines."

"No need, Miss Cornelia, no need. It is simply that the Lady Frances was a beauty, so much so that several illegal duels were fought over her, though she never once accepted a victor, always falling for the fallen, tending to their wounds. Your grandmother was a jewel of society and I remember her standing one evening with the arm of the Prince of Wales upon her own, beside the Brighton Palace, dazzling all society. You, my dear, are the recreation of that beauty, do you not see the resemblance now, Watson?"

Watson was indeed astounded. It was Lady Frances. He could imagine a different set of clothes, another place, another time...

"Holmes, you never fail to astonish me, how did you tell?"

"There is no great mystery, there could have been only one explanation. We knew Sir Oswald had no mistress, certainly none so beautiful as young Cornelia here, or else all London would be talking of it. The fact of the Hainsley ring, that she has the Hainsley face and that Sir Charles so recently trod the same course as us, all tie in to persuade me that she did indeed force Sir Oswald to forward her name and construct a story that she thought would be convincing. Vengeance can be a persuasive force, can it not, Watson?"

"It can, Holmes and is."

Cornelia bowed her head. "I sought nothing more than to go to Nürnberg, establish the facts, Lord Holmes. He was my father, it was simply a business trip according to my Mama, but when I discovered in which country it was and which town, I approached my Uncle Oswald immediately. It was entirely my idea, he could not turn my mind away from it. My father was the best that ever lived, I miss him so."

Holmes perceived tears were welling and he relented, turning his penetrating gaze elsewhere. "Watson comfort the gel, she's brave. No lieutenant, but any daughter of Sir Charles Hainsley is something for the Boché to consider. They have a formidable enemy now." He nodded to the girl. "Miss Cornelia Hainsley, out of respect to your father, welcome to the old firm of Watson and Holmes."

She could hardly believe her ears. Her bright but dewy eyes lit upon the great detective's face. "Then I may stay?"

"My child, you are under orders. We shall find the truth, discover just how your father died and by whose hand."

"Oh Lord Holmes, dear Dr Watson, I cannot say how relieved I am. How pleased I am that I do not have to continue to be a lieutenant. It did not sit well upon my shoulders, I must admit."

"Absurd," Watson declared, "nor a mistress, indeed I am quite relieved myself. Did you know that Holmes cannot refuse a damsel in distress?"

"I had not thought to approach him, nor indeed knew he was still a detective. But I must insist Lord Holmes that you remember that I am long out of the classroom and must not be treated like a child."

Holmes lifted one eyebrow. "I think ox-tail soup before the lamb, Watson," he said, hungry now another mystery was cleared up. "Then, after supper, there's maps and planning to go over. You can read a map, I trust?" Holmes enquired.

"Oh yes, I'm glad my father didn't bring me up a lady. We went hiking many times in these past years. Map reading was something we learned very quickly. My father could walk twice as fast as we; quite often all my young brother and I would see is the back of his head disappearing over some distant hill. It is funny how all maps seemed to lead to public houses, don't you think?"

Holmes broke bread. "Just like the sea," he answered, looking about him and smiling briefly at Watson, "just like the sea."

***

"I don't like it one bit, Holmes." Watson was protesting, clinging to the sides of an old Avro with grim determination. The flimsy, wooden plane tossed and plummeted with every stray air pocket, the ride was worse than a night in the channel. The roar of the engines throbbed in his sensitive ears. Even his leather straps hurt. Worse, Holmes would keep looking out of the only window for the dreaded Stukas that might at any moment strike at them from on high. Air travel did not seem to have improved much since the days of Alcock and Brown.

"Chin up, Watson, we're nearly there. We are over the Channel at least," Holmes told him, quite enjoying the experience so far.

"But Holmes, leaving our bath-chairs behind. It is a disaster, we shall never get about without them."

"Nonsense, Watson. It was unavoidable. This plane would not take off with them on board. No light, flimsy thing a bath-chair. I am assured a similar vehicle exists in Paris."

"But this is terrible, Holmes. We have already lost our baggage, now our bath-chairs. It will be our very boots next, I swear it."

"Don't worry about your boots," Cornelia called out to Watson, squeezing her way out of the cockpit to join her companions. "As long as you stay in them, Dr Watson, your boots won't easily escape without you."

"Well said," Holmes agreed, admiring her nurse's uniform for the second time and her splendid Royal blue cape.

"The pilot says we shall land in fifteen minutes, he is so sweet. His name is Howard Biggs, which are the very names of my two dogs, isn't that amusing, Lord Holmes?"

"Dogs?" Watson asked, mishearing, fearing that animals had now got loose in the plane.

"My two Border Collies, Howard and Bigsy. Oh I do miss them so," she said wistfully.

The pilot, a long term commercial flyer with Folkestone Air Ferries was delighted (if not a little mystified) to have passengers instead of freight. Happy also to have the lovely Cornelia to show all the controls to and boast of his exploits in Casablanca, or any other far off spot that sounded more romantic than Folkestone. The identities of his passengers was kept from him. Cornelia was a nurse escorting two elderly patients for recuperation in France. The waterways being too dangerous and their money being sound enough to hire their own plane to go in style (even if the plane was old and rough).

Holmes mostly kept silent, thinking only about his last flight to Europe, with Group Captain W.E. Johns, a distinguished pilot, a pioneer of air to air combat. Men of his ilk were not easily replaced by the Howard Biggs or Border Collies.

"We're running into a bit of cloud," Biggs shouted back. "I'm going to climb above it. Hold on gentlemen, it is going to be a bumpy ride."

"What is it they say about holidays?" Cornelia put to Watson with a smile. "Getting there is half the fun."

A Brush with the Boché

Watson was not amused.

The plane fell a clear fifty feet before picking itself up again and all of them hit their heads with great force upon the canvas roof. Holmes wished an aircraft with seats had been available.

"Damn and blast it," Watson exploded. "Hold onto your straps Miss Cornelia, this is no time for jests. This pilot could kill us off before we get within ten miles of the Boché."

"Have no fear, Watson, above the clouds all will be smooth sailing." Holmes informed them, having experienced this sort of flying before with Captain Johns.

Pilot Biggs did indeed get them above the clouds and here the sun was a glorious sight to see, set in a perfect blue sky. Even Watson relaxed, astonished to see a pure summer's day hovering above a sour December below. "Gad Holmes, so this is what flying is all about."

But Holmes, sharp eyed as ever, had noticed a speck somewhat to the left of the plane and coming their way.

"Miss Cornelia, go tell the pilot that we have a visit from the Luftwaffe."

Cornelia's heart missed a beat as she scurried back into the cockpit to comply with Holmes' instructions. However, pilot Biggs was no slouch and had already noted the aircraft, a Fokker single-engined fighter, not something he would want to tangle with at all.

"It's over French air-space whilst there is this heavy cloud," he told her, "he must be confident. Sit down, strap yourself in."

Cornelia quickly obeyed, scared the Nazi plane would shoot them down, crossing fingers, even toes for luck.

"He won't do anything to us," Biggs declared uncertainly, "we are over France, they haven't shot any of our planes down over France yet, not unarmed ones, perhaps they don't want to alarm the French."

"But we are British, we are at war with them," Cornelia pointed out, "our ships are sunk, why not ourselves?"

It was fair comment.

The Fokker came at them at full throttle, menacing, yet Biggs kept to his course, his heart beating wildly. At last, with only inches to spare, the Nazi plane zoomed by, engines screaming at their tugboat Avro, diving into the cloud, banking right and out again, readying for another 'buzz' as Biggs called it. Watson crossed himself, often.

"It's a game," Biggs announced, with possibly less confidence than before. "We'll keep this course, he's just trying to frighten us."

"He's damn well succeeding," Watson exclaimed; suddenly intensely aware he needed a bathroom.

The German plane, marked with a red flash on the side and the inevitable swastica, readied for another mock attack.

"As soon as he approaches," Holmes called out, "dive into the clouds pilot. I do believe that he is in earnest this time."

"No, Holmes," Watson protested, his bladder abandoning all hope. "We might provoke him."

But Biggs was worried too, not at all sure, as they flew over French open fields below, that the German would not practice his gunnery on an unarmed freight plane. Holmes and he shared that keen distrust of all foreigners. Cornelia just sat with her hands over her eyes praying that she would live.

The Fokker swooped down upon them and even without Holmes' suggestion Biggs knew he had to get out of the way. As he pushed up the flaps, the first spray of the German's sting grazed the sky above them, scaring them all. They dived, spiralling down into the thick clouds, bumping, wrenching, seemingly out of control, Holmes gripping a petrified Watson's sleeve, Cornelia breaking out in an unladylike sweat for the very first time. Biggs slowly pulled them out of the dive, only just in time, for the clouds seemed to go on forever, down to the very fields themselves. He levelled out at an alarmingly fast speed (possibly a record) hurtling over the French countryside, not looking back for fear of being pursued. French peasants were astonished to see so ungainly a plane hurtle over them at such speeds bringing to mind the heroics of the Schneider Cup and drew comfort from the fact that the English were at last taking aviation seriously. The Fokker did not pursue, his game was over. Had he known whom the old Avro carried, the outcome of the second world war might have been very different.

"Close call," Biggs shouted out, turning to Cornelia and giving her a thumbs up sign. She looked pale. "Those were real bullets," Cornelia protested, the entire experience seemingly unreal to her, save the uncomfortable feeling around her underclothes.

"Real as you or me miss. This route will be closed to British planes soon. The Boché will take France soon enough, their air force is a joke, last war stuff, not much to stand up to the modern killers."

Cornelia pitied France, but thought they would put up a good fight. She had read about Napoleon, he had had real fighters, al! France needed was another Napoleon, she was sure of it.

"Hold on," Biggs yelled back, "we're going into land."

The Hotel Paix was busy and full, more or less just as they remembered it from their last visit and the management still the same. Monsieur Reynaud took great delight in welcoming the two famous gentlemen in tweeds from England. "But Monsieur," he addressed Lord Holmes, "you do not wear your..." he searched his vocabulary for the word, "Deerstalker, your cape and where is the famous pipe?"

Lord Holmes allowed the small effeminate man a depreciating smile. "I prefer to be bare headed my man. Deerstalkers have not been worn in London for some years now. As for my Inverness, mere protection from the soot and grime that pervades London, a reasonable overcoat will serve purpose and the pipe, as with almost all my other vices, has been locked up by my 'friend' Dr Watson here, who wishes to prolong my life by making me miserable."

"I say Holmes, not fair. Not even true. The hat and Inverness went down with the baggage, that was surely no action of my part?

"No matter," Holmes declared, "we will go to our rooms. Miss Cornelia will attend us at 7 o'clock this evening." He turned to face her. "We will be taking a stroll and dining at La Cuillère Engraissé."

"A good choice, Lord Holmes," the manager told them, even though he wouldn't be caught dead in it himself.

The view from the Hotel Paix was not impressive. Watson had seen better brick walls, but Holmes, in the adjoining rooms was quite happy. "At La Cuillère Engraissé Watson, we will be looking for a Hugo Klauser, a Franco-German. The FO think he's tipped for a leading post here should the Nazis take France."

"It is to be hoped they won't take it this Christmas, Holmes."

"Never fear, old chap Their attention is focused on the Low countries and Norway at present. I think we shall have a pleasant Christmas in France. I suppose a little gift will be in order for Miss Cornelia?"

"Oh, I'll see to that," Watson told him enthusiastically.

"She has spirit," Holmes remarked, heading for the bathroom, "we cannot take that from her, despite her fragile appearance."

"In my experience as a doctor and a married man, Holmes, a fragile appearance denotes a certain strength and quality within, in direct proportion to their outward appearance of weakness."

Holmes thought on that a moment. "Exactly," opening the bathroom door. "Let's keep discussion to minor matters Watson, the walls may have ears, the keyhole spies."

Wide-eyed, Watson nodded, understanding completely. "Not a word of import shall pass these lips, Holmes."

"I'm sure it won't, Watson," Holmes replied mysteriously, shutting the door behind him.

4

Out and Down in Paris – not London

The Parisian streets were not as gay as remembered in the past. Just as in London the blackout had taken care of that. Yet the city remained determined and steadfast, Parisian restaurants stood bright and eternally full behind black shutters and roller-blinds. Everywhere was plunged into darkness. Whereas London looked almost normal in the nightly blackout, Paris stood crazy, unable to comprehend; violations everywhere one looked. Negotiating one's way by cab to La Cuillère Engraissé was no easy task, even for a Parisian cabbie who claimed to be able to get them there with his eyes shut. (Watson insisted that his eyes remained open). There was no fog, which was a refreshing change from London, but it was seasonably cold; a frost threatened, something Watson's chest feared most of all. He worried about Holmes as well. The man may seem indestructible, but Watson knew that weather like this played upon Holmes' old wounds (gained in part from that extraordinary escape from the swirling torrent at Reichenbach; Moriarty's evil deed, ever the dread scourge of Holmes' professional and private life).

Cornelia was in good spirits however, excited to be in Paris. It was not her first trip abroad but she was always astonished at the sharp difference of the architecture in Parisian homes, the castles, the elegance, the entire grand design of the city, the people too. How astonishingly different they all looked, how beautiful the women in their long gowns. She thought of the women in English society and had to admit that they were more than dull compared to the Parisian women. Even the peasants, dirty as they were, seemed to be charming. She was in love with the place and was thus transported, far from in the mood to play the role as nurse to Holmes and Watson. She was in need of care herself, so excited and happy was she, almost forgetting the purpose of her trip to avenge her father's death.

"May I suggest a little bromide in her coffee," Holmes muttered to Watson as Cornelia called out, "How sweet, how charming," for the one thousandth time since they had left the hotel.

Watson shook his head, fully understanding her excitement. Paris was infectious, only experience and respect for Holmes prevented him from crying out in praise too, as Cornelia pointed out one darkened detail after another. If anything, Paris was more interesting in the dark moonlight, for one began to notice much more, no longer distracted by the electric or gas lights.

"It is so pleasant to ride in these new Citroëns, Watson. The London cab could learn a trick or two from this machine. One cannot feel a single bump on this road. A far cry from the carriages of old."

"A godsend Holmes, a carriage on cobbles is good for nothing but piles, I should know, I treated enough at my practice. Cullingford my locum, was of the opinion that a poor diet causes piles, but I'm firm on carriages, the old bone shakers. Rapid decline in piles since the advent of the popular motor car, Holmes. Henry Ford should receive a Nobel prize for that achievement alone."

"I'll put it to the committee," Holmes told him with a smile hidden in the darkness.

With an abruptness that nearly had them all out of their seats, the cab drew up outside a church. The driver announced that it was as near as he would go to the restaurant, he, like the hotel manager, did not approve of the goings on in that particular place.

Holmes was cross, La Cuillère Engraissé was at least fifty yards away.

"Pourriez vous me changer un billet de mille francs?" Holmes asked.

The cabbie was most insulted. "Pas change, deux mille francs monsieur, regardez la meter."

"Je vous en prie," Holmes replied handing over a thousand francs and helping Watson out.

"I rather think he wants two thousand francs," Cornelia explained getting out the other side. Holmes ignored her, bustling them both away from the cab in the direction of the restaurant, a good distance away. "Bonne nuit, monsieur," Holmes called out, despite the cabbie's loud protestations. "These people will rob you blind if you let them. Two thousand francs and he doesn't even take us to the doors. Prices may be rising, but I remember a time when that ride would have cost no more than five hundred francs."

"King Louis has gone now, Holmes, prices change," Watson remarked, thinking it an amusing jest.

"Merde, les Anglais, toutes cochons..." the cabbie boiled away behind them, but to no avail, his fares had left him and there was not a policeman in sight, nor would he chase them to La Cuillère Engraissé for fear of losing his cab and his life. He surrendered and drove off swearing most vehemently as he went, vowing to never ferry another Englishman.

Lord Holmes led his mystified charges towards the dim, but well-signed restaurant.

"Nasty little Frenchman," Holmes muttered, never well disposed to the lowly rabble, believing the English cabbie the salt of the earth and a most treasured man. He had never once been overcharged there.

Watson felt Holmes was being a little unfair, but he knew Holmes was no Francophile.

"I am so hungry," Cornelia announced as they entered the crowded restaurant. Watson sniffed the food and smiled at her. "My gosh there's a few delicious odours in here, agree Holmes?"

"Je voudrais une omelette," Holmes replied, "nothing more."

Cornelia felt that Holmes had not quite got into the spirit of the evening.

Inside dense smoke, loud singing, shiny uniforms, busy waiters, and earnest, vociferous conversation assailed their senses. Cornelia was quite bemused by the difference to a British restaurant. She could not believe the people she saw, as they were guided to a corner table near to a window, a spot not as popular as the rest of the room. She wanted to be with the throng as they shouted at each other to be heard over the piano playing, but ever polite she remarked "so charming and so atmospheric." The waiter that led them there had such a shiny, bald head, she could practically see the entire restaurant reflected on it.

The piano was situated in a very smoky corner where a lot of men crowded around a petite, strange, waif-like woman, not young, but instantly arresting; her voice like the wailing of a broken heart, a catalogue of missed opportunities, at once tuneful, yet tugging at one's emotions. Cornelia asked who it was. The waiter shrugged, turning to look at the girl drinking back some wine, moving onto another sad song. He shrugged. "It is Edith, she comes, she makes us all miserable, she goes..."

Cornelia was impressed, no one sang like that in England. It all sounded so sad. Everything was totally different. Monastery tables, paper tablecloths, a menu written upon the wall. Not at all the type of place she suspected Nazis, even French Nazis to collect.

Holmes was being mysterious, but neither she, nor Watson felt uncomfortable. There was too big a crush for that. Their wine arrived in a carafe and Holmes tasted it, then poured, pronouncing it a, "mildly obnoxious little thing, but sufficient for our needs."

As far as they could tell there were no other foreigners to be seen. The men almost without exception wore short hair, shaved in that most unpleasant crop favoured by their mentor, Adolf Hitler, and there were quite a few sporting a moustache in the familiar style. Cornelia had noticed too, that the Charlie Chaplin film showing across the way from the restaurant had a lot of paint daubed on the posters advertising it. The word *juif* was scrawled across them. She'd seen the same thing in East London and hated it.

A young, arab waiter approached their table, his thin, rather hard face, worried by something. His eyes sought Cornelia's but she successfully avoided them, having never been served by an arab before and uncomfortable with it. She turned her eyes upon Holmes instead. "Who are we meeting?".

"A friend of the Duke's," Holmes replied, sipping his wine. "Do you think he's one of these men here?" Watson asked.

"I rather think not, Watson, now shall we order? The singer is rather interesting don't you think; Cornelia?"

She nodded, the plaintive song of a lost lover, truly exotic to her ears.

The waiter, a strange choice of employee for a restaurant catering to the proponents of the master race, swept a nervous perspiration from his prominent forehead, his eyes darting from Holmes to Cornelia, confusion in them as he wrote down their orders. As this tedious task was completed, he moved to adjust Watson's place setting and deliberately, (it seemed to Cornelia), upset Watson's wine glass, making a big fuss about it, wiping up everything in sight, saving Watson's knees from a soaking. At last he left, promising Watson a new glass.

"Poor chap looked most embarrassed," Watson said, amused by this time.

Holmes corrected him. "That upset was a necessary signal, though somewhat overdone in my opinion."

Indeed, both Cornelia and Watson noticed Holmes was burning a piece of paper in the flame of the table candle. A curious expression upon his thin, hawk-like face.

"It appears there is a change of plan," was all he said, as the young waiter returned with a new glass for Watson and a carafe of wine 'on the house'. "Since I cannot smoke my pipe, Watson, I think le tabac would be a blessing. A cigar perhaps."

"Cigarettes monsieur?" The waiter enquired.

"Cigar," Holmes affirmed.

"Pas cigar, cigarette..."

"Non merci," Holmes sighed, but the waiter still hovered.

"Ca ne fait rien," Cornelia told him, sending him away, dying to hear what was in the note.

Holmes resigning himself to not smoking, took a sip of the wine and bent forward towards his cohorts explaining in a low voice, "A man will join our table at half-past nine this evening. The Duke's friend is inexplicably detained. Although I am not certain, I believe the man will be Heinrich Döre, for the note told me a man of influence with the Nazi Government would be our man. For who else maintains such strong links with the fascist movement in England, France and Germany? He is a German living here in Paris, publishes an evil magazine called *Der Schuessel*, The Key. It promotes Nazi propaganda of the most perverted kind. It is published in French and distributed to schools, given away on street corners to stir up anti-semitic sentiments, already rife in all of Europe."

"Oh it is so awful, Lord Holmes. I hear such terrible things about the labour camps, even many dying there, can it be true?" Cornelia asked.

"Yes my dear, I fear that it is entirely possible." Watson answered for his friend. "I read a most horrifying article in *The Telegraph* on how they employ genetic science to decide on who is Jewish, or not; measuring foreheads, lengths of noses, everything. A loathsome idea."

"Then Mr Punch would not fare too well in Germany, Watson. Come now, this is not a subject for the supper table. You will seriously upset our young nurse."

"Perhaps you should," Cornelia said, sipping some wine, "I am very ignorant of these things, I think I should know more and besides are we not supposed to be pro-German."

Holmes looked at her in surprise, the young woman deserved constant reappraisal, not so weak and feeble minded as he had thought at first.

"Point taken, my dear. Your suggestion is quite proper considering our company, but nevertheless, I believe all races are entitled to a place in the sun, as it were."

"I can vouch for that," Watson affirmed, "the sun never sets on our empire."

"For now, but what of next year? What then Watson? Who will keep Singapore safe from an aggressive Japan? Could we even keep the Cape safe from German hands?"

"Surely we are strong enough Holmes."

"Empires rise and fall Cornelia. History is certain about this."

Cornelia shared Holmes' bleak view. Was anything safe in this world? "When will we go to Germany?"

Holmes frowned. "The trouble with women, Watson, is that they ask too many questions."

"One of the troubles," a voice added. It was a German voice, but his English was spoken with a refined manner. All three looked up to see the face of a young man of no more than thirty. He had a spare figure, thin, nervous fingers, steel grey hair, intense brooding brown eyes and a rapier scar over his dark eyebrows. His entrance had excited the attention of onlookers, who endeavoured to identify the three he had sat down with, but failed to do so. A waiter, a different one this time, appeared at his side. A few brief commands, imperious, but softly spoken and within seconds schnapps was upon the table, the music changed to Strauss and the tiny figure of Piaf had made a hurried exit out of the restaurant, followed by four or five hangers-on. It was not clear whether she left because of the new arrival, or that she had a new café to go to before the night was over. Cornelia got the impression it was because of their new table guest.

Watson was most uncomfortable and looked about the restaurant, noting a new, tense atmosphere. Only Holmes was relaxed; in command as always.

"Life can be so difficult, can it not, Lord Holmes – yet one cannot stress enough times the importance of realising its essential sweetness and desirability."

"Yet the road is fraught with danger," Holmes answered, as if this was a rehearsed conversation in some mysterious code. Instinctively, both Watson and Cornelia knew they detested this new arrival with all their heart and mind.

"Heinrich Döre," the German informed them, abruptly extending a hand for Holmes to shake. "It is a great pleasure to meet the world's greatest detective." He turned to Watson. "And the celebrated Dr Watson; the

Boswell without whom Lord Holmes would be but a plain Mister, an unknown theorist on the more astonishing crimes. And the young lady, a most charming, dare I say exquisite example of all that is pure and so good about the English race."

A vile, silken tongue, but wasted on the three of them. Holmes knew this sort of man of old. They would lie, cheat, exude noxious praises, yet were as trustworthy as Judas Iscariot, as dangerous as Brutus. One had to watch them very carefully indeed. This man had sick, twisted lips and if rumour was correct, his sexual perversions were so base that even Paris was astonished at their depravity. Holmes had no proof (when had he ever needed to look far for it) but just one look confirmed all his prejudices. At all costs young Cornelia had to be kept out of this man's reach. To lose one more Hainsley would be a calamity Holmes would prefer not to have on his conscience. "I understand you have a passion for Wagner, Lord Holmes," Herr Döre enquired, simply tossing back his third glass of schnapps, as if to demonstrate his iron-will.

"Indeed, Herr Döre. I have an invitation to Nürnberg, it is said that you are a man of influence…"

"Influence," he repeated slowly, enjoying the word. "Yes, people have said that." He smiled, not an easy or pleasant sight for one so young as Cornelia. "And why would you want to visit Germany at a time like this?"

"Christmas is an interesting time in Germany, Herr Döre and after all, Germany is the home of St Nicolas, the patron saint of Christmas." Holmes countered.

Herr Döre rubbed his nose, returning his gaze to Cornelia, who was thinking that St Nicolas was a Greek patron Saint, but kept it to herself. "And what is your interest in Nürnberg?" he asked her. Cornelia was not well prepared to answer this, but kept a cool head. "I have no interest in Nürnberg sir, but I am Lord Holmes' and Dr Watson's nurse. They can't be allowed out on their own without me. If I may speak for the good gentlemen sir, though I shall probably get into hot water for this, the gentlemen are rather old sir, as you can plainly see. This war with your country could go on for quite a time, for I'm sure we shall not give up an inch without a great struggle. Yet Lord Holmes' love for Wagner might be taken from them forever, he could be robbed of one last concert, it would be a tragedy if war destroyed all hope of music in England."

Herr Döre acknowledged her plea. It was a fact that Wagner could not be played in the Royal Albert Hall for the duration of the war. "Lord Holmes," he said, quickly casting a penetrating look into the detective's hooded, smoke-affected eyes. "Germany has not forgotten Von Bork! You are not perhaps on your way to conduct a case in Nürnberg?"

He frowned as Holmes appeared as bland and undisturbed as ever. "You see, I take a leaf out of your own book. Eliminate all the factors, the one that remains, however improbable, must be the truth."

"I say," Watson muttered, recognising this as one of Holmes' favourite sayings.

"Which is," Herr Döre went on, "that you wish to visit Nürnberg with Dr Watson and a pretty young nurse."

"I have never been to Nürnberg," Holmes informed him, wishing he had a pipe to draw on, making a mental note to purchase one in the morning.

"No? Then it would not matter if the Wagner memorial concert were held in Essen, or even Berlin?"

"No," Holmes confirmed, "save that it would be an embarrassment for my Government if we were discovered in Berlin. Nürnberg is not a strategic target – yet it is a sensitive area."

"So," Herr Döre said, with a sharp intake of breath, like a snake coiled around a large rat, "you have a need for duplicity, a quest for a Wagner Concert, a Christmas abroad, yet no great unsolved murder to investigate?"

"There is none that I know of," Holmes replied.

"Tell me Lord Holmes, how did you get out of the Reichenbach Falls? I have seen them, no other man could have survived."

Watson laughed, a nervous laugh. "Professional secret, old boy. Mustn't ever ask Holmes that. Houdini never talked, neither shall Holmes."

Herr Döre smiled, conceding the point. "I find it very strange that the famous detective should not visit Europe for several years, yet choose the moment Germany and England are at war to do so. Venturing to go to Nürnberg, of all places."

"I realise it is unpatriotic, that if the British press were to discover this I should be vilified from every editorial, but let us be sensible men, Herr Döre. I am old, your's is a young man's war. Furthermore, it is common knowledge that your forces will overwhelm England this spring, we are not prepared. It will be a terrible time for England. Perhaps many of us will die, I cannot pretend to like this, but if I can see just one more Wagner concert (yes, I confess it is a selfish decision) I shall be happy. Yes, I must admit that there is another side to our journey too. I confess it. We can plead England's case with those who might be close to the Fuhrer, insist that we be united by a treaty, without bloodshed. I saw the horrors of the last war, I should like to save England from the beastly conflagration. I do not want London flattened. I would not wish for a single English death. A war would be a piteous thing, the last was quite obscene enough."

Watson was amazed. Never had Holmes pretended to appeasement before, these were odd words to fall from his lips.

Herr Döre signalled to his waiter, some food was brought over for them all, Holmes' omelette done to perfection.

"We eat," Herr Döre ordered. "I will think on your 'special case', perhaps something can be achieved. These things can be arranged."

Both Watson and Cornelia wished that it could be arranged the sooner, for neither relished sitting and eating with this odious man for very much longer.

Herr Döre looked around the restaurant a moment, receiving nervous nods from one or two of the shaven heads in the room, but mostly he concentrated on his food. His eyes were fastened to his plate, his mouth crammed full as if this were his last meal for a long while, or his first. It was gross and unpleasant to watch. Even then, with his mouth full, he spoke to Holmes, though his eyes never left his plate. "And yet, you say there's no 'case' in Nürnberg?"

Holmes gave a quick nod to Watson, as if to say, "All's well." He pushed his food around his plate, thinking out his reply most carefully. "In times past, Herr Döre, the periods I spent inactive were most excruciatingly boring. Dr Watson has already recorded my decline into excessive use of cocaine as a solution to this boredom. What else could I live for? Without intellectual activity I am at a loss. I might as well be a pebble in the street being scraped by the never ending Baker Street traffic, a mere atom in the yellow fog that chokes the dun-coloured houses. What could be more dull and hopelessly boring? What use my gifts Herr Döre, when there is no business to put them to full use? England has forgotten us, crime has become so commonplace, so run of the mill, there are no challenges. Hence sir, a voyage to Nürnberg to hear Wagner once more, performed by Germans at a time when England does not wish me to go; at a time I might meet new people, new exciting minds, be stimulated by the grand new order of things. There is no case, Herr Döre, but if one was presented to me, I should leap at the chance, leap at it."

Watson was more than a little confused at this explanation from his friend, but just hoped that this was merely a ploy to encourage Herr Döre, but it was a shock to hear such words from a staunch Englander as Holmes.

"And of your business with the cocaine?" Herr Döre asked, "it is outlawed now y'know, or perhaps you have found some other drug...?"

"Oh he is cured now," Dr Watson declared most emphatically, "that great man Sigmund Freud cured Holmes of his addiction many years ago.*

"Juden," Herr Döre hissed sharply, quite frightening Cornelia. "Sigmund Freud is a Jew."

"It was necessary at the time," Watson informed him. "The fact of his being Jewish was not considered."

"They flee to Switzerland, but when the final program is complete, they will all go, Swiss or no Swiss. Judenhetzef"

Holmes had no wish to be side-tracked onto this distasteful subject, nor have his personal problems exposed to the likes of this man.

Herr Döre seemed amused by something, a malicious smile crept over his face. "Tell me, Lord Holmes, you still possess your full faculties? Can you tell me where I have been this evening."

It was always the way. Perhaps Jesus was persecuted this way, miracles on demand, always having to prove his sincerity. Holmes had no choice.

"Certainly," Holmes told him, for he had been studying the man ever since he had sat down with them. Herr Döre sat with the confident smugness of a man who believes his secrets impenetrable.

"You have spent most of the day in your printing press, where you drank coffee, ate sausage, taking time off for a shave and haircut around noon. I believe you returned to your printing press to discover that many errors had been made and a sudden re-setting of the entire paper would have to be done. The ink on your sleeves would indicate the job was a messy one, causing you much aggravation, the ink behind your left ear would indicate that you scratched your head more than once trying to cope with the problems. After your work, angry and tired, you took a walk with friends. Your boots scuffed and spattered with blood would indicate that you went by a nearby immigrants alley and kicked several of those unfortunates, causing much bodily harm. From the lack of marks upon your body and clothing, one can deduce they offered no resistance, or were tied up. You also used your fists, the blood under your fingernails the proof. Yet you are normally a fastidious man, I can judge that from the cut of your clothes. This evening you were pressed for time and the physical contact, coupled with violence, excited you, hence the slight cut on your bottom lip, bitten in a moment of intense excitement, not more than an hour ago, for the bruise is still rising."

*(*The Seven Per Cent Solution* by John H. Watson as edited by Nicholas Meyer.)

Herr Döre looked at Holmes in sheer astonishment, gaping like a fish. No word of confirmation was necessary, it was written in plain language in his mean eyes. He pushed back his chair, signalling to the waiter, hovering nearby. "I will settle the account tomorrow, kindly place my guests' meals upon my account also." He turned to Cornelia and bowed slightly. She was trying to calm herself after listening to Holmes' horrific account of Herr Döre's day. "It will be a pleasure to see you again my dear." His eyes pinned her to her seat, turning every muscle in her body limp with fear. "Lord Holmes and Dr Watson here will be joining our Christmas party at Chateau Vernet, just outside Strasbourg on the Rhine. A delightful place and our host, Karl Flohn a most interesting man, like you Lord Holmes, a man of science, but in engineering. He designs in concrete and steel, quite the modern thing."

"But this is rather sudden," Holmes said, not at all sure this was what he expected.

"Something a detective cannot do, predict where he shall spend Christmas. But your Wagner depends upon it, Lord Holmes. If I recall, it does not begin until January the 8th. Karl Flohn is already expecting you and your party. There will be many interesting guests there and that part of France (or should I say the disputed territories?) is very pleasant at this time of year. Note, too, that from Strasbourg to Nürnberg is but a distance of 290 kilometers. No great distance."

"When will we leave?" Holmes asked, resigned to a Christmas with this man. Realising that for all Herr Döre's airs he was merely a messenger boy.

"Obermorgen, the day after tomorrow. There is a train to Strasbourg and we shall travel together. I look forward to it with great interest..." Again his gaze had wandered towards Cornelia. Both Holmes and Watson noticed and duly recorded the fact.

"I shall contact your Hotel, Lord Holmes. Tickets may be purchased nearby, I daresay the Manager will deal with that himself. Good evening..." he paused a table away from them, "Just one thing," he smiled again most unnecessarily in Watson's opinion, "It was a cat I strangled. After all, if an immigrant is dead, who else will look after his cat?"

The man of compassion left forthwith, leaving three of English stock in a state of shock. "The man's a fiend!" Watson complained. "Strangled a pussy cat! Jove, Holmes, these Germans are monsters." Cornelia felt quite sick and quickly swallowed a full glass of wine to steady her nerves. Fortunately the atmosphere in the restaurant improved by almost one thousand per cent the moment Herr Döre and a few others with him, departed the restaurant. Yet the bitter taste of his visit was enough to signal that far worse was to come.

Cornelia was already in dread, to think of that man's dreadful bloodstained hands wanting to touch her, it was sheer horror itself.

"I have heard of this Karl Flohn," Holmes said at last, "it will be a fruitful meeting, Watson. Churchill will be pleased at our progress I think."

"You've heard of this man?" Watson asked, not at all surprised.

"The Flohn effect they call it Watson. His methods of production have made German factory efficiency what it is today. He has studied man and machine so well that it is said he has discovered the true harmony between flesh and steel, an inhuman slavery to production. His designs produce everything from tanks to butter, if we are admitted to the Flohn home, then we are admitted to Germany as 'bone fide' visitors."

"This is good news, Holmes, but was not Herr Döre suspicious?"

"I'm afraid his suspicions were somewhat suppressed by his sudden affliction for young Cornelia here and by an ostentatious display of my deductive powers. I might add that Herr Döre has an asthmatic disposition and that he is a weak individual addicted to alcohol. You noticed his eyes, the shaking hands, the way the schnapps hardly touched his throat. We have no need to worry about him, he is just our contact."

"Indeed yes, but..."

But Holmes bored of Herr Döre. "This is an odd restaurant to find in Paris, Watson. It is nothing but mock German. Oswald Mosley would find a welcome here, no doubt, but it would be a pathetic gathering I think. I vote we should seek out the real Paris whilst we remain, do you agree Cornelia?"

"Oh yes, Lord Holmes. I am quite overcome by this place. This isn't quite the Paris I know. The people look so serious. We should have eaten at Le Mal Herbe, that looked so nice."

"This is, I am saddened to say but a picture of Paris to come," Holmes informed her, a trace of regret in his tired voice. "Come, let us away. Herr Döre pays, we will be grateful for small mercies and squander our money in more cheerful places."

They rose and made their way to the door, ignored by most of the patrons. Holmes stopped Cornelia by the arm just on the threshold.

"My dear, I must think awhile, perhaps you will be Watson's escort for the rest of the evening. I must be alone." He turned to Watson. "Tomorrow, dear Watson, we shall find you a bath-chair, that I promise."

"Nothing too flamboyant, I trust," Watson commented, "but I thank you for remembering, Holmes. The old jezail bullet wound has lain quiet these past few days, but I have no doubt it will return by Christmas, it always does."

Outside, whilst Watson summoned a cab, Holmes spoke again to Cornelia. "You speak German, do you not?"

"Ja, Herr Holmes."

"Well that is good, tell no one of it, but listen well, you shall be our ears. We must beware of treachery, the spider does not invite you into his parlour without the surety of his ability to eat you up. Strasbourg is but a stop. No word about Dr Laubscher will pass our lips, but I would not be at all surprised if Herr Flohn did not turn out to know our Dr Laubscher very well!"

"You have knowledge of this?"

"Simple educated guesswork, but at last we are heading in the right direction. I shall make some enquiries this night, we have not much time. I suspect some hand guides us, I want to know why."

Watson rejoined them. "I have a cab," he announced. "Eight hundred francs to the Café Picard, you'll remember the Picard, Holmes. Good dancing to be had there if my memory serves me."

"It is to be hoped that it is still there, Watson. Much has gone on since the Gay Nineties."

"Oh I say, you may be right Holmes, but the Café Royal still packs 'em in, the Palais Dansant still goes on, why not the Picard?"

"I was just jesting, Watson. Do not get all fired up. Now see Miss Cornelia has a good time, make sure he does not tire you out my dear. Once Watson has the bit between his teeth, he can dance all night."

Cornelia laughed, pulling Watson towards the waiting cab. "Let's dance, Dr Watson, take me dancing."

"Holmes, Holmes," Watson protested as Cornelia led him away. But Holmes was gone, invisible in the night, the calculating automaton, the inhuman, yet so frail, machine.

5

A Scandal in Strasbourg

Watson was a wreck. Cornelia had danced him off his feet the night before and it was a very grateful doctor who had woken 'late' that day to discover a new and wonderfully upholstered bath-chair waiting for him downstairs in the lobby. A Delahaye, no less; the motor a Panhard singlex (similar to the solex, but quieter). He was a happy man. Holmes had dispensed with having one himself, preferring the use of his stiff, but improving legs.

Cornelia had managed to get her charges on the night train to Strasbourg and although the horrendous Herr Döre was on board as well, she considered herself safe for there were a number of other women; common prostitutes as far as she could tell, (not having much experience of them in Wales), consorting with the men in their cabin. Their screams and laughter kept her awake the entire night but at least she arrived in Strasbourg unmolested (if unrested).

And thus it was the party of six, Holmes, Watson, Cornelia, Herr Döre, Lucy Trishant and her sister Adele were in convoy, two cars bound for the Chateau Vernet. Christmas was full steam ahead.

Yet when they arrived, although there were servants a plenty there was no host. Even when all were unpacked and assembled for a lavish late breakfast, (though Watson had begged off, not having slept well on the train) there was no welcome from either Herr Flohn or his ladywife. It was most peculiar, even the staff had no idea where they were.

A Scandal in Strasbourg

Holmes, for his part, was not worried. Much would have to be arranged prior to Christmas; food to be bought, factories to be kept open as long as possible, all the usual chaos that passes for celebration. He was glad to see that the French did not seem to make such a thing of it as the English. Queen Victoria was to be blamed for that obsession. Christmas became an institution only because of her Albert and that sentimentalist Dickens (that and a need for something to do in the glens in winter). War, he hoped would set things to right for once and for all.

So it was, that all the guests from Paris were napping in their beds, when at last the Flohns came home triumphant from their shopping with friends, just flown in from Berlin. But the confusion and embarrassment was soon cleared up by the evening and by eight o'clock everyone was ready for a very enterprising and decorative Christmas Eve party, destined to be the talk of all Strasbourg the very next day.

Of course, preparing for that party took a while and to set the momentous events clear in our heads, it is necessary that we turn back the clock a little, to the early hours, just prior to the summons for dinner.

Christmas Eve is the traditional time of celebration in these parts and Strasbourg, though fiercely French, was remarkably Germanic in its habits. Thus it was that a Christmas tree was illuminated in the garden and inside, logs and fern, painted silver and gold festooned the Chateau's assembly room. Musicians had been hired for the evening. There would be no dancing, but a small trio from the conservatoire had gathered in a corner and were running through a delightful mixture of Strauss, Bach and even one or two American tunes for the benefit of Mr Onslow Wilson and his glamorous wife, Betty Wilson, a former star of stage and radio (though unknown in France, quite naturally).

All in all, it was quite a large assembly that was to honour Herr Flohn's Christmas and Watson could not help but feel honoured that they had been invited, though a little mystified as to exactly why.

Miss Cornelia was less mystified, knowing that the dreaded Herr Döre had designs upon her and she was thankful for a good old fashioned lock on her thick, impenetrable oak door. She was worried for all of them so far from home. However, as the long afternoon gave way to a particularly dark, snowy evening she went about her toilet relaxed, comfortable in the knowledge that the evening would be a very pleasant one, even though she missed her family and her dogs back home in the Welsh mountains.

Her main dilemma was what to wear. All the other women wore such fine clothes and although her own clothes were well made and quite stylish, nevertheless she had not planned for society evenings and was quite at a loss as to what she could wear. On her bed lay gifts for Dr Watson and Lord Holmes, bought by her with what little money she had, for the two old gentlemen had been so very kind to her, she could scarcely ignore Christmas. She had heard too, that Frau Flohn was amazingly beautiful, quite the image of the American actress Veronika Lake, just about everyone's favourite idol, her 'look' echoed in the face of half the girls of Paris.

There was a knock upon her door.

A moment's anguish, uncertainty. Was it the horrid Herr Döre?

"Who is it?" A nervous enquiry, her voice barely a whisper.

"It is I the butler, Miss Shand..." a querelous, aged voice croaked from behind the door. "I have a gift for you."

Quickly, Cornelia went to the door, hastily wrapping a dressing gown around herself, nervously opening the door. There before her stood a most remarkable old man. Shaggy white hair, disfigured spinal features that would be quite dreadful to see if it were not for the butler's suit that shone with an ebony brilliance. In his wretchedly long, bony fingers he held a parcel addressed to Miss Cornelia Shand. But before she could take it, the old man brushed past her and proceeded to the bed, laying down the box and immediately setting about opening it. In a quandry as to what she should do, endeavour to respect French customs and protect her gift and dignity, or do nothing, Cornelia chose the latter course and just closed the door. She was left standing there with her back to it staring at the old man as he worked away at opening the gift, clicking his tongue in a most irritating manner.

It was quite obvious from the box itself that what lay inside was a gown, a Paris gown, for the box was quite special. Fascinated she drew near as the butler, humming a few bars from the Ring, lifted the crimson silk gown out of the tissue paper. Cornelia instantly recognised it as a Coco Chanel design, straight out of the pages of *Vogue* magazine itself.

"Oh..." was one of the very few words she used to describe the dramatically beautiful gown. "Oh, it's so stunning. This is from Herr Flohn?" She took it out of the butler's hands and rushed to the mirror with it, dying for him to be gone so she could try it on.

"The dress is from a gentleman who did not wish to declare himself mademoiselle, I came as soon as I could."

Cornelia had a sudden unpleasant thought. "Oh heavens, not from that horrible Herr Döre. On no, it can't be. I should not wish to wear a gown given to me by that monster." There was an unusual force behind her denial.

The butler turned to go, saying, "To the best of my knowledge mademoiselle it was not from any German guest. I look forward to seeing you wearing it, there could be no finer gown in all Strasbourg, truly magnifique."

"Oh it is, it is. I shall wear it. This is my best present ever, I swear it. Whoever gave it will get such a kiss. I'm quite beside myself."

The butler smiled, aware that he was ignored and unnoticed, stepped out of the room, immediately walking along the corridor at a brisk pace until he came to a set of double doors at the end of the blue carpet, knocking only slightly and entering quickly, slyly closing the door behind him.

"What is this," Watson wanted to know. "This is an impertinence. I gave no permission to come in. Who are you my man, what do you want?"

"I am the butler, Sir John. I have come to help you dress."

Watson considered this a worse impertinence. "I can dress myself. I may be old, but I am not feeble. But I say, old man – you haven't seen Lord Holmes anywhere on your travels have you?"

"Non, monsieur, but is that Lord Holmes over there?" He pointed to the mountain view out through the window. Watson turned, looking at the window, seeing nothing at all. "I see nothing..." he said turning back. "HOLMES!"

"You look surprised Watson, come, be a good fellow and help me off with this wretched hump. I should not change places with a camel, I can tell you."

Watson laughed. "Holmes you rascal, you monster, you foxed me again. I should have known it was you. How do you do it? A remarkable transformation."

Holmes smiled, straightening up and undoing his shirt. "Foxed more than you, it seems Watson. Appears a butler just delivered a certain Paris gown to a certain young lady."

Watson clapped his hands together. "Capital, capital Holmes, she never recognised you, I am sure of it. My oath you are a one for games. How did she like the dress?"

"Quite overcome, Watson, quite overcome. As for the rest of the guests, a rare bunch is gathered here, that I can tell you. But," he sighed, "I will say that I am pleased to be back in this room. This disguise was fine for a younger Holmes, but it quite does me in these days."

"Here, let me help you with the hump," Watson offered, moving towards his mentor, "then, I think perhaps a drink of whisky by the fire whilst you explain all. I was quite worried, Holmes. You have been gone almost two hours." Then he suddenly laughed again, wagging a finger at him.

"Holmes, you and your disguises, so brilliant, had me completely taken in."

Holmes acknowledged Watson's praise in his customary manner, ignoring it and carrying on with his explanation. "Two hours is enough to discover that this is no ordinary Christmas party, Watson. I do believe our American guests are quite friendly with Herr Flohn. I have been in all the rooms, met most of the guests and as is the habit of those who live with servants, they ignored me completely, continuing their conversations in the most normal fashion. I have learnt much, but little that points towards events at Nürnberg. I have yet to learn the exact reason we were invited. This is the particular conundrum that worries me most. I suspect we might be tested in some way tonight."

"It is a complex matter, Holmes," Watson muttered, concentrating on removing Holmes' padding and apparatus. Holmes set about his face and whiskers.

"We must be down by eight o'clock sharp, Watson. We do not want to be missed and draw attention to ourselves."

"Of course, well, I do believe I am nearly ready, Holmes, but you have a long way to go yet. I fear the bath-water will be cold by now."

"'Tis no matter, I bathed earlier." He chuckled to himself as he sank into the chair by the fire, applying surgical spirit to his face, the eyebrows and all the accompanying whiskers coming away more swiftly than the afternoon they had taken to put on. It has been said that Holmes would have put the entire body of London's actors to shame, but being so intensely private a man, he enjoyed his triumphs in solitude. Donald Wolfitt and John Gielgud could rest easy.

"The complication of our situation lies in the fact that our information is so very vague," Holmes said a moment later, staring into the coal-fire. "Normally I can penetrate the atmosphere of evil, as well you know, Watson. This time I cannot quite grasp the significance of this Christmas rendezvous. Herr Döre was sent to fetch us. Now it was either to see if we are as pro-German as Unity and her friends, or it is an inspection to check if we are still a force to be reckoned with. It's the latter, I think."

"It has worried me too, Holmes. Perhaps all will be revealed downstairs."

"Perhaps, but perhaps not. Did you ever hear of the Wilson-Mason fortune?"

Watson shook his head, handing Holmes a small glass of whisky, produced from his handy flask.

"Thank you, Watson, perhaps this will clear my head. It is failing me miserably at the moment."

"The Wilson half of the Wilson-Mason fortune is the same Onslow Wilson who is staying here with his lovely ladywife," Watson deduced, sitting down to the fire with Holmes, noting that the time was past seven o'clock.

Holmes gave Watson a sharp appreciative look. "I'm glad to hear that your head is in good working order, Watson, this gratifies me greatly."

"It's the clean air, Holmes. Strasbourg seems to agree with me, though it is monstrously cold."

"Snow threatened I fear. Perhaps a little tobogganing, eh, Watson?"

Watson held up his hands in much horror. "Leave that to the young Cornelia. But say Holmes, what of this Wilson fellow?"

"His factories make many things, Watson, hold patents to many more. Here we are at war with the Boché and the Americans once again hold back from the brink. It would be an unfortunate thing if the Americans were to continue to do business with the Third Reich. Remember that America controls most of the world's oil. Standard Oil has many fingers in the German pie. IBM continue to do business there. They, like the Germans, tend to look at the balance sheet rather than the suffering and misery hidden away in camps."

"You mean the Americans could come in on Hitler's side?" Watson protested.

"It is no forgone conclusion they will support us Watson. England is perceived as weak, it is quite probable that we might lose. The American, Mr Wilson, will want to protect his investments, his interests. Think of Nazi Germany as an expanded business territory for German factories. Why fifty years from now there wouldn't be a British car in Europe, everyone would drive a Auto-Union or a Mercedes-Benz."

"That would be a tragedy, Holmes, but unlikely. The Rolls Royce will survive, people will always seek out a reliable Riley or a stout Hillman."

"Not if their factories were bombed flat and they are forbidden to build new ones after the war. We could be looking at American-German super conglomerates that surpass the power of anything that has ever gone before. This is the true enemy, a strangulation of the European economy by a few concentrated groups of men and industries. Adolf Hitler may be fighting for the realisation of his Mein Kampf and domination of the Western world, but even he cannot fight without shipbuilders, without businessmen, bankers, management. At one end a dictator, at the other, the accountant and the shareholder."

Watson shook his head. "You're saying big business wants this war? That American shareholders condone Hitler's Nazi ideals?"

"It is perhaps just that some don't understand all the implications Watson, or worse, they do. America sees Germany as a shining economic miracle, a model of efficiency. New machinery in every factory. If Hitler wins, which looks likely, what will result? Why nothing short of the revitalisation of all Europe and England, in much the same way Romania is being developed now. It will be the biggest explosion of economic investment the world has ever known. Germany could not do it alone, it will need American money and America will see that it has a share in it. For them to oppose this, turn their backs on such a massive post-war profit, well their shareholders will howl and demand blood. Business rules America, Watson. I have been there, it should not surprise me to discover America stays neutral in this war."

"That would be a calamity for England."

"Indeed, now perhaps you see the importance of our mission. Britain will stand alone. We have to discover whatever it is Dr Laubscher has to offer and guarantee to get it back to England. Mr Wilson's presence here makes our mission all the more urgent."

"I see Holmes, I see. Oh the villainy of it."

"Exactly, Watson, exactly. Now assist me with these trousers. I have a dinner suit to put on."

***

To describe the magnificence of Chateau Vernet is to delve into the art of superlatives. To do justice to the interior would be to compare it to the Palace of Versailles and allow the Vernet rooms (though not so plenty) to outshine, out-manoeuvre, outplay every facet. Yet as grand, as regal as the Chateau was, it was not cold. It was compact and warm, built by a man related to the great artist Horace Vernet (ironically enough the same man to whom the forefathers of one Sherlock Holmes were related), a man whose appreciation of life was roundly summed up in his observation, 'Life is not all summers'. A man who had the wish, from time to time, to gather fifty or so of his friends in some of the smaller rooms and shed their outer clothes, to dance, drink, converse by a roaring fire in the company of long velvet drapes, baronial tables and dramatic tapestries that told of grand deeds at the hunt, splendid steeds; 209 years of history told in pictures, told in the ceiling, told on the doors, told in a time before Kodak put it all on paper and placed it upon a shelf out of reach of the children.

The Christmas assembly were gathered in excited knots all over the room. Men in Nazi uniform, the French Nazis in an elegant military brown, Herr Döre looking particularly dashing, though not exactly festive. Only Mr Selim Markova and his wife, an industrialist up from Marseilles looked out of place, shunned by the majority of guests.

Mr Markova, Holmes and Watson were the only men there without uniform, but wearing dress suits. Watson thought that he and Holmes, despite their great age, cut quite a dash themselves. He was greatly moved to see such a table to one side of the room burdened with gifts and colourful name tags. He longed to stroll over and squeeze his parcel.

The ladies entered, to a ripple of applause from the men. Cornelia made a stunning entrance, quite reducing the other ladies to some drab netherland of fashion. The crimson was a coup de grace.

Watson dug Holmes in the ribs. "Our girl looks as magnificent as Scarlett O'Hara. She is stunning, beautiful. Oh Holmes, would that I were twenty years younger."

"Even at sixty-seven I should say you'd have a difficult time of it, Watson."

But Watson not listening. He was lost in a fantasy between himself, Vivien Leigh and Cornelia, too far gone to listen to Holmes' cold voice of reason.

Then, at last, it was time for their host and hostess to arrive. A hurriedly formed line was made for Herr and Frau Flohn, much bickering at the head of it from the Nazi contingent who (it was evident from much agonised hopping on one leg) stood on many French toes to be first in line.

Holmes studied the Flohns as they made their way down the line, pausing to have polite, somewhat distant chats with each and everyone. Holmes thought it strange that a rich and respected man like Herr Flohn should invite so many people to his Christmas celebration. Strange, for it was hard to imagine Herr Döre as a personal friend of the man like this, nor the hard nosed General Buchnort, a singularly unpleasant man, a hairlip lending a malevolent look to his already manifestly cruel face.

Cornelia caused quite a stir.

"And who have we here? A film star?" Herr Flohn asked, turning to his ladywife with a new light in his eye and pleasure on his formerly tired and withdrawn face.

"I am Cornelia Shand sir, nurse to Lord Sherlock Holmes and Sir John Watson."

"A nurse?" the master of the Chateau cried out. "An angel surely. You, my dear, shall sit at our table. My wife can be as angry with me as she wants, but afterwards. Tonight I shall endure your beauty with great fortitude."

Holmes received great satisfaction from this, Watson's little extravagance was a good ruse. He only sought Cornelia's affection (he would be upset not to be with her at dinner) but positioning her next to Herr Flohn was divine providence indeed. It was to be hoped they would assume her entirely ignorant of German, a stroke of luck for them all.

"And Sir John, Lord Holmes we finally get to you both. May I say what an honour it is to meet you. My wife has long been a great fan of your stories Dr Watson and I make the best honey in all the valley thanks to your excellent book on beekeeping, Lord Holmes. It is good to confirm with my own eyes that you did not succumb at the jagged Reichenbach Falls. Professor Moriarty did not make such a remarkable recovery, I hope? There is enough mischief in the world without his like amongst us."

"A dead man," Watson replied. "A dead man sir. Isn't that so Holmes?"

Holmes smiled with a curious curl of his lips. "He has not appeared by name, 'tis true, but evil abounds and there are times when I see his evil trace, times I have to remind myself he drowned, for that brand of villainy was the most singular force I've ever known, Herr Flohn."

Frau Flohn appeared much interested. "Oh, Lord Holmes, I sincerely hope he drowned."

"Well, you really are my honoured guests y'know," Herr Flohn explained. "When I heard from our friends in Paris that you were alive and well and staying there, that you wished to attend a Wagner concert, no less, in our glorious Third Reich, I took it upon myself to urge them to find you and invite you here. I mean to exact a price from you Sherlock Holmes. Tomorrow my wife and I will sit by the fire in our own living room and talk to you both until you are exhausted and even then we will urge your pretty nurse on, to revive you so we can discover more. It is really too bad of you, Dr Watson, to have given up your chronicles. What has Lord Holmes been doing these past years? And don't tell me tending his bees and writing up a treatise on coal-tar processes."

Holmes offered an embarrassed smile. "Coal-tar it is, Herr Flohn. The liquifaction of coal to distil petroleum has long been my goal. I hear the infamous Dr Brandt has a formula already with a working model in operation."

"Your information is remarkably correct, Lord Holmes, but..." he smiled weakly, looking quickly at his wife, "nothing more than we'd expect. You should talk to our American friend Mr Wilson, he has talked to Dr Brandt, though he remains unimpressed. But then the Americans have oil in their back yards. We European countries must rely on Arabs, not altogether a good solution."

"My own words exactly, Herr Flohn. It has been many years since Dr Watson recorded a case, but only because of his rheumatic hands and perhaps because of the delicate matter of the cases. If truth be known, I have become somewhat shy in my old age, preferring to let my rivals flounder about in confusion."

"Ah, I understand completely," Herr Flohn remarked, amused. "Le charme qu'on trouve avec le imbecile Hercule Poirot est qu'elle vous conduit indiscutablement a l'heureuse certitude que des sots vous n'etes pas le plus grand."

"Mon mots absolutement," Holmes replied, his French not what it was.

"What was that?" Watson wanted to know as their host moved off towards the gifts. "What did he say about Hercule?"

"Something terribly rude, I shouldn't wonder," Holmes answered amused.

"Poirot is quite impossible Holmes, an upstart, uses your methods and claims them as his. Same with Father Brown, plagiarists all. There are so many who set themselves up as consulting detectives these days, bounders every last one of 'em."

"Imitation is the sincerest form of flattery, Watson. We were first, we must take consolation with that."

"Onslow Wilson's the name," a fat hand attached to a large panhandle face, declared to Watson. "Lord Sherlock Holmes, if I'm not mistaken."

Watson was somewhat taken aback by the American's manners, but recovered sufficiently enough to answer. "No sir, you do make a mistake. This is Sherlock Holmes."

The American was not in the least bit embarrassed. He grabbed Holmes' hand and pumped it hard. "Damnit sir, meeting you is like meeting royalty. Better! Goddamnit, they'll never believe me back in Washington, came all the way to France and met the world's greatest detective. You are still number one with me Lord Holmes. You can keep your Sam Spades and your Nick Carters, and Philip Marlowes. Might be they can solve a crime or two, but no one's got class like you, no substitutes eh? No substitutes for the real thing."

Holmes extracted his hand from the American's rather sticky one, replying, "Your Mr Marlowe is adequate as far as he goes, Mr Wilson, but he lacks a stout and trusty Dr Watson at hand."

"You got it on the nail, Sherlock. No Holmes without Watson. My wife went out this afternoon to the bookshop, looked everywhere for a copy of *The Valley of Fear* (my favourite). She found a second-hand copy printed in Danish, can you believe that? She was hoping you'd sign the edition for her..."

"I'm interested in your uniform, Mr Wilson." Holmes replied.

Wilson seemed glad Holmes had mentioned it. "Neat, don't you think. It was Washington's idea, these Germans feel more comfortable talking to someone in uniform, so I had this made, call myself Commander Wilson. Got them doing goose steps everywhere I go in Germany. The French have got too much class to do an unnatural thing like that."

"Very interesting," Holmes replied, trying to get away towards the gifts table. "Dr Watson will be happy to sign the book, I'm sure."

They escaped the American and made it to the gifts table at last. Cornelia found herself flanked by Herr Döre, who was standing far too close and familiar, and another man, a German officer in his SS uniform. It was not a comfortable sensation. Fortunately she found a gift with her name upon it and concentrated on that whilst a row brewed between Herr Döre and the SS officer, over who saw her first. Her ears should have been burning, for they talked quite possessively about her; oblivious to her sensibilities and totally unaware that she understood every sharp and unpleasant word.

The gift was small, but magnificent none the less. A silver tipped comb of the finest craftsmanship and more than useful. It seemed Herr Flohn and his lovely wife had forgotten no-one. In despair she gathered Herr Döre had won this round, but the SS officer had loudly promised that he would not forget this sleight; one could be sure the matter would not rest there. Cornelia held her silence until again, Herr Döre again took her arm and suggested a walk before dinner to the glasshouse adjoining the main room. Perhaps she would join him in a glass of Rhudesheimer?

"Why, Herr Döre, you look quite flushed. Was that man arguing with you?"

Herr Döre adjusted his collar, a little tight after his tense discussions. "No, no my dear Miss Cornelia, it is just that I need a little fresh air and I believe the glasshouse to possess some of the most delightful Christmas roses."

"Then I shall certainly join you there, but presently, for I wish to watch my charges open their gifts. I believe they will be pleasantly surprised."

"As you wish. I shall attend you there, do not fail me Miss Cornelia. I am not a patient man."

'Nor a pleasant one,' Cornelia thought to herself as she watched him stride away, his leather boots polished to an absurdity.

Watson was the first to unwrap his gifts, the strains of Christmas carols washing over them all as he did so. Three gifts in all. Cornelia had given him a new, long scarf in a sombre grey, but much appreciated by him nonetheless, as he missed his other, lost at sea. From Herr Flohn he received a book, *The Sherlock Holmes Method of Investigative Disease and General*

Diagnosis, by Sir Henry Ottoman. MD. "This is a rare bird, indeed, a splendid gift."

"Should prove interesting, Watson. Probably bring you up to date in the field of medicine, a lot has happened since the day you graduated."

"Indeed Holmes, but look at the title. I shall have to have a word with this publisher, not a word to you or I about taking your name in vain. Camford University Press shall hear from me."

"Accept it as flattery, Watson and just pray the book is a worthwhile contribution to modern science."

Watson passed on to his third gift, this from Holmes (not normally one for such frivolities). Watson opened it and withdrew a large tin of best Virginia tobacco, moist and aromatic. "But Holmes, I gave up smoking thirty years ago."

Holmes cut him off. "Watson you have confiscated enough tobacco from me to start a tobacconist. This Christmas I am faced with an incredible urge to start again, you shall be the guardian of my vice, do not weaken in your resolve. I am determined not to smoke."

Watson placed a friendly hand upon Holmes' arm. "Accepted with honour Holmes. Though you must promise that you will not beat me about the head if you fail in your resolve and I deny you your supplies."

"Of course," he replied, turning to the table. "Now let me open my gifts, though quite what anyone can give me that I do not already have...?"

The first gift answered that immediately. From Cornelia he received a new deerstalker, just the right size and shade of green. It was a touching moment as he reached out a hand behind him and squeezed Cornelia's delicate wrist. From Watson, who knew of Cornelia's gift, a new Inverness, a cape so rich, so warm, so carefully a match to the deerstalker that Holmes was almost overcome. Yet there was one more gift. From Herr Flohn came a new lens, Ziess, with a built in lamp set in the handle for night work. It was a grand moment and there was friendly appreciation from all for Holmes' humble loss of words. "And the gown?" Herr Flohn asked of Cornelia with a knowing smile. "Who gave you such a beautiful gown?" Cornelia blushed so deeply one could hardly tell the difference between herself and the gown. "I do not know, Herr Flohn. It arrived at my room only this evening, yet it fits me so perfectly it might have been made for me."

Frau Flohn studied the gown a moment and smiled, "Chanel, my dear, you can be assured it was made for you. We shall stare at the faces of the men until we find the villain." Which in great humour they both did, coming only across protesting, innocent, smiling faces all, until they finally found the red-faced, hung-head of one Sir John Watson MD, who, despite much cajoling would not lift his head and indeed, thought his legs would give way. When he could take the well-intentioned ribbing no more he whispered (hoarsely) the magic words, "Bath-chair," whereupon Frau Flohn clapped her hands and signalled to her staff to fetch the velveted comfy chair. Cornelia ran to him and whilst Holmes gripped his companion under the arm, she hugged Watson fiercely with much affection, kissing him three times, as promised. This made his already delicate position considerably worse, although he would not have shunned Cornelia's kisses for all the world and would have gladly died and gone to heaven for just one kiss and hug from so beautiful a creature.

The bath-chair arrived and Holmes suggested a breath of fresh air whilst the other guests opened their presents prior to dinner. At the mention of fresh air, Cornelia remembered Herr Döre was waiting for her in the glasshouse and mentioned the assignation to Holmes.

"Go, my dear, Herr Döre is not yet expendable to our purposes. Go, but we shall be nearby."

"Be careful," Watson wheezed, sobering up considerably at the thought of his Cornelia in the arms of that dastardly evil Herr Döre. "We shall be very near," he re-emphasised.

Yet after allowing Cornelia time to get ahead of them, they found themselves delayed by the businessman, Mr Markova and his dumpy wife. Both professed much admiration for Holmes, enquiring whether a businessman, like himself, would be welcome in London, for they saw with trepidation that France was following the German vice of suspicion of foreigners with sickening slavishness. The Markova's having fled the Turkish massacres in Armenia once in a lifetime knew how to read the signs. They clearly felt out of place here, but it was his factories that Herr Flohn wanted to buy and it was Sherlock Holmes' opinion he sought on the chances of an Armenian running anything in France if Germany took over.

Holmes, who had experience in these matters, urged the man to sell and depart for America or Canada where people such as them gathered a plenty without harassment.

"Or California," Holmes added, "I hear there is much scope there."

Mr Markova obviously trusted his advice, but Mrs Markova was not well disposed to learning English, believing that everything would blow over soon enough. Mr Markova indicated he had decided to sell up. It was the best solution.

This business delayed Holmes and an impatient Watson for far too long. So it was that Cornelia stood alone in the glasshouse, pinned to a six foot cactus with the repulsive Herr Döre importunately and lewdly leaning up against her, trying to persuade his 'Jewel' to enjoin him in a kiss. He implored her to turn her head to look upon him, promising her the earth (which was not his to give), and her own apartment in Paris when the advancing tide of the Third Reich took over in the New Year. (He was convinced of it).

Cornelia was not impressed. Torn between being impaled by a cactus from behind and an altogether too bristly Herr Döre, whose physical intentions were fully impressed upon her, creasing her beautiful gown.

"Herr Döre, I cannot. I am engaged, betrothed to another in England. Upon his honour I cannot kiss you."

"He is far away and you are almost in enemy territory. He would understand, my pigeon. A kiss for me would open so many doors, can you not feel how strongly I need you... love you?"

"I can feel quite a lot Herr Döre, but little of it feels like love to me." How long could she endure this? Worse, the wine was sweet and his breath stank of it. Would Holmes and Watson never come?

He gripped her head and bending her further into the cactus forced himself down upon her taught, terrified lips.

Cornelia could not endure a second more. She was near to fainting. Her legs gave way and even as Herr Döre closed in for the kiss, she was suddenly no longer in his grasp, crawling out through his splayed legs as he continued to topple down with great inevitability to the long, thin, lethal spikes of the desert cactus, his eyes shut, oblivious to the whole affair.

Even as Cornelia scrabbled to her feet and ran to the doors, she heard a scream behind her and the most impolite set of curses she had ever heard in her short life. She turned around and there was Herr Döre impaled by his upper lip to the cactus, pulling himself away, clasping his hands to his bloodied lip and whimpering most vilely from the excessive pain, his eyes open wide in plain astonishment.

An officer ran towards her having heard the raucous shouts. "Vat is it? Vhy do you yell out so?" It was the young SS officer who had argued with Herr Döre.

"Not me," Cornelia pointed behind her, "him". Disgust strong in her voice.

He saw Herr Döre's bloodied hand, the cactus and understood everything in a trice.

"Your 'onour is saved Miss Shand," he declared, pleased at the outcome, placing his arm at her disposal. "I believe dinner is about to be served. I shall escort you to your table."

She accepted, little knowing her cruel fate would soon be revealed to her by this gallant, but deceitful young man.

"Arghh!" Herr Döre exclaimed, dizzy with pain, running up past them and on into the kitchen in search of first-aid.

"I fear Herr Döre will not be kissing anyone for some time now," the officer laughed, thinking it highly amusing.

"Oh I hope so," Cornelia asserted. "I do hope so."

A gong sounded for dinner.

As Cornelia walked into the dining room, Holmes came out from behind a pillar where he had been hiding and nodded. The girl was doing fine, he hoped she would listen well to their boasting this night, for these young men in their black uniforms were filled with zeal and enthusiasm for the Nazi ideal. Cornelia was his ears, but he did not like the company she was in. That young man had a curiously evil leer on his face that Cornelia might not understand. He would have to watch her well. It amused him that suddenly he had become Cornelia's nurse.

The London team found themselves pinned to the subject of war. Holmes seated next to Mr Markova and his wife, opposite Otto Von Hipplestar who was something in propaganda in Berlin, visiting the Chateau to discuss filming a piece on the glorious efforts and character of Herr Flohn. To Holmes' surprise the Germans seemed to know about the state of England's readiness for war better than the English themselves.

"There is indeed a fifth column in England, Lord Holmes. There has been for years. Stanley Baldwin, Sir Samuel Hoare, Captain Margesson, your powerful Sir Horace Wilson, Lord Stanhope and, of course, Mr Neville Chamberlain. Without them in power, Mr Winston Churchill would have whipped England into a frenzy and built up a war machine twice as effective as our own, for you had the money, the Empire. We had nothing but the will of the German people and our bare hands."

"Indeed," Mr Markova picked up the point, "with your Herr Göring and Doctors Schacht and Funk, much inspiration was given to the German peoples, a victory promised. It is always with astonishment I hear that the British people did not think a war possible, still do not think it, for the same men who pleaded for peace are running the country at war. There seems little urgency. I do believe England believes that France can contain Herr Hitler, that indeed, Mr Chamberlain relies upon it. Your shadow factories in

Coventry operate on a single shift system, you still have a million unemployed. Germany has none, everyone is busy making bombs."

Holmes was in no mood to discuss these matters, for it did no good to tell these men that he and one other loyal Englishman, the Right Honourable aforementioned Churchill were the lone voices of dissension. He did not want to be provoked into revealing his true colours. It was assured that they would try to trick him into jingoistic statements. He and Watson had to be on the defensive all the time.

"It was with some amazement that we learned that the Third Reich spent £1,650 million on armaments alone in 1938, Herr Hipplestar. This sum would indicate a great seriousness on behalf of the German people to defend their interests at almost any price. Yet may I ask... the term Blitzkrieg, that moving wall of man, machine and aircraft spitting flame, now it has been demonstrated to be so effective in Poland, do we now expect all of Europe to crumble at Herr Hitler's knees? Indeed, if all of Europe, the entire world, even America?"

Von Hipplestar looked at Holmes with interest, considering the question a while, then he offered a smile as he dipped his spoon into a fruit salad of a delicious pungency.

"I know of a movement afoot in England, Lord Holmes. Some quarter blame England's unreadiness for conflict upon the shoulders of that fifth column I mentioned. I am prepared to suggest to you that internal dissent will soon arise in England so severe that it will be ungovernable. To my mind, Chamberlain's Government is proof positive that democracy has proven its inability to adapt to the needs of the modern world. A new direction, a new mind, a new kind of man has to emerge out of this mess you grandly call Europe.

"Herr Hitler has a plan, perhaps you have heard of it? His plan is for a unified, glorious Europe; a common idea, a common currency, education, a pure, rational, logical league of like minded nations.

"Some will be invited to change with us, others will be persuaded. But liberation from your 'Guilty Men' is a necessity, Lord Holmes, a priority which it seems only Germany and our Allies, the Soviets, have the foresightedness and will to achieve. I think, in time, the Blitzkrieg will not be necessary. In time we will discover that we have over-invested in our military expenditure."

Flotenkonzerte des Barock – Vivaldi's 79 wafted over the assembly soothing Holmes' jangled nerves, for neither he, nor Mr Markova were happy to be sitting at Von Hipplestar's table. Watson was no happier, parked in a forest of German officers who spoke no English. He was just thankful he could eat from the comfort of his bath-chair situated alongside the table, his eyes never straying for very long from the young Cornelia's neck. She was seated next to Herr Flohn receiving many flattering admiring looks from almost all the men, much to the chagrin of the wives.

Of Herr Döre there was nothing.

So it was a veritable feast, serenaded, opulent in choices of dishes, eloquent in multifarious flavours and played much havoc with the indigestion, as did the distinguished Rhine wines produced locally, not far from the Chateau. Holmes, as was his custom when worried or thinking, ate little, preferring to nibble rather than sink like a battleship as most did at the assorted tables.

Cornelia's knowledge of German was a useful thing at the dinner table, for Herr Von Hipplestar took a moment to enquire of Herr Flohn the real reason for Sherlock Holmes' presence at the Christmas gathering, referring also to Herr Döre as that, "contemptible simpleton."

Herr Flohn answered him directly and pointed out that Herr Döre had proven to be a useful intermediary in the past and was the only man available at the time with ears close enough to the ground who could track Holmes down and persuade him to come to the Chateau. It was mere expediency that Herr Döre was involved at all and, as for Holmes, it yet remained to be seen if this was the man London were putting into the field. A test had been devised to gauge the extent of his mental powers. London must be desperate, he pointed out, if this was all they had to throw against Germany. But it was just possible that Holmes was the spy and thus a test was necessary to observe his famous skills. The 'operation' was now so far advanced that they did not want to waste valuable time leading Sherlock Holmes by the nose if he was not the man Churchill had sent. As for Herr Döre, he had performed his task and would be returned to Paris in the morning, perhaps still of some use to them all.

This much Cornelia heard from Herr Flohn's lips, but events continued apace and by the time she next met with Holmes, it was too late to warn him of any test.

Dinner was over, the ladies adjourned to the nether regions, cigars were lit and port was on its way round when Watson, fatigued by the excitement took himself off to bed. Some other gentlemen decided to do the same, and Mr Markova left to look for his wife.

Holmes, still undergoing a process of education from the irrepressible Von Hipplestar, stayed a while longer, restoring himself with the thought that these Germans were so confident of world supremacy, failure to achieve it never entered their heads. This, he felt sure, would be their downfall.

The scream that entered the assembly room seemed to have come from every direction at once. Yet Holmes knew from its diminished resonance that it had already travelled a long way before reaching his ears.

"A scream?" some voices were asking themselves, their questions immediately answered by another, much like the one before.

Holmes was already up and striding across the room when Herr Flohn, not quite past reason, despite consuming huge quantities of wine, called out in a drunken voice, "A case for Sherlock Holmes. A scream, Von Hipplestar, we must investigate."

But no investigating was done for all at the tables thought it was a huge joke and fell about with great laughter at the thought of Sherlock Holmes investigating. It was not apparent why, but Holmes attributed this harsh noise to the Germans' natural sense of malevolence.

Holmes seemed to have disappeared. Although the screaming had stopped, the corridors were alive with staff and guests alike, some fully dressed, some in nightgowns, confused, not understanding where the screaming could have come from. Some were of the opinion that it was the bedroom floor, others the cellars. The staff could shed no light on it and more than one guest kept asking for the old butler to assist, the one who had been so helpful in the afternoon. They would not be quieted when told that there was no butler. No one knew where the scream had come from, yet all had heard it and were of the uniform opinion that it was a young female scream they had heard.

Watson was out of his bath-chair, climbing the stairs, thinking that his services as a doctor would be needed and that the scream had sounded ominously like his favourite, the young Cornelia. His fears were considerably magnified when upon reaching the landing the bloodstained Herr Döre lurched out of a doorway and ran headlong down the stairs as if he'd seen a ghost! Watson was scared now, he had suspected Herr Döre of treachery from the first, but what could the blood mean? Whose life had been taken? He prayed that it was not Cornelia's and that he was not too late.

His feet turned to lead, fear descending upon him like a falling house. He knew he would die if a hair was harmed on Cornelia's bonny head. Steeling himself for the terrible ordeal, Watson flung open the door and to his utter astonishment Frau Flohn stood there stock still, holding a bloody dagger in her hands, tears streaming down her face. Beside her feet, gathered in an unhappy heap, was the newly late Mrs Judith Markova.

Another door opened on the other side of the house and quite a different scene presented itself to the sane eyes of Lord Sherlock Holmes. His pistol was at the ready, but he did not have occasion to fire. Yet in all his long and unusual, sometimes dangerous and unpleasant life, nothing had prepared him for this. If truth be known, he received the shock of his career.

"Cornelia," he called out in astonishment, anger rising quickly in him.

She was tied to a bed, hardly a stitch of clothing upon her body, gagged and obviously distraught, her eyes red-rimmed, her face swollen. In the corner stood the young SS officer, naked, arrogant, a phantom smile upon his contemptible face.

Holmes, dressed for duty in his deerstalker and Inverness had known all along that the screams had come from this quarter, but he had been foxed for a good five minutes while searching for the right room. This scene of wanton skullduggery and debauchery being conducted neither in Cornelia's room, nor this despicable young man's room, but Von Hipplestar's, presented a singular mystery.

Pistol levelled at the villain, Holmes advanced to Cornelia and removed her offensive gag (her own private things no less). She instantly began to cough, weakly muttering. "Oh, am I glad to see you Lord Holmes, am I glad..." but she could say no more before breaking down into uncontrollable, heartbreaking sobs.

"And you?" Holmes asked, waving the pistol at the man, feeling strangely inclined to use it. "This act of infamy will not be forgotten, you need pistol whipping, you beast." He turned to Cornelia suddenly, "I hope I am in time, Miss Shand?"

"Y-y-yes sir, but please untie me before the others get here." She was shaking with fright, confused by the Prussian's unnatural demands. Holmes understood at once. The sheer inhumanity of it. She was tied up for Von Hipplestar and whoever else may come. Moral standards were crumbling, collapsing with terrific rapidity. It was all the fault of that revolting book Venus in Furs, he was sure of it.

"I hope zat gun is not loaded, Herr Holmes," the young man complained. Holmes angered nearly out of his mind lashed out with the gun and bloodied the man's lip. "I want no word from you, you insolent dog. Pick up your things."

Holmes worked upon Cornelia's bonds, he was white with anger, hardly able to keep his code of honour and not shoot at an unarmed man. "You sir, get your clothes and leave immediately. You can dress elsewhere. If I were a younger man I'd beat you soundly. The villainy of this is beyond any conduct I've yet experienced. Now leave this instant, you beast."

The officer insolently saluted, "Heil Hitler", then taking his clothes he walked out of the room, soundly slamming the door after him.

"I shall avert my eyes," Holmes declared, knowing it to be impossible if he was to undo the ropes that bound Cornelia so tightly. He was quite affected by the sight of her swelling bruises.

"Oh no sir, your eyes do not have the menace I saw in his. I thought that this was my time. I have never seen such a look, I was nothing, tell me all love isn't like this...?"

"Hush, my child. Ask Dr Watson, he understands the mystery of romance, but this villainy," he hissed the word, a shudder crossing his soul, "this depredation is nothing but evil my child, best cast it from your mind or else it will trouble you, torment you forever."

Cornelia clutched at his arm. "Oh sir, oh I thought no one would hear. He said not to scream, but I knew their wicked plans. I knew they intended to have me, Herr Flohn as well." She sobbed again, burying her head into Holmes' side as he worked at a difficult knot. Her tears melted into his shirt and through to his very heart, long thought shut to a woman's hot tears. Nevertheless Holmes kept his resolve and squared away his own feelings. There was no time for sentimentality.

Her crimson dress lay on the floor, ruined, ripped apart. The SS officer was a monster, a coniving beast. Justice would be too good for him.

At last Holmes had Cornelia free. She explained, "I told him you'd come, you'd notice I wasn't about, for I know Dr Watson promised to say goodnight. But he said you'd be asleep, that you were old and useless, it was no use protesting, they meant to have me and that was that."

"Tonight you shall sleep in my bed," Holmes said, then seeing her confused expression, added, "and I in your's. Watson will be pleased to stand guard I'll say. This incident is no ordeal for a lady. I am ashamed to have allowed you to accompany us. It will rebound to my everlasting shame." It was a speech he most deeply felt.

Cornelia took his long bony hand. "I do it for my father, Lord Holmes. I would go through anything to avenge his death, do not think me wronged. These people are our enemy. Once I feel stronger it will strengthen my resolve. We must expect the worst."

"Indeed we must. Now gather yourself, my dear." He averted his eyes as she stiffly and not without some pain, rolled off the bed, gathering what was left of her clothes, not seeing Holmes' renewed embarrassment, as everywhere he looked a mirror reflected everyone of her most intimate parts to their resounding glory and his agonised shame.

"Here," Holmes said, hands around his shoulders and sweeping the Inverness off his tall frame down upon young Cornelia's slim body. It wrapped her completely, covering her down to her knees and the mirrors reflected his relief and calming of his knees.

"Oh, I hope all the gentlemen don't disappear in this war Lord Holmes. My Mama says the last war finished off ninety percent of them."

"War is an insidious thing," Holmes replied, hurrying her out of the room. "I will get you safely to my room, then I must investigate the whereabouts of Von Hipplestar. Something's afoot Cornelia. I knew it the moment I heard their cruel laughter at the time you screamed. Their plans will be thwarted."

Cornelia didn't understand what he meant but a quick look at his tense, deathly white face and she thought it best to remain silent as they stalked the empty corridors.

Holmes placed her in his room, surprised to find Watson's bed empty, no sign of him anywhere, his bedtime book, Huxley's *Eyeless in Gaza* unopened. His worry turned to a genuine concern.

"I must go," he told Cornelia. "I will lock you in, my dear. This is a strange Christmas night. It is not my choice I leave you alone, but..."

"I shall not sleep, I shall be too frightened until Dr Watson returns. I hope you find him soon Lord Holmes."

Holmes nodded retrieving his cape (with closed eyes) from the diminutive and saddened girl. She hastily put on Watson's enormous dressing gown.

"Have resolve dear Cornelia, I shall have Watson with you in a short time." He paused at the door. "This incident, do not mention it to Watson."

Cornelia couldn't have agreed more and watched after him until he departed and she heard the door lock, then falling upon her bed she began to weep, giving in to the horror.

For Holmes it was just the beginning.

Watson was in charge.

He had forbidden a thing to be touched. He had not allowed a soul to leave the room and no one had entered – save Herr Flohn, even despite protests of the most unpleasant and threatening kind.

Watson insisted Sherlock Holmes must be found and Mr Markova, whose wife it was laying unmistakably dead in the room.

Nothing could persuade Herr Flohn not to take the dagger from his wife's shaking hands, despite Watson's plea contrariwise. All in all though, he achieved a reasonable status quo and despite the overlong wait for Holmes to be found and the distinct resentment of all involved, there was a great relief when Holmes had bumped into the messenger and been directed to the unfortunate scene of such recent tragedy.

Mr Markova was sat outside in a kind of trance, rubbing his neck, totally unable to comprehend what was happening. His mind had quite collapsed and he was nothing but a corpse himself.

"Good man, Watson," Holmes declared taking in the situation at a glance, understanding that the good Doctor's familiarity with his work had ensured some evidence of what went on was preserved.

To those in the room, an audible sigh of relief was heard as Holmes had entered. At last something would be done. At least it was Sherlock Holmes and not some bumbling Inspector from the Strasbourg force eager for a quick solution and a transfer to Paris. To wait for such a man, one would wait all night and day besides.

Watson was explaining all that he saw to Holmes, beginning with Herr Döre and ending with much screaming and fainting at the door whilst he would let no one in or allow anything to be touched.

It might have seemed that Sherlock Holmes was a trifle insensitive to the sensibilities of the guests and host as he stalked about the room, inspected the dagger, the dresser, the very carpet; snipping samples from the pile, inspecting them with his new lens. He inspected Frau Flohn, the window, even the ladies powder room before taking the merest glance at the body of Mrs Markova. Yet when he did so, he stood up and joined Watson by the door. "It is really rather a simple case, Watson."

"You mean Herr Döre stabbed her and ran on? There is no sign of him anywhere. We have a search party on the lookout for him," Watson asserted, quite sure it was that evil man. Indeed, he wanted it to be so.

"No Watson, it was not Herr Döre who did this murder. I know that he was already bloodied from another, less sinister, occasion."

At that assertion there was much muttering, for all were in total agreement that it was the odious Herr Döre who had killed the guest.

A new arrival appeared at the door, Von Hipplestar, accompanied by the smug SS officer.

"So the caped crusader seeks truth and justice, this will be interesting sport Herr Flohn. To see Sherlock Holmes in action is a privilege indeed. I'll wager fifty thousand francs he will not succeed."

There was a shocked silence, but then, much to Holmes' consternation, there were numerous assentions to this monstrous wager. Herr Flohn, himself, wagered one hundred thousand francs that Holmes would find the culprit. He also offered, most kindly, to pay Mrs Markova's funeral expenses as well, which was a decent reminder to all that there was a dead body in the room. This seemed only to amuse the Nazi contingent at the door, who muttered and laughed quite freely amongst themselves. Their wagers alone reached the fantastic sum of 250,000 francs against Holmes. All the while Holmes said nothing, but quietly whistled, as was his custom when working. The case was quite peculiar and one of the most contemptuous he had ever had to solve.

"So out with it, Sherlock," Von Hipplestar exclaimed most rudely, confident he had won his wager already and eager to record the defeat.

Holmes was aware of his precarious position, yet concerned for young Cornelia back in his room. For this reason he quietly gave Watson the room key and asked him to run a chemical analysis on the dagger, even though there were no facilities to do this. Luckily Watson seemed keen to retire. With the dagger wrapped in his handkerchief, he left the room, hoping Holmes would be safe on his own with all those bully boys around him.

When Watson had gone, Holmes began his analysis of the crime, first seating the ashen Frau Flohn and having the body of the unfortunate victim laid out on the bed. While this was being done, he sat in a creaky wicker chair, leaning back, his eyes almost closed, his head sunk against his chest. When silence came to the room, he asked, "Pray tell me, Herr Flohn, when Mr Markova told you that he couldn't accept your offer for his factories in Marseilles – what did you hope to achieve by inviting him to your home at Christmas, a holiday Mr Markova does not normally celebrate?"

Herr Flohn was quite obviously stunned at such a question.

"I fail to see the relevance..."

"When Mr Markova again refused your new offer, a little more than half the true value of his factories, did you not also consider alternative means to persuade him to sell?"

"This is plain rudeness, Lord Holmes. I had expected better of you."

"Do not be alarmed. I know neither you, nor your ladywife, are guilty of this murder. I am merely establishing the reason for the Markova's being here. For no one would pretend that they were welcome company."

Pointedly there were no protestations.

"Von Hipplestar," Holmes continued, "offered to help Herr Flohn with his 'little difficulty' with Mr Markova. Yet he, too, is innocent of this particular piece of villainy." There was a knowing laugh at the back of the crowd that seemed to mock Holmes' announcement. But Holmes continued on undismayed.

"Many have observed that Herr Döre was seen running from this room when the murder happened. Yet I can establish beyond all doubt that Herr Döre was in the bathroom when Mrs Markova was murdered."

A ripple of interest went through the growing assembly.

"He was in there attending to a bleeding mouth, impaled by a cactus, the witness to that fact stands next to Von Hipplestar."

"Ja, that is so," agreed the SS officer, nursing his own lip, in no mood to help Sherlock Holmes solve anything.

"Indeed, Herr Döre must have been considerably surprised to find Mrs Markova sprawled as she was across the carpet, the dagger thrust into her side. The surprise would have led him to run away from the problem, aware that his own blood would not make for an easy explanation. His antipathy to foreigners well known. Mrs Markova was a guest of Herr Flohn, therefore untouchable.

"Yet who was in here before? While Herr Döre was in the bathroom?" Holmes stood up and walked over to the window, the curtains blowing in the breeze.

"Open, a footstep on the sill. Outside, illuminated by the electric light, footprints facing away from the Chateau. We could assume that whoever left, did so by using the window as his escape and making off through the snow."

"We must give chase in the snow," Herr Flohn spoke up, "follow the tracks. We will soon find the criminal."

"Little use I'm afraid, Herr Flohn," Holmes informed him. "The tracks would only lead to the front driveway cleared of snow and we should lose him. I believe the killer re-entered the building soon after the event and may even now be outside this room."

This comment drew a great deal of angry comment, but Holmes was not cowed. He walked across the room again. "Then observe this elegant dresser. The site of the dagger is plainly marked. The dust around the weapon evidence that the choice of weapon was not premeditated; an accident, or the first thing that came to hand. All right you say, so she was stabbed to death right here, outside a bathroom door where a man, albeit in pain, was applying cold water to his face to stop the bleeding, without much success it seems. Look again, carefully, at the site of Mrs Markova's body."

"Where was it exactly?" Herr Flohn asked, unsure now the body had been removed.

"Precisely why I advocated moving the body, a move no Scotland Yard detective, no matter how incompetent, would contemplate. Look closely. There is no blood." His magnifying glass focussed on the carpet strands.

"Which means she was..." an officer's girlfriend blurted out, instantly clasping a hand to her face, embarrassed and aware of all the faces suddenly staring at her.

"Which means she was dead before she was carried into the room." Holmes completed for her. "The murder was not committed in this room!"

Comment buzzed around the room apace. "Though one must ask oneself," Holmes added, "why would anyone want to stab a corpse? Indeed, why would the mistress of the house remove that dagger, an unpleasant, but possibly understandable Christian act."

"I could not bear to see..." Frau Flohn began, but her husband hushed her, fearing to discover more than was necessary.

"Observe," Holmes told all, guaranteed of a rapt audience, silent and fascinated. He squatted down beside the body of Mrs Markova and scrutinised her wrists. Five unpleasant bruises were the tell-tale marks of a cruel and vicious hand. "First she was pulled one way by one man," he inspected the other wrist, "then this way by another. The finger impressions being much larger on this arm. An argument between two men over the woman. Which men? Whichever man killed her, it was he who carried her up the stairs, losing her one shoe in the process, there flinging her to the floor; perhaps simultaneously hearing a scream, two screams out on the landing. Fearing the worst and hearing someone in the bathroom, he took fright, but he did not panic, for this man is a canny fellow. He looked about him, found the dagger, quickly stabbed Mrs Markova, just once in the chest, not even near her heart (for if this were all her injuries she might still be alive.) Schemer that he obviously is, abandoned all and hurriedly left by the window, leaving Herr Döre to take the blame. Devilishly lucky, diabolically unpleasant."

But all this is very well, but who is the killer?" Von Hipplestar demanded to know. It was not any of us, for were we not all smoking together with you, Sherlock Holmes?"

"Most of us, but several men were out of the room at the time of the scream," Holmes replied, a pointed stare at Von Hipplestar's young companion. "Mr Markova was with his wife."

"So you say Mr Markova killed his wife," Herr Flohn asked, anxious to have this unpleasant matter over with, pleased it was a foreigner and all seemed to be neat and tidy.

"No sir, Mr Markova did not want to let go of his wife, but was persuaded by means of a sharp blow to his head, inducing concussion; hence his obvious dazed and probably fractured state outside this room.

"We get now to the real horror of the situation ladies and gentlemen." He drew breath, appearing to re-examine the corpse. "The fact of Mrs Markova being poisoned."

"The chef, it was the chef all the time," Frau Flohn exclaimed with certainty, "it was the paté."

"It was not the paté," Holmes declared with some irritation, sensing things were getting out of hand. "Old fashioned strychnine was used. See how stiff and unnatural she is for such a recent death. No stab wound would produce a death like this." He stood up and swept the cape behind him.

"So we have a motive, the possession of a factory at half price in Marseilles. We have promises that with a little leverage perhaps Mr Markova could be persuaded to sell, perhaps frighten him so much he'd be glad to give away his factories."

"This is monstrous," Herr Flohn protested, flashing urgent signals to Von Hipplestar at the door.

"The truth is monstrous," Holmes remarked. "For the truth is, Mr Markova had given an undertaking to sell to Herr Flohn only two hours ago, at a mutually agreed price. This was not known by any, save the three of us, so the coercion could have been stopped, yet was not, perhaps to strike a better bargain? Perhaps too, Von Hipplestar thought he would be elsewhere by this time?" Holmes added mysteriously, staring at the man's bloated face. "That he did not think he would have to face me. Yet here we are and I can say with confidence that the smudges of engine grease, the button from his blue tunic, the footprint of a German manufactured leather boot, the fingerprints so carefully wiped off the dagger, but left upon the window latch, the bruises upon the wrist where she was dragged out to the Mercedes Benz outside and the leaves on her one shoe to prove it, all convict Von Hipplestar's chauffeur."

There was a shocked silence then, as Von Hipplestar turned purple with rage, a soft patter of applause for Sherlock Holmes was heard. "No question of it, Von Hipplestar. Under orders or acting alone, your chauffeur will have to confess all."

"Pay up, Hipplestar," were the first words spoken here.

"Where is the chauffeur?" another voice asked, one of the girls Herr Döre had brought with him.

"Asleep with the other staff most probably," Herr Flohn stated immediately, "drunk, I'm certain of it."

No one doubted his words on that.

"Then it is decided," Von Hipplestar announced, clicking his heels so violently the ladies winced. "We shall find the criminal, arrest and shoot him. It is a job well done Sherlock Holmes." His tone seemed sincere. He stepped forward offering his hand. "I have to admit I thought you an old buffoon, but this deduction business, sheer mastery sir. If you were on our side England would not stand a chance."

"Then you accept my word on this, Hipplestar?"

"Completely sir. Smit is a fanatic. He even asked me if Herr Markova's factories would make a satisfactory present for Herr Flohn. To my shame I ignored him. I am at fault sir. My apologies must go to Mr Markova."

"Please go and find the man," Herr Flohn urged, pleased the business was almost over, "and bring him to my study. Lord Holmes, I, too, owe you an apology. I, too, thought this might be a game we could play with you prior to calling in the police, but your expertise is second to none. I am proud to know you and more than pleased that we do not have to call upon the police in this matter, it is all too distasteful at Christmas."

Holmes had to agree, but he knew without police Von Hipplestar's justice would be the compassion of the lynch mob. However, on foreign territory he could not insist upon fair trials. The man was damned in any case. Strangely, Holmes felt he had passed a kind of bizarre test.

Frau Flohn sighed, shaking her head. "We shall all retire, the staff can take care of Mrs Markova. Please, everyone go to bed now, I insist."

Outside in the crowd there was no sign of Mr Markova anywhere, but Holmes knew the man had been listening. Suddenly a shot was heard from deep below the Chateau, people gasped and broke into a run.

"The chauffeur, I think," Holmes muttered, making for his room, having lost all interest in the case now it was solved. He was anxious to see how Watson and Cornelia were doing. Even as he reached his door and knocked four times upon it (their usual code) he heard another shot and a piercing scream, its echo bouncing up from the bowels of the Chateau striking fear into all but the stronghearted. "Mr Markova," Holmes added, totalling three bodies so far and only one hour into Christmas day.

Watson unlocked the door. "I heard shots," he gabbled, looking slightly ridiculous in his night cap and with a raised poker in his hand. "Has the world gone mad Holmes?"

"It is nothing, my dear Watson. Just the cold hard steel of justice, recrimination and the clear light of madness."

Young Cornelia was asleep, an empty glass beside her bed, the contents a sleeping draught provided by Watson. This pleased Holmes who had been more than a little distressed at her plight earlier on.

"Explain, explain," Watson implored him.

"Simple Watson. I found the chauffeur Smit guilty of killing Mrs Markova (probably under Von Hipplestar's orders). Mr Markova, in his grief and madness, upon hearing who was the guilty party, dashed downstairs and shot the chauffeur dead, an easy task for the man was most likely drunk and then, Mr Markova, fearing little justice from the Nazis for killing one of their own, shot himself. A tragedy, but not without precedent I think. These people really are monsters Watson. We are in treacherous territory and this is but the early days of the war." Holmes peered at the wall a moment, as if pondering more, but turned to Watson and placed a hand upon his arm a moment. "And now I believe I will wish you a happy Christmas, Watson and retire to bed. See that you attend Miss Cornelia most closely, for she had a fright earlier this evening that I should not like repeated."

"I shall watch like a hawk," he answered.

"Your life will depend upon it, Watson. She is a treasured being." He looked fondly at the mass of dark curls upon the pillow, then turned sharply for the door.

"I do believe you are as attached to her as I, Holmes," Watson remarked. Holmes merely took his leave with his enigmatic smile and wandered off down the dismal, yellow-lit corridor, pleased another night's injustice had been put to right.

Watson shut his door and stared at the sleeping girl in the other bed. "I do believe you will exhume the ghost of Irene Adler, my girl. But don't let a smile from Holmes deceive you. His heart is made of stone."

6

The Red-Headed Front Line

Christmas morning began with the news that the Sherlock Holmes party
would be given special dispensation to visit Nürnberg for two weeks
precisely, when it would be incumbent upon them to return to enemy
territory (France), or remain as free men in Germany for the duration of the
war, (which, they were assured, would last only six months at the most).
This was the reward for Holmes' previous night's effort, though not all the
Germans were happy with it. Privately, Von Hipplestar was saying Holmes
was too dangerous to have at large, but it was his game that had gone wrong
and thus he was cast in bad favour at Chateau Vernet, leaving earlier than he
anticipated.

Of Herr Döre, nothing was seen.

But the day after Christmas day in the town of Strasbourg, as Holmes and
Watson were attempting a stroll through the quaint medieval streets, they
caught sight of a very strange thing indeed. A bicycle with all kinds of
apparatus built onto it, with something that looked like a loudspeaker at the
rear, was standing outside an electrical suppliers. Holmes was fascinated and
observed the sleek lines of the most modern metal work, the black spokes, the
fretwork of steel that practically engulfed the whole machine, leaving only a
tiny space for the rider to climb into the middle of it. The wide saddle had
curious copper wires wound tightly around its base and continuing to the

rear spokes, where they made connection with more wonderful metal objects that were electrical in outlook. Dynamos, crystals, batteries, a dial on the highly polished handlebars that could be mistaken for a speedometer, but Watson knew to be a radio tuner from his own experience with the Home Service. The tyres were of double strength too, owing to all the extra weight.

"A most extraordinary thing," Watson remarked, "really a most extraordinary thing."

"Something on the line of a portable radio, wouldn't you say Watson?" Holmes remarked, "Friction powered. One would have to move at quite a pace to keep it working. Strong legs needed for a machine like that."

Even as they watched the bicycle (for they both knew watching brought results) they saw another on the horizon zig-zagging through the busy cobbled steets, the handlebars glistening in the rare winter sun.

"These really are most curious bicycles Watson. I believe we should study them quite closely, for if I am not mistaken, something of a revelation will strike us, I'm sure of it."

The other bicycle was in a great hurry it was plain to see, the rider lying flat, almost level with the handlebars, his behind high up in the air with all the aerials and equipment that accompanied this particular animal. His body made as little of the wind as possible; the legs threshed so hard on the pedals that no eye could see where the foot ended and the bicycle began. It was an awesome sight, a furious, grand sight and others, who probably had no business doing so, stopped and stared with wonder as the World Bicycle Land Speed record was most surely shattered.

At last they saw the rider lift his head, now discernible as a mass of red hair, an unusual sight in Strasbourg to be sure. Ten yards away from Watson and Holmes the rider applied brakes. Sparks flew from the metal pieces trailing on the lumpy cobblestone, showering passers-by who were astonished at their appearance. The brakes had been applied, the bicycle veered right and made a complete circle, coming to a precise stop next to the other identical radio-bicycle; almost as if this was a deliberate exercise and not some accident of gravity that deposited the rider with a flying leap to the ground, where he landed with the grace of Nijinsky.

"This grows more remarkable by the minute," Holmes remarked crossing the street, hoping to address the red-headed man. "I say," he began, but was too late, for the newly arrived cyclist had already entered the radio shop in great agitation.

Now there were two bicycles, identical in every respect and despite the addition of gears and racing pedals, they looked far too heavy for any man to

91

cycle at all, never mind the frantic pace at which this one had seen service. It was still hot and Holmes judged it to have been driven a long distance.

"This bicycle is of British manufacture, Watson. The radio, if I'm not mistaken, a Marconi design of the very latest type. I should be surprised if the owners of these machines turned out to be French. However, there is something about the design of the radio equipment that is decidedly un-French."

"Home-made, y'mean," Watson muttered. "Some boffin been at this one, one can tell, I never saw such a radio."

"Hmm, nevertheless, there being two of them, it would suggest that this is more than the work of an idle experimenter. We must be prepared to accept that there might be more."

"But why?" Watson asked, thinking the entire idea a puzzle.

They waited patiently for the two riders to come out of the electrical and radio shop. Yet when the two men emerged, Watson was studying Holmes' face and he was astonished to see it turn instantly pale as every drop of blood drained away, leaving Holmes looking older, not even half the man he was before. Yet in another second he recovered and looked as good as new as he approached the men with a hearty, "Good-day gentlemen."

The two red-headed men in green cyclists' overalls with cloverleaf motif looked quite astonished.

"English," one said, "Oh Lord, an Englishman and us off our bicycles. You have not been tampering with anything, I hope?"

Watson immediately took offence. "How dare you sir. We were just taking an interest."

"No wait a minute, gentlemen," Holmes instructed them. "I am curious to know what two Irishmen are doing in Strasbourg on radio-bicycles. This is an amazing conundrum gentlemen, I think it owes something of an explanation."

"No sir, it does not. We have here what can only be called a secret."

"Some secret," Watson declared. "Anyone can see as plain as day that these are mounted radio-cycles - English made."

Watson could perceive he had made some impact on these two Irishmen. "Now see here, my friend Lord Sherlock Holmes is a scientific man himself, he would be most interested in your experiment."

The two men were immediately impressed and dismayed at the same time.

"This is no experiment," one declared importantly. "Where is your proof you are Sherlock Holmes, how do I know you are not German spies?"

"Because we are gentlemen," Watson answered.

The complaining Irishman could not disagree. "Then it is a pleasure to meet Sherlock Holmes and you, sir, must be Sir John Watson, the chronicler of his case notes?"

Watson nodded.

"Then this is a most momentous occasion to be sure."

"And what might your names be?" Watson enquired.

"They might be O'Connor, or O'Reilly or Duncan," they answered. "But we are sworn to secrecy. The street is no place to talk."

"Then coffee gentlemen, I'll buy you both coffee," Holmes offered.

"Nor coffee house, hot bed of gossip, sin and spies. There's nowhere safe for our bicycles."

"I see you came for new valves," Holmes observed, noting the boxes they carried.

"That we did, sir. Valves will become an ever increasing rarity as the war goes on. We are cycling from radio shop to radio shop mustering all the valves we can. Trouble is, French tubes are a little uncertain, not reached a high state in development compared to the Murphy valve, but there's a singular lack of them in these parts."

"Few Murphys in all of France, I'd say," Watson ventured.

"'Tis the truth you speak, sir. The Murphys are a home loving creature. I know for I have an Uncle who never left his village in all his life, not even when the British tried to smoke them out."

"Those days are over," Holmes told him, taking a new pipe out of his pocket and beginning to suck on it.

"Is that a German pipe you're sucking on?" one asked.

"It is," Holmes replied, "a gift from a grateful host. It would please me more if there was some tobacco to be had."

"You are to resist the urge," Watson urged him, ignorant of the pipe until that instant.

The two Irishmen were of another mind though. One suggested, "We ride to meet another, Lord Holmes. Perhaps we could share this pipe of yours. Sean has some of the finest shag in all of France, brought with him from Ireland and that in turn from America where our cousins reside."

Holmes smiled, his ruse had worked. "That is a most capital suggestion what say you Watson?"

Watson had studied the sweaty faces of these rough, but affable Irishmen and come to the conclusion that they weren't all they seemed, yet a good shag shared would not do Holmes much harm. "I'll be glad to join you, perhaps if I might be allowed to fetch my bath-chair situated around the corner..."

"An excellent idea Watson. I will ride on the back and we shall go under power, for one cannot expect such cyclists to walk."

It was mutually agreed then. After only a moment's delay, whilst Watson fetched his bath-chair, Holmes attempted to draw the Irishmen out of their little secret (to no avail for an Irishman will not be parted easily from a secret and Holmes would never attempt a bribe.)

Soon though, the gentle throb of the approaching Delahaye bathchair could be heard and Watson sped around the corner, vibrating most violently on the inhospitable cobbles. He hardly slowed at all to pick up Holmes, who leapt on the back and clung with a grim determination as all three vehicles sped along the street avoiding the towns' dogs, cats, traffic and buses as best they could; the two radios on the bicycles blaring out *Irish Eyes Are Smiling*, to the puzzlement of the French population and the amusement of Holmes.

"I should like a radio in my bath-chair, Holmes," Watson informed him as they motored through open country, the fields brown and exposed, the trees stark and bleak at the roadside. A few minutes later they approached a railway bridge some way from the city, beside a church, little used from the look of the overgrown graveyard. A babbling stream flowed nearby, over-full, swamping the distant fields, the Christmas snow having melted with a vengeance.

As was promised, waiting to meet them was another man possessed of a bicycle with radio contraptions. This fellow was a foot taller than the others with a large ornament of a nose yet, predictably enough, a bright red crop of hair grew on top of his head. So bright was his hair Watson was almost sure it was a wig, but was assured upon enquiry that it was not and indeed was the pride crop of all Kilpatrick where this particular carrot-top hailed from. He turned out to be the man called Sean.

"This is really most astonishing," Holmes declared after the pipe was filled and all four (they excluded Watson) continued to pass the pipe around under the bridge. So intent were they on enjoying the excellent Virginia shag they allowed the pipe to become so hot each could hardly hold it for very long, thus ever increasing the pace at which it revolved.

Watson sat in his bath-chair avoiding the smoke, munching some Pontefract cakes, much needed for a stubborn condition.

"Remarkable," Holmes was saying, "to find three red-headed Irishmen pedalling radio bicycles on the border of France and Germany. It is a pity these radios only receive light music, for it would be a useful thing if they could be used to relay messages from Germany to your roving cycles and leave you to relay that message all the way to London. But, of course, three would not be enough, there must be limits, nor would I have the correct crystals to contact you…" It was a bait, but would they swallow?

"Three?" The tall Irishman called Sean exclaimed importantly. "There's more than three. Eleven more like, perhaps even thirteen, valiant Irish radio officers, red-headed all. We are posted from the Mediterranean as far as Verdun."

"That is truly remarkable. The thin red line," Holmes mused.

"The thin red-headed line," the smallest of the men corrected him.

"But I was not aware that Eire was involved in the coming conflict?"

"There is much you may not be aware of Sherlock Holmes," Sean told him, turning up his radio to cover the conversation. His legs did not seem to be tiring at all, despite maintaining a constant spinning of the rear wheel (suspended by a metal, hinged ramp to give him stability). *The Hills of Kilkenny* filled the entire under-bridge area and provided a most wonderful effect.

"It is a simple explanation I am offering you, Lord Holmes, because there is no complicated one. I give you an explanation only because you so cleverly noticed us and I know from your queer and demanding reputation that you will not rest until you know the truth. It is best that we tell you the truth and that you swear by the God Almighty and the Virgin Mary that you will not reveal the secret to anyone, even under pain of torture. That goes for the old tub in the bath-chair as well."

Watson was not over-fond to be called a tub, but he, like Holmes, swore to secrecy.

"Swear by the bond that binds all red-headed men everywhere."

They swore again, Watson noting for the first time that the bicycles had no reflectors, surely a danger at night and at variance with the law?

"This, then, is the truth," Sean confessed, scratching the top of his red head and allowing his eyes to search both before and behind him for spies with air guns and the like which were, they were informed, much feared in these parts.

"It is well known that France lacks behind in radio technology." Holmes did not know this, in fact, but nodded sagely all the same.

"So it was a natural act on France's part to cast about in panic for some assistance when news of Adolf Hitler's intentions were known. Eire, as you understand, Lord Holmes, would not think of sharing its radio technology with England, which country is damned in the eyes of the Lord anyway."

Neither Holmes, nor Watson rose to the bait. Watson concentrated on the music and his stiffening arms, always a bother in the cold.

"France found us, gentlemen. The newly-formed Brigade of Radio Bicycles, more mobile than a car in cities and less detectable. And a determined lot we all are."

Privately Watson was a little puzzled. He had thought that Eire was all for a victory by the Hun against the English, but he held his peace.

"There is a bond between Ireland and France that cannot be broken, Lord Holmes. France turned to us in desperation and immediately we set out for Paris. Cycling many days to the ferry, then across to France until, finally, you find us here."

"Here?" Holmes asked, the bridge a curious setting for a brigade of Irishmen. The pipe came back to him again, burning his hand, though he showed no pain.

"Inside this bridge and set below where no bomb can reach it, lies every tube, valve and crystal in France that we could lay our hands on. Even now France is in uproar for not a valve can be found in Paris; their factories are unable to cope with the fantastic demand."

"But who pays for all of this?" Watson asked, ever practical; thinking it a tall order and waving pipe smoke away from his face.

"The French. But things will be put to right soon. We have secured enough now to continue a war of monitoring and sending out messages about troop movements in Germany for as long as the war might last. A year, two years, more... we have the valves, the crystals and even a spare bicycle."

The three Irishmen looked pleased with themselves and expected Holmes to be, though his face showed no emotion at all. This prompted Sean to add, "there are some problems, of course." The other two protested, but Sean hushed them pretty sharply. "No there are, we have to admit it. Not one of us speaks any German, nor French, but this is no obstacle, worse things have happened in Ireland."

"True," the others concurred, "the County Tyrone disaster, for one."

Even Holmes knew of that debacle and removed his hat briefly in remembrance of that time.

"But one thing is in our favour. We can tell the difference between French and German," the shortest Irishman explained enthusiastically, sucking deeply on the red-hot pipe.

"I can see that you are eminently suited for warfare," Holmes remarked. "The Maginot line is one thing, but yourselves are something else entirely."

"Never better put," said Sean, "we are now France's first line of defence. If the Germans attack, if they move an inch, our barrage of information will speed, like Mercury, back to Paris to warn them."

"Speed onto Dublin too," one remarked, "for radio waves can continue for many miles in the mysterious night ether."

"So France will be saved. No surprises for them, all is in hand," Watson declared, pleased to hear it. "It is good to know the best of Irish technology is put to work in the defence of a good cause. But pray tell me, why does the German radio broadcast only Irish tunes?"

There was an easy answer to that, the Irishman showed some surprise that Watson should ask at all, "This is a Dublin-built Marconi," was all he said, as if no more need be explained.

Holmes thought it best not to continue this investigation. All he knew was that if he were French, he would not sleep well in his bed at night with this as the nation's first line of defence; though, to be fair, there was a lot about modern warfare he did not know. Instead, he said, "Gentlemen, that was a truly remarkable shag. Now, we have an appointment with a young lady, perhaps you'd like us to wish you a good war?"

The three men nodded sternly. "A good war," they chorused, mounting their bicycles as one, gracing the much-polished saddles with the care of men who respected their steeds, who understood the subtle blend of approach needed between an Irishman and his bicycle. Sean kicked down his ramp, stopping his rear wheel and, momentarily, the music.

"It was a pleasure, Lord Holmes." He stretched out his hand and gave Holmes a tiny, blue crystal. "Here, take this, for emergencies. If you are ever in need of help, eight dots, six dashes repeated will bring help. You can be assured of that as the word of the Red-Headed Brigade. Are you going to Germany, by any chance?"

"It is a secret," Holmes told them, raising his forefinger to his lips.

The three red-headed men gaped a second, then with sly, all knowing smiles acknowledged this indiscretion and solemnly turned their bicycles in the direction of the afternoon sun. They rode off into the strong glare on the country road; the sound of *Sweet Molly Malone* accompanied them to a very distant, verdant horizon.

"Physiognomy teaches us about the face Watson and we know from their determined faces that those are brave men, but what does it tell us about red hair? I think perhaps a study on the effects of red hair is a much needed tome, don't you think, Watson?"

"Anything you say, Holmes," Watson replied, trying to get his engine started. "But I fear their's is an uphill struggle, though I can see they are brave men."

Holmes took the key from Watson's shaking hand and inserted it into the ignition, starting the engine immediately. "The war," he said, mounting the back of the bath-chair, "is one surprise after another. Come Watson, we promised to meet young Cornelia for tea."

***

Young Cornelia was almost recovered from her ordeal in Von Hipplestar's room, preferring not to think of it and most relieved that nearly all the German contingent had gone back over the river to Germany. In her opinion they ought to have stayed there anyway, for was not France and Germany at war? It was not proper that they were allowed over for festivities. Even though they themselves, were seeking the same.

The talk of the town was all about the scandals in the Chateau Vernet; the shootings, about how three bodies were buried in the garden, their heads and hands removed. This was not true. Mrs Markova's body was sent back to Marseilles along with her husband's; the other body was flung in the river well weighted down with gravel bags. On and on flew the rumours, following Cornelia wherever she went in town. People said the police had been bought off by Herr Flohn, which was probably true. People also said that the legendary Sherlock Holmes had unmasked the villains, but no one payed much attention to that, preferring their own Hercule Poirot and Francois Le Villard. To each and every opinion did Cornelia listen as she shopped around the town for trifles, as instructed by Holmes. She liked the idea of being useful and buying clothes such that a nurse might wear off-duty in Nürnberg. Holmes thought of every detail, as usual.

She had also heard a man assert, "...You know how he became a Lord? The English King lost his horse, his favourite, and summoned Sherlock Holmes (already famous the world over for his acceptance of the Order of the Legion of Honour) and asked him to find it. Well it seemed the King's horse had already been taken by mistake to the abattoir. Tragic, yes, for Silver Blaze was a champion horse, formerly run to great success by a Colonel Ross and sold to the King for stud. But Holmes with the aid of root dye, a team of hairdressers and an expert French horse trainer managed to substitute an imposter for Silver Blaze and the King never knew. Better still the new Silver Blaze astonished all by winning the Derby, twice.

"For this he was given his title Lord Sherlock Holmes of Baker Street. I know this is true for I read of it in the English *News of the World*."

But Cornelia did not believe a word of it.

Holmes was in good spirits when he and Watson at last located the discreet little café Cornelia had chosen for their rendezvous.

Holmes was quiet at first but after his first cup of coffee and some of the proprietor's Suchard chocolate, the best from Germany they were assured, he entered into a very conversational mood, almost in top form. Watson had not seen him this way in years, the subjects he chattered about changed like rapid gunfire. He spoke on the Passion play, on Celtic poetry, the rare beauty of North Wales, an area he got around to visiting all too infrequently. He spoke on the rising tide of Muslim culture, how one day they would rise up and seize their own lands from the Oil Barons and on the Jet plane, about which he had become interested when Mr Whittle had filed patents back in 1930. It was Holmes' opinion that not enough was being done, if anything at all. The turbine was the future, the piston engine had far too many parts. The limit for them had come with the Merlin III built by Rolls Royce. He was afraid that England had not taken Mr Whittle's ideas seriously enough. He mused on Germany's obsession with rocketry and his conversation with Mr Wells. How Mr Wells had told him that London could come under a reign of fire from rockets fired across the channel. The future of war in the hands of a monster like Adolf Hitler would be startling in its cruelty and ingenuity. Whitehall had no ideas, no answers. England entered this war blindfolded, expecting gentlemen's rules. He spoke, too, on the simple beauty of ripples in his coffee starting in the centre and working out to the rim, something Watson found fascinating. At 87 it was a new way to look at coffee.

Holmes spoke on each subject as an expert, a man who had spent a lifetime studying these very subjects. It was encouraging, a great experience to witness this performance by Sherlock Holmes and Cornelia wondered at his mental powers, so acute at 83: how much stronger forty years before, at the height of his fame?

Watson was quite obviously pleased to see his friend in so uncommon a fine mood and was anxious to find out what had caused it, but in this young Cornelia thwarted him. Even as Holmes began on a new assortment of Stoller chocolate and ate it with obvious relish (perhaps to squash the new appetite for tobacco he had acquired under the railway bridge) Cornelia stood up saying:

"I have a surprise for you Lord Holmes. Close your eyes. The owner of this café was most interested to hear that you were in town and immediately enquired as to whether you had lost your musical appetite. He has heard all about your passion for music Lord Holmes and here," she clapped her hands and from behind a curtain the proprietor of the Café Zola emerged with a beaming smile and a prized Stradivarius in his arms. "Open your eyes".

Holmes was beside himself. Now he needed possession of that Stradivarius immediately and with an almost frantic urge he took it over. After a minimum of tuning he stood up with a stern but appreciative smile at Cornelia and began to play.

It was uncanny. Watson had not heard Holmes play the violin with such virtuoso. He had never heard the solo from Bizet's Symphony in C Major, played with such imagination. Holmes treated them all to compositions of his own, not the sombre material he normally played, but light, almost military and decidedly Wagnerian.

This event did much to improve British-French relations in Strasbourg throughout the war. It was once again a triumph for music and a personal victory for Sherlock Holmes, Peer of the Realm.

Transported into some dream world Watson, quite against habit, ate some chocolates with a keen appreciation, treating the occasion as if it were a night at the Proms. He felt growing inspiration, so much so, even whilst Holmes played, the urge to write came upon him and thus it was that *ten Café Zola cream, starched napkins filled to the very edges with closely-packed handwriting became part of the Holmes-Watson heritage and proof of the mission Winston Churchill had despatched them on.

And yet, unaccountably, just an hour later, Watson and Cornelia had the most severest of headaches and had to retire early, whilst Holmes declared that he had never felt better and spent the entire evening discussing the most intricate and important plans with Herr Flohn. The German was most keen to impress his astute and intelligent guest with details of his progressive, streamlined factories, an indiscretion he would one day regret.

It was not until some time later that the seemingly innocent excitement at the Café Zola and their supposed over-indulgence became significant. It was a shock still to come, and would have been ignored by a lesser man than Sherlock Holmes.

Another result of Watson's unfortunate malaise was that there exists no record of the New Year's Eve celebration for the year 1939 and no word at all until Holmes and Watson had embarked on their journey to Nürnberg with the papers furnished by Von Hipplestar himself, with all the necessary Berlin stamps. Only here did Watson begin his diary once again.

Herr Flohn had provided them with a driver for his wife's Horch 12, a delightfully comfortable vehicle, ideal to take the three of them across the border to Appenweier and its newly important railway station.

The British Library Literary Notes Collection: Holmes:Napkins:Notes '39

But imagine their discomfort when at the last moment Herr Max Millhapt, a friend of Herr Flohn and a fellow engineer ran out of the house to join them, squeezing himself in besides Cornelia and squashing her terribly.

"You vill excuse me, Lord Holmes, Fraulein Shand," he apologised. "But I have urgent business in Berlin."

"By all means, Herr Millhapt," Holmes answered. "Make yourself comfortable, perhaps you'd be good enough to inform us of the current state of Germany's communications and roads. Watson here makes a great study of roads."

The Horch drew away (the bath-chair secure under tow behind) and the Chateau quickly receded into the distance. Cornelia watched it fade away with mixed feelings, her first Chateau. It would not be her last.

"Of course, the German road is vastly superior to the British road," Herr Millhapt was saying, annoying Watson instantly. "Here we are in 1940 already and it is a fact that England hardly has one inch of autobahn. Your crooked little roads are quite useless for modern tank er...traffic. Where are your Reichsautobahnen, Deutsche Alpenstrassen?"

"We have an excellent rail network between cities," Holmes informed him. "It is a foolish notion to encourage excessive motoring, increase one's dependence upon oil. Your autobahn will be your downfall Herr Millhapt, mark my words. There is only so much oil in the ground, finite resources."

"Indeed sir," Watson stressed, leaning forward. "England is streets ahead on road surfacing. Your uneven pave is a disgrace about which all Europe knows."

At this Herr Millhapt visibly paled, his eyes narrowed to slits as he sought to counter Watson's harsh words. "Soon all traffic will use the autobahn, the country roads will be irrelevant. Our cars will lead the world, nothing will defeat the ever increasing power of Auto-Union and Mercedes-Benz. We shall conquer the roads of the world with the designs of Dr Porche and Herr Eberan von Eberhorst, his chief engineer. They will be the first world cars, a design for all the people."

"It is hard to imagine a road without an Austin," Cornelia ventured, knowing Watson's fondness for the little cars.

"Never," Watson declared quite angry. "Impossible."

Herr Millhapt laughed most cruelly. "The Austin is an English joke. There is nothing in Britain to compete with superior German technology. Not one car in the 5000cc class, mein Herr Caracciola is a god amongst ordinary mortals."

Watson snorted. "Dick Seaman could have taken him anytime. God rest his soul."

Herr Millhapt just sniggered, slapping his knees. "You make another good joke Dr Watson. He had his chances." He stared out at the countryside as, coincidentally, they passed a section of new road leading to the border, a wide, concrete, military road.

"Now this is a good road, but even this is not as good as a German road. I must tell you Dr Watson, the last time Britain could truthfully be said to have possessed a road system was during the Roman occupation. This will soon be remedied. Within a year we shall march on London and begin building straight roads."

Watson snatched a quick look at Holmes, but Holmes merely smiled. "You will have to win the war first Herr Millhapt, how do you propose to do that?"

It was Herr Millhapt's turn to lay back in his seat and smile. "Superior military technology, superior roads, superior people on a balanced diet, a vision, a clear idea of nationhood, a superior leader and a grand plan for the unification of all Europe, including England. One cannot defeat an idea. This is not war, we have declared an open invitation to all Europe to join us."

"And if they don't?" Cornelia asked, her eyes glittering with a quiet tightly-reined anger.

"They will be liberated, freed from slavery by the ruling classes. This Nazification is a revolution like none other before. In twenty years history will have been rewritten, there will have been no other history. The world will be German; pure, a miracle rebirth for all mankind, a new chance for the human race to save itself from utter disaster."

"Sounds reasonable enough, Herr Millhapt. If only that could be achieved without bloodshed. However, I believe that the German word for what you describe is Mondscheinfischer..." Holmes declared wistfully.

Cornelia smiled. Moonshine fisher, it was a good word.

Holmes noted the approaching border reinforcement. Every sign of military activity, yet a total lack of sophistication. Not much progress had been made since the last great war. France looked unprepared, it did not bode well for this nation. Their thin red line of bicycles was no match for the military might of a Deutschland inflamed.

"It's going to snow again," Cornelia remarked as they slowed for the border. "Are there mountains in Nürnberg, Herr Millhapt?"

"I believe so, they will be covered in snow, to be sure, it has been cold there, I hear."

The French side was easy to navigate with no complications at all, but Holmes worried about the German Zolluntersuchung. He had left things too much to trust and allowed Herr Flohn to arrange everything. So far he hoped

Watson, Cornelia and himself had not given any grounds for suspicion. Herr Döre's decision to allow them through to his influential friends was partially due to Herr Flohn's own interest in him, but in part also due to Döre's obsession with young Cornelia, an obsession not to bear fruit. Now by the misfortune of others, they were being sped to their ultimate destination. He hoped it was a series of accidents. Holmes' ever suspicious, alert mind worried that too easy access into Germany might suggest that they were suspected spies; even being watched. Yes, he had to be prepared for that.

"Der Pass," came a gruff request.

Herr Millhapt handed all five passports out of the window and the customs officer took them with him into his little hut. The swastika was imprinted everywhere, on everything. There was no going back now.

"I hope there's no problem, Holmes," Watson said, looking back at his bath-chair under tow behind. "We won't have difficulty with my transport I hope. Since that little soiree you gave Holmes, I haven't been myself at all. I swear French coffee is the most vile substance."

"Acorns," Herr Millhapt stated. "They make it from acorns."

"Ja," the customs officer said, who had re-approached without them noticing. "The French adulterate their coffee with chicory, acorns, anything, it's a disgrace. The Fuhrer will put a stop to it, that is most certain."

"I hope so," Holmes agreed, with a tight smile. "Adultery is a punishable offence in England."

The customs officer's eyes lit up. "This is so? Things are much advanced in England, no? What kind of punishment for adulteration of coffee?"

Watson would have corrected the man, but Holmes firmly but discreetly tapped him on the knee. "Five years," he said with a wink to Cornelia who suppressed a giggle. "Wir haben nichts zu verzollen. Wann geht der Zug nach Nürnberg?" Holmes asked.

The officer shrugged. He didn't know. "Ich weisse nicht."

"Your German isn't so bad, Lord Holmes," Herr Millhapt declared.

Holmes shrugged. "Just a few useful words, I'm not always sure what they mean."

"Well anyway, the customs officer wouldn't know what time the train leaves, they are pretty isolated here."

The passports came back fully stamped.

"Guten Tag. Heil Hitler," the officer said, saluting briefly before returning to the warmth of his hut. Soldiers ahead raised the barrier and they were in Germany at last, set amongst a forest of swastikas. It was like entering another world entirely.

"We got through," Watson sighed, mopping his brow. He had been worried about Cornelia's false passport.

"Your Berlin seals are good," Herr Millhapt told them, glancing at Cornelia's black eagle and swastika. "This stamp is from Goering's office. Herr Flohn has some very useful friends."

"Indeed," Holmes agreed thoughtfully as the car pulled away onto the open road once "Herr Flohn himself is to take us around one of his newest factories in Nürnberg. The most efficient confection factory in the world. Chocolates, I think."

"So? An honour Lord Holmes. I am a jealous man. I who designed that very factory have never been in it. My time is too precious now.

"I have dedicated my life to the total onslaught Lord Holmes. You will find a different Germany here. A land blessed with the gift of a true leader. It is a time for destiny, a time for the very gods themselves to cower and cringe with envy. We shall master the earth, it will be a glorious future. Heil Hitler."

"Heil Hitler," Holmes muttered weakly, trying to get into the spirit of things, hoping his scheme to meet the elusive Dr Laubscher would be adequate, that indeed this famous man was still willing to share his secret with them. It was a dangerous mission, yet with God's grace and luck they should remain above suspicion.

"Curious you did not choose Bayreuth for your Wagner concert," Herr Millhapt commented.

"It would have pleased me very much to go Bayreuth, but it is a tradition yet to be revived. I did attend in 1911. Wagner himself was there. The Festspielhaus never offered such a superb occasion. Perhaps we might be allowed to pay homage to Wahnfried and his grave."

"You will like Nürnberg, however," Herr Millhapt told them as they entered the town, heading for the station. "It is a most charming walled town. There is an excellent hotel near the Hauptbahnhof, but I forget its name."

"We have a hotel booked," Holmes told him. "Frau Flohn put us in Der Deutsche Hof. Which is the best hotel I believe."

"Ja, verstehe."

"I fear it's getter colder," Watson fretted, "you were right Cornelia, it will snow."

They were out of the car, unlocking their baggage, supervising the bath-chair when Herr Millhapt hurried back to them. "A train for Nürnberg leaves in fifteen minutes. It is the only one today and there is space."

"Good man, Millhapt," Holmes told him. "We must hasten. I shall go ahead and purchase tickets. Nurse, keep a good eye on Watson, summon a porter if there is one to be had."

And thus it was the Holmes party caught the Nürnberg train, a journey that was not to be entirely without incident, however.

During afternoon tea, Watson suddenly became concerned about a man sitting at the far end of the over-full restaurant car. A man well padded against the winter cold (despite the warm carriages) and wearing a strange wide-brimmed white hat. Although Germanic in his features, it was not the usual attire of any German they had seen.

His eyes never left their party, switching from Holmes to Watson to Cornelia with great regularity. Certainly the man's interest in them was beyond the bounds of common decency.

Even as tea finished and Holmes rose with his party to return to their carriage, the inquisitive stranger also rose, following at a discreet distance, either unaware they were onto him or indifferent to their privacy.

"This is a mystery," Holmes muttered. "I do not believe this man to be German, yet he follows us as if a spy. We must observe him closely."

"We must see if he gets off at Nürnberg," Watson said, hurrying Cornelia along.

"It is very likely he will," Holmes pointed out, "this train terminates there."

"Ah," Watson nodded sagely, trying to keep a steady foot as he walked along the swaying corridors.

"Should I talk to him?" Cornelia asked, thinking that this would be a simple way to clear things up.

"I advise against it," Holmes replied, "remember you speak only English Nurse Shand and that's an order."

But they had not been sat down more than ten minutes when the man appeared outside their door, slid it open, poked his pale face inside and asked, "What news of England?"

An American, no less. He shut the door behind him and uninvited sat down next to Watson, introducing himself.

"Richard Moore, Dick. Special representative of the United States Government." He flashed an identity card which proved his word, although the photograph was far from persuasive. In fact Holmes was immediately sceptical, but held his tongue, inspecting the man thoroughly.

"I knew you guys had to be English, no one in Germany or France dresses this way. What are you doing so far from home?"

"Wagner in Nürnberg," Watson answered, not at all impressed with this American and intensely suspicious of him.

"Is that so, he playing or conducting?"

Cornelia laughed, for she thought everyone knew he was dead. "That's funny, huh?" he said, wanting to know what he had said wrong. Cornelia noted his hands, large with flat, chipped fingernails.

"I was getting kind of desperate, haven't met a soul who speaks English in weeks, a guy can get pretty lonely away from home."

For some reason Holmes did not believe this and decided he would make public his suspicions. "That is very odd, I should have thought you would have been able to find someone who speaks English in London, for that is where you were yesterday."

The visitor dried up suddenly, his mouth opened and shut in considerable surprise, his piercing blue eyes looking to Cornelia for support.

"Furthermore, although you speak with an American accent, your nationality is German, Mr Moorehaus. Your clothes are American, yet you wear German shoes made in Stuttgart. The ticket stub impressed upon the sole of your shoe, no doubt caused by stepping onto a wet platform at the station shows that you left Victoria yesterday at ten o'clock in the morning. It would be extremely unlikely that you did not speak to anyone on that train given your outgoing nature."

Instead of denying Holmes' assertions, the man seemed exceptionally pleased to hear them. "You are a remarkable man sir. But you have given yourself away." He laughed, raising his left hand, scratching under his hat, winking at Cornelia. "I took a bet with myself that you were the famous detective Sherlock Holmes and this here Dr Watson, of literary fame. The nurse had me puzzled, but I guess she fits in naturally enough."

"Then the mystery is over," Watson declared, much relieved.

"No sir, it is not." Holmes asserted. "Pray Mr Moorehaus, what is your occupation? It is with machinery of some kind, is it not?"

"Aviation, Mr Holmes. I sell airplanes. As it happens I use German patents. The Heinkel engine. Business is booming. I was kind of hoping I could do a deal with England, you'd be just the guy to help."

Sherlock Holmes began to feel his suspicions were unfounded. Perhaps this man was genuine. Perhaps he really was just a man on the lookout to increase his wealth. After all, there was nothing intrinsically wrong with an American doing business with Germany, they were not at war with one another.

The American dug out some cigarettes from his inside pocket and offered them around, finding no takers. Although Cornelia would have loved one;

her nerves were not what they were. "Of course, I don't reckon this war is going to last too long, no disrespect to you, Mr Holmes..."

"It's Lord Holmes," Watson interrupted testily.

The American was impressed, but carried on just the same. "Well, whatever, Lord Holmes. England just ain't prepared for war, you know what I mean? You haven't got the planes, the men, the guns, the ships. Your technology lacks behind Argentina in sophistication, your cars still incorporate ideas around in the last century. You're just not equipped to defend yourself, and an attack is right out the picture. Believe me I know, our company ran an analysis of British cost-effective performance rates in a war situation and I have to tell you, you're going to lose, hands down. But, and here's the ace, I could save your ass!" He looked at Cornelia suddenly, noticing she was blushing. "Oh, sorry Miss, I could save your behind."

Cornelia felt that neither expression would do, but she was fascinated. She had never met an American before, the man was like someone from the fairground. He claimed to be in aircraft, but no Englishman would conduct business this way.

"Now I know you're short of engines, worse you're short of planes and men. Now it just so happens I have a whole lot of Heinkels and pilots lying around doing nothing in Spain."

"But Spain is a Fascist country," Watson countered, wondering how an American could possibly direct the Spanish Air Force.

"Maybe it is, General Franco is one hell of a guy though and he's got a whole lot of Heinkels, or rather he had. I bought 'em, they're in mothballs. Spain needs the money and they aren't fighting nobody this year. My company back in New York is looking for buyers, first-come, first-served. Eighty-six of 'em, brand new, and fifty American-Hispanic pilots all dying to get into action in this war. They don't care which side as long as they get action, know what I mean?"

Holmes knew what he meant, but resented the man's tone of voice. No trace of dignity in this fellow, to be sure.

"Anyways, I turned up in London yesterday, tried to get to see your Air Minister. Boy did I get the runaround! No one knows anything about business in Whitehall. They treat you like dirt, like I was trying to sell them scrap-iron. The dumb jerk couldn't give me an appointment until April, soonest.

"Well I don't know about you guys, but I reckon the war could be over by April. Germany's got you by the balls, but eighty-six Heinkels could be just the thing you need. Think of it, the German pilots wouldn't know what was happening, you could fly right into German territory and take out as much as possible without a shot being fired at you. As long as the Germans fly Heinkels you've got it made. It is a stroke of genius, right?"

Holmes had to admit the idea had its merits.

"Now, all I want is twenty thousand pounds per plane. That is a bargain, believe me, a never to be repeated bargain. The pilots want British officers' salaries and the usual pension scheme for the widows and orphans. It's a classic business deal. One hundred and seventy two thousand pounds believe me, it's for nothing. New Heinkels cost nearly thirty thousand pounds fitted out and I can even do a deal with the spares we make back in Trenton, New Jersey... good prices too."

"What do you want from me?" Holmes asked, fearing the worst, suspicious again.

"You got twenty-four hours, Lord Holmes. Call your Government and tell them I've got this deal set up. They can call my office in New York and deal with my boss Peter Weinstein at Grobbler International."

"Weinstein?" Watson remarked, surprised, "with German war planes?"

"Hey don't knock it, doctor, business is business. Now I'm just on my way to see some guy called Ribbentrop. He's mighty keen to do business with me. Of course it helps I'm the Heinkel rep. And you're right Lord Holmes, my family name is Moorehaus, but I'm a loyal American. My heart belongs to business. Say, you ever meet my hero when he was staying in London?"

"Hero?"

"Lindy. Now there's a guy. Champion aviator, tragedy with his kid and yet he comes back strong. He knows America has to stay out of this war. He's going to make sure we don't get suckered again."

"Yet you want to make money out of this war." Cornelia remarked acidly.

"War is genuine profit machine. That's why FDR signed the neutrality act in November. He knows he can't take us into war, but he knows there's money to be made off it."

Holmes didn't think his little joke amusing. Nor was he well disposed to this remarkable offer. It had to be a trick, but he decided to play along a little further.

"I'd need some proof of your ability to offer these 'planes," he said, "but I must tell you I have no unofficial way of communicating with HM Government, nor any influence within that body." He couldn't help feeling that this offer was, in some way, a test to see where their loyalty lay, to England or the Third Reich. It was a time to remember that they were already deep into enemy territory.

"You could not do this without a commission of some sort, Lord Holmes," Cornelia piped up, surprising them all. "My father would have definitely secured some sort of commission." She was certain of it. She had been to enough of his boring business meetings in London, to know how things were done.

The aviation salesman relaxed, crossing his legs, pleased his fish appeared to be biting. The craggy lines of his unshaven face creased into a smile. "Now we're talking business. Five percent off the top."

"Only five?" Cornelia protested, despite hostile stares signalling "No" from Holmes in the corner. Of course, neither Holmes, nor Watson were wise to the ways of commerce, but perhaps they felt it was not proper for their nurse to conduct their business for them.

"OK young lady, eight percent, tops. For a nurse you're some lady."

Lord Holmes kept mysteriously silent, thinking that eight percent would represent thirteen thousand pounds and would not look amiss in his pension fund.

"Hell, to think I'd given up on England." Moorehaus said pleasantly.

"Von Ribbentrop is likely to offer more if he knows there is competition for the 'planes," Holmes mentioned.

"Or nothing at all," he replied. "He could decide to march right into Madrid and take 'em. But I bought them from Government Surplus fair and square. Dealing with Berlin is a hairy occupation sometimes, luckily they don't seem too keen to annoy America right now, so I might be lucky and make the deal. Of course, I'll give you time to make an offer."

Holmes stared at the man a moment, making a judgement, then he slowly leaned forward and spoke in a soft voice, barely perceptible above the clack of the rails. "We want this war to end very quickly, Mr Moorehaus, buying your planes might prolong it."

The American nodded. "That's good thinking, Lord Holmes. If England fights, the war is going to drag on, maybe a whole year, and I can tell you there's a lot of business in that. If Germany wins, well their economy is geared to war, not peace, the next target will be the USA. I have the notion that a Heinkel agency isn't going to be worth much then. So I've got to keep this war going, single-handed, if I have to."

"Logical, Mr Moorehaus, logical. I admire your candour. But I doubt if we can help you. We are on holiday y'know and I doubt we could make a phone call or send a telegram to the Air Ministry with an order to buy Heinkels from German or Spanish territory. We are at war, as I've no need to remind you."

The salesman looked disappointed. "Well I'll be in Berlin on the 6th, you've got until then to make contact if you want to change your mind."

"We'll do our best," Watson declared before Holmes could stop him, "England must have Heinkels." He thought the idea a wheeze and had not detected Holmes' scepticism.

Holmes tried to get Watson's attention, but he was not looking his way.

"If I was younger," Watson was saying, "I'd go to Spain and fly one back myself, if I could fly that is."

"Oh you are brave," Cornelia told him with a smile. Watson did not detect the mockery in her voice and straightened his back accordingly beaming a proud smile back at her; still wishing he was twenty years younger, he was sure she would have fallen for him then, positive of it.

"Watson would have made a good night fighter," Holmes told them all. "He drives with his eyes shut."

"Oh I say, Holmes, I do not!"

"You do. When Watson emerges in his bath-chair on Baker Street a bell rings and the entire street clears for fear of an accident. Tried to get him to wear his glasses under his goggles, but he's a stubborn man".

Watson was clearly annoyed at this slur on his driving ability. What had happened to the spirit of all for one and one for all? Holmes was obviously entering one of his nasty moods again, it was clearly a time to be quiet, stand back and let him have the field.

Holmes was satisfied that he had silenced Watson for a moment or two before any remark revealed more to this German agent than was necessary. He returned his attention to the bewildered Mr Moorehaus.

"Of course, it might simplify matters if I gave you a letter to Winston Churchill himself and sent you back on the next train to London, but speaking personally, I doubt London will respond. Your deal will suit Germany better. The British pride being what it is, they would not like to admit they need Heinkels."

The salesman sighed. "Yeah that's why I can't miss this opportunity with Ribbentrop, but you have to try..." He rose to leave. "Hey, look you guys, if you need help anytime," he flipped a business card, a Berlin address and telephone number. "Just call me. Berlin's a fun place. We could do the town and I know there's a whole lot of guys who'd really dig to meet you. Hell, you're a legend in your own time."

"Apparently," Holmes answered with modesty.

Moorehaus looked at Cornelia, "Wagner huh? He as big as Glen Miller, Bennie Goodman?"

"Bigger," Holmes replied, annoyed. "Germany's heart beats to his music, the very rails sing his melodies. The factories grind to his rhythms. Wagner created modern Germany, though few people understand that. He makes the blood boil."

The American pulled a face. "This must be some guy, but me, I'll stick with Artie Shaw. Nice meeting you guys. If I see you again, it's dinner on me. You're a piece of history, Lord Holmes. I just got to hear about Jack the Ripper and all that jazz."

And suddenly he was gone.

"I think the man must be mad," Watson declared pulling down the blind. "Who is Artie Shaw?"

But Holmes weighed more important things.

"His offer is feasible, but was it a test? I have to admit to being a little confused, Watson. The world has changed so much. The American is another breed entirely. If we pass word to London, they might be looking for our method of transmitting messages, suspecting we really are spies."

"But if it is genuine?" Cornelia pointed out, "England should have those 'planes."

"A dilemma," Holmes muttered, frowning, his long fingers rapping impatiently on his forehead. He stared out of the window, the scenery nothing but a blur.

At length, he abruptly brought down his fist on the armrest stating, "I say the whole thing is a pack of lies!"

Watson started, swallowing a whole butter-drop.

"They are searching us out, seeking a betrayal. Moorehaus may seem an American, but he's a German. Eighty-six Heinkels, Cornelia, but if our mission fails, England may befall a greater danger, this we must think of and the vengeance upon your dear father's enemies."

She bit her lower lip. "You are right, Lord Holmes, I'm sure."

"In this world," Watson said, a little hoarsely, the butter-drop having stunned his larynx, "one must choose between science and wisdom, Germany chose science. I agree, we should avoid temptation, cast away Satan's apple."

"Well put, Watson. By jove, well put. Satan's apple indeed."

"You mean that it was all a kind of trial?" Cornelia asked, incredulous.

Holmes nodded, closing his weary eyes. "Remember Dante's Inferno, the Trojan Horse. We must be alert. They might throw up Englishmen, Americans, all kinds of traitors set to catch us off guard. We must appear sympathetic to this Nazi vermin, but anxious for reconciliation.

Remember we do not want war, we want peace. Buying Heinkels would have revealed our true feelings. Note too that he calls Lindbergh a hero. We know a different Lindbergh, a man who wears Görings gold medal.

"The tricks will come, Watson, Cornelia. Question everything and just when everything seems logical, throw out the logic and what is left is the truth. Buying Heinkels is anti-Nazi, to contact London would jeopardise everything."

"Jove Holmes, the Germans have a difficult conundrum fathoming yourself."

"True, Watson, but now I'm tired. I think a nap before we arrive in Nürnberg will do all of us the world of good."

"Seconded," Watson declared, already well on the way.

"I'll read," Cornelia said, "someone should keep watch."

Holmes smiled at her, then settled back into the carriage seat, dropping off to sleep instantly.

Cornelia opened her *Conti-Atlas*, trying to place exactly where Nürnberg was in her mind, in case of problems later. If she was to escape, she wanted to be sure to run in the right direction.

7

Watson Makes a Deal

Their arrival at Nürnberg was uneventful. They were discharged stood waiting at the Hauptbahnhof looking across the grey afternoon expanse of the square, a cold wind adding to the austere atmosphere. The view was large and uninviting, instantly a reminder of the war, four young soldiers lounged at corners waiting to be drilled. Cornelia looked out for their American, but saw no sign of him, puzzled he didn't show.

A taxi was found for Holmes and Cornelia, but Watson, ever concerned for his bath-chair, preferred to wait until the elegant machine was wheeled up the platform and released to him by the station staff who expressed great interest in it.

"It's a Delahaye," Watson explained, but no one understood. Worse, when Watson climbed in, strapped his cane to one side, his case to the rear, the electric start would not work.

"Varta." A nearby porter exclaimed, pointing to an enormous advertisement up on the station wall. "Varta batteries."

Watson knew there was nothing wrong with his battery, it was probably a loose connection. He went through the laborious process of extricating himself from the chair and inspecting the battery stashed on the side. Sure enough the battery connection had jolted loose. Soon he was reinstated and the motor fired up first time, much his relief and three cheers from the station staff.

But even as he motored out of the station area, he realised that in his anxiety for the well being of his bath-chair, he had neglected to get directions from Holmes. Which way was 29 Frauenforgraben? There was no way he could ask directions, little chance he would find any English speaking person. He could see signposts for Ansbach, Sulzbach, Weissenberg, but nothing that seemed to indicate the town centre.

Nevertheless, after the drizzle began to fall over the ancient walled town and Watson had successfully discovered Albrecht Durer's house, crossed the dull, rather pungent Pegnitz twice and got himself thoroughly lost in the narrow streets of the old town, only by luck escaping again, he found himself depressed, cold and hungry opposite Oesterlein's OPEL garage and enquired there.

Many amazed faces asked him whether he was English and Watson felt bound to admit that he was, especially considering the large spanners wielded in their rather large, oily hands. But they did not seem to mind him being English and did not ask for his papers, it was the bath-chair their greedy eyes admired.

"I'm looking for my hotel, Der Deutsche Hof." Watson tried again, a little frightened that they did not seem inclined to reply. "Which way to the hotel?"

Luckily a man stepped forward at that point, his hair well greased and parted in the middle, a small moustache the echo of someone, but he could not think who. His face was quite fierce, but it was the result of an unfortunate skin condition so it did not scare Dr Watson.

"You are lost mein Herr?" he asked, as if he did not know. "I am the manager."

Watson felt a great deal of relief. A man of responsibility and one who spoke English, what was more. "Thank God, you speak English, good English, too. I'm confused my man. I'm looking for my hotel, Der Deutsche Hof."

The manager did not answer immediately, instead he inspected the bath-chair very thoroughly, running the palm of his hand along its surface; patting the sides with a great sensuality, a look of uncontrolled lust in his eyes.

"This is a very good machine, mein Herr. I offer you five hundred Reichmarks for it."

Watson was quite taken aback. "No, no. I do not want to sell it. I want to find my hotel."

"But mein Herr, you cannot drive a bath-chair, not a Delahaye, in winter. It will snow tonight for sure. Tomorrow at the latest. The roads will be impassible for a bath-chair, you need a good Opel. I will do a very good deal..."

114

"I cannot drive an Opel," Watson told him, gripping his joy stick with great determination, understandably a little panic stricken, yet aware from rumour just how persuasive a car salesman could be.

But he reckoned without the German's desire to make a deal. "I'll tell what you want, mein Herr. Five hundred and fifty Reichmarks will buy you a brand new Opel Kadette, our latest model, twelve horsepower, it's a '39, sweet little thing, very economical..."

"But you don't understand, I don't want a car, Mr...?"

"Schoeck. Really, mein Herr, you should have a German car. They are the best and weatherproof, which is more than I can say for your Delahaye."

He could see Watson was weakening. "Furthermore, just to show German goodwill for the English, despite our present arguments, I'll throw in a set of new tyres and we will forget about the odd fifty marks. That is a bargain. You'd get no change out of one hundred and fifty pounds for this Opel in England. A most respected car there, sister to the Vauxhall, but better built if I may say so, mein Herr. I, myself, have taken a week's vacation in London and saw the factory there. Such old machinery, shoddy work. Buy an Opel, Herr Englisch and see Germany in all her new glory."

"I'd rather think about it," Watson said, realising at once his fatal remark. "Tempting as your offer is, I am rather attached to my bath-chair."

The motor salesman was not so easily defeated, a smile like a newly opened tin of treacle poured over his face as he rubbed his hands readying for the kill. "No, no, there's no hurry to make such an irrevocable decision, you will leave your bath-chair here tonight and you will take the beautiful blue Opel over there to your hotel, drive it for a day, you will love it. Believe me, if you do not like it, you just call me on the telephonieren and we will exchange back, no obligation at all. Ja?"

Watson did not see how he could refuse the silken tongue and the intimidation was complete, he sighed, looked at his bath-chair for one last time, a hard lump in his throat and said, "Oh very well," as reluctantly as he could. It was a fatal error to show weakness in the face of a car salesman, he now knew he had won.

In no time Watson was extracted from his bath-chair, pushed into the mock-leather seat of the Opel, instructed by a big, gruff, oily mechanic on how to operate the controls, assured that it had petrol, that it was manufactured in late '39 and would be guaranteed for a whole six months.

"But I'm still lost," Watson wailed, engine started, confused and already missing his bath-chair.

The manager was installed in the bath-chair, revving the engine alongside the Opel. He handed Watson's cane and suitcase to him through the open window. "Der Deutsche Hof is just five streets from here, mein Herr. Turn right at the fifth street and not more than one hundred metres further you will arrive at the hotel, it is unmistakable. Ask for General Direktor Farber, he is a good friend of mine."

"Thank you, Herr Shoeck, thank you." Watson sounded most grateful and relieved. But it fell on deaf ears for the salesman had driven off at high speed to road test his bath-chair, a proud man.

Watson engaged gear and immediately stalled, this was not the best of beginnings. Cursing the car and his own frustrations he went through the tedious procedure of disengaging gear and restarting the engine, embarrassed by the entire situation and desperate to get away from the mocking eyes of the forecourt.

The car burst into life, he crashed into first gear and whizzed away careering off the concrete onto the narrow pavement. With eyes firmly closed he set course for five blocks, determinedly sticking to the pavement; crashing off the curbs, rolling over the crossing roads and bumping back onto the pavement again, only occasionally opening his eyes to ensure his way was clear, doing his best not to hit the lamp-posts sited every fifty feet. It was the safest course in his opinion. The road was far too dangerous for a beginner Opel driver.

Courage took hold of Watson for the last hundred yards when he spotted the distant neon announcing Der Deutche Hof and so he attempted the smooth road (leaving only one pair of wheels on the curb). He even managed a run through the gears and by the time he began to feel quite confident, he was nearly there. The Opel did not pose as great a threat as he had supposed. His only remaining concern was Holmes. What would he say to him? He could be so devastatingly cruel.

And thus it was, Watson, in a state of much confusion and depression eventually arrived at the hotel, where an anxious Sherlock Holmes stood waiting on the steps, his eyes resting somewhere into the distance, no doubt scouting the horizon for a wayward bathchair. Watson rather sheepishly parked his blue Opel (with some difficulty) and climbed out of it walking to within four steps of Holmes before he started with surprise, greatly amazed to see Watson before him without his loyal bath-chair. Luckily Holmes had a quick mind and he saw the car, Watson's solemn face and deduced the problem. "That is an Opel car, Watson. You cannot drive a car, pray explain?"

Watson was too embarrassed about the whole thing. "Cannot, Holmes. I merely stopped at a garage to ask and..."

It was immediately obvious to Holmes. "A motor salesman talked you out of your bath-chair. Was he by the name of Schoek by any chance?"

It was Watson's turn to be surprised.

"Yes, Holmes, how the devil could you know that?"

"I thought as much. Herr Schoeck is the most successful Opel agent in the south. We now know why. I trust you remembered to remove my little box."

Watson sighed with relief. "I have your box. You're not angry with me then?"

"A Delahaye is a valuable bath-chair, but an Opel is a jewel that can carry three in comfort, shielding us from the elements. A fair exchange I think."

"Lucky thing Cornelia can drive," Watson commented, going back for his suitcase.

"Let the porter get your things, Watson. Come, a hot bath awaits you and then an early dinner. There is much to plan."

Watson turned around again, more cheered. "A bath and dinner is a most welcome idea Holmes. I confess to being down in my spirits after driving about lost all this late afternoon."

"Nothing amiss, Watson. Tomorrow you shall be my guide. Dürer awaits us, the delights of Konigstrasse. The old town is quite fascinating, I hear. A sort of triumph between barbarism and teutonic mysticism. Gothic in an early, unrefined form. This is the city of Tannhäuser and Hans Sachs, the poet. Peter Vischer worked miracles with brass here. The first pocket-watch and the first clockwork toys were invented here and delighted adults and children alike. The Clarinet was made here and that geographical globe you have in your study, it was invented here. And that is why we are here Watson."

"Because of the globe?"

"Because it is a city of invention Watson. A place of ideas and secrets. Cornelia will drive us up Marienstrasse tomorrow, we must look like devout tourists, our image is most important Watson, all important."

Holmes took Watson's arms and helped him up the steps. "Don't fret yourself my dear chap. We have failed but rarely in the past. Churchill might consider this a challenge, but believe me, if Nürnberg has a secret, we shall unearth it. You can be sure of that."

Watson stalled at the lobby, looking up at the old, heavy woodwork, dominant, unmistakably German. "Holmes, I'm afraid I might let you down. I'm a feeble old man, I cannot keep up the pace as I once did. I become confused. Look I abandoned the bath-chair and it was a machine I admired most dearly. Instead I have a vehicle I can barely drive except with iron-will and clenched teeth."

Holmes simply smiled and studied the images on the wall, the standard flag of the Third Reich, a lurid, red silk affair with the Iron Cross and black eagle atop a swastika, four more in each corner. A painting of the Fuhrer hung alongside. Holmes noticed Watson staring at this display.

"If ever your strength falters, if ever your heart fails you, look at that flag, mark it well and imagine it flying from the roof of the House of Commons."

Watson gasped. "Holmes, it could never come to that."

Holmes' impassive face revealed all. "It won't Watson, we will succeed. We have little choice. We have donned the mantle of consulting detective once more, we shall succeed, or die in the attempt."

The hotel was quiet, the other guests invisible as two weary old gentlemen mounted the wooden stairs looking forward to that hot bath.

***

Watson emerged first, pink as a new morning rose, steam rising up through his white dressing gown.

"I feel twenty years younger, Holmes. That pine-scented bath is a miracle cure. Those Norwegians know a thing or two."

"I shall have a bath presently, Watson, but I wonder if you'd bring your hand to your mouth so..." Holmes clasped Watson's hand over his mouth, puzzling his friend. "I think some of these Norwegian exercises are very good for your health, Watson. Perhaps you'd hold this a moment and stand very still?"

Watson could not understand, but knew enough about Holmes' methods to hold his silence. Furthermore he had nothing to hold at all, as Holmes tapped the walls, the furniture, crawled under the bed, acted out a very strange pantomime indeed.

Holmes at last gave something to Watson to do.

"Enough silent exercises, Watson. Now, I wonder if you'd switch on your radio, some music perhaps?"

Now it was Watson who was concerned for Holmes' mental health, for the man was listening to the far wall, taking great strides towards the radio itself, just as Watson found some music, a German military band playing *Going To The Cork Fair*, an unlikely choice, but without doubt everything was strange since they had left England.

"Louder Watson, good exercise music, what?"

"Certainly Holmes, quite invigorating," he replied, quite certain that at least one of them had gone mad.

Holmes felt under the table on which the radio stood and his fingers came across something quite interesting. A microphone (only four inches wide), a very satisfied smile broke out on his face as he squatted down beside the bed and ran his fingers along the table's inside edge, following the wire, cleverly spliced into the radio power supply. The wire and power supply parted company at a point just behind the bed and into the wall. Holmes had now to think on whether to accept the one, or go further and go with the "two microphones" theory.

The music, he mused, would tend to drown out conversation and prevent their eavesdroppers from hearing their voices, but what if there was a device in the bathroom?

Holmes stood up, slightly giddy as the blood rushed to his head, then switched off the radio. He would look in the bathroom now, even if it meant missing dinner. The running bathwater would mask his activities there.

"An odd game Holmes," Watson remarked, impatient to hear what was going on.

"No game Watson. I'll explain at dinner. Meanwhile I will take my bath. I believe we join Nurse Shand at seven-thirty tonight. I think I shall be looking forward to my dinner this evening, I have worked up quite an appetite."

"I'm glad to hear it," Watson replied, "but not surprised. All that exercise, bound to give one an appetite."

"Exactly, Watson, exactly."

But there was so sign of a microphone in the bathroom, not even in the skylight, nor under the basin, or toilet bowl. The bathroom was safe. Their spies would have little to listen to now, of that they could be sure. All important conversation would be conducted in the bathroom, or outside. This was a new way to fight a war, but Holmes could see the logic of it. It amused him to think of the German's having possession of a recorded disc with the dedicated drivel of one of Watson's conversations upon it.

But he would leave the microphone untouched. The longer they thought it undiscovered, the safer they would be. Frau Flohn had reserved this room for them. It was possible they would be spied upon all the time, their innocence as tourists never taken at face value, of that he could be certain.

He had only a few minutes to reach the dining room before it closed. Watson and Cornelia had gone ahead and sat down, believing Holmes would not be in time. Cornelia smiled at Holmes as he sat down. "I fear your companion is being most difficult, Lord Holmes. First he insists we sit at another table to get out of the draught, upsetting the staff no end.

They complained most forcefully. Then he's been in a depression ever since he opened the menu. Your most urgent services are needed I think, for I cannot get him to smile at all."

This was serious. If Watson would not smile for Cornelia, then something very serious must have happened.

"Come Watson, out with it, what ails you?"

Watson sighed, laying down his menu and pulled a very exasperated expression indeed. "Sausages, Holmes. Five, heed that, five different würsts for dinner and two different sour cabbages, the only alternative being pigs' trotters. I am at a loss I vowed no more sausages, never again."

Holmes laughed at his friend's lamentable fate.

"When in Rome, Watson. Did you not know that Bratwürst was practically invented here. Months of hardship with sausages should have made you immune. Choose the one you dislike least and then perhaps order an extra ration of roast potatoes."

Watson cheered up at this suggestion.

"I hoped there would be veal at least," he declared peevishly.

"Well there is wine and it should be excellent. Buck up Watson, I have some interesting news for you." Then, looking at the table and thinking of the microphone upstairs he added, "And congratulations for changing tables. For I should have done so myself and will do so daily to defeat their best-laid plans."

And so, after they had ordered, Holmes explained his bedroom antics to an amazed twosome. It was a fantastic tale and emphasised to them their dangerous position. Watson was horrified, amused, upset to discover their room was not sacrosanct, and readily agreed, as did Cornelia, to restrict their conversation to more private areas, rather exchanging notes and burning them immediately afterwards if something urgent needed to be said. The microphone was a salutary lesson to them all that their innocence was not presumed.

***

They had three days in hand before the Wagner Concert and thus they had ample time to plan their cover activities as tourists. The night was whiled away in front of other guests, mostly German officers from the nearby camp and local police, all of whom seemed to know of Sherlock Holmes; and not a few who walked by to inspect the nurse. Cornelia played her part well, affecting great concern for her two charges and was seemingly oblivious to all around her. Yet she was listening well, watching for signs of hostility or personal remarks directed against them. She heard none. The local populace was of the opinion that the day of Sherlock Holmes was over, the two old men were just that, two old men, little use to anyone, a relic of a past world.

The longer they continued to think that, the better Lord Holmes' chance of success.

"I can't help worrying about this secret formula idea, Watson," Holmes was saying by the fireplace in the sitting room. Cornelia was sewing in the corner. "Nürnberg is a likely place for secrets yes, but what could it be, so startling it could change the fate of this war? There is little heavy industry. In Stuttgart yes, but not here. Nor should I have expected Herr Flohn to build a chocolate factory here. There is not the manpower, no dormitory town for the labourers."

"There's a camp for undesirables," Watson remarked, having overheard a reference to the place whilst waiting for Holmes at dinner. "They'll need to earn their keep."

"Good point, Watson. But I am of the opinion that that is not the particular labour pool I was thinking of. If I remember my Mein Kampf well, there is no place for such folk in the German order, not even in a camp. I should think they will send them all away in time, they are inhuman enough to do it. Personally I think either Herr Flohn has reached a new high in automation, or this factory is more sophisticated than we assume and requires technical staff as opposed to basic unskilled labour."

"Well there is a large college here, Holmes, that should supply enough of those. I passed it twice earlier this evening."

"You are becoming very observant in your old age, Watson. Excellent. That would provide a highly educated labour force indeed, a valuable observation. We must walk the city walls with Cornelia. The Kaiserburg is most impressive I'm told. Make sure we find the Sinnwellturm, the round watch tower. It might give us a good view of any new factories outside the ancient walls."

Pleased to have solved this problem, Holmes cast his eyes about the room, smiling briefly at Cornelia, who looked most industrious with her sewing.

"Have you noticed how shabby the cloth of the ordinary folk is Cornelia? How ill-made the uniforms. How much used is the table wear and carpets of this hotel?"

Cornelia looked up, surprised the remark was addressed to her.

"It does look poor, Lord Holmes. But I imagine a lot of money has gone into providing for this war."

Holmes nodded. "You are an intelligent woman, my girl. The war has indeed already drained their resources. Yet Watson and I can remember a time when German clothes were the best, such excellent quality. Did you not notice, too, how few men there are? Young men not in uniform are a rarity."

"I have scarcely seen one individual not in a uniform, sir. Uniforms seem terribly important here."

"That is so, now if you will excuse me, I must go up into my room and think. Tomorrow morning I hope you will have an interesting time young Cornelia. Watson and I will miss your company." Cornelia smiled as Holmes stalked from the room, Watson watching him go.

"It is good to see him with a problem," he said. "Holmes has been so restless, we must hope this mystery is solved satisfactorily, yet not too swiftly, for the return to the commonplace will do him no good at all."

"Oh I'm sure Mr Churchill will find him something to do," Cornelia said, instantly biting her lip, remembering that she was forbidden to utter the First Lord's name. She looked about the room, but no one seemed to have heard and Watson was almost asleep anyway. She sighed. She had been thinking a lot about her father of late, wondering what really became of him. She half hoped he would be still alive, but it was a slim hope; no more than a flickering candle hope. She knew the dastardly German reputation, their inherent cruelty.

Eventually, of course, it was bedtime and sleep came to all.

But the morning brought a new problem.

"I can't find them Holmef."

Holmes eyed his old friend with mild annoyance. "What is it you can't find?"

"My teef, liften to me, Holmef I floft command of my speech. Oh my goofneff, wherever can they be?"

"Well don't look at me like that. I may be a detective, Watson, but I'm not a nursemaid. Now try to remember where did you have them last?"

"At dinner, I diftinctly remember having them then, couldn'f have made much headway with the faufagef without 'em."

"Indeed, but if you continued from the dining room by way of the sitting room to bed, it should not be so very hard for you to deduce where your teeth are."

Watson heard a mildly sarcastic tone in Holmes' voice. He knew the man was annoyed with him, but dammit he could not carry on without his teeth, things were bad enough and young Cornelia might laugh at him, something he would not relish at all.

Holmes took out his notebook, suddenly remembering where he had left a useful German reference book back at 221b, it was in his old Gladstone bag. He cursed the haste with which they had left London.

"It wasn't the fitting room," Watson muttered, scratching his head. "I am abfolutely fertain I put them in the glaff befide the bed. No queftion of it."

Holmes ignored Watson and concentrated on his notes. He had no time for such minor problems. Watson would find his teeth, of that he had no doubt.

Watson knelt down on the thinly carpeted floor and searched the under-bed area and even under the carpet itself. There was no sign of his teeth, or the glass he had put them in. It was extremely vexing, they were best porcelain, the finest ever made, in his opinion.

"No teef here," he muttered.

Holmes looked up, intensely annoyed now. Obviously he would get no peace at all until these teeth were found. "You are sure they are not in this room?"

"Fertain of it, Holmef, do you think the room maid took them out with her?" A fearful look came over Watson's perplexed face, visions of the precious teeth being tipped into the sink with all the crockery. Holmes had to think. What had Watson done after his supper?

It was whilst he gave thought to the problem that a familiar flash of inspiration took hold as his eyes fell upon Watson's tweed jacket, slung over the desk chair.

"Is there anything you'd like to tell me before I reveal to you exactly where your teeth can be expected to be found?"

"You know then, Holmef?"

"I do not know, Watson. I can only apply method to the search." Watson heaved himself off the floor and sat on the softly sprung bed. "I have no anfwerf, Holmef, none without my teef."

"Very well, you see your jacket is in need of a brush, not uncommon after a late dinner with biscuits and cheese. Your lapels bear the mark of crumbly biscuits and some of that awkward hard cheese they serve here. You say you ate your dinner then proceeded to the sitting room with your teeth, but I maintain there is no mystery. Your teeth, Watson, never entered this room last night."

"Never? They did not?" Watson cried out in plain astonishment.

"No Watson," Holmes stood up, put on his Persian slippers and instructed Watson likewise. "We must pay a visit to the pantry."

"My teef are not in there, Holmef. I fear you make a miftake. I have never been to the pantry."

"Well Watson, if there were a jury sitting, I should soon have them convinced you had."

Watson trotted after Holmes along the corridor to the stairs and together they descended, nodding to the other guests attending their morning affairs. Watson was shaking his head all the while.

"You're wrong, Holmef. I hafe to say thif, but you are wrong."

"The pantry is this way, I think," Holmes said, stalking the teeth with a grim resolution, convinced he was on the trail. "You know, Watson, this reminds me of that strange tale Dr Mortimer told us once."

"Oh?" He asked, unfamiliar with any personal story from that Dartmoor personage.

"In his earlier days he once attended a patient in Exeter and forgot his teeth. A trifling matter, one might say, but the difference between, 'Madame you suffer from shock,' and, 'Madame you suffer from pox,' is a mighty large one and to this day no doctor with false teeth has made a successful practice in Exeter. Ah, the pantry."

Watson was relieved at that, but disappointed the Exeter story would not turn out to be an untold adventure after all.

"Now we will see testimony to the great missing teeth mystery," Holmes declared, turning to look at Watson with a broad smile. "Brace yourself for a shock Watson." Holmes' hand was upon the door. "I contend that your difficulty with the cheese last night has an explanation in this very room. The fact is, my old friend, your teeth left the table before you did!"

He opened the door and switched on the light. It was cold in here and the odour was quite overpowering; predominantly rotting meat and cheese, but essentially sweating sausage. Holmes glanced along the rows of cheeses and finally his eye fell upon the very cheese tray that had been offered them the previous night.

"Observe, Watson, how finely contrasted a pair of porcelain upper and lower sets are with this yellow cheese. How finely clenched they are, or to be more precise, embedded."

Watson stared with disbelief at his teeth, locked onto the wedge of cheese he had spent a good ten minutes wrestling with the night before. He felt terribly embarrassed; at a loss for words. Naturally Holmes sought to help him out and lifted the glass cover over the cheese and extracted the teeth from their prize.

"They say you can't build a better mousetrap, Watson, but I think a short note to the patents office is in order." He smiled, presenting the teeth to his old friend, who quickly wiped them off and slipped them in, happy to be human again.

"Now let's away, we have urgent business to attend to. This Dr Laubscher has to be found and Herr Flohn's factory worries me, my nose twitches, and you know what that means Watson. I would not be surprised if they weren't up to something in there, anything is possible."

"Really, Holmes? Perhaps they intend the chocolate for British troops. Trying to poison them, eh?"

"No, Watson, too damn subtle for the German mind. Besides the British Army Catering Corps will beat them to it. Come let's go, the cheese has had its day."

***

After a light breakfast, Cornelia had returned to her room, shed her nurse's uniform, pinned up her hair and slipped on a plain dress, one of the those she had bought in Strasbourg, and sensible black shoes. She donned a coat, dull, unimaginative, unmemorable. Stepping out without make-up, she hoped she resembled one of the countless drab females which seemed to inhabit Nürnberg. Certainly she hoped to get about without a soul being suspicious of her or suspecting her foreign origins.

She opened her door, making sure no one was watching and quietly, yet unhurriedly, made her way along the corridor to the staff stairs. There she descended to the ground floor, unnoticed and slipped out onto the paved road.

Immediately she felt the frost on the ground and the cutting wind that pierced through her coat and thin dress with a cruel force. She walked on, her eyes watering from the wind, hoping her disguise as a German girl would work, not daring to think about what would happen if it did not. She worried about her German, unused for over a year, hoping that it would be convincing and that her Bavarian accent was as remarkable as her dear Papa had tried to convince her it was.

She passed the Lorenz church and slowly she was absorbed into the old town, mindful of the important task Sherlock Holmes had given her.

And of those two gentlemen...?

They, too, partook of a light breakfast of sausages and coffee, Watson full of protest as was usual. Then well wrapped they climbed into the new Opel Kadette and set off with a map of Nürnberg, following closely behind the Number Two tram travelling east into the business section, a newer part of town, where the old narrow streets gave way to a broad, modern interpretation of what a town needed to survive in the fourth decade of the twentieth century.

Holmes was driving (something he was loath to do). "This Opel's remarkably simple Watson. Steering's a masterpiece of precision compared to a bath-chair. I'm surprised you clung to them for so long."

"A bath-chair is a comfortable thing Holmes. At my time of life an Opel is like a fish out of water to me. Now slow down, this isn't Brooklands and we are nearly at our first address."

Holmes pulled smartly into the curb, narrowly missing a young delivery boy on his bicycle, who angrily shook his fist at Holmes before speedily accelerating away.

"No manners, children have no manners these days Watson. I blame the radio, it subverts the young mind, it's entirely responsible for the spread of urban crime, I'm sure of it."

"Didn't know you listened, Holmes."

Holmes harrumphed. "Besides the point, Watson. Anyway, I have listened, you're always sneaking it on when I have my bath. Apart from Mr Well's talk that you used to like there's precious little else; I fail to see what amuses you."

Watson frowned. Holmes was irritable this morning, he obviously had not slept well.

"So what have we here?" Holmes asked, his fingers drumming on the wheel.

"Dr Laubscher. H.C. Laubscher, specialist in leg injuries and spasms."

Holmes shook his head. "This does not sound like our man. How many Dr Laubschers are there in the telephone directory?"

"Five, Holmes. It will take all day to cover them all."

"Perhaps not. Our man is not a specialist as such. He probably has no practice at all. I'm betting our Dr Laubscher is not a practising healer but a research scientist. We would do well to remember the German habit of calling engineers, theologists and the like, Herr Doktor, our man could be an electrical genius or a musician. We can hope that he is one of these five, but don't be too disappointed if he is not any of them. Our man is important, he may not like his name to appear in the phonebook at all. So the next?"

Watson looked at the hotel's phone directory. "Just a little further along the Marienstrasse, I think. We could walk."

"Nonsense Watson, we have a modern car, a heater. We shall drive everywhere, we have resisted the car for too long. It is a lot more comfortable than the hansom cab. Takes the effort out of this dull policework."

"But more useful with a driver, Holmes."

"True, but our driver is busy elsewhere this cold morning."

"I hope she is all right," Watson said pensively. "I'd despair if any harm came to her."

"She will be fine, Watson. Come on, we will walk after all, the road is quite blocked with traffic. It must be market day judging from the many peasantry wandering about the town, not to mention musicians. I have seen more than a dozen posters announcing the Wagner Concert already. It will be a big occasion, I'm sure of it.

"Now to business. We must make sure none of these Dr Laubschers we see have an inkling we are looking for a Dr Laubscher, if you see what I mean, Watson. Each one we come across, we wish merely to make an appointment to see them if they are a physician and if they are an engineer, I will use my judgement to gauge their significance to us. Now, is there any sign of that Ford that was following us?"

Watson turned, his eyes opened wide in astonishment. "Holmes, it's parked less than three cars behind!"

Holmes' eyes narrowed to a mere slit. "I thought as much. They don't want to lose sight of us for long. Methinks we'd better take in a few churches, a shop or two before we look for the next Dr Laubscher."

"I've a mind the German National Museum might be a patriotic move to make, Holmes."

"Capital idea, Watson. You always come up with the right idea. We shall go there directly after lunch when we have seen our third doctor. I'm determined we should eliminate all five by late afternoon."

"You sound so sure they will be eliminated."

"Instinct, Watson. There are many surprises to come. Sir Charles Hainsley didn't die because a doctor with the recipe for a new cough linctus contacted HM Government. We are looking for something devastating, world shattering. Four men have already died, it was something the Germans are very keen to protect, very keen."

***

But it was more by chance that any advance in the case was made at all, though it must be said, chances taken can reap rewards, the risk justified by the discovery. It was just that way with Cornelia.

Holmes had instructed her to go 'walkabout' something he had learned of from research into the oddities of the Australian aborigine. It was the best way he knew on how to pick up gossip; listen to tales of hardships, find out about how life was really lived by the population of the town. So she listened to shop talk, about shortages, the lack of men, the new jobs available in various institutions, factories. Which roads were no longer in use to the public, buildings where guards had appeared where none were before. Sudden changes in the town, new people. In short, all the talk of the town, which she could then relate to Holmes and allow him to sift through it all, extract the nuggets, piece together a portrait of the town and by logical deduction, perhaps even discover Dr Laubscher's secret by this backdoor method.

But by late afternoon, Cornelia, tired and hungry, her feet sore from the endless walking decided that what she needed most was a cup of hot chocolate at the next Kaffeehaus. With luck going her way for once, on the very next corner a quaint, dimly lit Suchard sign announced the Kaffeehaus was open. It was in the prettiest part of town; the walls pleasantly rustic, the cobbles neat, a bridge clock tower spanned the street up ahead, indicating 4.35 in the afternoon. She was sure she had walked every street in town.

Schokolade Aller Art it said on the door of the Kaffeehaus and the smell inside was heady and inviting. Inside there was coffee, chocolate, and ladies in warm coats sitting at tables eating rich, expensive cakes, not one of them in need of a bite more.

"Hilde, willkommen" a woman shrieked, completely taking Cornelia by surprise.

"Es ist Hilde, Peter's junge madel," she told everyone.

Cornelia realised the mistake at once, but the proprietress seemed so sure that she was Hilde (a poor, plain creature to be sure), it was difficult for her to extract herself from this predicament. She had never expected to be recognised. She cursed her hunger and her weak self for not going straight to the hotel as she had promised she would.

"Diese junge madel singt ein liibsches lied, Margot." The proprietress exclaimed, patting Cornelia on the head, smiling happily. "Ah, meine Hilde, Du sprichst nicht?"

Cornelia dare not speak. She understood, but fright took hold of her. She attempted an excuse, the doctor was always good for a try. "Leh fuhle mich nicht sehr wohl heute abend. Der Arzt..."

Just mentioning the doctor had the two women up and fussing over her.

"Vielen dank," Cornelia sighed, trying to look as ill as she could.

"Möchten Sie Schokolade?" A woman asked, a worried tone in her voice.

"Sofort, Matilde."

"Ja, Margot. Ich hätte gern einen tasse heisse schokolade," Cornelia replied, beginning to cry, the tears coming much easier than she thought for she was nearer to tears than she thought. The womens' hearts were breaking all around the room. For they knew this Peter she was supposed to be going about with. He was a young devil with the women and as far as they were concerned, with Hilde's normal robust constitution, if she had been to see a doctor, it meant only one thing, it was not chocolate she wanted, but a quick wedding. Consequently they did not demand anything of her and after giving her the cup of hot chocolate with some cake on the side, they let her be. Although some women came up to her and smiled before leaving the Kaffeehaus, one grim woman cursed her, shaking her fist and crossing herself. She quite obviously did not approve, but Cornelia shook her head and cried a little more leaving Margot and Matilde to drive the insensitive dragon out.

As she drank her chocolate, remembering to smile at the two women occasionally, she listened as an old man complained about his chocolate cake, calling it foul. This quite obviously offended the proprietress, Matilde, who declared that the best chocolate in all of Germany was manufactured in Nürnberg, that the Fuhrer would eat no other but Dr Laubscher's chocolates, as it was well known.

The name of Dr Laubscher jolted Cornelia into life, though she covered her shock by noisily blowing her nose.

"Dr Laubscher's Spezialitat. Nicht Perrero, nicht Munster, nicht Suchard, Tobler, Stoller. Der Fuhrer mochte Dr Laubscher Schokolade," Margot confidently asserted.

"Ich mochte Dr Laubscher Schokolade?" the old man demanded. "I want Dr Laubscher's chocolate. Why does he have to have it all? All of Germany has to make do, he gets the best. Is his money better than mine?"

"Our Fuhrer gets the best, because he deserves the best," Cornelia found herself stating, gaining the loud approval of the women. She hoped that this remark would redeem this poor girl Hilde.

"All the same," the old man said, "I hear the reason he eats so much of it is because it keeps you young."

Matilde pooh-poohed the idea. "It isn't him that eats it all, it's her, Eva Braun. She wants to get fat!" This was apparently funny for the ladies fell about laughing.

The old man did not see the humour of it. "What makes the chocolate so special?"

"Ask the Fuhrer," Margot told him, hooting with laughter, making Cornelia laugh too, its sheer bulk of hilarity so infectious.

"But Carl, you old goat," Matilde called out to the old man. "You know Herr Flohn's new factory will soon provide plenty of chocolate for everyone. Hilde is working there."

Cornelia started, she was back into the conversation. She knew she had to leave, the impersonation had gone on long enough. She began to fish for her money. Matilde walked over and closed her hand over Cornelia's, pushing the money back into her pocket. "Nein, Hilde. Auf wiedersehen," a tender smile upon her well-fed face.

Margot was still talking as Cornelia got up and bashfully walked out of the Kaffeehaus. "Dr Laubscher just returned from Berlin. He delivers his chocolates by hand. But I hear the new factory will make chocolate for the army, perhaps we might get some of his chocolate then."

Cornelia closed the door behind her, walking away into the dark street as quickly as she could, the beginnings of a snow flurry swirling around her feet, grabbing at her exposed ankles. Now she had news for Lord Holmes. It had to be! This had to be the Dr Laubscher. But a chocolate maker? Could her father have been killed over such a simple matter as a new chocolate factory? As she ran along the streets she shook her head, trying to prevent the tears which froze on her cheeks as fast as they slid down them. Herr Flohn had been mentioned, his factory which they were to tour very soon, the same factory? More than coincidental? She would have to allow Lord Holmes to work that out.

The sound of violins and trumpets, a cacophony bruised her ears as she turned a narrow, ill-lit corner. Her immediate view was through a courtyard over the road where she could see a dozen or so musicians practicing in a hall, the lights illuminating them inside. Two unmistakable silhouettes were in shadow against the wall. Sherlock Holmes and Dr Watson taking in a sneak preview of the Wagner concert.

She smiled to herself and hugged the new information she held, or rather the unfortunate Hilde held. The poor girl's reputation would be permanently blackened and much confusion arise out of this meeting with an imposter. Cornelia sincerely hoped she would never have to impersonate Hilde again.

Tempted as she was, she could not risk being seen with her companions either, especially out of uniform. Spies might already have discovered that she really was not in her room. Watson had instructed the people in the hotel not to go in and disturb her for that day. But what if they came knocking or...?

Watson Makes a Deal

She ran on past the rehearsal hall towards the hotel, retracing the steps she had taken in the morning, using the staff entrance. Now it was her turn to anticipate a hot bath, her heart beating wildly, excitement mounting within her as she thought of Holmes' face when she told him her news.

She could hardly bare the suspense. Would he be disappointed? Would he dismiss it out of hand? She wished they were at the hotel so she could find out immediately. It couldn't be, it just couldn't, but she wanted to hear Holmes say it before she doubted it herself.

8

A Night on the Tiles

"I cannot believe it, Holmes. There must be some mistake. This couldn't be the right doctor. There must be another one."

Holmes sat in his velvet dressing gown and weighed the evidence. Young Cornelia sat in her bed, demure and sleepy, for Holmes had woken her up to remind her to dress for dinner and see how she was. They had just returned from their outing and Watson, frozen to the very marrow, stood before her warm fire, defrosting his breeches.

"What Cornelia has written down is quite comprehensive, Watson. (They were conscious of those confounded microphones). However much I value your inestimable opinion, this time I think I'm right. We have seen five Mr So and So's and yet not one seems remotely like our man."

"Yes Holmes, but..." damning the cursed microphone which might or might not be listening, it was impossible to speak any sense if one had to scribble everything down. Holmes signaled for him to calm down.

"And yet," he continued in a low, mild voice, "young Cornelia here has told us the remarkable truth. It is diabolical, Watson. I can scarcely believe the magnitude of the problem. I never suspected the will of the Third Reich could reach so far."

"What is it, Holmes?" Watson asked, concerned, seeing Holmes' face stern and pale.

Holmes tapped his head. "Not all is revealed to me yet, Watson. It will develop, more thought needed here, much more thought."

But Watson knew Holmes had it, he knew that look well.

"Do you think that my Papa...?" Cornelia began, but Holmes put a finger to her lips.

"No conjecture, you have done well, very well, my girl. This case might have remained confused for another week at least. I bow to your success my dear. Much will become clear very soon, of that I'm certain." He wrote a quick note to Cornelia.

> *I've a notion we are meant to discover something in this town, but I'm sure it will be a false trail. Your accident at the Kaffeehaus has saved the day. I am sure that your Dr Laubscher is the man we want.*

There was a sudden knock upon the door and without waiting for an answer, a woman walked right in: Holmes dashed to the fire and flung the message, only partially read into the flames, nearly knocking Dr Watson over in the process. Nobody quite knew who was the most startled.

"I've come to air the bed," the maid told them, not at all sure what to make of two old men falling about at the fireplace and a half dressed young nurse lying on the bed, her bedclothes a mess. But then, she had been asked to make sure the nurse was really in there by an interested party, she could only report that she was. No wonder she was tired if these sort of goings on were occurring at all hours, before dinner too. It was a disgrace.

"Dinner in fifteen minutes," she told them, all eyes on her, guilty eyes too, one could not trust the English, even if these were special.

"I'm glad to hear that," Holmes told her with a gracious smile. He turned to Watson and Cornelia, "And then perhaps a game of cards, or a little music. I do think we could get more in the mood for the coming concert don't you agree?"

Cornelia smiled. "I'd love to play cards, but if you gentlemen will leave me, I'd like to dress. Thank you Dr Watson for coming to see me, I'm sure I will be well again after some supper."

Watson nodded, understanding her little ruse. "You would be if there was more than ruddy sausage to look forward to. Do these people think of nothing else?"

"Oh Dr Watson," Cornelia suddenly shrieked, catching all of them and the maid off-guard. She burst out laughing at their faces and blurted out, "Chicken, I saw the menu tonight it is chicken!"

Holmes laughed, the maid could not make head or tail of it and Watson's eyes lit up a smile from ear to ear.

"I'll be first down. I shan't wait mind, nothing will part me from chicken Holmes, nothing."

"You deserve it Watson, you truly do."

But it was a crestfallen Watson who ordered chicken and found nothing less than a chicken würst on his plate that night. Not even a celebratory champagne livened his spirits. It was a mournful occasion in the end, but nothing dampened Holmes' enthusiasm. He had the scent and he meant to follow it that very night.

***

It was already one o'clock in the morning. Snow was still falling quite heavily outside, softening the edges of the gothic town, transforming dreaming spires. Holmes was well wrapped against the cold; some Vicks vapor salve rubbed well into his chest and wearing two pairs of woolly vests. He was already out on the roof of the hotel, jumping (somewhat precariously) from ledge to ledge, careful to keep low and out of any stray light. Down below in the street a man stood coughing, stamping his feet, trying to beat off the cold, cursing his luck he should have this job, of all jobs. The one place his eyes did not venture, was up. His orders were to watch the doors of the hotel. His Ford, stood gathering snow, not more than ten metres away. He worried as to whether it would start again. His eyes strayed to the end of the street every few minutes or so, anxious for his relief to come and take over, even though he was not due for more than an hour.

Holmes had already noted that the guard changed every four hours, but in this cold it was too long and a form of narcosis took over after little more than one hour. It was too cold to stand and just watch, even with exercises.

Holmes on the other hand was already showing definite signs of overheating, the strenuous effort of keeping upright on snowy rooftops was no easy matter for his aging, spindly legs.

At last he found the fire-escape he had noted earlier that afternoon, one that would take him to ground level more than eight houses removed from Der Deutsche Hof. From there he intended to briskly walk back into the old town passed the German National Museum and fetch the old bicycle he had purchased after lunch that day and hidden in a cold, unused alley way.

A Night on the Tiles

It was with some relief when he eventually reach ground level and found his alleyway. Everything was already much covered in the powdery snow and the memory played tricks in the altered townscape. In addition Holmes' feet were achingly cold, he had forgotten to line the soul of his shoes, but fortune was with him, the bicycle was still there and, more importantly, dry.

Of course, he knew it was more than a little foolish to be out cycling in the snow covered streets of Nürnberg at such an hour, it being below freezing or very nearly. It was a risk to his own health and the entire campaign, but the thick snow was ideal cover and it would ensure he would get about town quietly, possibly unnoticed. He would not use his lights and his white coat made him almost invisible. He only hoped that a car would not find him so, if one ventured out on such a bad night and at such an hour.

He had in mind a house he had seen earlier in the day, one set back in its own grounds, a high wall around it. Guards stood discreetly just inside the gates, Himmler's men, he was sure of it, for although they were unobtrusive, their uniform was black and although his glimpse had been but brief from the car, he thought he had seen the SS insignia on their uniforms. This was no innocent house, to be sure. Barbed wire was liberally strewn on the tops of the walls. Holmes already knew from enquiries he had made in the phone book and casual questions put to hotel and shop staff that this was not the house of the Mayor, nor a lawyer, professor or rich merchant, for none of these men would warrant the attention of the SS to keep out the curious. Or perhaps, just perhaps, it was to keep the occupants in?

It was a strange house, quite mysterious, well worth Holmes' attention. The snow lent the building a gothic appearance, the four towers covered in a thick layer of glistening snow, a sudden reminder that this was the country of Hansel and Gretel and other atrocities. There was a snow-drenched monkey-puzzle tree in the garden, an alien beauty, but Holmes had no time for the romance of wintry town houses, his mind was on one thing.

This house he believed to be the house of Dr Laubscher. There was little proof, save the alleged SS guards. No general lived here, for there was rivalry between the Army and Himmler, a general would have soldiers outside. It was said Göring himself owned a villa in Nürnberg, yet this was not it, of that he was sure. Holmes, standing in the shadows of the street opposite this house, was certain that this was the house of Dr Laubscher.

One learns so much from observation. Holmes was the master of that maxim. But as he had so often proved, seeing a house was not necessarily an act of recording all the facts.

The snow showed no sign of letting up, but it did hide him as he stood like a rock listening to the heartbeat of the town, the whispers of the house, its upstairs light still burning brightly. The two sentries, stood smoking, stamping their feet to keep warm, talking in a low monotone as sentries do, their voices carrying quite clearly to Holmes' ear, but nevertheless remaining unintelligible.

To one side of the house stood a large shed, the roof of which was flat and steam poured from several pipes. Not a household boiler, there were no fumes in the air associated with that. No, this steam was altogether quite different. To Holmes' mind, an expert in chemistry himself, something was cooking, boiling away in that shed. If this was the famous Dr Laubscher's house, then perhaps this was the equally famous chocolate on the boil? But Winston Churchill had spoken of a secret formula. Men had died trying to get at the information. It was Holmes' sincere belief that those men's lives, Cornelia's father for one, had ended for something more than Adolf Hitler's chocolate. He hoped fervently there was more to it than that. Surely the association with Herr Flohn was more than just a commercial exercise in the exploitation of Hitler's Darkest Secret – a nutty full-creme whip or a hard, thin slab of dark chocolate, bitter, yet long lasting and much appreciated by connoisseurs of the cocoa bean?

He hoped it was more important than that. His last case had to mean more than obtaining a secret recipe from a vain confectioner who sought patent exploitation of his 'secret formula' world-wide. Boxed treats of Hitler's Choice Chocolates may be what the world was waiting for, but he, Sherlock Holmes could not, would not accept that this was the end of the case. He would not agree that this was the inevitable outcome of months of soul searching in the Baker Street Bunker, weeks of vile liverwürst, any würst at all, the entire immersion theory gone to waste on a tasty bar of chocolate.

He could not, would not accept it.

Holmes turned around, brushed the snow from his bicycle seat and with a heavy heart began the slow run of a cycle ride home and a long climb, the back way, to his cold bed.

Life had never seemed so bleak as of that moment. It was not a good hour in the life of Sherlock Holmes.

Nor was it a good moment in the life of his bicycle.

Holmes, more than a quarter of a mile from his hotel, engaged action with a large snow covered brick, carelessly abandoned in the road. The impact was as severe as if he had collided with a stone wall.

Holmes was flung from his bicycle and fell headlong into the powdery snow, thankfully a good two inches thick. Nevertheless, Holmes grazed his hands and bruised his forehead so severely, that it was several moments before he was able to get up again and he lay there, breathless, in pain and dazed, knowing that it was foolhardy to stay in this position. It was already nearly three o'clock in the morning, he needed rest and had to get back to the hotel unnoticed, or all would be lost. They would know he was up to something. It was imperative he continued on.

With a determined will, only a man like Sherlock Holmes can summon when all seems lost, he urged his tired, ageing body up off the ground.

Gingerly, with aching, frozen hands, he brushed the snow off his white coat and although it was dark, he imagined he saw blood. He thought he was going to be all right; he was not as fit as he used to be, old age was the final unsolved crime, accidents tended to have unwanted side effects. There was a light in his eyes that was not there before, a dizziness. The street began to sway, his knees began to wobble. He took a step and bent down to remove the useless bicycle off the road, but slowly, relentlessly he found himself sinking lower and lower until it seemed his very nose was buried in the snow. It was a ridiculous situation. He could not move. Here he was, a quarter of a mile from the hotel, bent double over a prostrate bicycle, himself paralysed, his legs slowly, inevitably, giving way until he was almost completely flat, sprawled in a most unattractive fashion over his machine.

A car!

He heard a car engine, it appeared to be driving on his side of the road, but there was nothing he could do. His heart was barely beating at all, no urgent commands to his limbs were getting through. The blow to his head must have been more serious than he had first thought. A torch, there was a torch in his right hand pocket, his hands did not want to respond: they completely failed to move. With a fatalistic certainty Holmes knew his end had come. An ignominious end it was too. Sprawled upon a bicycle. He could see the car's headlights dancing in the snow up ahead, hear the motor was running fast, much too fast for the snow, but at least he had the comfort of knowing it would be a quick death, the car would break his spine.

Poor Watson. He tried sending a message, concentrating his thoughts into one tight beam, aimed at Watson's sleeping head. 'For God's sake, don't go it alone. Leave for England, take Cornelia.' It was his only hope, the Morgenthau method of thought transfer had worked in Innsbruck, why not here, right now? 'Watson, you are my best and only friend. Go home!'

The car was upon him. Holmes clenched his teeth, said a prayer and took his last breath...

Never was a bicycle so well missed, never was a swerve at forty-five miles an hour so neatly executed. The big Mercedes-Benz SS Coupe was slammed right and left and right again, spinning in a complete circle, its engine roaring as the driver sought to bring it under control, the ground shuddered as the five-litre two-ton machine made impact with the curb, squeezing out a bank of fine snow that curved in the air and fell with a heavy 'crump' on Holmes. For himself, the paralysis seemed to have left him as quickly as it had come and although he was stiff, he was less rigid and his breathing was returning to normal. Although near to faint and dizzy, he was still aware of his surroundings and predicament.

The driver's door slammed. The man ran over to Holmes, shone a torch down on his head and never were two men more surprised.

"Sherlock Holmes!" The man exclaimed, "how the hell...?"

"Mr Moorehaus," Holmes croaked, amazed to meet a man who knew him at all.

"Stay still, stay absolutely still. I want to make sure you don't have any broken bones."

"I have no broken bones Mr Moorehaus, it was my head that received the blow."

"You were attacked?" he asked, astonished, squatting down beside Holmes, brushing snow away from the old man's face, getting a grip under his shoulders.

"No, no, my bicycle met with some resistance. If you'd be so kind as to get me to my hotel, I have not lain here too long, I just need rest..."

"Mr Holmes, I mean Lord Holmes, I shall get you there in no time at all. But surely a hospital?"

"Dr Watson can attend me," Holmes snapped, the very last thing he wanted was to go to a hospital.

"OK, OK," Moorehaus agreed, worried about the large bruise on Holmes' head. "Just let me get the car and I'll be with you in a jiffy. Just what the hell were you doing out here on a night like this?"

Holmes realised that he needed some sort of story.

"I am a well known insomniac, Mr Moorehaus. The bicycle helps me relax and the town is so peaceful in the snow."

It is to be doubted Mr Moorehaus believed this story.

It is a matter of unrecorded history that Sherlock Holmes was thus delivered back to his hotel sans bicycle, right under the nose of the sentry posted outside. He was almost carried in by the strong American, yet no report was made of this, so the authorities were never aware of Holmes' night on the tiles. The sentry saw them come all right, but in the snow, the two gentlemen mounting the stairs looked more like drunken off duty officers to him and he would not be one to interfere.

Only Moorehaus knew and as he practically shoulder-hoisted the wounded Holmes (who was too hurt to protest the indignity) he asked, "You didn't contact England by any chance?"

"It is useless, Mr Moorehaus," Holmes replied weakly, remembering that he judged this man to be with the enemy. "Germany is poised to win. We both know this. I will have nothing to do with prolonging this war. Germany needs Lebensraum, living-space. We can do nothing to stop her."

Moorehaus nodded, yet he was confused by Holmes' answer. He had never considered Holmes to be such a defeatist, but if this was the voice of England, as Intelligence supposed, then their judgement of Holmes as an agent was wrong. Perhaps the man did sympathise with the Third Reich. It was known many did. Well time would tell, he would contact the doctor soon if he was an agent, if he lived, that was. He did not look to be in good shape at all.

Holmes, still stunned, allowed himself to be transported to his room, where Watson, awake and highly agitated, awaited Holmes' return.

"Holmes, Holmes – my God, Mr Moorehaus, what has happened to Holmes?" It was a moment of confusion and emotion.

"Nothing a good rest wouldn't cure, Dr Watson. He's your patient. Keep him in bed tomorrow. It's a lucky thing my trip to Berlin was delayed or your Sherlock Holmes would be a goner for sure."

Moorehaus explained the accident and Watson was soon in such a state about it that the American was almost forced to put both of the men to bed. But at last he left them in their room and went about finding his own bed at his hotel, for what was left of the night.

Outside in the street he noted a man sitting in his Ford Taunus across the road from him. Holmes' sentry no doubt. He smiled. Little did Himmler's men realise that with Holmes one did not just simply post guards, one would have to turn a whole town into spies and even then there would be no guarantee of catching him out.

Exercise? Insomnia? He didn't think so. Sherlock Holmes was their man, he was sure of it, banking on it. Exercise? It was laughable. The man had never spent as much as an hour in keeping fit unless it had some relevance to a case. Moorehaus had read enough of Dr Watson's accounts to know that much about the man. Still it wasn't his concern. Nürnberg must look to itself, or suffer the consequences.

9

The National Prescription

By mid-morning it was common knowledge throughout the hotel that Lord Holmes was ailing. His non-appearance at breakfast triggered the alarm and the sight of Nurse Shand, pale, worried and dashing out more than twice for medicine from the pharmacy confirmed everyone's worst suspicions.

However, whether at Holmes' instigation, or Watson being an old fashioned doctor at heart and possessing a fanatical belief in the benefits of fresh air, at eleven o'clock that very morning, the snow stopped, the sun began to melt the night's snow and Watson made a decision to get them out of the hotel. The sky was a rare, beautiful sight, one of those pale eggshell-blue, almost transparent skies, quite tempting for even the most jaded to take a stroll under it.

Cornelia emerged first from Der Deutsche Hof, pushing one of the hotel's own rather antique bath-chairs with a well wrapped, nay, almost mummified Sherlock Holmes inside it. Watson followed soon after, obviously greatly concerned, leaning heavily upon his stick, talking to himself, shaking his head. It was a pathetic sight, enough to break the hearts of those who knew Holmes in his more vigorous times of old.

Catching Cornelia up, Watson, guide book in hand calling out the sights, led his tiny ensemble towards the Hauptmarkt, passing the timbered Rathaus built in the 14th Century and famed for it's dungeons hewn out of the rock. In this square they could watch the world go by and whether from the market place itself or the Kaffeehaus across the way, the world could watch them.

Cornelia, emotional, yet professional, true to her new calling as a nurse, constantly reviewed Holmes' temperature, sticking the thermometer into the blankets, taking it out, shaking her head, shaking the thermometer just to make sure. When Dr Watson saw this, he sighed and then fed more pills to the reluctant mummy and sat by him, talking sporadically, sometimes maintaining silence as he wrote, catching up on his notes, occasionally ordering a coffee for Cornelia from the nearby Kaffeehaus, or a beer for the occasional passer-by who came to sympathise. It seemed the whole town knew of Lord Holmes' sudden illness, a swollen head, cancerous some said, so terrible he could not show his head in public.

The conductor of the forthcoming Wagner Concert himself sought them out, having already witnessed Holmes and Watson's interest with his work the previous night at a rehearsal. Holmes had looked well enough then, but much older than he had imagined.

"Herr Holmes will recover, I hope?" he asked, shaking Watson's hand, casting an anxious look into the bath-chair, seeing nothing but a breathing lump and some hair. Holmes obviously did not want anyone to see him.

"I pray to God that he will be, Herr Professor. This treatment is severe, but if it brings down the swelling, then I shall be a happy man. It will disappoint Holmes greatly if he has to miss the concert."

"Us too, Herr Holmes has a keen reputation as a connoisseur of Richard Wagner. I myself saw him at Bayreuth only once as a youth, eighteen I was. A keen flautist even then."

"Holmes met the composer too," Watson boasted. "They even exchanged autographs. Holmes stuck his above the bed, it is his most treasured possession. I wish he were awake now to tell you about it."

The professor, a young man of fifty with a white streak through his hair and the inevitable silver swastika on his lapel looked very worried. "It will grieve us terribly if Herr Holmes cannot attend." He peered into the bath-chair then turned to Dr Watson. "Tell me honestly Herr Doktor, was it an accident? He is no longer a young man, like yourself..."

Watson confessed. "He fell in the snow last night, a chill set in. I've had to sedate him very strongly. But I know Holmes. He will attend tomorrow night. He wouldn't want to miss it, not for all the snow in Siberia."

The professor smiled, taking up one of Cornelia's hands, frozen, quite blue.

"My dear nurse, you are so cold. Come with me a moment to Frau Zelda's shop. I will purchase some mittens for your beautiful hands. And do not protest. The hands that nurse Sherlock Holmes must be warm hands and Herr Doktor, you must not take the English obsession for fresh air too far. You are both cold enough, you need not demonstrate to us how hardy the English are."

"Nonsense, Herr Professor it isn't cold at all. But I grant you I have been remiss in not considering Nurse Shand's condition." He felt quite guilty all of a sudden and blushed deeply.

"No sir, I..." Cornelia began.

"Mittens, junge Dame. I insist," the professor said, pulling her from her seat. "Sherlock Holmes is a lucky man indeed to have such a beautiful nurse." He pressed his lips to her icy hands and then gently, but forcefully tugged her away from Watson and Holmes. There was nothing Watson could do about it, he could not abandon Holmes. But he reasoned the conductor had good intentions and he waved with as big a smile as he could muster as Cornelia allowed herself to be led around the corner.

"Oh dear, oh dear," Watson wailed. He felt things were not right, not right at all. What he would have dearly liked was a copy of the *Daily Telegraph* and news of the war, even bad news, as long as it was news.

***

Two fat iron eagles adorned the wrought iron gates of the Kaiserhof, they were reflected in the window of A Lugger, Buchhandlung, a faded antique bookshop, its stock much depleted, if not banned outright.

An old man, dressed in rough peasant cloth, a cap tightly pulled over his head, carried a box, cleanly and neatly wrapped. Clearly it did not belong to the old man, its heritage much more of the Upper Marienstrasse, which was a long way from the heritage of this disheveled old man, who seemed too old for any kind of employment. Surely there was a pension for this unfortunate, no need for him to lug heavy, wrapped boxes, it was a disgrace that a man like this should have to work at all.

Yet this poor creature with the box, crossed the road and advanced towards the iron gates of the Kaiserhof. There were two sentries, SS men, for they wore black uniforms and they eyed this peasant with great indifference.

"Diese sachen sind fur Herr Doktor Laubscher," the peasant mumbled, shoving some dirty paper with Dr Laubscher's name on it.

"Schokoladewaren und sonstige Dauerbackwaren," he spat, having obvious difficulty with the words. The sentries were used to deliveries of chocolate ingredients. After all, Dr Laubscher's chocolates had to be made fresh, with only the best ingredients. However this delivery man was hardly the person they were used to delivering the doctor's supplies.

"Who are you?" they asked, not particularly interested.

"I'm the cleaner at Braun's Liefert," the old man replied, breaking into an unpleasant cough that offended the bored, young sentries no end. They waved him on, out of their way. They did not want to catch any germs from this uncouth peasant. They hoped the box was well sealed.

"Take it in, old man," they told him, "and stop your coughing." Miraculously the coughing stopped and the old man limped up the slushy pathway to the rear of the house. The sentries turned their gaze back to the street to watch a pretty girl go by, a lovely honey blonde who shyly averted her eyes as she passed them by, something she had to do two, three times a day, much to the sentries' delight and the girl's torment. She had not enjoyed Dr Laubscher's rise to fame, not one bit.

The back door was enormous, a child sat there playing with a ball, bouncing it up and down in front of him. Bored, fat, listless, he took no interest in the old man, old men were not interesting. Beside the boy stood a broken toy, a tin soldier with the head bitten off, not the sweetest child that ever lived.

The old man groaned with his weighty box, brushed past the boy through the open door and stepped into a steaming cauldron. The Laubscher kitchen was a hive of activity, luncheon was being prepared, cabbage was steaming and sausage was on the boil. Kitchen staff circulated in a mad frenzy of preparation. Creams were being whipped, bananas creamed; sponge mix beaten; flour, sugar, cabbage leaves, spoons, knives, rags, dishes everywhere and the all pervasive steam.

"Schokoladewaren," the old man croaked, endeavouring to be heard above the hiss of the steam. A young girl with a mass of black hair lying against her sweating face pointed in the general direction of the opposite side of the kitchen, the old man nodded and near exhaustion, staggered through the mad house with his burden, stumbling through a wide door on the opposite side.

Here again was another transition, a calm ante-room with still, quiet pictures on the walls of lakes, mountains, picturesque views of Hessen Eisenbach in all its glory.

The old man set his box down and fetched out a filthy rag to wipe his perspiring forehead. A charming picture of Der Dutzendteich lay on the table and he admired it whilst taking a rest. This room was obviously the Fruhstuckszimmer, the breakfast room; the preserves on the sideboard confirmed it.

"Who are you?" A harsh voice demanded suddenly.

The old man looked up and saw a man who was instantly recognizable as the butler.

"Schokoladewaren," the man repeated once more. "17.50 Reichmarks."

The butler seemed taken aback. "We ordered no supplies today. Where is the regular man, Boris?"

The old man shrugged. "Ich weisse nicht. I don't know." His hand still held out before him.

The butler looked at the box. "17.50 Reichmarks?" He shook his head, "das ist zu teuer, too much."

"Herr Doktor ordered it specially," the old man pointed out.

However, the butler did not agree. His voice rose by several octaves.

"I shall fetch Doktor Laubscher and we shall see, we shall see!"

This was obviously intended to frighten the old man, but he stood there quite resolute with his grubby, long fingered hand still held out for money. Determined to sort this out, the butler left to fetch the Doktor. The old man allowed himself a hesitant smile, he had no time for pompous butlers.

Soon the sound of heated conversation in the passage heralded the arrival of an angry and impatient Dr Laubscher, who was not impressed to be dragged away from his experiments by his butler or by filthy old men. He stormed into the breakfast room and began a tirade against the old man, shouting at him in the most unpleasant manner, telling him that he never paid more than 7.50 Reichmarks for his additives. It was time shopkeepers forgot the way of Jewish traders, it was criminal to extort this kind of profit when Germany was at war... and so on.

The old man bore it with as much good will as he could muster, but at the end of it he merely held out his hand again and said, in a voice that was calculated to surprise the doctor, yet not alarm the offensive butler, whose ignorance he thought he could count on.

"17.50 Reichmarks, or perhaps you'd prefer to pay in sterling?"

The doctor stood back in surprise, then recovering quickly, he smacked his head and attempted a silly laugh, cursing himself for forgetting his November order. He took to castigating the butler for not realising that he had ordered extra ingredients for the Fuhrer's special chocolate cake.

"These are the supplies I ordered from Belgium, from Brussels."

Embarrassed, showing obvious anger with his butler, he invited the old man to bring the box into his study where he would receive full payment and a little more as an apology for the butler's mistake.

The butler, red in the face and with an angry glare at the old man, withdrew to the kitchen, no doubt to curse the kitchen staff for letting the man through at all.

Dr Laubscher turned and marched up his dark passage, the old man following in his wake, clutching the heavy box.

"I had not expected to receive those ingredients at all," the doctor said, as he opened his study and laboratory door. "I have ordered the box three times already, yet it never came. The war has made communication so difficult already."

The old man entered the room, placed the box on the table and began to look about him. It was odd, he had expected some devastatingly, incalculable thing in this room, but was disappointed. Instead, banks of chemicals stood stored in a corner so dark it was as if it were made from a black rock, so thick and permanent it seemed. The ceiling was a maze of wires and gurgling pipes that exited at the far end through the wall.

There was a distinct electrical hum audible and a subdued, barely perceptible vibration below. A powerful generator was working somewhere in this building. On the far side stood a bank of dials, a forest of complicated gauges to measure temperature, velocity, density; it was the laboratory of a rich man. Not a book, not a machine, not a tool was short in this place.

The doctor had opened his box, taken out the special ingredients. Ten pounds of sugar and a tin of Cadbury's Flakey Chocolate drink mix.

"Well, it all seems to be here," he answered smiling, enjoying the joke a little, glad his butler did not have to see his "special ingredients". But when his eyes again fell upon the old man, he was astonished to see that the vagrant had grown at least three foot or more and was sitting comfortably in his own favourite chair.

"And so contact is made Herr Doktor, may I present myself, Lord Sherlock Holmes."

Dr Laubscher simply could not believe the transformation. "But where...?" he asked, looking about for the shriveled old man he had entered the room with.

"Gone," Holmes said, "gone back to the thicket, slinking like a serpent, as well he might. That disguise is no easy burden for my poor back."

The doctor sought a chair and fell into it with a long sigh, "Mein Gott," he repeated several times. "At last... I had given up." He looked up at Holmes watching him with a steady eye. The doctor nodded, smiling to himself briefly. "It is an honour. To receive you sir, it is an honour." Then thinking of the seriousness of the meeting, he leant forward, his voice beginning anew with a more urgent tone. "This meeting is so dangerous," his eyes grew wide with a new fear. "They spy on me. The butler, he is one of Himmler's men, I'm sure of it. Herr Hitler does not allow me visitors, you cannot stay, the butler will expect you to leave immediately."

Holmes understood. "We must meet, you say you have a secret formula, three men have died trying to get to you, Sir Charles Hainsley..." The doctor held up his hand. "I told Sir Charles everything, but they came in the night to his hotel and took him away. The gestapo... I know he told them nothing, for I am still here, making the Fuhrer's chocolates."

Holmes' heart sank. All the rumours were true then. This adventure was all about chocolates. The doctor took out a handkerchief and mopped his brow, giving the appearance of being a highly nervous man. "They must be one hundred per cent pure. Everything is inspected, all my ingredients regularly checked, the Fuhrer trusts no one. I can tell you, Herr Holmes, that he eats three pounds of chocolate a day. Three pounds! He and his mistress, Eva Braun. He is obsessed with chocolate. Have you not noticed that everything he wears is a different shade of brown? That there are brown shirts everywhere? Rommel's army is brown. He seeks to turn Germany into a brown country, everyone must wear brown around him, he paints all his walls brown. It is clear to me that all is not well."

Holmes' patience was being sorely tried. "Dr Laubscher, I have not endangered my life and I should like to think the others have not wasted their's just to gain knowledge that Herr Adolf Hitler is addicted to chocolate. It is common knowledge that the King likes gum-drops, but the news is not considered catastrophic enough to bring the downfall of all England. Even though I will admit that a man who eats three pounds of chocolate a day will suffer, his bowels are not to be envied."

Exasperated, the doctor called out, "No no, you do not understand, Herr Holmes. Chocolate is merely the key to the problem. I am forced into experiments, the entire German people are forced into a most grotesque and horrible experiment. Already Herr Flohn's factories produce my chocolate for the army..."

A knock on the door interrupted him. Holmes at once resumed his disguise and leapt up from his chair saying, "It is good to meet a man who likes Richard Wagner, Herr Doktor. Are you going to the concert tomorrow night?" The doctor nodded, reaching for the contents of a small box. "Quick take this," he tossed a small bag of chocolates at Holmes. "It is the Fuhrer's, no one but him can eat it. Do not attempt to eat it, whatever you do. I must tell you everything, perhaps an exchange of programmes at the concert?" He anguished suddenly.

"But they will watch us so closely, they know everything."

Holmes nodded. "My nurse will greet you with the word 'Mycroft'. Exchange with her." Another knock, more loud than the last. The doctor began to show signs of panic, he ran hurriedly to the door, opening it. "Ah Herman, please show this old man out, he's come a long way with his box, he must be so tired." The butler bowed slightly and Holmes bent into his former shape, limped out of the doctor's study. He was disappointed that he had not been told more, but from the laboratory layout and with the aid of his near photographic memory, he felt sure he would be able to think upon this meeting further, and its consequences. Once more he was led down the dark windowless passages and out through the kitchen. The kitchen staff shouted at him as he went through, complaining bitterly about him getting the butler into trouble, but Holmes could not follow their conversation. Outside on the step the small boy smiled. No doubt he had been sworn at too and saw in Holmes an ally. He offered Holmes a cigarette card, urging him to take it, a sign of friendship. Holmes looked at it and was shocked to see it was the Nazi flag again, the black eagle on swastika. First Issue, number 43 Truppenstandarte der Nebeltruppen. Holmes thanked the boy and took out of his pocket a biscuit, offering it to the boy who solemnly took it, impressed to receive an exchange he could eat. He smiled again and darted away into the garden. Holmes pocketed his card and trudged away from the house as quickly as he could, the sentries laughing at his limp, calling him names. In the distance the sight of the former prison and torture chamber Burggrafenburg, with its pentagonal tower, mocked him also. Undaunted, he swayed and limped away to a nearby alleyway, some one hundred metres from the doctor's home.

There, concealed in the darkness stood an old hotel bath-chair with an impatient and nervous Dr Watson standing beside it. Cornelia was at the other end of the alley nervously keeping watch.

"Holmes, Holmes, I thought you'd never get back. Our air-pump packed up, our mummy stopped breathing over an hour ago."

"No matter, Watson, our ruse worked, I hope?"

"Rather, no problem at all. Here let me help you with your disguise, did you discover anything Holmes. What is Dr Laubscher's secret?"

But Holmes didn't answer, he was thinking and concentrating on returning to his normal appearance, permanently shedding the old man's filthy disguise. He saw Cornelia looking at him from the far end of the alley and waved briefly.

"We must get back to the hotel, Watson. We have work to do. Miss Cornelia must get me chemicals. A busy afternoon ahead, Watson. There's a mystery all right, but it confounds me. Chocolate is not a word that will impress the British Cabinet, yet I'm afraid it is the one word I'm going to have to say."

"Chocolate?" Watson queried, quite astonished to hear Holmes refer to it in the context of their investigation.

"It's a diabolical thing, Watson, but if I'm right, Sir Charles died trying to get that word to the First Lord."

"And the word was chocolate?" Watson exclaimed.

"Precisely, Watson. Now advance, I'm in an urgent hurry to be in our room."

Soon the trio could be seen trudging the streets of Nürnberg. Holmes was a tad heavy for Watson to push alone and to a discerning eye, one would have noticed that both Cornelia and Watson were using considerably more effort to push Lord Holmes now than they had earlier in the morning, when indeed, the young Cornelia had pushed the bath-chair all by herself.

It was not something that escaped the notice of their guardians in the ever present Ford. They had circulated the town in sheer panic fearing they had lost their charges, desperately running into shops, alleyways, everywhere, scared to report to the overseer that they had lost the English spies.

So it was with relief they overtook Holmes' party and no surprise to Holmes that for the rest of the journey their 'guardians' actually preceded them to the hotel, a ferret faced man staring out of the rear window at them all the way. Holmes marked that face well. He looked down into his lap and stared into the bag of Hitler's chocolates, amazed to see that each and every piece had a tiny swastika stuck on it. He brought one up to his ever keen nose. Peppermint. A peppermint swastika. What further secrets did it hold? What was the vice that caused the little corporal to eat so much of it? He was determined he should discover the secret.

"The Baedeker says there is a magnificent restaurant here, Holmes. Does the best veal in all of Germany, I was wondering..."

"Perhaps tomorrow luncheon," Holmes told him, smiling to himself, "I promise we will find you a day without sausages soon, Watson. Did I see you with new mittens, Cornelia?"

Cornelia reddened a moment. "Yes sir, the conductor bought them for me, he insisted. I could not stop him."

"It is well," Holmes told her, cutting off her apologies. "You are a great distraction my dear. I do not know what we would do without you."

"Why thank you, Lord Holmes."

But Watson could not help wondering what Holmes was up to. He rarely, if ever complimented ladies without some secondary motive. The answer was short in coming.

***

Their large hotel room was filled with smoke, so much so Cornelia doubted her ability to continue breathing and she sat in a chair by the window, only partially open in deference to her sensibilities, for Holmes preferred the windows shut quite tightly when he was conducting experiments.

He sat at his deck, hastily rigged apparatus boiling away all around him, a foul stench with yellow smoke billowing from the last of the test tubes. The portable microscope sat on the other end with a sample of Hitler's chocolate under the glass. Holmes, closely involved with his science and making copious notes, as bottles bubbled in front of him, ignored the others in the room. The radio was kept going full blast with dancing music to drown out the microphone which now had a blanket stuffed around it to block their words.

Watson, for his part, had no easy task. He sat less than a foot from the suffocating Cornelia and observed. This was not fetish on his part. Cornelia had entered into the spirit of the experiment with great willingness, even if she was experiencing great discomfort with all the fumes. However, she drew comfort from the nearness of Watson, who from time to time took one of her hands and squeezed it tight, asking her if she was all right, searching her eyes for signs of trouble. He wished it were he undergoing the test. The odd thing was, Cornelia could not exactly tell if she was all right, though she did know that she felt very queer, very queer indeed.

"Nothing?" Holmes asked, looking up from his desk momentarily; the desk light catching him in a strange eerie way so that the eyes in his head appeared to glow like a hollowed-out pumpkin. Cornelia let out a little cry of fear, he seemed to her like a ghost.

"Little effect," Watson muttered, taking up Cornelia's hand once more.

"Increase the dose," Holmes ordered, turning back to his test tubes.

Watson was doubtful, but complied. Cornelia was not keen either.

It was the bitterest chocolate she had ever tasted. Not a bit like the Terry's Assorted she preferred at home.

"Just another slab," Watson told her in a sympathetic voice, "not even half the packet yet. Spit out the swastika if that bothers you so."

"No," snapped Holmes, who had not eliminated the swastika yet, "all of it."

Reluctantly, Cornelia reached out and took the chocolate from Watson, breaking off another slab of the dark substance, taking two swastikas by mistake, spoiling a neat row. Then, her eyes closed, she placed it in her mouth, hardly chewing it at all before allowing it to plunge down her throat to the pit of her tiny stomach and immediately attack the digestive system.

Watson immediately set about observing her with renewed vigour, checking his pocket watch and watching her eyes for signs of uncontrolled, unconscious movement; feeling her pulse for a quickened pace, a signal the chocolate was penetrating her blood stream and from there to the heart.

This time the effect was almost immediate.

Cornelia began to feel the top of her head opening up. Light was pouring in from all over the universe. Her weight fell away, the music on the radio entered her very soul, turned her inside out. "Holmes," Watson called out excitedly, "Holmes, it's started."

And indeed it had. Cornelia stood up, struggling with her balance and oblivious to all began to sing the theme song from Fred Astaire's *Top Hat* which coincidentally was blaring out on the radio. She entered into the spirit of the song with such gusto and obvious pleasure, as if a spotlight was upon her, that Watson burst into spontaneous applause and could not remember a better floor show in thirty years.

As the chocolate took hold her performance became more dramatic. She stepped back, wrapped the full length drapes around her and began an erotic siren dance, more stunning than even the sensuous Dorothy Lamour. It quite gave Watson the palpitations, not least her lovely voice, the smile on her happy face quite radiant as she acknowledged a grateful audience.

Holmes stood up and walked over to her, to observe more closely. Inspecting her eyes, actually touching and manhandling her with all manner of tests whilst she went on dancing.

"As I thought, she is in a trance. I was right, these chocolates are drugged."

"Drugged?" Watson exclaimed in sudden anguish. "But Holmes, we can't give our Cornelia drugged chocolate. She isn't a stray cat, one cannot experiment upon her, it isn't fair."

Holmes shook his head, "Science, Watson, is never fair." They watched her finish her song, take a bow (two bows and cry off an encore) discard the drapes and begin to lie down on the floor mewing like a cat, crawling up to Watson's leg and clawing him, calling, "Daddy." Watson was quite overcome with emotion and angry with Holmes. "This is scandalous Holmes, you deliberately made her a guinea-pig, you don't even know what drug it is. I hope to God it isn't poisonous."

"Tut-tut, Watson. Think carefully, where is your logical mind? Cornelia is eating," he whispered, "the Fuhrer's chocolate. The very last ingredient that is in that substance is poison."

"Then what is it? What makes her so wild? Oh Holmes I hate to see her so, there must be something I can do?"

"Nothing can be done, Watson. The chocolate is already absorbed into the bloodstream."

Watson writhed in anguish for his Cornelia. "You mean to tell me, Holmes, that 'he' goes like this every time he eats chocolate?"

Holmes sighed, walking back to his desk. "Sometimes I wonder whether your medical training ever made any impression upon your mind, Watson. Cornelia writhes because this is the first time she has experienced the exhilarating rush of cocaine."

In horror, Watson turned so fast to look at Cornelia he cricked his neck and cried out in agony. "Oh damn, damnation Holmes, my neck, my blasted neck."

Holmes understood the pain, he had pulled enough muscles in his time. He rushed over and taking a firm grip under Watson's chin, placing his knee firmly in the man's back, gave him a short, sharp wrench. There was a sickening crunch of bone grinding somewhere in Watson's body and then, much to Holmes' astonishment, it went limp and collapsed into the chair.

"Watson, Watson, my dear fellow," Holmes exclaimed, bending over to look into Watson's red face. It was as he feared, the man had fainted. Something had gone drastically wrong.

Cornelia began to sing again, but was rolling about on the floor as she did so, upsetting things, getting dangerously near to his desk.

"Cornelia," Holmes said sharply, "Cornelia, pull yourself together. It is supposed to relax your body, stimulate your mind. This behaviour is a disgrace."

But it was useless, she did not heed his word for even a moment and the chocolate still had some way to go before the effect would wear off.

This was chaos in Holmes' orderly, logical world and there was nothing he hated more than chaos. He rushed back to his work desk and inspected the contents of his test tubes, blowing out the candles, taking the final residues in their respective test tubes and sealing them with a cork.

"Most interesting," he muttered to himself, walking over to the leaded windows, flinging them open, the smoke instantly pouring out into the freezing evening air, the room clearing quickly, a blast of cold air causing everything to flap and rattle in its wake.

This soon put Watson right. He snapped to with a roar, "My God, the cold air. Holmes, your chest, I cannot allow this." It was apparent he had completely forgotten his neck, he rushed up to the window and began to close it. As he did so, he observed a man in the street below looking up at him, quickly stepping back into the shadow, his footsteps running away into the cold darkness. The odd thing was, Watson had the distinct impression that the man below was none other than the odious Herr Döre. But he dismissed the notion as a trick of the light.

Cornelia was barking at Holmes, alternatively laughing at some secret joke. Holmes sat in a chair making notes and shaking his head, glad the poor girl could not see herself so transformed.

"It's a strong dose, Watson. I fear she will be decidedly ill later tonight. She must remain with us and be closely watched."

Watson bent down and with considerable effort persuaded her to jump up into his arms, barking joyfully, instantly commencing to lick Watson's face and snuffle in between his head and shoulders.

Holmes observed her bark, the short whimpers and her general attitude and deduced... "Border Collie," he said, recognizing the breed.

Watson gaped at Holmes in amazement but ignored it. "Look here, Holmes. If Cornelia gets like this, how could he 'run' anything? Surely..."

Holmes looked at his test tubes and then again at his chart, frowning. Cornelia's barking and snuffling was becoming quite uncontrollable. "Here," he called out to her, taking a biscuit out of his pocket; one of an eternal supply he always kept for emergencies since he had given up smoking. "Here, sit, take this, settle down..."

Cornelia took it in her mouth and quite happily began to chew it, calming down into Watson's lap, Watson's big arms around her and himself not altogether so upset to have her so close to him, even though now she thought herself a dog.

"One must bear in mind two things, Watson. Cornelia is inexperienced, even a little of that chocolate, given time, would have been sufficient for her to experience more than the equivalent of a double dose of the seven percent solution. Perhaps more, the whole packet could be equivalent to a quarter ounce..."

"Oh it's criminal, Holmes. To think of this virtuous young girl contaminated with that. I remember that young actor Noel coming to us two years ago with the same..."

Holmes cut him off, reminding him to keep his voice below that of the radio, now spouting the news. "Listen to me, Watson. I have made calculations, they are not complete yet, but I'm almost certain (I will not fix myself upon this position though) that I have computed the extent of our doctor's astonishing work."

"Already, Holmes? Only you could begin to solve such a mystery from the contents of a packet of chocolates. But I must warn you, I can allow no more experiments on Cornelia. No matter what you say. Statistics say that exposure to the drug can induce reduced responsibilities, a dangerous withdrawal from reality. I forbid Cornelia to be used like this, if you'd hinted that you'd suspected the chocolate to contain cocaine..."

"You would not have allowed me to use her, Watson." Holmes declared, wiping his face with a damp cloth, removing some of the soot from his eyes.

"It's true," he said defiantly, "proponents of the drug claim its curative value, but it is just so many untruths."

"Ah," Holmes said knowingly, "untruths." He smiled to himself.

Watson stared at him a moment, annoyed. Holmes had once been in the grip of this vile substance. He wondered if he was tempted again.

"No Watson, Cornelia has suffered under a good cause. It might interest you to know that this chocolate is more than twenty per cent cocaine and other substances, some of which I've identified, some I have not."

Watson made some rough calculations of his own as Holmes went on.

"Think of it, Watson. He eats three pounds a day, or at least he and his mistress do. What does that suggest to you?"

"That the man is an addict. How could he possibly cope with running the country so afflicted? Look at Cornelia on just a nibble."

"It's more than that Watson, think man. He needs three pounds a day to satisfy himself. It suggests to me that the man is strongly dependent upon the drug. We say it is non-addictive, but it is mentally addictive, one develops a chronic dependancy. I know that feeling well enough."

"It's terrifying," Watson declared, "the world's strongest leader in the grip of that mind debilitating drug."

"More than that, consider the subtleties of the situation. Quite obviously 'he' does not regard this addiction to his chocolate as wrong in any way, on the contrary, he sees it as a necessity to get through his long day. By all accounts he works prodigious hours. The chocolate eaten at a sustained pace is merely his emotional crutch, his hidden strength, the stuff of myths. He cannot be seen injecting himself, but with chocolate produced under a cloud of secrecy, under guard, maintaining that purity image he is so fond of. Others may admire this stand, others might see this personal obsession with chocolate the private eccentricity of a genius, the secrecy surrounding it a necessary step to prevent poisoning. It's a foolproof way to maintain a myth. Think of Göring, Goebbels, Heydrich, how jealous they must be of their leader's endless strength. How they must wish to know his secret. One can assume Herr Himmler knows, but those two are like two kings in a conspiracy against the world. Neither will divulge the other's secrets for fear of weakening themselves."

"Astounding, Holmes, you really think he is so concerned with his image?"

"Most certain of it. He wishes to be in control of everything, to do that one has to be awake most of the time and for the time he is asleep, his control over people works to his advantage. He has rewritten the military text books. His tactic is to spread fear, create terror, sow mutual suspicion, prevent anyone from forming cliques aimed against him. A fiend, a diabolically, brilliant fiend. But there is something more sinister than this behind the scene."

"More?" Watson asked, thinking this information of Hitler's addiction good enough to take back to London. Intelligence could do a lot with that.

"Herr Flohn. He has always been at the centre of this plot."

"Herr Flohn?" Watson asked, his eyebrows meeting in his forehead like menacing clouds.

"My conversation with the doctor revealed very little new information to add to what Cornelia had already told us. But piecing things together, Herr Flohn's new super efficient factories built in Stuttgart, Koln, Berlin, Landshut and Nürnberg all will soon be mass-producing chocolate to our doctor's recipe."

Watson blinked. "You mean, all Germany will soon be eating the same chocolate as Cornelia ate?"

Holmes shook his head. "I don't think so. Not so strong, but similar certainly and it will be for the Armies, the Luftwaffe, the Navy. Think of it Watson, an army marching on a diet of this stimulating chocolate. They would be invincible. They'd feel no pain, they'd never tire. How else could they achieve that inhuman exercise, the 'Goosestep', marching into Europe?"

"It's a terrifying thought, unthinkable. An army that never tires, daily subjected to this chocolate. It's a stimulant to the nervous system which will abolish fatigue, breathlessness. Tank drivers could drive as long as there is petrol in their tanks. I remember the Indian Post runners, Holmes. Ate about half an ounce of cocaine a day, prodigious feats of running, never been equaled, poor blighters."

"Precisely, Watson. Now what would happen if they were deprived of this chocolate?"

Watson knew the answer well enough, he had seen Holmes lounging about in fits of great depression when he had either run out of the substance, or he had confiscated the bottle. "They'd grind to a halt completely, Holmes. The longer they have been subject to the dose, the longer the lethargy. The cocaine would have dulled their mucous surfaces, blunting hunger, so they would be ravenously hungry. Yet it is a medical fact that continued dosage causes emaciation, loss of memory, sleeplessness, a general breakdown of the central nervous system."

"Unless there is a supplementary diet Watson; such as the chocolate loaded with vitamins and perhaps a graduated dosage increase."

"It's incredible Holmes, absolutely incredible. The entire German military structure dependant for its strength on Erythroxylam coca and Theobroma cacao to use their proper names."

"Exactly, Watson, now look at this information more closely, what do you see?"

"See? I see nothing but an invincible army, Holmes. It frightens me. London will howl with anguish when they learn of this."

"On the contrary, you can see the problem. You fail, however, to reason with the vision. You see only the wall of indomitable Boché."

"Then pray, for God's sake, tell me what lies beyond that wall?"

Holmes stood up and walked to the radio, turning up a concert being broadcast direct from Berlin. Schubert's Quintet in A Major Op114, *The Trout*.

Cornelia appeared to be fast asleep in Watson's lap, looking for all the world like a tiny child, her cheeks rosy red, a reaction no doubt to the contaminated chocolate. Holmes picked up his new Zeiss lens and inspected the contents of one of his test tubes in a peculiar introspective manner, characteristically back in his old thinking mode. He suddenly abandoned this work and stalked over to Watson, scooped Cornelia out of his arms and walked into the bathroom with her, dumping her into the empty bath, turning to beckon Watson into the bathroom too. Watson complied, shutting the door behind him as Holmes turned on the basin tap, indicating to Watson to sit on the edge of the bath.

"We have dealt with the possibility of Herr Flohn's factories being used to manufacture chocolate to make the Third Reich armies invincible. This, I feel, is a reality, hence our doctor's great concern for their wellbeing must concern him deeply. His alarm has summoned us, and our unfortunate predecessors. Yet here we are almost in full command of the knowledge he wishes to convey to London."

"It seems so, but we have still to get back to London," Watson reminded him.

Holmes nodded, looking at Cornelia suddenly and throwing a warm towel from the radiator over her, sensing her need in that cold metal tub.

"And here is the conundrum Watson, there is a complete other side to this problem. Suppose we accept my supposition. The enemy is marching on cocaine, their invincibility secure. Our task then, the British task, is to attack their line of supply."

"That's it, Holmes, by jove you've got it. Cut off the cocoa bean and the cocaine at a vulnerable time and the military machine would be a ruin within forty-eight hours, craving for chocolate, hungry, angry and not the least bit inclined to fight."

"Agreed Watson. The British must open up a second front – South America. They could apply that well-known Boer invention, the scorched earth. The English army must go to South America, the Caribbean and wipe out every cocoa plantation not in our own, or American, hands. Destroy all the cocaine at source, which I understand is grown in Columbia. Our submarines could sink every South American ship laden with cocoa beans. Germany will never take to carob powder, a chocolate substitute will fool no one."

"So the war could shift from Europe to South America as Germany seeks to defend its chocolate supplies. Herr Hitler wouldn't let us get away with this without a struggle."

"That is correct, Watson. If Britain can hold Germany off just a few more months, we could have the chocolate industry of the whole world ground to a halt, the German armies in Europe in total disarray. Hitler himself a wreck, for we strike directly at the Fuhrer if we deny him his regular supply."

"He'd have to turn elsewhere," Watson declared ominously. "Japan and China, Russia even. Their pact will be worthless if he tries to seize their chocolate factories. Think of it Holmes. Germany would have to sue for peace for they could never attack the Far East and ourselves at the same time."

"Which would be none of our concern, eh Watson? Jove if all this is true, the war could be won tonight, right in this very bathroom."

"When do you talk to our good doctor again?" Watson asked, adjusting his rather uncomfortable bottom on the cold bath edge.

"No more words, Watson. I will speak to you about it later. If he confirms all that we conjecture, I move we return to England immediately the concert is finished, perhaps see if we can't sneak a few photos of Herr Flohn's factory with your Brownie tomorrow, eh?" He shook his head and stood up, turning off the basin tap. "It is a wonder I did not tumble to this secret when we spent that afternoon at the Café Zola in Strasbourg. We ate German chocolate all afternoon, remember? How ill you and Cornelia were. I should have looked more closely. I'm getting old Watson, this brain doesn't work as fast as it used to."

"It has done well tonight."

"Tonight yes, but tomorrow?" He sighed. "The longer we delay in getting back to London the greater risk we now take." Holmes flushed the toilet, to hide further conversation.

"Is this what Sir Charles died for?" Watson asked.

"I'm certain of it. It's a dastardly plan Watson. I shall be pleased to see the faces at the Cabinet table when I'm asked to sum up my mission in as short a way as possible, their usual habit, I'm afraid. Imagine their faces when I simply say 'Chocolate'."

Watson laughed, a slow rumble that began somewhere in the barrel of one of his legs and crept up through the expanse of his stomach, growing louder all the time until it poured out of his mouth, rolling out onto the floor landing against the door, rattling with a great jocularity, reverberating in the tiny, white tiled bathroom until the noise of it was so intense young Cornelia opened her eyes. Taking one look at Watson, crimson with laughter, Holmes, gaunt, hunched over the basin staring at her with mixed emotion in his pale face, she could do little else but burst into tears; huge sobs, attracting the instant attention of a quickly sobered Watson. Holmes spoke on.

"Tomorrow we visit the chocolate factory. This will be a great test of my theory. We must obtain samples at all costs, discard what they give us, aim for the genuine article."

But Holmes might as well have talked to the wall, for Watson was busy comforting an almost hysterical Cornelia, who kept wondering why she was in the bath and her mouth was full of biscuit crumbs.

"I think an early night's sleep will do us all good," Holmes added, opening the door. "Order Cornelia some tea Watson, better get some sandwiches up too, she'll need them now and she'll not thank us for allowing her to miss supper."

Indeed, Watson was not so delighted to have heard this either. The mirth left him instantly. They had all missed supper, it was a disaster. Holmes had tricked them both.

A resentful silence immediately ensued, both Watson and Cornelia busy thinking up the most expensive sandwich they could order. Spying, taking part in experiments was all very well; something one did for one's country. But go without supper? Never!

10

The Strange Case of the Fruit Dip Whip Machine

It need not be a matter of conjecture that the young Cornelia was unwell the following morning. Indeed, at dawn she had been attacked by a renewed and desperate last stand by the drug-filled chocolate and had spontaneously run through the entire repertoire of Jesse Mathews' songs before the morning girl brought her early morning coffee. The sudden knock on the door and the consequent quaffing of the entire contents of that pot of coffee soon brought her to rights, but it confused her the entire day that she had acquired a sore throat. It was quite a puzzle, for she was unaware that she knew any Jesse Mathews' songs at all. Indeed she had always quite detested *Evergreen*.

So Cornelia was somewhat ravaged by a restless night, her head, throat and stomach in sorry want of repair. Watson brought all guns to bear on the problem and was up, even before breakfast, scouring the town's pharmacies for vitamins and substances he had calculated would restore her natural vitality. Although pleased Holmes had solved the mystery, he was annoyed Cornelia had been the guinea-pig. It was a dangerous game Holmes had played and indicated a certain callousness.

Cornelia had the remarkable qualities of gentility that reminded him of his dear departed first wife, Mary Morstan. If Holmes had married such a woman as Cornelia, the child would have been a genius, another Einstein, or some such famous personage. Progeny to the Holmes' strain was sadly lacking. Mycroft had had a son, of course, but he had been wasted on the battlefield of the Somme; only the daughter, Isobella Holmes, married to some American diplomat in Washington, was left to carry on the genes. Watson severely doubted there would ever be another Sherlock Holmes, such a 'genus loci' comes only once in two hundred years. The genes bloom once, a lone flower in the desert of mankind.

This day, being an important one in the life of Sherlock Holmes, he was up early, keenly anticipating the coming Wagner concert, the zenith of the entire German trip. He was already planning the next stage of their journey, the return to England. The day promised other things, of course. The visit to Herr Flohn's factory (he was in town for the concert), luncheon with various visiting dignitaries from Berlin in Nürnberg to review some military installations outside the town. These things did not impress Holmes. Military installations were an obvious target of intelligence work and he was not interested in the obvious. He was more interested in the heavy security outside a fertilizer plant on the outskirts of town, it meant only one thing to him, the nitrogen was not destined to raise crops, but to mow them down.

Holmes had planned a motoring trip; he wanted to take in Bayreuth on the way back to London, one last glance at the Haus Wahnfried. The Opel was ideal transportation back to France, only a little small to accommodate themselves and the baggage. Some ingenuity was needed to increase the car's carrying capacity and it was on this errand Holmes employed himself after an early breakfast alone, Watson having his food with the invalid in her room. It seemed a natural thing to Holmes that the first place he should look for a luggage rack would be the Opel garage and this was where he went, deciding to fill up with petrol and oil whilst he was about it.

The garage was busy, no one seemed particularly interested in yet another blue Opel driving onto the forecourt. But Holmes was immediately interested in them, for there in the showroom, the centrepiece of it no less, stood a Delahaye bath-chair. A sign read: BRAND NEW only 100 kms. Rare, beautiful and a must for any collector at a bargain price of 2,500RM.

Holmes got out of his car and walked over to the showroom window, shaking his head. He had paid less than half that price for the machine and it was barely new then, having been previously owned by an ageing Marquis in Paris. Now here it was, rejuvenated and selling at the same price as an

Opel Kapitan alongside it. Obviously there had been a serious miscalculation on Watson's part as to the real value of his bath-chair. It was difficult at his age to come to grips with this new disease, inflation.

A man ambled up to him, shaking water off his large, red hands. Herr Schoeck himself, the ace car salesman, scourge of all bath-chairs everywhere.

"Can I help you, mein Herr?" He asked, sizing up Holmes, deciding that he wasn't a local; he never bought the Opel he was driving from him, but, as an Opel driver, he was entitled to a warm handshake and a friendly smile. Both of which immediately went into operation.

"Ja, you can help me," Holmes replied, tearing his eyes away from the bath-chair.

"Well, my name is Schoeck. I see you're admiring the bath-chair. A brilliant piece of engineering. One of the last ever made, you wouldn't be thinking of trading in your old Opel for it would you? I could give you best price, of course. 500RM for the car, 550RM if we were talking cash."

Holmes put his hands in horror. "Nein, nein," thinking the man a first class thief. Sells the Opel to Watson for the bath-chair one day; next day offers to make himself nearly two thousand Reichmarks on the deal. Shylock would have approved.

"I need a roof-rack," Holmes informed him, hoping his German was adequate for his needs here.

The car salesman made a funny grimace, showing intense disappointment.

"Oh I wish that I could supply you with one sir. It would be a happy day if I could supply anyone with such an item. Have you not heard of executive order B16/63?"

Holmes frowned, experiencing great difficulty in understanding the man, but he caught the sense of what he was saying.

"Nein, Herr Schoeck. Was ist es? What is it?"

"B16/63 has changed things in Nürnberg, I can tell you. There's not an ounce of spare brass, not a piece of silver or chrome, not a rod of spare steel that hasn't been requisitioned by the factory."

"Oh really?" Holmes remarked, greatly interested. "I come from Munster we have no B16/63 there, though the brass is being collected to be sure. The German navy needs all it can get."

"Well our's isn't going to the navy, you can be sure of that. It all goes into the factory. Who knows what they do with it. They'll soon be searching our very houses for silver-plate. Any precious metals are needed, gold, even platinum, but where would you find such a metal here?"

"Well," Holmes said, making a joke of it, "I hope they don't melt down my car."

The car salesman turned white, even staggered back a foot or two.

"Ja, Ja," he agreed violently. "It might come to that. Already they talk of cutting down car production to half. Imagine it. Don't they realise the car industry is the backbone of the nation? What goes for Opel – goes for Germany, I always say. Our fortunes are intertwined."

"So I shall not find a roof-rack in all of Nürnberg?" Holmes asked, trying to extricate himself, yet pleased this metal collecting activity had come to his notice, very pleased.

"Go and see Herr Hartnack at the saddlery, he might make you some straps. It is back to the early days of motoring, I can tell you. There's going to be hard days ahead for the motor-trade."

Holmes could not but agree and walked back to his car, paid for his petrol, he needed no oil (as well it might not). He might have left and never thought more on the subject if Herr Schoeck had not thought of a little joke and walked to wave goodbye to Holmes.

"That is a very fine pocket-watch you wear mein Herr, watch out Herr Melnick doesn't get it for his factory."

Holmes looked down at his gold pocket-watch and nodded. "I shall guard it closely," he replied, "these are difficult times."

"Too true, mein Herr. Just look at that bath-chair, I'm giving it away."

"Quite," Holmes replied, letting in the clutch and lurching out of the garage forecourt back onto the main street. His mind was already at work processing the information given to him, cross checking it with the legendary mental filing system. That there was no immediate result was not a cause for disappointment. The search for precious metals was a natural thing for a country at war to do, very natural. Soon England would wake up to that fact and once again the railings, door knockers, statues would disappear into the ironmongers' furnace. But Holmes was still in search of a contraption to hold his baggage. Straps did not appeal to him at all, never had. In a moment of inspiration he called in at a piano manufacturer located in the oldest part of the old town. There he was pleased to discover a harmonious hive of activity as old craftsmen and young girls (the boys had long ago joined the army) beat large 'Grand' frames, strung piano casings already made and lacquered almost completed pianos in a sealed off dust-proofed corner. Over nine pianos were in production and the name of Blintz, though not a renowned marque, was nevertheless a respected musical factory and their pianos were highly prized by European music-halls and comedy theatres. They had even sold one to the Empress of Japan who, had a passion for the music of Mozart.

Herr Klaus Müller was the man Holmes spoke to about his luggage problem and the man who solved it, despite the fact that Herr Müller immediately noticed that Holmes was English. This was easily overcome for Herr Müller was also an avid fan of Richard Wagner. Whilst he fashioned a ready made luggage rack out of piano wire (first carefully felting the corners of the roof) he discussed some particular musical issues dear to his own heart.

Holmes looked at his watch, Herr Müller noticed this. "You must watch out our Herr Melnick doesn't see that. He'll soon have it for his factory."

Holmes was surprised to hear Melnick's name twice in such a short while, but quite reasonably supposed it was inevitable if the man was scouring the town for precious metals. He would have visited a piano factory, of that Holmes was certain.

"He seems to be quite a menace in Nürnberg." Holmes remarked, admiring the handiwork of the pianoman. Herr Müller wiped his brow and nodded. "He employs small boys to raid the premises of metal workers and even private homes, it is a scandal in the town. I wish I knew what they did with it all. One must ask oneself, is a piano safe?"

"Or bicycle," Holmes added.

"Now you said it," Herr Müller declared forcefully, letting go a taut piano wire with a great snap against the roof, tightening it down, strumming the wire until it sounded just right. "The Nürnberg bicycle scandal has to be heard to be believed. One hundred bicycles stolen between October and this very day. No bicycle is safe. Right across Germany bicycles are disappearing as fast as they are bought. The padlock I have on my machine is one of the best, but if your bicycle is tethered to a lamp-post, they'll take that too! Nothing is safe."

"So it's not just precious metals," Holmes asked, even more interested in this weird phenomenon.

"In the main it is, but a bicycle has spokes on its wheels and chrome on the handlebars, a hundred bicycles is a whole lot of spokes and chrome."

"A singular case."

"You wouldn't be thinking of taking up the case would you?" The piano man asked in surprise.

"No indeed not. We know who the villain is and we know the reason for the crime, there remains only justification."

"Ah, justification," Herr Müller repeated, savouring the word, looking for a German equivalent and finding none.

"This is an excellent job you've made on my roof, Herr Muller. The luggage I take it fits under the wires and one merely tunes them here at this ridge for tightness. It is an ingenious device."

"It will last as long as the car, or until Herr Melnick sees it."

"We shall be away tomorrow on our way back to England."

"So soon?"

"I came for Wagner, to delay longer would be bad form."

The pianoman considered this a moment. "Wagner would have understood," he said, after a while. "Heil Hitler."

Holmes frowned, he could not bring himself to respond in kind. "How much do I owe you?"

"Fifty-five Reichmarks to you. I shall be at the concert this evening. It is one I have looked forward to for a long time. The whole town will be there, those that have tickets, that is. A hard commodity to come by is a Wagner ticket".

"I am sure." Holmes paid the man and climbed back into his car.

"It is good to see an Englishman in a German car," Herr Müller yelled at Holmes through the glass. "Auf wiedersehen."

Holmes drove off quickly. He had a rendezvous to meet Herr Flohn's driver outside Der Deutsche Hof within ten minutes; little time to ready himself for their tour of the chocolate factory. Now they knew its guilty secret, it was but an important formality.

As he got up speed on the cobble road he could have sworn he heard a choir of angels following him. It was an uncanny noise, almost haunting, eerie. A portent of death, perhaps? Though Holmes was never one to harbor superstitions in his mind. It was some moments on and with much relief that Holmes discovered the sound was not the sinister summons of an early demise, but the tuned piano wires on his roof being strummed by the force of the wind gliding over the Opel at speed. When one got used to it, it was all rather pleasant and Holmes imagined with a little more refinement and a few profitable patent applications, the tedium of motoring long distances could be instantly alleviated by such a device as a musical roof-rack.

The more he thought about it, the more interesting the project became; a gaggle of cars streaming through the city with roof-racks tuned to Wagner's Siegfried or Beethoven's Ninth. Freeflowing traffic would be a joy to hear, a boon to civilisation. Of course people would need a licence, could not let a thing like that get out of hand, or into the popular music field. The sheer horror of half a million Austin Sevens rushing about playing a Bing Crosby tune was unthinkable. And it was upon this subjected that he reflected as he made his rapid way back to the hotel.

Young Cornelia was the first to greet Holmes, indeed, she had heard him coming from a long way off. She and a few others turned out on the street to discover what this strange noise was. She was most excited to see the roof contraption and would not believe it was just accidental that the roof sounded like the swing section of Henry Hall's band.

"It is a delicious sound, Lord Holmes, you are a genius. Watson will be tickled by it, I know he will."

Holmes offered up an involuntary smile (for he was quite embarrassed by the association with Henry Hall) and instead remarked on the condition of his nurse.

"You're looking remarkably changed, my dear. Fresh is a word that comes to mind, don't you know."

Cornelia smiled, an open, endearing smile and ran forward to give Holmes a quick hug. "I feel marvellous. Dr Watson filled me up with every drug he could think of Vitamins A, B, C, D, absolutely everything. I'm awash, I cannot believe how spiffing I feel. Look at my eyes, I can hardly blink."

"Hmm," said Holmes, looking into her bright but glazed eyes. "I rather think Watson has overdone it, but never mind, I'm happy to see you are well my dear. Your contributions to the happy outcome of this case are immeasurable. Without you and Cole Porter this case might have taken months to crack."

"Nonsense, Lord Holmes. I will accept no praise. I am merely an instrument in your hands." But she did wonder what Cole Porter had to do with it.

"Ah, here you are, Holmes," Watson hailed from the top of the hotel steps. "I have just received a message that Herr Flohn's car will be here within three minutes."

"Good man, Watson. Do you have the items I listed?"

"Certainly, and your hat. I'm sure that we can expect rain or snow, it is not a clever thing to be without one's hat." Watson climbed down the stairs, beaming at young Cornelia.

"An excellent job, Watson. Cornelia looks quite ravishing today."

"Indeed," Watson enthused, "should keep their mind off the chocolate, eh?"

Holmes smiled, he had been thinking the same. Watson was looking at the car.

"I say, what's that business on the roof of our car? Not another portable radio, Holmes?"

But Holmes had no inclination to go into explanations. He saw that a long limbed limousine had turned into the street and was bearing down on them at a respectable speed.

"Time to go," Holmes said, signaling to the approaching Mercedes-Benz. "I trust you put the film in your Brownie, Watson."

It amused Cornelia to see Watson's face turn very red, his mouth open in silent excuse for, of course, he had completely forgotten.

Holmes merely smiled as they climbed into the attending limousine. When they were seated behind the solid divider that separated them from the driver, Holmes produced a roll of Kodak, giving it to Cornelia to load into the camera, thus sparing Watson's difficult hands.

"The thing of it is," Watson remarked, when they were passing the heavily guarded fertilizer factory (Holmes surreptitiously taking two quick snaps with the Brownie), "I don't actually like German chocolate!"

There, it had finally been said. In actual truth, it must be revealed that the British party spent the rest of the journey making great play with the subject of how little they liked German anything. Watson lead the way with a long list of complaints, from sausages and the coffee to the garages and the bitter chocolate. It probably did them all good to get it off their chests and with a chauffeur who could not overhear, they all felt quite safe. It was a much needed safety valve and thus they arrived at the Nürnberg Schokoladenfabrik exorcised of any residual aggravation and with such a powerful catharsis in operation that they quite looked forward to the forthcoming factory tour and promised luncheon.

"Be natural," Holmes ordered as they arrived at the factory gates. "And Watson, you have your orders."

"Yes Holmes, I have my orders."

"And mine?" Cornelia asked brightly.

"Stick close to Herr Flohn, Cornelia. Smile, keep his attention. Remember they will give us samples, but it isn't those we are interested in. We must obtain the chocolate off the production line itself. (Your faint is all important, Cornelia. That way, we can be sure what we get is exactly what is given to the soldier at the front. Timing is everything."

Cornelia nodded, she understood and began to smile immediately, for Herr Flohn was approaching even as they climbed out of his car.

"Miss Cornelia, Lord Holmes, Watson, this is indeed an honour. Come this way, this is a big day in the life of the Nürnberg Chocolate Industry and Lord Holmes," he wagged a finger at the detective's gaunt, smiling face. "I defy you to tell me you have ever seen a more efficient and grander confection factory than this."

Just at that moment Heinkel warplanes flew over in an almost continuous wave, drowning out all possible conversation. The sky was black with them and the noise was like an impossible ten minutes of constant thunder, shaking the ground and the glass in Herr Flohn's spectacles. It was an impressive and awesome sight. So big and widespread were they it was impossible to count them. At last they disappeared over the opaque horizon.

"Good news today," Herr Flohn said, resuming his smile. "Spain donated eighty-six Heinkels to the cause. General Franco is a generous man. Eighty-six aircraft will make a difference. It is a good day for Germany."

But not for England, or Mr Moorehaus, Holmes thought to himself. He followed his party into the massive, yet functional factory entrance, the size of which was so enormous that the famous West London Hoover factory would have fit snugly into the foyer alone. Holmes could not help but feel that this factory was the largest he had ever seen, whether car, cloth or confectionery. The Third Reich must have a very sweet tooth indeed if this was the size of just one chocolate factory; it was cavernous. It extended so far into the distance that a bus served the staffs transport needs. The width of the factory defied belief, it was the eighth wonder of the world.

"What is the extent of this factory?" Holmes asked Herr Flohn as they entered the initial processing chamber, the actual place where the cocoa nibs were ground to a fine powder. This space alone was bigger than St Pauls and Watson was heard to remark that there was room for the entire world crop of cocoa in this very place. A thought worth considering if a strategic blockade was to be introduced. No use shutting the door after the horse had gone. Quite obviously the Germans would soon be prepared for siege.

"I cannot answer that, the exact size of this factory changes all the time. It expands almost daily. Demand is so high from the furthest outreaches of the Reich. We can hardly keep pace," Herr Flohn told them. "You had better redirect that question to Herr Melnick, the general manager."

Melnick! The very name exploded like a well-placed bomb in Holmes' mind. He stood riveted to the spot. Could this be the same Melnick who was the scourge of Nürnberg's bicycles and lampposts? Enemy to all pocket watches and roof-racks alike?

"I would be very interested to speak to Herr Melnick," Holmes told Herr Flohn, stepping aside to allow through a woman pushing a huge vat of chocolate powder. Behind her, and as far as one could see, the same scene was repeated thirty or forty times by white coated women; clouds of chocolate powder hanging over them in a white haze. It boggled the imagination to think how much chocolate could be produced by such a vast factory. Probably more than the output of all British factories combined. It was a good thing that the British palate was not partial to German bitter substances. The ancient factories of Cadbury's would be overwhelmed, Bourneville could become a wasteland of unemployed chocolate workers.

"One hundred and fifty different types of chocolate are produced here. And here," said their host as they entered yet another enormous chamber where machinery clattered and performed with great energy and noise, "is my greatest achievement." Herr Flohn boasted, pointing to the machinery with streaming conveyor belts pouring out of one wall. It all converged on a terrifying bank of towering metal where chocolate slurped and splooted from countless funnels, leaving millions of blobs on the conveyor belts where they passed onto more devices which shaped them; cutting, whirling, dipping and curling. From there, their destiny lay either in the vast freezers where they set instantly, or the equally vast flash-ovens which baked those that needed baking.

Holmes understood what the great achievement was instantly. "No people," he whispered. "The entire production process is done without people."

Herr Flohn beamed, clasping Holmes' hand. "It's the miracle of the Third Reich, Lord Holmes. People are needed at the beginning only because that is cheaper than heavy handling equipment, and at the very end where it is necessary to test, sample and pack the finished product into the boxes and tubes. My factories remove the drudgery of factory work, release much needed manpower to the armed forces. Not a man on the labour force except Herr Melnick and the security guards."

"My congratulations, Herr Flohn. May Watson be allowed to take some photographs of this wonderful process. I'm sure England will be most impressed to see them."

"No need, my general manager, Herr Melnick, will issue you with official photographs. I am very proud of this factory, I had pictures commissioned especially."

Holmes' mind engaged gear and was roaring away at some incalculable rate. Herr Melnick (if it was the same one) spent his days scouting the towns for precious metals, to what purpose? The factory was built and functioning, what possible need..?

"I have heard of Herr Melnick," Watson said unexpectedly. Herr Flohn turned to face him, his smile dying on his concerned face. "Oh yes, Herr Doktor?"

"Yes at the hotel. The young receptionist, a pretty girl, Marthe; she was upset that all her mother's silver had gone, seems Herr Melnick came around and paid a ridiculously low price for it. Apparently you have a chronic shortage of silver paper..."

Herr Flohn's smile crept back, yet it seemed to Holmes that the man had breathed an inward sigh of relief. Why?

"Ah yes, with the total onslaught against Germany affecting everything, it is a great problem to get the materials we need. Silver paper, gold wrappers, all kinds of packaging. Herr Melnick is a genius at acquiring the raw materials, but soon the German chocolate eater will have to get used to plain paper around his chocolate. Each and everyone of us must make a sacrifice for the good of all."

Watson accepted this reply at face value. Silver paper was a necessary part of chocolate to keep it fresh. Naturally Herr Melnick would do his damnedest to secure supplies. Needless to say, Holmes was not convinced. Silver for silver paper he could fathom and accept. Bicycles, iron, anything in steel, all precious metals, he could not. There was a mystery here and he was determined to find the answer to it.

It was the time for one of Holmes' little ruses to go into operation.

They passed the ovens section, which was fearfully hot, and they entered the section where the baked chocolate items moved in their thousands towards another machine that stamped them whilst still warm with various designs and insignia. The varieties of chocolate were quite staggering, the shapes enticing and extremely hard to resist.

"Right now we are preparing our Easter line," said Herr Flohn. "Last year the old factory sold over one million chocolate Nibelungs; the dwarves of darkness were their most popular line. 'Nibble a Nibelung' proved to be an irresistible catchphrase. This year we shall make five million chocolate dwarfs and I do not think it will be enough by half."

Cornelia said she was impressed and wished she could have a chocolate dwarf to take home to England with her for her young sister, Charlotte. And it was here, in the almost unbearable heat where only the enormous electric fans suspended from the ceiling prevented the chocolate from spoiling, that Cornelia judged her feint and performed it whilst admiring a multi-coloured wafer machine. She tripped against an electric cable falling headlong, saved only from hurting her fragile head by the lightning responses of the two security personnel accompanying them.

Herr Flohn fussed and flapped, bending down, worrying over her, plucking her out of the guards' hands into his own, pulling her up, brushing her down, flicking dust off her short dress in what could only be described as a licentious manner, but noticeably Cornelia did not protest. She thanked her rescuers and clung in a most forward manner to Herr Flohn whilst she inspected her heels.

It was just as well Herr Flohn and the guards were fully occupied by the femine wiles of Cornelia, the nurse, for Sherlock Holmes had spent a frantic fifty seconds grabbing as many chocolate samples as he could and stuffing them under his hat. All the while his heart beat wildly lest he should be discovered. He hoped that they fitted under there without any messy protrusions until another moment might avail itself when he could transfer the stolen chocolate to somewhere more suitable.

The party resumed their tour with a slight change. Herr Flohn's arm slipped through Cornelia's, "just in case she should trip again and injure herself." Holmes trailed the rear, crossing his fingers for another development to divert his host's attention. Together they approached the chocolate-box production line, where ready-mixed blended chocolate was poured over shortcake and candies of all descriptions. They watched caramels, creme fudges, eclairs; all hurling with a never ending rush towards a franking machine which expelled them with great velocity towards a shape-sorter, where it in turn propelled them onto vast trays that disappeared through an instant flash-cooler to the first hint of humanity lurking beyond the wall, the sorting and boxing room.

"Flash-cooling completes the task much faster, extends chocolate shelf-life and it will not melt as easily as ordinary chocolate, ideal for use by a soldier at the front, who would not like to eat soggy or soft chocolate. The best brains in Germany went into this process. This factory supplies German armed forces all over Europe with the best and longest-lasting chocolate."

Which confirmed Holmes' theory that Dr Laubscher's chocolate was army intended. It gave him no comfort to confirm his worst theory. He noted that they had not been allowed into the mixing section, for that was where the chocolate recipe would be blended, the cocaine introduced. The fiends.

It was just at this moment that Herr Flohn, then Holmes (who had stalled the discovery as long as he could) noticed Dr Watson was missing.

"But where is he? I thought he was behind you?" Herr Flohn demanded to know, obviously angry, turning to his guards and snapping, "Did you not see him go? He is at large, you dunderheads, don't look at me with amazement, he is gone, you were supposed to be the escorts."

"Perhaps we lost him at the last bend," Cornelia suggested stepping forward as if to go and look for him.

"No, no," Herr Flohn growled at her. Then suddenly realising the tone of his voice, softened. "No, my dear. The guards lost him, they must find him, they shall be severely reprimanded. This factory is not yet completed; you, yourself, fell down. Dr Watson could stumble – and who knows?" he indicated the myriad of chocolate processing machines, "who knows what flavour he might be by then?"

He laughed, a most cruel laugh and although Cornelia and Holmes joined in, they were singularly unamused by it and Cornelia's tummy gave her a queer turn as she eyed the chocolate for signs of tweed caramel or a fruit dip whipple with two fat bushy eyebrows and a pale grey moustache.

"Oh dear me, Dr Watson is so dithery these days, Herr Flohn. This morning he forgot his shoes. You must not be too cross with him, he is an old man."

Herr Flohn bowed to her. "No, no, my dear, I am not angry with any of my guests, it is my pleasure to have you here. But for the guards to lose one of you…" he indicated his throat and slid his finger across it.

He did not say any more, but if he had shouted, "off with their heads," she would not have been surprised.

Holmes made the most of the occasion to filch some more of the chocolates and proceeded to fill his pockets with several samples, rejecting the uncooled ones. He had a nervous moment when Herr Flohn inclined his head to whisper something into Cornelia's ear and he suddenly darted his eyes in Holmes' direction, catching him in the act of licking his fingers. But a quick reaction by Holmes and a muttered, "must stop biting my nails," hopefully forestalled any embarrassing enquiries.

At last shouts were heard, a great clatter of stomping feet barely touching the ground. The guards were taking Watson's arrest far too seriously yet, suspiciously, all three of the men had a tell-tale smudge of chocolate around their mouths. Watson had been apprehended when he was bodily removing some samples off a production line. He had finished taking pictures with his Brownie, and amazing pictures he thought them too, when the guards found him, a good hundred feet from where he was supposed to be. To cover his actions he had hastily swallowed an almond-ripple, confessing as much to the guards, who, much to his surprise, did precisely the same, one eating four in quick succession. Obviously the almond-ripple was a favourite. It was a conspiracy of thieves. They walked Watson back to the corner where they covered themselves by roughly picking him up under his arms and hauled him up before Herr Flohn.

Herr Flohn knew what had happened. An old man had been seduced by the chocolate, and it was unfortunate. Something would have to be done to

Dr Watson, confirming the carefully orchestrated objective. It was entirely regrettable that any chocolate had been eaten, but not yet a tragedy. Meanwhile he ranted and raved at the guards once more and accused them of all manner of treachery. Slightly overdoing it, Cornelia thought, looking Watson over and failing to spot the Brownie.

Watson himself was worried what the chocolate might be doing to his insides. He did not want to be bursting into song during the company lunch, that would not do at all. It vexed him greatly, the almond taste still on his tongue.

Holmes also had noted the Brownie was missing and he wondered how best to approach a polite enquiry.

Suddenly a great siren went off. Six female technicians rushed into the building waving their arms in alarm, dashing about switching off machinery, turning wheels, raising levers. They were followed by a very agitated older man, sporting a goatee beard, who immediately ran to the most prominent trouble spot and began to inspect a distant production line, much to all the guests' interest and Herr Flohn's distress.

Soon all was put to right. The machinery was restored to full working order and the bearded man went around the production lines eventually reaching Herr Flohn's tour with a large piece of chocolate in his hands, the size of two boxes of chocolate, an angry glare in his eyes.

"This must belong to one of your guests, Herr Flohn," holding it up for all to see.

Watson hung his head, he had failed again. Cornelia stifled a desire to laugh and Holmes, feeling downcast, stepped forward to claim it. "Dr Watson's Brownie has a frightfully regular bias to go missing, mein Herr, my apologies."

He handed the chocolate covered camera to Watson, who, it must be said, was quite impressed at the way the chocolate had set on his camera, enhancing the simple lines most attractively.

"I'm truly sorry," Watson began, "I got lost, I put it down momentarily. I didn't see that it was a conveyor belt."

Herr Flohn drew some satisfaction from the event, the film would have been spoiled. "No matter Dr Watson, it is a good job you are not an industrial spy, you would make a poor living."

Watson felt compelled to laugh, but it was a nervous titter that escaped his throat. From that moment on he resolved to be on best behaviour, yet he had seen, he had actually caught a glimpse of something the other side of the factory that he had tried to capture on film before the huge metal doors had closed. A vision of something altogether outside his comprehension, strange and monstrous, nothing less exotic and horrific than a dragon or the mythical Jabberwocky. It was in there with its scaly skin, breathing fire. He had only a glimpse, a mere half-second glimpse, but something had lurked there and whatever it was, it was not chocolate.

"I think it must be time for luncheon," Herr Flohn remarked when they reached the rows of chocolate packers. "And I'm not forgetting you'll be wanting some samples, Dr Watson. A gift box awaits you in my office, for all of you."

"Oh lovely," Cornelia rejoined. "I'm ravenous. All that chocolate has made my stomach ache with hunger. I could eat two whole boxes right now."

Holmes considered this unlikely, but admired Cornelia's enthusiasm.

Herr Flohn smiled, offering his arm once more. Holmes smiled at the ladies in the packing room, all of whom turned their heads to see the visitors. The face of one of the packers took Holmes by surprise and caught Watson's eye too. A young girl, poor to be sure, but identical to their own Cornelia. Perhaps someone with eyes less well-trained would not have spotted her; after all, the white uniform, the drudgery of the job, was hardly one to inspire the imagination or encourage one to substitute the natural radiance that was written in Cornelia's face. But it was identical nevertheless. The two men passed on into the welcome cold, midday air and thought briefly on the coincidence that was immediately creating possibilities for them not considered before.

Holmes found an opportunity to remove the chocolate from under his hat and stash it in his pockets, regretting the melted state of most of it. He turned to Herr Flohn as they approached a new building. "The entire factory produces chocolate in the same way?"

"Of course, Lord Holmes, although further along there is storage, repairs, a design centre and administration. A factory isn't just production lines. There must be systems, directives, but I can guarantee that this is the world's most modern plant, everything is here, all in one vast complex. I must point out that we are not yet at full capacity. When we are, we shall produce more chocolate here at this facility than all the factories of our enemies combined."

"An amazing quantity. Herr Flohn, you are to be congratulated."

"And Herr Melnick, too,' Herr Flohn added. "Without his dedication this factory would not function. We approach the executive canteen now."

"We will meet him, I hope in better circumstances," Holmes remarked, with what he hoped was the correct amount of interest. The Brownie episode had not augured well for such a meeting.

"Oh you shall, but he is a busy man, a very busy man."

But Holmes was very sure that his activity was not all connected with silver paper. He considered the whole thing about silver paper quite spurious.

Watson was quiet, wondering if his Brownie was ruined forever. He just seemed to trail along, a little overawed by all he had seen and growing anxious for his delicate stomach and brain since he had eaten the almond-ripple. The guard had eaten four. No doubt he did not mind in the least if he broke into the chorus from *The Pirates of Penzance* during his lunch. Watson fervently hoped he would be saved that embarrassment.

It was no surprise to them that the first person they met at the executive office reception was Herr Melnick, carrying an armful of heavy metal through a side door. It looked distinctly like platinum to Holmes' trained eye, the white-silver metal being quite distinctive.

Herr Melnick obviously did not expect their arrival and was embarrassed to be caught with the heavy metal ingots, looking at Herr Flohn to rescue him.

Herr Flohn was not perturbed however, inviting his guests into the conspiracy. "More silver for your smelter, Herr Melnick. It is so good to see your dedication to this silver paper problem." He turned to Holmes. "You see Lord Holmes, what English factory general manager would be so dedicated to this supply problem we have?"

Holmes had to agree. "The German general manager has a excellent disposition to his job, but then he is lucky enough to have the shining example of Herr Hitler to guide him."

This answer was well received and Herr Melnick's attitude definitely softened, perhaps overcoming the initial hostility incurred by the Brownie incident. Indeed, he even attempted a smile at Watson, despite the heavy load straining his arms. He spoke up, revealing a row of bad teeth;

"Perhaps Herr Doktor would like to purchase a superior German camera now his own is spoiled? I have a brother-in-law in the camera business and I'm sure he would be pleased to sell you a new Zeiss."

"I'd be pleased to meet him," Watson muttered, worried that his chocolate Brownie seemed to be setting quite hard.

"Goodrich Cameras is the name, mention my name. Incidentally, it would give me great pleasure if you would let me keep that camera you have, Herr Doktor. It will look fine in our display cabinet, quite a droll item."

Watson was immediately on guard, the film was still in there. Besides, he was also attached to the chocolate Brownie. If they got the film and exposed it (if it was not ruined already) he would be damned forever as a spy.

"I, er-er," he blabbered, confused, not at all sure how to avoid this debacle, all eyes upon him.

"Oh, no," Cornelia exclaimed. "Oh please don't let Herr Melnick have it, Herr Flohn, I was hoping that it would be our souvenir of your brilliant factory, oh please." She hung on Herr Flohn's arm and flashed her eyes, as convincing a performance of affection Holmes had not seen since Sarah Bernhardt had quit the stage. If he did not know better he would have sworn the girl was afflicted of the heart with the German industrialist.

Herr Flohn relented, squeezing Cornelia's hands.

"Of course my dear, if you want it, you shall have it. Herr Melnick, see that Dr Watson receives the official photographs of our factory. I would hate him to be without them."

"It shall be done," Herr Melnick replied, disappearing through the swing door with his heavy load, a loud crash came from within and cursing following very shortly which politeness forbade enquiry thereof.

"And now luncheon, may I take your hat Lord Holmes?"

"Of course, this tour has really been most interesting, Herr Flohn, most intriguing."

But as Holmes removed his hat, it was evident that he had neglected to remove all the chocolate from his head, one rather sticky slab remained on top. Cornelia let out a little shriek and Watson dropped the Brownie in surprise, which luckily distracted Herr Flohn's eyes from Holmes' head. Cornelia allowed a moan of disappointment about the camera, simultaneously jumping up towards Holmes' head, snatching off the offending chocolate as he instinctively bent down to retrieve bits of the camera.

Luckily Watson managed to expose the entire film (by affecting more total confusion and stepping on the end of the spool whilst pulling it all up off the floor). It was a remarkably smooth operation all round. With Watson clucking, "Oh no, all those pictures of the town." He shook his head at his own stupidity. "Holmes, you must think me a clumsy oaf indeed. Herr Flohn, you see before you a remnant of my former self, a toothless baboon, not worthy of anything but the dark closet of an old age home. I'm the clumsiest of fools and have ruined your Brownie, Miss Cornelia, please forgive me, please."

Cornelia was too worried about what to do with the piece of chocolate in her hand to worry over the shattered camera, but she knelt down beside the humbled Watson and winked. "Oh dear Dr Watson, you really are in a state today. But it is no matter. I cherished the camera it is true, but I'm just glad it isn't you down here on the floor. I think you must be in need of your lunch."

"Yes," Herr Flohn declared, much irritated by Watson's apparent stupidity. "Let's have lunch, we have guests to meet and I have business to attend to."

"Of course," said Holmes, "we would not dream of keeping you from your business, not dream of it."

And so they passed through the doors to the executive canteen. Holmes was burning with the question of the need for platinum; Watson still worried about his contact with the monster lurking in the factory and Cornelia, still with chocolatey hands, found herself unable to fend off Herr Flohn's touches and suggestions that were most personal, most personal indeed.

There were two impressions instantly imprinted upon their minds as they entered the executive canteen. The first was that it was immense, lavish, most ultra-modern and the second, it had the most spectacular view of the whole of Nürnberg, falling away in the distance, sweeping up to the Castle dominating all. The view also took in a wall close by, belonging to another, older warehouse building and carrying an advertisement for the new chocolate factory's closest rival, imploring people to buy *Fine Almond Elisen Spiced Cake... Haeberlein-Metzger...* a portrait of Kaiser Maxmilian 1 finely reproduced on the wall. Herr Helnick saw them looking at the portrait.

"They won't last," he announced with a sneer. "Our cakes are better than their's. They won't last. We can bake two thousand cakes to their one, soon *Haeberlein-Metzger* will just be a memory, their 13ozs tins a collectors' item, no more than that."

"People must change with the times I suppose," Holmes remarked. "The traditional ways no longer profitable."

"Besides," Herr Melnick added, "we have the entire Bavarian chocolate supply sown up. They will be forced to use substitutes. We will not, we will bake only the best. It is the only way. The German soldier expects it. Soon we shall build another factory in Peenemund, Denmark."

This was a revealing remark. Holmes wondered if this was an unintentional slip, that here was a clue to Denmark's destiny. Hitler intended to grab that kingdom too. He ignored the boast and said, "Still it is good to have a rival to keep you on your toes, eh Herr Melnick? But then you have all the silver paper, they obviously do not. I was interested to hear of all your activities in the town. Is there really such a shortage?"

It was a leading question. Herr Melnick looked to another man, one of the Berlin guests for assistance, but none came. "In war..." he struggled, his English suddenly faltering "...lines of communications...uncertainties of supply, we must stockpile..." His face was red with the effort. Holmes was amused at the obvious attempt to lie, hide the real reason. His suspicions were already aroused.

Cornelia returned from washing her hands and was about to enter into some light frivolous luncheon banter with the Berlin guests, some of whom were keen to meet her, when quite suddenly the air was filled with the most awful screaming sound which seemed to rip through the very factory. The windows began to rattle, the whole building began to shake, people began to raise hands to their ears experiencing real pain. The scream was building with such force on the floor, each man and woman vibrated with it. A deafening crescendo blasted and assailed them from all sides.

"What is it," Watson asked, hands over his ears, fearful of his eardrums bursting.

Herr Flohn was plainly seething with anger and he stalked out of the room towards a sign which read Telephonieren. No one could hear a word anyone was shouting, Herr Melnick had already raced out of the room to see what the problem was, his face having turned deathly white at the sound of it. The piercing scream seemed to come from the depths of the factory, seemed to ooze out of the walls and it continued at this roaring, high-pitched caterwaul for several minutes, alarming every living soul in the room, quite uniting them in real, tangible fright. Cornelia still had an image in her mind of Herr Melnick's pale face, his hair standing practically on end, his eyes set in an exact imitation of sheer panic.

Now Holmes saw things more clearly. With platinum, silver, noises the like of which he had never experienced before, the ashen face of Herr Flohn, he knew that he owed it to England, owed it to himself, to investigate the source of that noise, if not immediately, then later, in private.

Watson was convinced it was a dragon, albeit that it was against logic for a dragon to be made of metal, but it was a terrifying noise, filled with pain, straining to the outer limits of endurance. It was urgent that he convey to Holmes what he had seen, a private word, but it was impossible while all eyes were upon them.

Cornelia had her fingers in her ears and stood against a wall afraid the ceiling might crash in, not able to comprehend the screaming at all, wondering if it was not some sort of bomb or automatic machine that had gone out of control readying to explode any minute?

Abruptly the noise abated. Herr Flohn re-emerged, nervous perspiration covering his brow and his hands, his mouth steadying a nervous tremble as he sought the right words to excuse the screaming, the shock of which still rang in their ears. "Gentlemen... Er Fraulein Cornelia, there has been a sort of... accident. Our smelter, sudden water contamination has led to an explosion. I am very sorry but I have to attend. I am very sorry, but please, each your luncheon. It is unfortunate, but accidents do happen."

"Of course," Holmes told him, sympathetically, "is there anything we can do?"

Herr Flohn shook his head. "No, no. I must go. Now please Lord Holmes accept my apologies, do not forget to take your chocolates, compliments of this factory, and my chauffeur will drive you back to your hotel after lunch."

Obviously much distraught and most angry, he disappeared leaving the three English facing a wall of indomitable Germans.

The Berlin guests were staying at the Nazi Party Palace on the Party Estate, the Reichsparteitaggelande, the Fuhrer's showpiece, almost an entire city outside the city. It was fortunate for the visiting party that the Reich's Fuhrer had no need for a winter rally. Nürnberg would have been intolerable, overburdened, awash with Brownshirts anxious to overplease, SS officers strutting about, as was the custom, abusing the local, peace-loving, population. More than once on this trip, Holmes had remarked that he found it strange that Bavaria, a normally hospitable place, known for its civility, should be the host to the Nazi party. To him it was an incongruity.

The Germans sought to find a topic of conversation as distant from the terrifying scream of the smelter explosion as possible. But no one was fooled. No smelter that any of them knew about sounded anything like a scream. A hiss yes, but a scream? Certainly not for a continuous five minutes. It was a subject all were crying to discuss, but like the last passengers on the *Titanic*, the rising water was something best ignored in the vain hope it might go away.

To Cornelia's mind it had sounded like a volcano, not that she had ever heard one explode, especially in a chocolate factory. Holmes was now impatient, aware of only two things. He wanted to get back to the hotel to think and take a bath, remove the chocolate from his head and pockets.

"You have visited Der Burg?" A bloated Berliner inquired, inviting the English visitors to partake of a chilled Riesling, his nearest companion heaping a huge pile of chicken mayonnaise on a silver plate for his own consumption.

Watson's eyes grew as large as saucers as he stared at the mounting food.

"The five cornered tower is most interesting," the German pointed out, "I have a copy of the *Torturer's Handbook* if you'd like to borrow it."

"Ja, ja," another Berliner enthused, "the Iron Maiden is one of the best examples I have seen."

Cornelia didn't want to discuss tortures or torturers. She wanted to eat lunch without being regaled on the delights of torn, smouldering flesh. She had been forced to read Foxe's *Book Of Martyrs* once and that was quite enough.

Luncheon was eaten, forgotten, a hurried event, despite the amount of it. Every man and Cornelia wanted to be somewhere else, the constraints of keeping face a genuine torture for all of them. At last the chauffeur came to collect them. Holmes left the Berliners with a friendly shake of hands having, as far as Cornelia could tell, persuaded the men that Britain sought accommodation, a guaranteed right to exist. Poland was a lost cause after all. How Holmes could say things completely contrary to his nature was beyond her, but earned him yet more of her respect and admiration.

It was apparent to her though that the Germans had no opinions of their own, other than what their Bible, *Mein Kampf*, had told them. There was no deviation. She heard the same phrases from everyone. No concern that democracy seemed to have been abandoned to a token rump, a rubber stamping parliament. Seated in the car as they swept out between the iron factory gates, Holmes remarked:

"The German citizen would rather salute a uniform than be bothered with a vote. They are sheep. Herr Flohn is a man of vision, but his partners are mere zombies, Cornelia. It defies logic, but it seems more than just sinister to me that from the lowly man in the street to the highest industrialist and officers in the SS, they have all abandoned thought, imagination, individuality for a set of values that makes Hades seem like an attractive London garden suburb. Adolf Hitler is a popular man, he appears not to have an enemy in the whole of Germany, yet I suspect he is thoroughly disliked by his friends."

"Hear, hear," Watson agreed, shivering slightly in the sharp air, the car's heater barely perceptible.

"And as for you, Watson," Holmes said, bringing his attention to bear upon his bumbling friend, "I believe you know more about this strange smelter of their's than you have lead us to believe so far. I saw your eyes back there in the factory. I can read you like an open book. Out with it man. What did you see when you got lost?"

But Watson shook his head, pointing to the glass partition, partially open. Holmes noted it and signaled that he would wait until they reached the hotel, even though they knew the chauffeur could not speak English.

It was the most unbearable journey all three had ever endured, but at last it ended and at half past three in the afternoon they were deposited back at Der Deutsche Hof with their box of chocolates, some four hours before the Wagner concert was due to begin.

There was much to do, much to think about and chocolate to be sampled.

***

"No, a final time, NO!" Cornelia asserted, stamping her foot. "I won't eat any of their chocolate ever again."

Holmes was irritated at her intransigence, but could hardly blame her for refusing. "Look Cornelia, we have been given samples, we do not know if they are actually from the Nürnberg factory, we must verify that fact. Now with these samples I have collected from the production line, we know for sure that they are the genuine article. Watson has already eaten one with no ill effect, but I'm assuming it takes six or perhaps a steady diet to give the required dosage. All I want you to eat is two chocolates. I know from experience that if there is the slightest residue of the drug in these chocolates (which we must assume there is), then you will experience similar symptoms of light-headedness, but none of the power of the last chocolate you ate. You have my word on that."

Cornelia's gaze met Holmes' intense blue eyes, searched his face for sympathy but found none. His hands were firmly implanted in his blue dressing gown pockets, his impatience all too evident. This was for science. Holmes was merely an instrument of science, she a helpless laboratory mouse.

Watson sat in the corner with his sketchbook trying to reconstruct the scene he had witnessed through the factory's sliding metal doors, affecting great flourish with his pencil and rubber, his tongue pressed hard up against his top lip.

Cornelia sighed. "All right, but under protest, Lord Holmes. I do not care if I never eat another piece of chocolate as long as I live."

"Good girl," Holmes said warmly, holding up a partially melted piece of chocolate covered nougat. "You eat this and I shall busy myself with the identical ones in their sample pack."

Sighing, resigned to her wretched fate, Cornelia ate the chocolates. She sat down in the only armchair and waited for the worst to begin, watching Holmes taking chocolate samples from the gift pack to his makeshift test bench, dissolving items bit by bit, boiling off substances in candle heated test tubes, blackened and immensely hot, the inevitable fumes filling the air.

Holmes saw her studying him and nodded to her, knowing she sought explanations. Getting up from the table, he walked over to the radio set turning it up louder, making sure the rug they had stuffed under it to smother the microphone was secure. It was. He knew they would not hear anything through that and was amused by the thought that each time they left the room the microphone would work perfectly, recording hours of brass band music.

He went back to his test bench, pouring off some of the boiling liquid through a gauze, exposing some to acids and some to litmus papers.

"This chocolate is very similar to the samples Dr Laubscher gave us," he confirmed at last, looking directly at Cornelia. "In these two test tubes I have still boiling, I have the chocolate you are eating at this moment."

Cornelia gulped, looking inward a moment to see if she was experiencing any weird sensations, failing to find anything untoward as yet except mild indigestion from the heavy lunch.

"Personally I hope it's mildly active," Watson chirped from the window. "I could do with another selection from Cole Porter. This military nonsense on the radio is quite nauseating after a while."

"Agreed," Holmes said, "but if it puts you off radio, Watson, let it play on."

"Cole Porter?" Cornelia asked, not following the conversation very well.

But Holmes ignored her query. "I'm convinced that chocolate is not the only thing they make at that factory. Everything points towards manufacture of some large metal object and I think we can safely dismiss trains, boats, anything of the normal run of the mill contraptions. They would not resort to disguising a factory that uses precious metals without good reason."

"You suppose their chocolate dwarves, the Nibelungs, could be a new fangled grenade covered in chocolate to fool us all?" Watson remarked.

Holmes shook his head, there was nothing so obvious as that going on in the factory, but something secret was going on, he was sure of it.

"It was a calamitous mistake for them that their smelter, so called, had to play up during lunch. Most embarrassing I'd say. It's a funny thing too, but I could swear it sounded like a turbine out of control, not in the least like a smelter, though it's revealing enough to know they have their own smelter, that they do not contract out for silver-paper. A most self-sufficient factory, don't you think? Unnecessarily so."

"Indeed," Cornelia agreed, "so thoroughly automatic it is a wonder that they have not invented a machine that eats chocolate as well."

Watson let out an enormous guffaw. "I say that's a pretty smart comment, my girl. Chocolate eating machines, ridiculous."

"Not so," Holmes replied, "Remember Southsea Station, Watson? Five years ago? Our trip to the sea?"

Watson thought hard for a moment, then exclaimed in sudden remembrance.

"Jove yes, Holmes. The dreaded penny swallower. Quite a mystery there Miss Cornelia, quite a mystery. The chocolate machine, Nestlés, don't you know, would swallow a penny and patently refuse to cough up the goods. Gawd knows how many people it caught before Holmes. But he complained after threepence had disappeared into the mouth of this villainous machine."

"It was monstrous, my dear," Holmes continued, impassioned. "I exposed an entire crooked little empire of dwarves who actually stood inside these machines every day for the best part of a year. Soon as a penny went into the slot, it found its way into their pockets, not an ounce of chocolate was given over, unless it was a station employer who would be certain to protest. Imagine it. Six machines on every main station in London and all down the line to Portsmouth Harbour, a dwarf in practically all of them. I exposed that pretty sharpish, I can tell you."

"The Southern Railway Company gave Holmes and I free tickets for six months as a reward, but we found very little enjoyment in Southsea; quite impossible to walk on the pebbles and the public houses are a disgrace. Ruffians everywhere. I recall we saw a wonderful production of *An Ideal Husband* at the New Theatre Royal with Michael Wilding and the lovely Dulcie Gray. Quite a gal, but even so, Portsmouth quickly runs out of charm."

"Quite," Holmes agreed, closing the subject. "Any results yet, Cornelia?" She shook her head. "I must confess, none at all."

Holmes studied her face a moment then nodding to himself he brought his fist down hard on the table, shaking everything. "Then it is just as I thought, Watson. Something's afoot and I think at the bottom of it there lies three damn fools!"

"Fools?" Watson enquired, finishing off his sketch, hoping it was as exact as he remembered it, taking pride in his skills as an artist (not inconsiderable, as his anatomical sketches made fifty-eight years before reveal).

"There, Holmes, come and see my monster."

"No horns I hope, Watson," Holmes queried, walking over to the window.

"No horns," Watson replied with a smile, feeling a little foolish now the fear of the monster had subsided, exorcised by the drawing of it.

He recalled momentarily a night more than fifty years before when he thought he had seen the legendary Dartmoor Hound, the spectral black dog. Holmes had found a logical enough explanation then, he felt sure he would find one now.

Holmes regarded the pencil drawing made by Watson most closely, scrutinising every detail. He cast himself in Watson's fear-filled shoes, attaching the incredible mechanical scream to the image before him; impressed with the execution of the drawing, lost in conjecture, unaware of the keen eyes of both Cornelia and Watson upon him, awaiting his opinion. "You've done well, Watson. This is no monster, but it is monstrous."

At length Holmes took the drawing to the fire and in silence all three watched it burn and continued staring until the last sparks and shimmering carbon ash had floated away up the chimney.

Cornelia could tell Watson was upset, but years of such treatment from Holmes had dulled his protests. However, Holmes had his methods and it would be foolish to be caught with such a drawing in their room.

"Dr Laubscher is a fraud," announced Holmes suddenly. "I am convinced of it. Tonight we shall prove it, or Sherlock Holmes is not my name."

A loud percussion roll on the radio announced the usual *Horst Wessel* chorus and the news was expected. That *Horst Wessel* should be so sanctified was the most degrading aspect of this perverse country to Holmes' mind. One of the most degrading, the list was endless.

"Explain," Watson demanded, getting over the loss of his sketch, looking to Cornelia for sympathy.

"Explain, Watson? That would be a hard task even for a magician, but I'm telling you that Herr Doktor Laubscher takes us for fools and worse, we have shown every sign of being perfectly cast, better suited than Harold Lloyd or Laurel and Hardy."

"Strong words, Holmes," Watson remarked, not at all sure he liked the expression on Holmes' face. A dark cloud had settled there, make no mistake about it.

"Why is the chocolate we stole from the factory exactly what it claims to be, Cornelia?"

Cornelia started. "How do you mean?"

"It is just plain chocolate, that is what I mean. Chocolate that you or I could eat until the cows come home without much effect other than an overabundance of caffeine-like substances in our system. Dr Laubscher stated that this factory was producing chocolate to his recipe for the army. Thus we manufactured an entire theory that centered on South America and the blockading of cocaine and coca nibs. Did we or did we not conjure up that idea, Watson?"

"Yes Holmes, we did. The second front, the great South American war. It's a stunner, our troops will enjoy a holiday or two in Trinidad, but I'm willing to bet that the war office will find it all hard to believe. Probably only do so on production of evidence and your infallible word."

"Precisely, Watson, precisely. My word is infallible. All of Whitehall will testify to it. As for evidence, we have it in abundance; the chocolate Herr Hitler eats and this newly manufactured, neatly packaged box right here on the table, laced with the purest cocaine."

"Yet my chocolate had none in it," Cornelia interjected.

"Excellent, now your brains are working again." He paced the room, excitement mounting within him and his observers. "The world is full of the duped and the dupers. I could happily go back to our First Lord and persuade him of the urgency of a mission in South America, the instant diversion of troops, ships, submarines into that area. He would be appalled to hear of ruthless German soldiers marching on such a drug-filled diet, the knowledge of it would strike fear into any British soldier's heart. Inhuman, robotlike, machines marching on Belgium or Paris. The world would shudder. But what have we really got here?" There was no answer.

"We have plain, perfectly ordinary, not even excellent Nürnberg chocolate. You have both eaten it and there is no ill effect. It suggests to me that our Dr Laubscher is a liar and if he is a liar, this chocolate is deliberately put our way."

"Then that is what they want us to believe," Cornelia finished for him. "Oh Lord Holmes, it's a bluff, they've played us as finely as a deck of cards."

"Exactly, whether Herr Hitler eats that chocolate, or not, the whole fantastic idea has been blown out of all proportion, to achieve what ends?"

"To frighten Britain," Watson offered, "because, by golly, I was frightened."

"You are half-way right, Watson, but you do not pursue your fear far enough. Imagine if we had left tomorrow, taken back this contaminated chocolate, persuaded the First Lord to act in South America, deploy all forces in the southern hemisphere, send in team after team of saboteurs to enter German territory and blow up chocolate factories, warehouses, plantations. Think of the calamity, Watson, England denuded, drained of its soldiers, its Navy, its submarines..."

"It would be wide open for attack, the Hun could sail from Hamburg or Cadiz under the cover of darkness and by the morning all of our ports from Portsmouth to Folkestone would be in German hands, they could march on London and all would be lost!" Watson took in an emotional breath. "Oh my goodness Holmes, we could have destroyed an Empire, done Hitler's job for him, paved the way for the first conquerors in England since 1066. Our names would be mud for evermore. The calamity of it. They had us duped, befuddled, to think we could have ever thought a war could be fought over chocolate."

Holmes, his face drawn tight, the muscles exposed under the thin flesh nodded in agreement.

"The position is, if chocolate is NOT what this war is about, why, Watson, why did four good men, which includes Cornelia's father, die?"

Cornelia stood up suddenly. "To fetch you Lord Holmes, my father died to fetch you." She was plainly excited and the words tumbled from her trembling lips. "I always went fishing with Papa, Lord Holmes, I know all about fishing. You use bait to catch fish and smaller fish to catch the big ones."

"Your father was no small fish," Watson interjected.

"No indeed, Dr Watson, but Lord Holmes is a very large fish indeed."

"Enough of fish. Pish fish." Holmes declared.

"But after you have caught your fish Lord Holmes, you always refer to the one who got away and it gets bigger with the telling, until it is easily the largest fish that ever lived. They attracted my father with three small bait then to give the whole story much more credence , then they killed my poor father too. Now the First Lord sits up and takes notice, he sees four of his best agents have perished trying to obtain this secret, each time the name of Dr Laubscher is prominent, each time he gets word out that he is still willing, the big lie assumes a greater importance with each agent that dies."

"Perhaps I should retire," Holmes remarked, quite genuinely amazed. "You are perfectly logical young Cornelia. One can indeed see how we were drawn into the maw of this giant salmon."

"Salmon?" Watson asked confused.

"Nürnberg is a city of great significance to the Nazi party, it's symbolic and perhaps almost amusing that we should be intended for sacrifice on the altar of their lies and deceits. You are right, Cornelia. We are the big fish and their aim is to get us to swallow a big lie, take it home and ensure England's total defeat and enslavement."

Watson understood this all right. He shook his head and felt a sudden desire for a good whisky and began to search for his flask.

"One wonders at their confidence," Holmes confided in them, his brain churning in turmoil, searching every avenue for possible alternatives. "Yet one has to remember their absolute faith that they can make no mistakes. No other city would have done for this scheme, not even Munich. It had to be Nürnberg, for here is the Party Estate, here is this chocolate maker, Hitler's personal chocolate maker. (I'm inclined to believe that part of this story is true at least, but doubt if even the Fuhrer could stand such a high dose as poor Cornelia suffered). The tour of the chocolate factory was necessary too, to convince us of the total strategy of this chocolate perversion. No factory in England is so vast, so all encompassing, so indomitable. We were impressed, we are impressed. We know that six of these factories exist already, a seventh planned. Are all these to produce chocolate? Well I think yes and no. They will all be chocolate factories, an innocent party in an evil masquerade. Lurking behind the gentle brown ooze is something more sinister, horrific, world shattering and they do not mean us to discover it."

"But I saw it," Watson declared, finding his flask at last.

"Yes, Watson, but the planning that has gone into this is remarkable. They know chocolate factories are not strategic targets, the British won't bomb them, even if they believed our story in London, the attacks would have gone to source in South America. We, in England, always play by the rules. If we make a weapon, we manufacture it in a weapons factory, or, at second best in a Rover or Austin works, whichever.

"The Germans, cunning fiends that they are, conceal their secret devices in chocolate factories and it is sheer ill luck that today something should chose to go wrong and they lost track of Watson. I must congratulate you both in enabling that to happen, your fall was splendid, Cornelia. Your drawing, Watson an admirable feat. I do not know what it is, but I can tell you that I am not leaving Nürnberg until I know exactly what that foul machine is and what it is meant to do. England's survival depends upon it, mark my words."

"A tank perhaps?" Watson asserted, "some kind of giant machine that could roar across the ground, terrify our soldiers."

"But you say it belched fire," Cornelia remembered, wishing she could have a drop of whisky too.

"Indeed, Cornelia, my dear. It shook and blasted hot flame, never have I been so frightened. Men were running in all directions, so confused were they."

"A long cylindrical object, heavy, made with precious metals, it baffles me." Holmes admitted. "Perhaps you are right Watson. A machine designed to scare men to death. We have to get into that factory, we must photograph that monster of yours, Watson."

"But my Brownie," he protested.

"That man's brother-in-law owned a camera shop. A Zeiss," Cornelia reminded him.

"I'll get onto it right away."

"Good man. Now we must ready ourselves for Richard Wagner. Cornelia you know your orders with Dr Laubscher. By all accounts we must leave the Germans with the impression that we are glad to leave tomorrow, that we believe in Dr Laubscher's information completely. It is clear to me now that the entire journey was planned by them from the very beginning. Their beckoning fingers reach as far as London itself. Perhaps even the invitation to me to attend this concert was just part of a well orchestrated scheme guided by Herr Flohn and his associates. It is as if they pull the strings of Whitehall from here."

"The First Lord wasn't to know you had an invitation," Watson remarked.

"No Watson, but I wonder who prompted him to remember us eh? Who have the Nazis got in Whitehall? That is what we have to consider, what mole lurks there setting up the most famous trap of all time?"

"You don't think there's a spy in Whitehall? Never, Holmes."

"Yes, Watson, we cannot eliminate the idea. The fifth column has always lurked as a spectre in British affairs. Remember Admiral Wolkoff of the Russian Tea Room? If our suspicions are correct he leads a nest of spies with direct connections to Whitehall. Our journey here is part of some grand master plan to invade England without meeting resistance. To think that it might have worked irks me dreadfully. We will take what Dr Laubscher has to offer, but we must gain entry to the factory."

"You have a plan?" Cornelia asked.

"A simple device," Holmes replied modestly. "Tomorrow morning we leave Nürnberg as planned in our Opel car. No doubt we shall be followed, but we shall take the Bayreuth road and, if I'm not mistaken, pass by a secondhand car lot. If we drive fast and with verve, we should outrun our escorts momentarily, giving us time to park in the car lot (quickly removing our luggage) assuming the air of a car on sale. After they have gone by we shall simply trade in our Opel for something older and less conspicuous, returning back to Nürnberg at night. There we shall drive to the factory, gain entry by way of the warehouse roof next door and then we shall see what this mystery is all about."

"I'm not sure I'm up to climbing rooftops, Holmes."

Holmes nodded sympathetically. "You will not be expected to, my dear fellow, but you will be in the field behind the factory with your car. Cornelia will be climbing with me and the new camera." He laughed suddenly well pleased with events. "This is a new adventure, Watson. Not chocolate, it never pleased me that my career should end up in the heart of a caramel fudge. But a genuine, fire breathing monster, by jove, we are on to something here, I know we are." He clapped his hands, stirring Watson. "Watson, the camera man. Cornelia help me put away the test tubes and then you will go and buy a few things we will need for tomorrow. Our work has only just begun."

But all was not to go so smoothly.

11

Twilight with the Gods

All the best of Nürnberg society was present. There was a tide of exhuberance and jostling eagerness that was rare in a musical audience known for their more reserved, funeral reverence for what should be, after all, a celebration of what is the highest form of art and expression. Richard Wagner, in Nürnberg, his *Siegfried* and *The Valkyrie* were the pinnacle of that astonishing capability of heart, mind and soul, the music written expressly for the birth of Nietzche's *Superman* – no matter Wagner and Nietzsche's subsequent disagreement. Music that equalled the power of Thor's celestial choir, perhaps even excelled all the music that had ever been written before. The orchestration of every nerve in the body to a sensory orgasm, becoming the very breath you breathe.

Society had come together as gods to bathe in the glory of Valhalla, worship at the shrine erected to themselves, the swastica surrounding them in acknowledgement of the growing power, a symbol to the world that the prophesies had come true. At last the gods have been reborn on earth, in Germany. Today, this day, the rules were changed for a thousand years, nay, for all time. The day of reckoning was still ahead for those who opposed, but as in the days when the legends were still being made, there could be no mercy. Mercy was a signal of weakness.

"Here walk the gods," Holmes whispered, as he sat down and stared up at the giant podium where the orchestra would soon play. "This is a great moment, Watson, a great moment."

Watson was silent, overawed by the enormous concert hall, built for ten thousand persons and filled to the very roof with every dignitary, every officer, all the right people of Nürnberg and beyond. A hive of activity and waves swept between people from either side of the hall; suppressed laughter, repressed coughing.

"It's astonishing, Holmes, I doubt even the Albert Hall could get this many people in it, and certainly not to a Wagner concert."

"This will be a good night, Watson. I never thought this ambition of mine would ever come true, but here we are in Nürnberg and there's a good cause into the bargain." Holmes leant back and observed the audience. They had the best seats in the house, their company the elite of the town. Almost the entire officers' corps of the SS and their wives, lovers, boyfriends and, naturally, the Berlin contingent they had met at lunch, some of whom noticed Holmes and nodded in a friendly way. Cornelia's seat was empty. She, attired in newly pressed nurse's uniform, was attending to last minute details, without which, plans would most surely fail. She had lost her programme, in fact all the programmes and in a panic was back in the foyer to obtain three new ones. She was amused to catch a glimpse of their usual escorts dressed in the unfamiliar dress suit, looking most awkward, trying to hide behind a pillar so she would not notice them. No night off for them, but there was no chance Holmes would be anywhere else, nothing would keep him from his Wagner.

She was escorted back to her seat by a young girl, a brown-shirted pretty fifteen year old who marched with a certain over-important style in front of Cornelia, showing her to her seat by pointing at it with such a severe expression on her face. It reminded Cornelia of detention at school and quite filled her with dread for a good five minutes thereafter.

Watson was asleep already and snoring!

Holmes had a cure however (for he detested snoring) and produced a feather from his top pocket with which he began to tickle the palm of Watson's right hand.

Watson sat bolt upright, blinking in astonishment. "By jove, don't tell me it's over, Holmes. Don't tell me I've missed the whole damn concert."

Cornelia laughed, amazed at how well the feather trick worked.

Holmes, knowing Watson's habits of old did not restore the feather to his top pocket, but kept it primed ready for the concert proper. Wagner could be stirring, but it was also a powerful drug for a perfect nap and Watson was ever prone to one of those.

It was at that moment Holmes caught sight of Dr Laubscher, who sat, by some miracle, only four rows to the left of them. But it was obvious from the way he rigidly kept his face in the opposite direction that he knew where the Holmes party were located and pointedly did not want to be associated with them in any way.

The orchestra began to come onstage and the English party prepared themselves for the inevitable propaganda and salute to the Fuhrer that preceded gatherings of any kind. It was no comfort to know that Wagner would have probably wanted it so.

The programme was the legendary opera *Lohengrin*, which was fine by Holmes and a relief to Watson who had feared it might be *Parsifal*, not one of his favourites. From the moment the conductor came out onto the podium stage right, the atmosphere was electric and with the last thirty seconds to go, ten thousands throats and noses were cleared, for no one wanted a weekend in a concentration camp, guilty of desecration, there were few more heinous crimes.

It began. Watson, dozing, missed the singer's entrance, saw no swan, heard nothing.

So there remained only the interval and the promised exchange. Cornelia was nervous. If Holmes was right and they meant for this information to reach them, all well and good, if they did not and Dr Laubscher was risking his neck, all eyes would be upon her and perhaps him. As it was Herr Flohn's eyes burned into her from two rows back and she had received invitations from three SS Officers to a rendezvous after the concert. Even while she sat there next to her companions, the notes were appearing miraculously in her shoes from time to time.

As the hall broke into a tumult of applause, the walls reverberating with shock, people leapt up all around to escape the inevitable rush and make it down the aisle to the bar before the slowest clogged the aisles.

Cornelia was up and already being swept along by the tide, carried by an impatient aggressive mob, charged by the music and whether by intent or coincidence, she found herself walking between Herr Flohn and the dreaded Dr Laubscher. Here was a dilemma. Were the men in league or not? It was an uncomfortable moment. She did not know what to do, worse Herr Flohn had his hand pressed firmly upon her behind in a most intimate manner, making good use of the skin-tight nurses' uniform; the pressing crowd so tight and crushing that he could have undressed her there and then and not a soul would have noticed or done a thing to stop him. Dr Laubscher smiled at her and she at him, using her free hand to try and prise off the lecherous industrialist's hand from her bruised derriere. No privacy for code words either.

"It was a superb concert don't you think, Herr Doktor," Herr Flohn remarked, thus acknowledging he knew the doctor, "allow me to introduce you to Fraulein Shand, a visitor from England."

"Oh really?" The doctor replied, "this is a rarity. A welcome from Nürnberg, my dear, you have chosen Germany's finest city to visit."

"I know, it is breathtaking," she replied, "this hall, it is so big, it is a miracle that such a large roof can hold up. *Lohengrin* suits it well."

"Ah I'm so glad you like it." Herr Flohn purred, "this was a recent project by my company, the largest cantilevered roof in all the world. The acoustics are rather fine don't you think, doctor?"

By now Herr Flohn was standing ahead of Cornelia, his hand placed behind him in what could only be described as an affrontery to decency itself, a licentious intimacy that she could do nothing about and made all the worse by those who pressed from behind. A man shouted a greeting to Herr Flohn who turned to hail him back. As he turned, a nervous but efficient Dr Laubscher whisked her programme out of her left hand and substituted his own, a speedy and precise operation, made only just in time for they arrived at the foyer and (much to Cornelia's relief) Herr Flohn could no longer take advantage of her. Indeed, both he and Dr Laubscher quickly vanished from her side, leaving her with the only safe recourse, the ladies' room, to which she fled, preferring the queue there to any bad manners from the German industrialist.

Even in the ladies' room bad manners persisted as queue jumpers, SS wives, claimed cubicles ahead of others and the language was an education in itself. But at last, her own turn came and she rushed in, shut the door, opening the programme. Inside were four typed sheets of information on the flimsiest of paper which she immediately folded into a very tight bundle and inserted into the safest place, her brassiere, remembering to keep the programme on her, which would be expected by those observing her. She found her nervousness gone with the accomplishment of the mission and she congratulated herself on a job well done. It was not unlike exchanging secret messages at school, the same thrill was there.

She got back to her seat only seconds before the house lights went down and she had a sense of accomplishment about her she had not experienced before. She felt part of Sherlock Holmes' world in a real and intimate way now, really part of them and the exhilaration of it combined with Wagner's music was such that she was quite overwhelmed and in a state of euphoria for the remainder of the concert. This was in marked contrast to Watson who slept through the entire second half; Holmes allowing it only as long as he did not snore.

In the end, with one glorious finale, in the full glow of the music, Cornelia was one with Holmes who staggered to his feet with the ten thousand and roared his delight, his heart filled with emotion, his eyes misty like never before. As if he sensed Cornelia's new found love of Wagner, he reached out for her hand as they stood watching the bows being taken and gently squeezed it, a flow of energy and affection exchanging between them both as father to daughter, as teacher and pupil. A moment she would always remember.

***

It was almost as if they had returned from an arduous day planting the last rows of a huge potato crop. Holmes and Watson were plainly quite exhausted, the mental and physical exertions of the day had drained every last vestige of energy out of them and even though charged with the Wagner spirit, nothing would persuade either of them to attend the reception afterwards. Holmes did apologise in person to the conductor and thank him for a brilliant performance. Holmes also refused to allow Cornelia to attend the reception by herself. This was no vindictive spoil-sport decision, but mere security. She could not be left alone, there were too many lusting eyes and straying hands.

And it must be admitted, Cornelia herself did not wish to attend for the same reasons, having had her bottom pinched, fondled and bruised quite enough in her country's cause.

So three weary, but elated English folk took themselves off to their hotel and by midnight were all safely in their bedrooms looking forward to a good night's rest while the snow once again fell softly outside, covering a multitude of sins.

Cornelia closed and locked her door behind her and with relief shed her nurse's uniform as quickly as she could, wondering if there was any hot water for a bath.

She looked into the mirror for signs of damage to her delicate flesh, relieved her behind seemed to be taking the wear and tear. Her body, slim and quite firm, stood up well to examination, even if the lack of bruises did not bode well for any attempt on her part to aspire to royal blood, if the princess and pea episode was to be taken seriously.

Suddenly she decided that she really did want a bath and she went to her cupboard to get a dressing gown. She opened the door, turning to the bed to see if her slippers were under there or not when two hands lunged out at her, encircling her throat so tightly that faint was instantly near, as she turned naked and petrified to face her attacker.

Herr Döre! She would have screamed but for the tight hold on her soft, white throat. She would have died if not for the pain.

This was a different, horrible – more horrible than can be acceptably brought to the page – face than it had ever been before. His lip, swollen, bloated, twisted; a large scab as long as three inches, cut a swathe from his nose to his chin. He was a monster and his bloodshot eyes stared crazily at her, as he dragged her almost lifeless body to the bed. He let go of her throat, but still Cornelia could not scream. She lay in abject terror, her own hands at her throat trying to soothe the intense pain his pincer-like fingers had induced there.

"So at last I have you my pretty wench," Herr Döre sneered (but to tell the truth the words fell out a mumble for speech was almost past him). "You'll pay for your frivolous behaviour, you'll regret the day you ever snubbed Herr Dore." His hands fondled her roughly, his clothes stank of oil. Cornelia already regretted it. Her wits were returning. If she wished to be free, to go unravished by this creature, this crazed monstrosity, then she had to scream, she had to – naked or not – run to her door and escape, even though her legs were weak with fear.

She made as if to faint, then with the speed of light she bounced off the bed and ran to the door, grabbing the key to turn the lock screaming, "Help! help, please help," her eyes streaming with angry tears.

"Oh no you don't," cried Herr Döre, jumping up after her, a snarl of hatred in his throat.

Cornelia couldn't open the door. "Help," she screamed again.

Then suddenly the stars burst in confusion all around her head and she fell, sinking fast into a deep, dark well of unconsciousness, claimed by the waiting arms of her abductor, his twisted lip breaking into a smug sinister smile.

The Curse of the Nibelung

*****

Holmes could not sleep, he was worried. He had seen the way Herr Flohn looked at Cornelia during the concert. He knew from Cornelia's instinctive aversion to him that he had made improper suggestions to her and that with his wife away in Berlin, the girl was vulnerable to his advances. It was perhaps only half an hour after Holmes had got into his bed, yet his concern for the girl was so great, he got up once more, put on his dressing gown, his Persian slippers and journeyed along the corridor to Cornelia's room.

The first thing that disturbed him was evidence of water in the corridor, someone had traipsed into the hotel wearing boots covered in snow. What was more interesting was that the water rested outside Cornelia's door. It began to look to Holmes as if he was too late. Herr Flohn had already got there before him. He listened at the door, but heard nothing. So, using his rights as Cornelia's guardian, he tried the door handle. Much to his surprise it was unlocked and he quickly entered the room, switched the light on and stood there with astonishment. The room was wrecked. Every item of Cornelia's clothing was ripped to shreds, her bed torn asunder. Anything and everything she had touched was smashed or torn. And worse, she herself was gone.

Never one for delay (though his heart beat with a sickening emotion, for he was strongly attached to the girl), he began a systematic investigation of the room. It was obvious she had been abducted, what was not obvious was by whom? He had already dismissed Herr Flohn, he harboured no insane grudge against the girl, quite the opposite, but it was hard to think of anyone who could possibly hate her so much.

Holmes opened the cupboard, a vile smell of oil immediately assailed his nose and at least he now knew where the villain had stood. He also knew the man had dark, greasy hair, for there were loose strands stuck to the cupboard ceiling. This was enough. What he needed now was a good tracker dog. Years ago he could have called upon Toby, a particularly smart dog that had led him half across London trailing tar, or Wiggins, a street arab who could summon an army of urchins to come to his aid. But this was Nürnberg and he was quite alone. It was clear to Holmes that Cornelia had been carried off by some madman, to track her down might not be such a great difficulty as it might appear, after all was it not snowing outside? But such a man who had ripped everything the young girl owned and more besides, would he not do the same to Cornelia? Urgent action was called for, very urgent.

In seconds, Holmes was back in his own room dressing for the cold, snowy night as fast as he could, having woken Watson and told him the bad news. Watson, bless his heart, could not help the tears and fell back stricken in his bed. It was all Holmes could do to make him realise that every moment Watson lay prostrate, Cornelia was getting further away. Watson creaked his body up and began to dress.

"I shall be on the trail, Watson. You must alert the authorities, find Herr Flohn, tell him. I'm sure this is not part of their plans with us. I'm positive that it isn't. Now hurry, Watson, Cornelia won't thank you if you dither anymore."

With that Holmes vanished and in a twinkling of the eye, dressed in his familiar deerstalker and Inverness, he was downstairs talking to the hotel manager roused from his accounts, not having gone to bed as yet.

Holmes explained the catastrophe to him and enquired whether there was a good hound to be had to put him on the scent. Alas, there was not.

"But Lord Holmes, I have a cat."

"A cat?" He stepped back in surprise. "One cannot go on the scent with a cat," he protested, dismissing the idea.

"Frederik is no ordinary cat, Lord Holmes."

This was no time to argue. Anything had to be tried and something had to be done.

Frederik the cat, a siamese of a most extraordinary nature and glossy, cream coat, with enormous saucer eyes and a haunting 'miou' arrived, reluctantly snatched from golden slumbers and quite roughly handed over. Holmes, as reluctant as the cat, quickly carried him upstairs to Cornelia's room to familiarise him with the oily cupboard and pick up the distinctive odours of hair grease and, trample the delicate scent of the young Cornelia in her shredded nurses' uniform. This done to Holmes' satisfaction (if not the cat's, for he was quite bewildered at all the orders to sniff this and sniff that), pocketing a piece of Cornilia's dress, Holmes attached a lead to the cat's jewelled collar and they began work.

It was just at this moment that Watson flew out of their room, excited and almost beside himself, slipperless and only partially dressed.

"Holmes, Holmes, thank God I've found you. Herr Döre, yesterday I saw him out of the window. I did not think to mention it for I did not believe my own eyes, but if Cornelia has an enemy in the world..."

"It is the odious, unloved, Herr Döre," Holmes finished for him. "This then makes matters far worse, for we know what manner of man Herr Döre is. I fear for the worst, Watson. I fear for the worst. Call Herr Flohn and tell him what you have just told me. We shall need help, I'm convinced of it."

Watson noticed the cat and was unsure of how to react. "On the trail, Holmes? With a cat?"

"A sensitive cat, Watson, a sensitive cat."

"Miou", the siamese informed Watson, who turned away as if he had understood every word.

The cat led Holmes to the staff staircase and it was this they descended to emerge in the snow-covered street. It was obvious to both cat and Holmes that Herr Döre was not concerned about leaving his tracks in the snow and that from the deep trenches his feet made it was evident he was carrying Cornelia in his arms.

Frederik was obviously not partial to traipsing in the snow at one o'clock in the morning, nevertheless he must have sensed the urgency of the problem, for he hopped along at quite a pace ahead of Holmes, keeping an unswerving course on the trail of oil fumes. Holmes was convinced it was Herr Döre they were after, the crime fitted a familiar pattern.

"Now, Frederik," Holmes instructed him as they came to a main road junction, the snow already worn away by the traffic, Herr Döre's tracks obliterated. "We shall have to hope the tracks resume the other side, but if they do not, your best skills will be required."

Frederik did not exactly acknowledge either direction, he just forged ahead, straining at the lead, Holmes struggling to keep up. The tracks did not continue the other side as Holmes had feared, but the cat, with eyes and ears flitting back and forth, his nose firmly to the ground, circled a large area in the road itself, pulling Holmes around and around until he grew dizzy.

Suddenly Frederik's tail shot up in the air and he was off. Holmes, caught off-guard, took one step forward and felt his feet giving way under him and in one great spectacular somersault he was down on the road landing upon his bottom, grazing his ankle – the fragile ankle already much afflicted by a certain bull-terrier, the scars still terrible to see. Holmes was hurt and indeed exclaimed most loudly, but he was up in a trice pursuing a fast cat who had been freed of the constraining anchor on his lead.

"Frederik," Holmes called out, limping along, trusting to luck that he was following in the right direction, cursing his ageing legs. "Frederik don't go so fast, cat, don't go so fast."

But even though Holmes pursued at quite a lick, he had lost the cat and lost his way entirely. Cornelia would not thank him for that. It was an ill-starred night and did not bode well for the day, for he could not hope to gain entry into the chocolate factory without her help. It was almost impossible as it was, one could not ask Watson to climb anything.

He heard the distant rumble of an approaching military truck and Holmes, true to instincts born of years in the shadows, shielding himself from unwanted questions, moved into the side of a building and slunk low, invisible, as the large truck went by. It was filled with crying, moaning people under heavy guard. He heard children's voices. To what end did they cart children off in the night? To what purpose?"

As the truck moved out of earshot, Holmes stood up again, thinking he heard a cat. He advanced around the building and within seconds he became convinced he could hear a cat and the distant sounds of pebbles colliding with one another. The River Pegnitz flowed through this part of town, situated on either side of this unpredictable river. The cat's miou was definitely discernable over the other sounds of the night, but even Holmes' keen ears could not pinpoint which direction Frederik's distinctive voice was coming from. But sound travelled down-river rather than up-river in Holmes' experience and using this rule he descended a narrow, slippery pathway which led past derelict homes to the river and its cobbled bed, it's level low since its source lay frozen up in the hills.

Behind him he could hear cars, still some distance away. Had Watson succeeded in alerting the authorities? If so they would be following his tracks, but they had no cat to guide them to the river.

Frederik's mious were very strong up ahead, but Holmes began to fear that he had deluded himself, that this was just the standard night call of a cat in heat. In which case this cat was going to get quite a surprise.

The pathway became very slimy indeed, it was evident a recent flood had deposited a lot of mud on the path and cold and foul as it was, rats darted out in front of him sliding into moss-covered crevices in the stone walls. Holmes was chilled to his bones. The stench nearly choked him. This was the last refuge of the low-life of Nürnberg, the souls with no place in the new Reich, the last stronghold of the outcasts before the inevitable rounding-up into the workcamps; the haven for all undesirables. All part of the total strategy. Suddenly Holmes' keen nose detected oil! The air was full of it, overpoweringly so and coincidentally the miouing of the cat abruptly stopped.

"Frederik?" Holmes whispered, "psst, Frederik, Frederik?" It was dark, too dark; no street lights penetrated this far. Instinct told Holmes that trouble was near, but he was blind down here, his nose saturated with oil fumes.

There was a sudden wild leap from out of the corner of Holmes' limited vision, a white blur. He had but a second to dart his head back as a wild, hissing cat flew past his head, claws extended, fur frizzed high as it zoomed by and landed with the most savage animal scream in its throat, slashing the throat of its victim, only inches from Holmes himself.

A man let out a piercing yell and Holmes instantly understood that Frederik had come to his defence as an axe fell to the stone path and a cursing, yelling Herr Döre fell backwards down into the Pegnitz.

The fierce cat, claws sunk into his eyes, blood spurting from every place, determinedly fastened to the brutal, inhuman head.

It was plain to see Herr Döre had lain in wait to murder Holmes. It was all a trap to lure himself into this hell hole. Quickly he stooped, picked up the axe, feeling the edge, as sharp as a razor. Cornelia would be somewhere near, he had no doubt and he felt sure Frederik was more than a match for a blinded Herr Dore.

"Cornelia, Cornelia," he called out, climbing over a heap of rubble into what would have formerly been a riverside garden. "Cornelia?"

He heard nothing, but from the strong smell of oil in this building, he knew this was the right place. Wet, mouldy, derelict, an ideal stage to play out an execution scene, an abduction, an assassination.

He could only hope that the axe had not already seen use this night, if only he could be sure that Herr Döre had selected only Sherlock Holmes for this purpose, this madness. The question as to how, or why he was there at all he would leave until later. All his efforts were concentrated on finding Cornelia, worried, too, that she had no clothes, the cold alone could finish her. He took out his lighter (a smoker may give up tobacco, but never his lighter), lit it, holding it aloft, calling out Cornelia's name.

He did not see her at first, but he sensed she was near, "Cornelia?"

He lit the flame again, their eyes met, they blinked. Holmes could only stare aghast. She was suspended by her arms, bound by a rope to a hook in the wall. She was covered in a rough, worker's coat, gagged, her cheeks were red from the blows she had received and her arms and feet were covered in oil. The room was an oil store. The flame grew unbearably hot suddenly and Holmes had to extinguish it, but his eyes, scandalised by the sight of Cornelia once again so abused, had marked the sight well. In the dark with one deft swing of the axe he brought it down between her bonded wrists and with one blow they were severed. Cornelia fell to the ground, her arms still up in the air, bloodless, stiff, only agony promised.

Holmes would have whipped the gag from her mouth too, but a light step at the door alerted him and he suddenly crouched picking up the lost axe, the hairs on his neck bristling with a new found apprehension. There was no need to ignite his lighter, he knew from the smell and the heavy breathing that it was the resiliant and murderous Herr Döre. Wither Frederik? Had he lost?

"Holmes, Sherlock Holmes," Herr Döre announced, his voice barely intelligible. "I know you are in there, Sherlock Holmes. But you shall not escape, no you shall not. I have you both and cursed you are, you ruined my life, made a mockery of me. She rejected me and now Germany laughs at me. You cannot kill me with a mere cat. You meddler, you spy..."

Enraged, Holmes could do little else but stand up again and angrily fling that axe with all the strength he could muster. With a sinking heart he watched it sail past the villain's bloody face into the darkness. Now Holmes was defenceless, trapped, just what the madman intended. Herr Döre smiled a putrid grin, his face a hopeless mess, his twisted lip an open wound. He had a bottle with him, a bottle filled with petrol and a petrol soaked rag sticking in it. A match flared, a sudden burst of flame and the bottle was thrown clear over Holmes' head, exploding a second before it hit the far wall, a shower of glass cascading to the left of them both.

Immediately everything was an inferno. Holmes, Cornelia, the floors, the walls, all covered in oil were ablaze in one blinding flash of flame. Heard above all was the hysterical laughter of the madman Herr Döre, who turned away from the heat and once more staggered off wounded into the night, his dark soul rejoicing at his foul deed.

Holmes was ablaze, his cape and deerstalker, everything. The oxygen had all but evaporated from around him, his eyes blinded by a thick, oily smoke. But he had not come to the end of his days to die in the Reichstag flames.

He crawled, inched forward towards the helpless Cornelia, found her, bodily lifted her off the burning floor and with one mighty surge impelled his frame towards the opening. With a roar from Holmes, they crashed out the flaming room, rolling down the hard slippery steps, still ablaze, flesh and hair exposed to the hot touch of naked flame now their clothes were burned. Cornelia's gag fell away, but she was in too much shock to yell. Holmes pulled her close to him, at the very border of his last strength and with a last massive surge and a foolhardiness that comes with desperation and heroics, he plunged them off the pathway into the freezing Pegnitz below, landing in a shallow but welcome nine inches of icy water.

Instantly Holmes buried their faces into it, rolling them in the water until they were both soaked and stood more chance of freezing to death than dying by fire. And then, exhausted, unable to move another muscle, Holmes lay there in pain, but alert, breathing, and alive. By sheer luck neither of them were burned beyond superficial wounds to the arms and hands. Their clothes were the main casualities. The speed of the evacuation had saved their lives. They lay coughing the smoke out of their lungs, allowing the cold water to numb the pain, wash the tears from their eyes.

Suddenly something stirred, Cornelia, her legs still bound, unable to move with Holmes' weight alongside her, felt something wet slimy and cold crawl over her, making its way towards her face.

She wanted to scream, but could not find her voice as it relentlessly made its way up her body. Suddenly it was there and something rough, a hot tongue, licked her face before sitting across her bruised throat and in a croaking pitiful, but victorious voice cried, "miou," and stretched out a wet paw to her swollen lips.

"Frederik," Holmes gasped, lifting his head, turning to look in Cornelia's direction. "Frederik you are an excellent cat."

But Frederik already knew that.

"Holmes, Holmes, where are you, Holmes?" Watson's familiar voice came out of the darkness, echoing in the night air. They heard more voices, saw the flickering torches.

"Holmes, Cornelia, are you all right? For God's sake answer man. We have him, Holmes. Herr Döre is a dead man, we have him."

Cornelia stretched out a hand and took Holmes' wet one, turning slightly to look at his face. Leaning a little closer to him and, cat upon her throat, or no, she inclined her head and kissed Holmes' forehead with the passion of a princess freed from the tallest of towers; her tears flowing faster than the river itself, her body beginning to shiver.

Holmes squeezed her hand tight, taking necessary strength from her. She had come through this well, deserving recognition for her bravery. He was indifferent to her thanks and affection, but there was a new admiration for this much-maligned soul beside him.

"There'll never be a man like you again, Sherlock Holmes," Cornelia whispered. "I'll never know a man with a greater love, I'll never love another as much as I love you."

The cat also stretched out a paw to Holmes and dripped blood into the tired almost submerged face.

"Holmes, Holmes?" Watson shouted again, his voice filled with, emotion and worry.

"Miou," Frederik shouted loudly and suddenly the torches were upon them.

"There they are, there they are," a great shout went up. And it is recorded by Watson that they and the cat were saved.

12

Chocolate Soldiers

From such an ordeal one does not recover easily. On Dr Watson's orders they had been forced to endure a whole hour in the hotel sauna smeared with wintergreen. They had not been permitted to leave even for a moment, then plunged into cold showers and finally boiled again and wrapped so warm neither could hardly breathe. But Watson knew that both of them could have died so easily of hypothermia. The mere fact that neither Cornelia, nor Holmes, developed 'flu or even a fever was remarkable enough, considering how cold the Pegnitz was. Dr Watson put it down to adrenaline. Both had been so concerned with surviving the ordeal they had completely ignored the icy waters. But stiff, sore and bruised as they were, their survival was a sign to all of them that their mission was meant to succeed. The hand of death was stayed and that strengthened their purpose. Herr Döre had been no Siegfried, no hero, and he had suffered an ignominious death as befitted him and his kind.

There was no question about it, they would have to spend the entire day and night in bed. There was no question of them leaving Nürnberg. Neither Watson, nor the German doctor called in by Herr Flohn, would countenance it. Holmes had burns about his head and neck, blisters mostly, for he had been well wrapped in that tortuous inferno. Cornelia was suffering, too, having received several cuts from broken glass on her body.

By some miracle her face was unscathed, although her feet were sore and swollen with blisters. Her beautiful hair was so singed, it practically had to be cut to within half an inch all round, enhancing her youthful, boyish looks more than ever.

There was no contest between Holmes and Cornelia as to who ached the most, it was considered a draw.

Talk of Herr Döre was kept to a minimum. He had been shot by one of the permanent tails assigned to Holmes, who, alerted by Watson, had gone off in hot pursuit, choosing the river as a likely spot by accident. The madman, bloody and shouting hysterically had tried to run when confronted by the man and his gun, refused a request to halt and was thus despatched with a well-aimed bullet in his back, a death entirely appropriate to a man of his ilk.

By noon, the morning after the night before, Holmes and Cornelia were able to sit up in bed (Cornelia in Watson's bed for safekeeping.) It was clear to Holmes that some readjustments would have to be made. Especially now, as Herr Flohn had induced the security force guarding Holmes' party to double their strength and provide an escort for their eventual car journey to the French border.

Of course they had accepted it all as an honour, aware that the Germans were anxious for Dr Laubscher's secrets to get to England safely and as quickly as possible. These secrets obtained by Cornelia during the exchange of programmes made interesting reading for Holmes for they supported his entire earlier theory almost to every detail, also providing a list of chocolate and cocaine suppliers outside Germany (mostly centered in the East Indies and South America). It was a comprehensive blueprint for an all-out South American war. England could not have failed to act upon it if he, Holmes had recommended they did so. They would not get that recommendation.

Now he had to think on the German alternatives. If he, Holmes was discovered trying to penetrate the real secrets of the chocolate factory, surely the same fate that awaited Cornelia's father would overtake them. The ramifications of that would be that Winston Churchill would assume the secret of Dr Laubscher to be even more important and despatch yet more agents into the field. This time, if they succeeded, one could be sure the war would fatally shift to South America.

He could not fail and neither could Watson. It was a question of readjusting, reawakening those skills Watson had learnt with his regiment in India and Afghanistan, for himself conjuring up the Gallic genius of his forebears, the Bohemian ingenuity. Cornelia, he knew, had the advantage of youth and, despite her wounds, could be relied upon to come to the ramparts once battle commenced.

But the years he had spent in Sussex had softened him, he did not have the grip on his body like he used to have, he cursed the lure of fresh air and bees. Finding oneself with nature was all well and good, but it did not keep a sharp mind keen, only a city could do that. But now he wondered if his move back to 221b had not come too late to rescue his decomposing brain cells. He wished that he had his great 'index volume' with him, too, for within that encyclopaedia were many answers and useful jogging for a sluggish memory trying to retain eighty-three years of accumulated mystery and intrigue.

But Holmes was not all maudlin, he did not dwell on the useless. There was none of the usual torpor that came so easily with inactivity. Indeed, with Cornelia in the bed alongside him, he experienced a new feeling of comfort long thought the exclusive province of Watson. (It it not recorded if Watson was at all jealous. His resentment of him vanquished by events.) Indeed Cornelia was interested in neither, because she in turn was comforting the injured Frederick. Suffering from cuts and bruises of it's own it revelled in the attention Cornelia lavished upon it. She held it close and Frederick signalled his happiness with loud purring.

At length, when all three were finally alone, the radio on, the microphone stifled with a rug, Holmes turned to Watson and simply stated, "We must do the unexpected, Watson. This rest is all very well and well deserved, but when would be the best time to investigate that factory?"

"When they least expect it."

"Precisely, Watson. When would that be?"

"Well it would be impossible today, your condition, Cornelia's..." But Watson could see from Holmes' face that impossible was not a word he understood.

"It may sap the last of our energy, Cornelia, but today, this afternoon, of all afternoons they would not expect us to be poking our noses into their business."

"Oh no, Holmes," Watson protested, "you aren't well, if you should fail, Cornelia's feet..."

"We are at war. War is won by tactics, Watson. Our pain is secondary."

"I'll do it," Cornelia said bravely, though she doubted she had the strength. "But please, Dr Watson, couldn't you arrange for a cup of tea, I'm desperate."

Holmes nodded, "An excellent idea, Cornelia. What better way to convince the Germans we are in for the day other than ordering tea. And it is true, a cup of tea would go down very well. Order it Watson, perhaps some muffins as well, if such things exist here, then I have one or two things for you to do. We must get the essentials into our car, we may find we will be leaving this town in rather a hurry."

Watson complied, but he had to confess to his notepad that he had a sudden urge to go into retirement, the emotional stress he felt could not be cured by a mere cup of tea.

***

"Guten Tag, Hilde, how are you? I didn't see you leave."

"My mother is sick again, I had to see the Workers Compensation Board, there's only me earning now."

The security guard shook his head. "It's a hard life, you'd better get in now, or they'll be missing you," he smiled at her, looking at her as she removed her scarf, "and I like your hair short like that, the new style is it?"

She nodded, tossing him a coy smile.

"Anytime you want a new boyfriend, don't you forget me."

"I won't," Hilde answered walking off, unusually nervous, turning left at the end of the corridor and heading into another long, depersonalized corridor; her feet echoing ahead of her. Ascertaining she was alone she had to try three different doors before she found the right staff changing room, her brave smile made ready for the guard, a dim memory already; her nerves making her extremely jumpy. She was expecting to bump into someone at any moment and be revealed as an imposter, for this was not the Hilde whom the factory listed as an employee, but Cornelia; her insides so churned up with worry she thought they might fall apart any moment.

Holmes was right, as she knew he was right. They would not expect an impersonation and she was almost identical to the German girl, Hilde. She had never seen her, herself, but the guard, an employee and a cyclist in the town had all greeted her as an old friend. It seemed Hilde was popular, but Cornelia was not tempting fate.

She was not going to take this impersonation to its furthest extreme and try to take Hilde's place. That would be a foolhardy thing to do. No, having gained entry to the chocolate factory (made easier by the common clothes given her by the hotel manager, her passport to a worker's identity) she had to find a hiding place and stay there until the nightshift had gone home.

206

She realised that if caught she could only expect the worst.
Death would be merciful, there were no mitigating circumstances. Holmes
was right to go in when they least expected it (let alone her sore feet) but she
was scared to death, petrified.

But thus far she remained at large.

Herr Flohn had not made her task easy however. The Nürnberg factory
was a miracle of modern design. The changing room was open plan, the
clothes hung upon numbered and locking hooks, there simply was not a
cupboard to hide in. There were, however, six spare, freshly laundered white
overalls lying on a table and she quickly discarded her awful frock for the
uniform, a safer disguise than any other. But oh, how her feet ached from
the burns, still sore despite Watson's careful dressing.

She had just dressed and was busy stowing her clothes on one of the
hooks when she heard voices in the corridor outside. Two women entered,
one, an older woman, was bleeding from a finger and complaining loudly
about it. There was no place to hide, no way to escape confrontation.

"Hilde, fetch the first-aid box, it's by the Fernsprecher."

Once again these women accepted her as Hilde. Biting a nervous lip
she quickly ran to the window and grabbed the battered first-aid tin half
hidden beside the phone and came back with it, already open, saying, "I
must get back."

"Ja, ja, they will notice if all of us take a holiday," the uninjured woman
agreed, immediately cleaning the wounded finger. The wound was deep, in
need of a stitch or two. "I keep telling them to trim those racks, this is the
third cut finger this month."

"They don't care about our fingers," Cornelia said, trying to sound like a
hard-done-by working girl.

The two women stopped their activities a moment and looked at the
rapidly retreating figure of Cornelia and their faces confirmed a sudden
kinship. "She's right, Eva, she's right. They don't care." It was a moment of
confession rare in the chocolate workers' lives. Cornelia wished she had not
been so smart, but she could not unsay it. She rushed out of the changing
room and ran up the corridor once again, all the way up to the very last door
which was left open. She entered quickly her heart beating wildly.

Closing the door behind her, she discovered to her utter astonishment
that she was standing in the most enormous chamber, almost as big as the
Hendon Airship building she had visited ten years before. She stared amazed
at the contents. It was filled from the bottom to the very top with molasses.
The brown, sweet smelling crumbly produce stood in giant heaps

everywhere and women stood at the far end with shovels watching a large funnel disgorging huge amounts of sugar from the roof. There was a heady sweetness in the air, suffocatingly so. The brown heaps dwarfed the five or six people in the warehouse. She noticed two conveyor belts at the far side, two women shovelling the molasses onto it with a monotonous rhythm, their efforts being transported through a hole in the wall, steam pouring back through it, engulfing the powerfully built women.

She deduced that this was where the molasses were processed. Cornelia had no idea that chocolate needed so much sugar, but at least in this warehouse there was the possibility of a hiding place. She circled a sugar heap, making sure the working staff could not see her as she approached a long, enclosed workbench. Above it was an emergency hatch through to the next chamber, its bolt unfastened.

The sugar continued to pour in from the roof, the mountains of molasses began to spread and a sudden slip off one side sent half a ton of the sticky substance plunging down just behind her, covering her feet and legs. It was not a way she had envisaged hiding herself and the stench of disturbed molasses was quite awful, making her giddy. She extracted herself, thinking all the while about the sheer amount of sugar in the warehouse and the many dentists Germany must need to cope.

At last she was free and she found herself at the workbench, quickly checking around her for enquiring eyes. Seeing none, she climbed into the workbench through a narrow door and nestled in beside brackets, tools and some unidentifiable metal objects that dug most uncomfortably into her flesh.

Here she felt safe. There was just enough air and although it was not comfortable by any stretch of the imagination, she needed to spend only a few hours there at the most and her feet needed the rest. She clutched the box of matches and the lighter fluid tightly, as she lay looking out along the warehouse through a chink in the woodwork, waiting, waiting.

And so it was the Nürnberg chocolate factory blew the whistle at six-thirty and all work ceased for the night, to resume at seven thirty in the morning. Cornelia was not discovered in her hiding place, which was just as well for she had fallen asleep at five o'clock and her exhausted body had little inclination to reawaken.

***

Holmes' plan was quite simple. Cornelia would be in the factory when everyone went home (the guards would only see one Hilde leave and be happy with that). At nine o'clock precisely, with the aid of a match and a little petrol, Cornelia would start a fire outside the factory in the yard. This would summon the security staff together in an urgent panic and in the throes of the diversion, Holmes, who would already be on the roof of the warehouse next door, would jump. He had gauged it only four feet at the narrowest point, and he would enter the factory with the aid of a rope through the office skylight, meeting Cornelia in the canteen.

This was the plan.

But a plan made from a comfortable bed does not necessarily become so easy once it is put into action. For one thing Holmes' body was so stiff he could hardly walk, let alone jump four feet. The new security staff was brought into the hotel itself, no longer discreetly placed outside in the cold. Watson had grown so excited, he had choked on his sausages at supper and was in no fit state to drive Holmes anywhere, or lurk in some damp field behind the factory until all was done.

Yet it had to be done.

"Eight o'clock, Watson, the action begins."

Watson buttoned his coat, looking glum. He did not give this operation much chance of success. Climbing roofs, evading security guards was for younger men. Now there was the very real prospect of death. He had to agree to Holmes' commands, he always had. But as a doctor, as a man with a modicum of intelligence, he knew that all should be abandoned, their chance of success was negligible and it was foolhardy to continue. Sheer nonsense.

"You know what to do," Holmes told him wrapping the rope around his waist plus an entire wardrobe of tools stolen by Holmes from the hotel storeroom during the dinner hour.

Watson sighed, "I wish this were not happening, Holmes."

Holmes frowned, then realising Watson's dilemma, he nodded, walking over and gripping the old man's shoulders, speaking tenderly, "Watson, my dear chap..."

Watson looked up into Holmes' steady eyes, his own were glazed with emotion and the hazards of old age. Holmes' face was pale, there was no question of it, the fire had taken a lot out of him.

"Look, Watson, we have to go on, there is no choice. Cornelia is already there waiting for us. You care for her a great deal, do not fail her, do not commit her tender life to the Gestapo and the horrors of the concentration camp. Strength Watson, no matter our frail bodies. Take strength from your heart, we cannot, we will not let her down."

Without a word, Watson turned, picked up his hat and opened the door, walking straight out into the corridor, his medical bag in a firm grip at his side. The security guard was standing at the landing by the stairs. In halting German, Watson told him, "I am going to Der Apotheker. Lord Holmes is very sick. Please escort me, I do not feel safe walking alone."

The German ran this information through his head and when he finally put it together he assented. He had his orders. No one leaves the hotel unescorted. Dr Watson would be accompanied, he would do it personally. The man downstairs would take over outside Holmes' door.

"I have locked my patients in," Watson informed the man, brandishing the key. "It is safest." This impressed the guard, he nodded his approval and meekly followed Dr Watson down the stairs.

Holmes immediately appeared in the hallway, followed by the limping Frederick.

"Not this time Frederick. You have earned a long rest."

The cat looked most disappointed and sat watching him, puzzled as Holmes quickly closed the door after him. He had left the radio on to indicate that people were still inside. The guards would not check as Watson would entrust them with the key. That would be their security. Stiff and aching but ever determined, Holmes was down by the staff backstairs and inside the Opel, behind the front seats, before Watson had even left the hotel for the car park. When he did arrive, he came with the upstairs security man who was obviously regretting his decision as it was cold and he did not have his coat.

"This car has a heater," Watson told him, "why don't you travel with me, your old Ford looks a very draughty thing indeed."

The guard did not understand but he got into the car with Watson anyway.

"I have to go to a special place," Watson said slowly in his halting German, "a special medicine."

The man nodded, unable to follow Watson's German very well, his mind on the cold and his inability to stop himself from shivering. Watson got the car started and moved out onto the Frauentorgraben while the German, head down, fiddled with the heater controls, cursing his mean and lowly job and the English for coming on holiday in the middle of a war.

It was a good five minutes before the man looked up at the road, satisfied at last with the heater. He was somewhat surprised to find them on the route out of town, going towards the new industrial complex.

"But-but," he began, "wie weit ist es? How far is it? How far is this Apotheker?"

210

Chocolate Soldiers

Watson pretended not to hear. It was eight forty-five already, enough time had been wasted, Cornelia would be ready, waiting.

"Dr Watson stop. This is the wrong way."

"Nonsense," Watson replied, slowing down for the chocolate factory turn off, "we need something special."

"But this is the road to the chocolate factory."

"Yes it is and this, my man, is where you get out."

"Get out?" His surprise was quite apparent, his voice rose several octaves, "me get out?" His hand slid to the inside of his jacket for the inevitable gun.

"I wouldn't touch that if I were you," Holmes informed him, sitting up in the rear seat training his own small pistol on the man. "Don't worry Herr Security Man, you will not be left out in the cold. Stop the car Watson."

This was quickly done.

"Now get out," Holmes ordered, "and don't try to run away, I am fully prepared to use this gun."

The man didn't understand the English, but he followed the conversation all right. His hands went up in the air and he winced as Watson withdrew the gun from his holster, pocketing it as his own.

Holmes followed the man outside around to the back of the car. "Get in."

"What?" The man asked, more than surprised.

"Into the boot, get in."

The German, in Holmes' observation, rarely argues with a gun. It is always good to meet a man who respects a gun and this one was quite willing to climb into the cramped boot of the Opel without any trouble whatsoever.

"This won't be for long," Holmes said, though he knew it was a lie. The unfortunate man took one last breath of the cold night air and that was it. He was locked and sealed away, the events of the night could proceed uninterrupted until the hotel discovered the birds had flown, or something went wrong at the factory.

"You have the camera and flash, Watson?"

Watson nodded, starting up again, moving off quickly. It was ten minutes to nine already. He turned off the headlights so as not to alert the chocolate factory guards.

"I hope this desperate escape will bring us rewards, Watson, or we shall have egg on our faces if all we find is a smelter."

"There is a monster in there, Holmes, make no mistake about it. It was no chocolate Easter bunny I saw. I am convinced villainy goes on in there, convinced of it."

"Pull in here, Watson. You are on your own now. Get this car to that field we discussed, let us hope that the map is true and we can find the farm road to the main highway. Do not loose your German yet, we can find a suitable place for him later." Holmes took one last look at Watson. "God Speed, old man, you can be sure he is on our side."

It was a comfort to know that as he let out the clutch and lurched forward, looking for the country road.

Holmes took a deep breath. He had quite a climb to make. It was fortunate that it was a dark, black, cloudy night; a relief it was not snowing, but nevertheless the surface was slippery. A fire escape to the old three-storey warehouse was there; he knew it was there for he had seen it from Herr Flohn's executive canteen. But what the canteen window had not revealed were the endless rolls of barbed wire at the base of them. It was impassable and he did not need to look at his watch to know young Cornelia would be preparing to set off her diversion. This was a calamity, everything had seemed to work so well, but this, his only access to the factory! He had no fall-back plan. He stood there in the uncertain light, the only source of illumination coming from the factory grounds, bathing him in a pale yellow glow. It was a catastrophe.

One minute to nine. He was going to fail Cornelia, it was a tragedy of the worst kind, a betrayal. She would curse him for ever more.

Holmes walked to the main gates contemplating a bluff, but he knew not what sort of story he could use that would fool these guards. Nor would one pistol defeat guards armed with the very latest machine gun, one of the deadliest weapons ever invented in Holmes' opinion, heinous indiscriminate things, most unsporting.

It was nine o'clock precisely!

Cornelia had woken with a start and knew from the way she felt that she had slept deeply. A look at Watson's wristwatch confirmed it. It was already ten minutes to nine and she was not even half way prepared. Lord Holmes would curse her. She crawled out of her hiding place and stood up to stretch and do some rapid exercises to loosen up her very cramped body. It was a moment before she noticed that the giant molasses warehouse was not as dark as it should have been. She inched forward to get a broader perspective of the place when her eyes caught signs of movement to the right of her, shuffling. Someone was there and making a curious sucking sound. Nervous, wondering how she would ever get out of the place by nine, she turned to look for something to protect herself with. The light was coming from a section near the two far walls. The conveyor belts were still in motion, automatically feeding themselves from the interior of the molasses, no person seemed to be in attendance, but it was obvious that someone was in the other chamber operating machinery, for automatic machines did not need so much light.

A sudden screech behind her made her heart miss a beat, she spun around, her eyes better adjusted to the light now and what they saw confirmed that there were no people on the molasses heaps but rats. Huge, sleek, sticky rats sat gorging themselves sick; fifty, no a hundred of them, squatting on their dinner. Her stomach churned as she fought to hold down a surging desire to vomit. Rats were all around her. She had been sleeping in the middle of them.

However, there was a positive side, it confirmed to her that she was alone and taking stock of herself, trying as best she could to avoid the stinking molasses. She made her way to the emergency exit situated at the far end wall. The rats scattered at her first step, running shrieking in every direction under her feet, scaring and revolting her.

The door, like most emergency doors was blocked by empty barrels and rubbish of every kind and although it was a hindrance to her, it did provide her with the means to start a fire.

The emergency door was most definitely designed by a male. It was the roll bar kind one pushes and it automatically frees the latches, but it was new, probably never used and no matter how hard she pushed, the door would not budge, not even when she kicked it, the sound of which echoed everywhere scaring her half to death.

It was five to nine already.

She remembered something her father had told her. 'The French fight one another when an order cannot be obeyed, the Germans await new instructions, the British compromise.' Holmes wanted the fire outside, well it was not possible; at least not this way and so, if the problem was to be solved...

The fire in the molasses warehouse began spectacularly. The empty barrels proved to be excellent combustion devices and within seconds almost everywhere there was the unpleasant stench of burning sugar.

Perhaps the only unfortunate aspect of her act was the speed of the flames, forcing her subsequent flight from the intense heat. Now she worried the fire might burn itself out before discovery, thus defeating the object of the exercise, even resulting in Holmes' capture.

She need not have worried. Alert factory security guards detected the strong smell of burning sugar long before they located the actual fire and the alarm sounded within three minutes of the flames shooting up in the warehouse.

"Schnell! Schnell! Fire! Get the hoses, the sand, the masks," orders went out as men everywhere ran about in confusion to their pre-arranged assembly points. Hoses were unrolled, water turned on even before the fireman had entered the factory to locate the actual fire.

Cornelia thought it best to escape whilst she could, thinking it odd that so many men were out there ready to fight fires. Surely a chocolate factory would only need five or six men to guard it, not fifty, for that was how many there seemed to be, judging from the noise they were making. She only knew one safe way out and it was not the doors. The firemen would use those, the conveyor belts were the only solution, she and the molasses would discover which part of the factory they were headed for. She could only hope it was the one part Sherlock Holmes was aiming to explore.

Holmes had heard the shouting. He could not see a fire, but knew Cornelia had achieved something for it was on the dot of nine that the trouble had begun. To his surprise and luck, two men rushed to the heavy main gates and proceeded to open them. In the distance behind him, Holmes could just make out the sound of an approaching fire-engine. Proof of Cornelia's good work. The open gate was before him. He waited, he could afford to wait; the fire was his passport to forbidden knowledge.

"Where is the fire?" one guard wanted to know.

"Next to the distillery," another replied, his voice filled with awe. "If that goes up, we are dead men."

"Gott im Himmel! The distillery! There are thousands of gallons in there."

Holmes was very interested to hear that. Distilled what? Not liqueur fillings for the chocolates he was quite sure about that. A chocolate factory with smelters, distillery, precious metals was all very suspicious. Distilled...? To distill meant alcohol, pure alcohol?

Were they making vodka, or was it some new method for making engine fuels? Germany had no fuel source of its own, research was constantly being done, experimental cars run on alcohol. But no, Holmes shook his head. Nürnberg was not the logical place for such a development.

He readied a disguise, taking an oilskin from his lightweight canvas bag, donning his sou'wester. It was a rough and ready disguise, but in the dark, a shiny black oilskin and helmet-like sou'wester could be mistaken for fireman's uniform. Besides, it was all he had. He would have to trust to luck on this one. He had planned for a fire and this outfit was merely to protect him from the water he had calculated they would spray onto the building. The risk of impersonating a fireman at the gates amidst the chaos and confusion was one he was prepared to take.

Suddenly the fire engine was upon him. Two of them. The instant the first was slowing at the gates, Holmes jumped onto the rear of it and was driven through the factory grounds at quite a pace, until it came to a halt outside the giant molasses warehouse. It was quite clearly the source of the fire with flames leaping high into the air. Men were milling around, pumping water in through the axed emergency door. The molasses themselves were on fire, whipped up by an enormous updraught that made a mockery of the flameproof concrete walls and asbestos roof.

Holmes slunk off into the dark. The flames casting long shadows everywhere, sending bursts of light scattering over the yard. But there was no denying the success of the operation. Holmes was within – yet without.

A man, an officer, came running out of a side door, straight past Holmes, shouting orders, only part of which Holmes understood; "It's coming through, the flames are coming through, the tanks, the tanks..."

Holmes darted in through the closing door and found himself in a part of the chocolate factory that was definitely not part of their tour. It was the distillery. He immediately discarded the oilskin and hat which were too hot in the intense heat.

Watson had once led Holmes on a tour of Maclaren's distillery in Scotland and although this effort was on a far larger scale, here the principles of distillery were demonstrated to be the same. The towering metal structures, one hundred feet into the air shone brilliantly; the lofty platforms with gauges, pressure valves. This was no mere distillery, it was more like a refinery, the fuel storage tanks stood like huge indoor mountains on the far side, twice the size of a London gasometer, the largest tanks Holmes had ever seen before.

It was fearfully hot. The heat was coming through the walls from the warehouse next door and was unbearable; the fumes from burning molasses stifling the last breathable air. Their worries were obvious, the storage tanks would be holding combustible refined alcohol. Holmes noticed that as tall as the tanks were in the air, the same was buried in the ground. The entire factory could blow up, taking an area the size of Chelsea with it. It would be a spectacular end for them all.

As keen as he was to defeat the Germans, Holmes found himself hoping the firemen could do their job. He looked for a place to keep out of sight, yet make progress towards other parts of the factory, aware that he had to meet up with Cornelia. Fortunately there was no one about. Everyone was outside helping with the fire. Men, plenty of them, another blow to the myth that only women worked in the factory. Quickly Holmes took out the camera, adjusted it for the bright light conditions and took several shots of everything, nervously twisting his head to one side after each shot looking for signs of returning personnel.

"Molasses," a familiar voice called out from behind a bubbling filter. "It's molasses that goes in here, tons of it, coming through on a continuous conveyor belt which pours into this huge vat here."

Cornelia appeared soaked, sticky, dizzy from behind the filter. "This is where they make fuel for the engines," she added, "but I don't know which engines. I also wish I wasn't so sticky."

Holmes was astonished to see her. She looked terrible, but clearly happy to see Holmes. He would have shaken her hand had she not been so unhappily messy and if there had been more time.

"I escaped on the conveyor belt, but it just dumped me in the vat. It's filled with drowned rats and," she nearly sobbed, but held it under control, "if the fire hadn't shut everything down I'd be sucked under into this here," she pointed to the filtration plant. "I nearly became five litres of pure alcohol, Lord Holmes." Her voice was quite pitiful to hear, it was surely the result of a great shock. "I believe it is 100% proof, might even be higher. I saw some chart..."

Holmes remained calm, as always, eyeing the works with a keener understanding. "Some kind of engine fuel. Romanian oil is not enough apparently. Fuel from molasses. This is their project independence, Cornelia, but why? Why does a chocolate factory get involved at all? What kind of engine needs 100 proof alcohol."

"Come we must get out of here," Cornelia said, "they'll come back."

Holmes shook his head. "The fire will keep them busy yet. See? It grows hotter by the second. You are a brilliant arsonist, my dear, quite brilliant. Now, what is through that door over there?"

"I didn't go there." Cornelia stumbled a moment, it was evidence of her exhaustion. She was hardly able to carry on. Holmes quickly let the camera dangle around his side and marched up to her, leading her over to a wash basin in the wall, a place where delicate instruments were cleaned, filters rinsed out. A place where a sticky Cornelia could be doused and quite readily she submitted to her second soaking in twenty-four hours. But it was with a sense of sweet relief that the hot water gushed out of the tap and swirled away all the sticky stench of molasses. Holmes drowned her in water from her head to her toes, then ordered, "Strip, take off your clothes." Unhesitant, she complied. Holmes took the sodden mess over to the vat she had recently emerged from and threw them in as Cornelia took down two men's overcoats from the wall and put them on, pleased to be warm for once and not be bothered with having to dry long hair. The heat coming through the walls was enough to dry anything in a very short time, indeed. Flames were beginning to lick the conveyor belt from inside the molasses warehouse, darting yellow tongues into the distillery side. Time was running out for the factory and themselves. A sudden shouting from outside indicated that they thought they had the fire under control at last. Any moment now they would be in the distillery to make a defence there. "Let's go," Holmes ordered, now wearing a white coat himself, hoping against logic that, if discovered, they might be taken for engineer and student. They ran as best they could through the maze of pipes, machines and wires. "Why did you make me change?" Cornelia asked, "it could have waited."

"Your overalls in the vat will delay them. They can't switch on again until they know how they got there. Perhaps they might even look for a body. It is just a delaying tactic."

His candid reply pleased her. "I see," she answered, thinking him quite remarkable. Here he was; grey, exhausted, ill with fatigue, yet able to press them on, ever forward, seizing the moments.

"This is the opposite side of the factory we toured, it is also almost twice the dimensions," Holmes remarked as they reached a pair of doors set within larger fireproof doors. "The railway siding comes along side here, thus linking the factory with all the trade networks for the molasses."

"There are tons of them in there, it burns strangely, like gas or something."

"That would be the rotting substance below generating a great methane bubble, your fire would have been an inevitability one day. But this factory is built on such a large scale. I wondered at all the chimneys that seemed to be enclosed in the roofline. It is obvious they utilise their excess gasses for heating and additional power. This is truly a most advanced design. Herr Flohn is everything they say he is."

They had the door open, just in time, for men began to enter the distillery behind them, shouting, making quite a play of running the hoses in. It was dark inside the area they approached, but enough light entered from the roof windows, the well-illuminated yard contributing a dim iridescence that was difficult to adjust to after the bright distillery. But here again Holmes was confident that they would not be apprehended by any guards. Everyone had been drawn to the fire and even as they walked in, closing the door after them, they heard a great cheer that signalled that the fire would not be a problem for much longer. Meanwhile Holmes felt confident enough to use his torch. "Here," he gave it to Cornelia. "You hold it whilst I take some pictures, London will prefer to have visual evidence of all we see." Cornelia shone the torch directly in front of her and from both of them came a sharp intake of breath as their eyes focused on Watson's monster. There it was in all its enormous, astonishing beauty. It was a dragon, the like of which no St George could have tackled for it was as big as a mansion, lying quiet, work still to be done on it. It possessed a strange sadness, resembling a shining bare metal beetle with a huge mishapen belly, a true monster. Cornelia could say nothing.

She had never seen anything quite so big, so utterly alien. The tyres it stood on were as big as a tractor's, but virtually nothing else looked familiar. Holmes quickly took five flash photographs, walking around the aluminium monster. Cornelia's torch illuminated much of the craft, but did not readily provide explanations. It towered above them, fat, as big as a Short S.25 Sunderland and that, as Holmes knew was eighty-five feet long. But it was becoming obvious to him what use the distillery was being put. Fuel for this machine, for want of another word. "It is the strangest craft I have seen, Cornelia, but I believe it is an aircraft of some kind. It must be thirty feet off the ground."

"But it has no wings, no propellers," she protested.

"That fuel out there is for a new kind of engine," he surmised, "a jet engine. I'm sure of it. Ever since Mr Whittle let go his patents on the 'jet' for want of five pounds in 1935, I have been expecting to hear news of a jet development. The only one so far is in Italy, the Caproni-Campini, but I have not heard any news of it flying as yet. The axial flow turbine has been a closely guarded secret. This craft, I am sure we shall find, is modelled closely on Mr Whittle's design. If so, it is a most ambitious design. A daring aircraft design indeed."

"The jet runs on molasses?"

"No, but the alcohol made from it, quite indubitably. It burns it at a great heat, thrusting against the air, pushes itself along, so to speak. If the Germans have this engine so far advanced that it is already installed in an aircraft, we must curse the laxity of the British Air Ministry.'

"But how can this be an aircraft if it doesn't have wings?"

Holmes made no ready answer, looking at a metal plate that announced the manufacturer's name, Messerschmitt. So that was their game, a complete secret factory. All British eyes were on the obvious, the two major Messerschmitt factories. But... away from prying eyes in a chocolate factory, of all places! He needed proof, he had not seen propellers, he had only assumed jet by deduction. He would need proof. London would need proof. He knew, proof was unnecessary for him.

Suddenly they heard voices coming from more than one direction, running feet on the concrete, men shouting, lights coming on all around them. "Quick," Holmes ordered, sensing there was no time for them to run away this time. "Up the ladder, quick, Cornelia, up the ladder into this machine."

Cornelia wasted no time. She raced up the ladder, even though her feet ached with pain every time they made contact with the rungs, even though she was afraid to climb in. Holmes ran up so close after her, he almost climbed over her, impatiently urging her on. "Quick, hurry, hurry," he snapped as overhead lights came on.

They crawled into the vast, hollow gut of the creature. A workbench stood in one corner, a desk light already switched on revealing complicated wiring diagrams on it and the folded half of an engine sketch, enough to instantly confirm that it was an axial thrust turbine. Alongside it were sketches of a smaller jet aircraft designated ME 260B.

Holmes quickly adjusted his camera for focus and with the last two flash bulbs took pictures of both the diagrams, no need to know they were top secret.

"It's not finished," Cornelia whispered, pointing to wiring still unsoldered in the walls.

"This area is not meant for people," Holmes whispered, noting the long trapdoors set into the floor. He knew enough about conventional designs of warplanes to piece together this craft. "This is a bomber, a jet bomber. Twice as fast as normal planes, it looks as though it can carry twice the load. I knew it would happen. We ignored our Air Force for so long, but then Germans are smart, they know where the war is going. Jets, Cornelia, not chocolate, that is the simple truth. The sky filled with murderous, screaming jets that will cut down our antique Fairey Swordfish and Hurricanes in a twinkling of an eye. Come quickly, let's venture to the controls."

Outside on the ground the guards were assembled. Something was happening, perhaps the smoke pouring from the distillery had something to do with it, for great shouts were going up and Cornelia made out that orders had been given to move the craft they were in. The great metal sliding doors were being opened in front of them, they were playing safe.

An enormous tractor started up its engine, making ready to tow the unfinished plane out of the building. They could see everything, the cockpit provided a good vantage point. The controls themselves were completely different from any they had ever seen before, a long way from the joy stick and compass from the old days. The ground far below them.

"Now you see where all the precious metals went," Holmes explained, extremely satisfied to see such a complicated array of instruments, himself not in the least nervous of their predicament. "Instrumentation, the metal cladding of the aircraft, the jet engine turbines generate massive heat, special alloys would have to be made to prevent melting, the fans themselves would have to be incredibly strong. This is no experiment, Cornelia. I only wish this was an English factory we were in, I should have more confidence at the outcome of this war."

Cornelia was not so impressed. She was more concerned about how they were going to get out of this situation. Here they were sitting in the cockpit of a secret German warplane in a secret factory with twenty, thirty armed men standing around just looking for an excuse to kill someone, for it would be quite understandable that none of them would want to take the blame for the fire. Nothing would give them greater pleasure than to discover foreign saboteurs, none more famous than Sherlock Holmes. What a show trial! She didn't want to think about it.

The tractor began to pull them out of the hangar. Smoke was pouring in from behind them, whether steam, or a new fire breakout, they were unable to tell.

"You're wondering how we shall escape this predicament," Holmes told her, placing a hand on the damp and nervous Cornelia. "Well, observe my dear, there is nothing more precious than this wingless aircraft, all their attention is being spent on protecting it. A factory can be rebuilt, molasses imported again, even a jet-fuel distillery can be rebuilt. But a prototype jet aircraft, this is a most precious thing indeed. A baby that requires the best attention, the best security.

"What's that?" Cornelia asked, pointing to a long enclosed glass tunnel with a giant propellor at one end.

"A wind tunnel." Holmes exclaimed, most interested. "By jove, look at the model inside it, it is this very craft, Cornelia, with wings. Note the swept back wings, the idea is quite aerodynamic with the wings in place.

Aerodynamics my dear is what the future is all about, fine tuning the skin of the craft to engineer better passage through the air. This is no Dodo after all."

Holmes adjusted his camera once more and clicked away.

It was one risk too many.

"Wer? Gott im Himmel," a guard shouted. "There are two of them in the cockpit."

They began to shout at the tractor driver to stop, but the aircraft was already outside the building before they could make him comply. A gunshot sounded, a man was waving at them, ordering them to come down and give themselves up. They could hear others shouting for a ladder. Within a minute they would be overwhelmed and it would all be over.

"Sit tight," Holmes ordered, "strap yourself in."

"What?" Cornelia asked. "What?" Her voice squeaking with a new-found fear, looking up at Holmes's determined face.

"No wings, Cornelia, we can't fly home, but we can at least try to give them a run for their money."

Holmes, who had been studying the controls for some while, understood two things; a jet engine switched on would propel the craft forwards once it had reached enough thrust to overcome the weight of the craft itself and the power would build unless throttled back. He understood the basics of flying, but only attempted to fly once, in a Sopwith Camel, without too much success, having had to donate two new trees to an irate farmer.

"May God go with us," he cried, turning two switches, pleased to hear a hum as the electrics turned on. A simple fuel gauge indicated virtually empty, perhaps indicating that the fuel would normally be stored in the wings and for tests they might carry out in the building only a small supply was on hand. Then he pressed a button.

The noise was more deafening than if they had sat upon Mount Vesuvius at the moment of eruption. The guards around them looked up in horror, scared to death. The ladder party stalled and fled, caught downwind of the new ignited turbines. Even though they were interminably slow to start, the noise was terrific. Though it was a fact that a brave guard could have boarded the craft, still stationary, and shut down the engines, none did. Whilst the warming up process carried on they were either too surprised or fearful of the whole aircraft blowing itself up, as it had tried to the other day, when the throttle stuck wide open.

"Our smelter is slow," Holmes joked nervously, wishing he could understand the flickering dials and warning lights flashing from all quarters, the din of the cockpit just as loud as outside. On the tarmac itself, Cornelia was relieved to see the tractor driver take his vehicle away at quite a speed, sensing disaster no doubt, as did everyone else around them. The guards held their hands over their ears and ran for safety. Something terrible was about to happen, she was sure of it. "Why are they running like that?" she asked, growing more nervous and deafened by the second. Holmes had to shout back.

"You must ask yourself why haven't they boarded us, why don't they shoot at us? Remember the morning we were here, this engine screamed like this for a long time, perhaps it caused some damage. I think they are more afraid of it than we are of them."

Suddenly Holmes knew it was time to set the craft in motion, he looked at the controls again, selected four levers, flipped up a red switch that said 'Bremse' and eased the levers down towards him.

They shot forward with the speed of a bullet, immediately entering a dark, blind area as the concrete became a narrow strip heading out over the field. Blind, the engine building up power all the time, their speed increasing so fast the 'g' force had them fastened in their seats as if they had been punched in the stomach. On and on they hurtled down the strip, keeping a tight straight line with a primitive half moon steering wheel, approaching 200 then 250 miles an hour, two anguished, petrified humans at the frontier of science, doomed, scared, the blood drained from their faces. The Jet shuddered, shook, lurched, rattled, swayed, hinted at flight, but like a clipped eagle could not flee the ground. Then, as abruptly as it had begun, the fuel gave out and the twin turbines began to wind down, reversing the scream to a protesting whine. The engine dead, the steering became more manageable, but their fear did not subside.

"But we are still travelling at a hundred miles an hour," Cornelia protested. "Oh Lord Holmes, we are out of the frying pan into the fire, oh dear God, we shall crash."

"Nonsense," Holmes retorted, taking the wheel, turning the craft so that it gradually left the concrete and cut a giant curve in the long grass surrounding the factory. It immediately slowed them down, though the ride became violently bumpy and most precarious as it pitched them up and down. But it worked. They slowed to sixty miles an hour, rapidly falling, so that by the time they caught sight of a lone car bumping along an old farm track flashing its lights at them, they were only doing approximately forty miles an hour when they overtook it. At last they encountered a slight hill that took all the steam out of their sails, as it were.

"I think that this is where we leave, Cornelia. They will have got over their shock by now, soon cars and bullets, no doubt, will be in hot pursuit." The aircraft came to an uneven halt and with no delay the two aviators climbed out of the cockpit and quickly fled the metal craft, Holmes wishing he had just one more flash bulb as he jumped to the ground. They ran, Cornelia leading down the slope to the approaching car, praying it was no mistake. The car slowed, a head popped out of the window.

"Sorry I'm late, had a puncture."

Holmes smiled, Watson was there, that was what mattered, trustworthy and true. They quickly climbed into the car and Watson moved off again, grating the gears all the way up to third.

"I'm afraid I had rather a time of it with our friend in the boot Holmes. He wouldn't let me have the tyre. It's one thing to lock a man in your boot, quite another to make him change a wheel."

Cornelia giggled, her nerves quite shot. Watson was a tonic to restore her sanity. She watched him trying to cope with the rough road, concentrating hard, but failing to choose the smoothest route, the steering wheel proving to be quite an enemy to reason.

"Faster, Watson, they are coming after us," Holmes urged, in desperate need of a cigarette, or two.

"Oh dear, well you'll blame me I suppose. But I couldn't kill the chap. It's just not me Holmes, a doctor doesn't kill people. I pointed the gun at him and whether he was convinced I would use it or not, he agreed to change the tyre if I would let him go free."

"One could see his point of view," Holmes said, sinking back into the rear seat exhausted, quite happy to let Watson ramble on.

"That's what I told myself. Anyway he did a good job, tightened the nuts well, then just as I was going to say, "You can go," he flung dirt into my face and ran off into the night. These Germans have no idea about an Englishman keeping his word."

"They need a lesson in manners I think," Holmes replied, "keep going my friend, there's no going back now. Nürnberg will be alert to our disappearance, they will connect it to the events in the factory. We shall be lucky to get out of Germany alive, but at least we have discovered the truth."

"Not chocolate then?" Watson asked, turning onto an ordinary road and choosing the Neustadt road, a route that would by-pass Nürnberg, as they had planned.

"A new kind of bomber, Watson, Messerschmitts are in the act, a Jet bomber and judging from our test 'flight' just now, a formidable weapon indeed. Astonishingly fast. I felt as though I had been tied to a Guy Fawkes' rocket."

"I smell molasses, Cornelia," Watson remarked, sniffing the air. She smiled, leaning forward, slipping her arms around Watson's neck and hugging him. "Cleopatra bathed in goat's milk, Watson, I bathe in molasses, it's supposed to keep me eternally young."

"Well," Watson replied, a warm glow coming over him, "well whatever next."

"Whatever next indeed, Watson," Holmes sighed from the darkness. "We must change vehicles. Find something to exchange this one for. They know it too well and I fear the roof rack is too distinctive for us to pass ourselves as being just any Opel."

"Steal one?" Cornelia asked, quite intrigued. "I am amazed at you Lord Holmes. First you try to outpace Mr Howard Hughes back there, now you plan to be a common criminal. Dr Watson you must remonstrate with him."

"Exchange," Holmes replied, "exchange is no robbery."

Cornelia was not listening anymore however. She suddenly fell fast asleep on Watson's neck and Holmes, distrustful as he was of Watson's night-time navigation, fell into slumbers too, his mind and body having been extended to its furthest limit.

13

Stormrunners

Watson stood guard, his coat collar huddled around his neck to keep out some of the driving rain. It was a cold wind, not a pleasant dawn; hardly improved by their hunger and thirst, nor by the task Holmes had set them in dumping the reliable Opel. He had given more thought to the problem and since they had managed to evade the Nürnberg net as far as Buchen, it was evident that to let them spot the Opel now would allow them to ascertain where they were going and by which route. It would be foolish in the extreme. It was dishonourable, but in war almost anything was excusable, they would have to steal a car and this was the reason Watson stood guard.

The farmhouse was already roused. Dawn was the official time for farms to wake up, or before, for some especially keen farmers. They had walked two miles already, cutting across sodden fields until they saw the village ahead and the farm to one side. This was Odenwald, good farmland and the traverse path they took had not been the most direct owing to a compound of errors and a natural deviousness instinctive in Watson. But they had put a great distance between themselves and Nürnberg. The Rhine and then France was only one hundred and fifty kilometres away, as the crow flies, but only if they could reach Karslruhe and beyond to Lauterburg in French territory which was the nearest point and one probably most guarded.

Holmes was occupied in an old run down shed with Cornelia. She sat at the wheel of a 1925 Renault that was plainly in daily use for the battery was still fully charged and the petrol tank three-quarters full. Their only problem was to get it started and away from the farm before anyone noticed it was gone.

A dog was barking the other side of the house, a cock crowing, cows stamped their hooves and complained bitterly about the cold from their fields. As the morning grew noisier they hoped it would be easier to extract the Renault (the only car they had found with a key in it, other than a tractor).

"Someone's coming," Watson called out urgently. Sure enough a large man in farm waders, muttering and cursing about the weather, wandered up the cobbled yard towards the house, striking a match, lighting his first cigarette of the day. An early worker had arrived. Holmes wondered if they had made a mistake in trying a farm car, too many people about. Suddenly an opportunity came their way, a truck could be heard coming up the farm driveway, either bringing more farm workers or come to fetch something. Holmes gripped the Renault's starting handle and signalled to Cornelia. On the very second turn the engine caught fire with an enormous backfire, scaring even themselves, shattering the morning peace, silencing the animals. The farm truck came into view, Watson and Holmes piled into the car, waited for the truck to pass, instinctively knowing that every man, woman and animal for miles around would have-heard that backfire. Only providence would attribute it to the truck which rumbled past them at that very instant.

"Now," Holmes ordered. Cornelia slammed the complicated gears into reverse and backed out, the car belching black clouds as she did so. She swung it around, changed gear, the clutch as stiff as a rusted gate, and with a vast lurch forwards, accelerated away from the farm at such a fast speed that casual observers would have thought a bank robbery was in progress.

The truck driver saw nothing but the smoke. Although the farmer did poke his tired head out of the window, he merely heard the noise of an approaching engine, saw the smoke and thought no more about it save pity for the truck owner; for black smoke meant that his truck was in as bad a state as his own blasted Renault. The valves all gummed up, it was destined for the scrap heap. French spare parts were notoriously difficult to get.

Holmes clung to the sides of the car. Watson hung on for dear life in the back, objecting to all the black fumes engulfing him and a sharp spring under his seat, his teeth rattling in his head.

"It's in terrible condition," Cornelia remarked, sniffing something that smelt remarkably like burning rubber.

"Ill-luck, Cornelia, we have stolen a wreck. This will never get us to France." Holmes told her, angry and disappointed. "How can these Germans let their cars get into such bad condition, this car is barely fifteen years old."

"Same with their horses," Watson remarked, "no respect for beast or car, a callous race."

"So it would seem, Watson, so it would seem."

Cornelia came to a fork in the road and could not tell which direction to go. Fatally she slowed down and with a sudden change of heart the engine coughed and abruptly seized; instant junk metal, the radiator hissing, pending explosion. They cruised to a stop only six miles further on from the farm; too dangerously close, as it was now daylight. Only trouble could come of this.

"Oh dear," Cornelia mumbled, head down, biting her lip.

Holmes patted her shoulder. "It isn't your fault."

Watson was out of the car already, hauling his case with him. He was determined he would get his notes back to London, the Germans would not get them, he would rather burn them first.

Holmes followed suit, discarding his white Lab coat as being too conspicuous for the day and stood up in his tweeds, the last of his dry clothes. Cornelia wore a pair of men's trousers and Watson's striped shirt and tie with a scruffy overcoat on top. She found herself quite comfortable in all of this and much warmer than her normal attire.

They stood at the roadside with the remainder of their things, waiting for Holmes to suggest something, though they knew it could only be a long walk that he would command.

The ill-luck Holmes had feared arrived in the shape of a car. A long, black Mercedes-Benz came over the hill, moving at a leisurely pace, an SS flag flying from the chromium mast at the side. They could do nothing about it. Doom closed in on them.

It slowed down, eventually stopping beside them, the occupant inside very interested in them. The driver wound down his window and asked them what was wrong.

"Engine seized," Cornelia answered in German, "my grandfather and his friend will be late for the hospital."

The driver turned to explain and Holmes wondered why the SS man had stopped. Their reputation was not one of compassion.

"Get in," the driver ordered, surprising them all. "Schnell."

There was no choice, Holmes herded his entourage into the warm car, Watson clutching his case close to his side. Cornelia had to sit on the floor, pleased to be near the hot air vent.

The SS man turned out to be very old himself, a surprise for all of them, though his uniform was new and crisp, the gold stars a sign he was an important man. His face was pale, tired. There was a distinguished look about him that was hauntingly familiar, a man who had seen much and lived through it. His eyes studied tham all with a practiced instantaneous judgement that was the trait of one, Sherlock Holmes. They did not look dissimilar, though Holmes was older, taller and had a sharper nose.

"I am Colonel Mundt," he said, signaling the driver to go on. "I should like you to look at these pictures of some very dangerous enemies of the Reich and tell me if you have seen them in this area."

Watson took them first. If he was surprised, he held it back well, for he was looking at a drawing made many years ago of himself and Holmes probably taken from the Tatler. It looked familiar. He passed them to Holmes who looked with only cursory interest, passing them in turn to Cornelia, remarking in German, "an evil looking pair of Capitalists I'll say."

"These must be old pictures," Cornelia remarked, "the clothes they are wearing are so amusing."

The SS man agreed, wondering at the peasant boy's excellent German. "Nevertheless, they are the Reich's biggest enemies. I await more recent photographs, but I am told they travel to France, two old men and a girl. That only one, Sherlock Holmes, speaks a little German."

Cornelia was more nervous now than she had ever been since she left England. "But Sherlock Holmes was the great English detective, no."

"Yes, sonny, it should be easy to find two old men with an English girl should it not?" His leer was hard to comprehend. Cornelia wondered if he suspected them.

"But why did you stop us," Holmes asked, struggling to sound like the Prussian who had tried to teach him German almost seventy years before.

"Because we must leave no stone unturned. Spies are everywhere, there is a total onslaught against us, old man. You could be a spy, where is your permit to go to hospital?"

Cornelia looked at Holmes, then back at the SS Officer. Did he know she wasn't a boy. Was he playing a cruel game with them? "We have no permit," she answered. "Grandpa visits grandma, what is this permit? I have not heard of it at the farm."

The SS officer looked at Cornelia; scruffy, dirty-faced, muddy boots and smelling of molasses, a typical farm boy, but with a curiously light voice, quite attractive really, but not manly. The farm boys of Germany were supposed to be manly, but then this was a backward area.

"Personal – Ausweis, Führerschein – identity cards, driving licence," he demanded, making a decision to let these simple people out, they looked nothing like the drawings anyway, far too old and decrepit to have been able to destroy the Nürnberg Experimental Factory. These old men could not destroy a piece of straw without trouble.

Holmes dug deep down into his inner lining and produced an I.D. card, one made for him by the Special Services in London. 'Henri Bergman, Leipzig born, aged eighty-five retired.' The SS officer inspected it and nodded, handing it back to Holmes. "You are a long way from Leipzig," he said, his hand out for Cornelia's and Watson's cards. Neither was in possession of one.

"One cannot farm in Leipzig," Holmes replied, "one's grandson moves so far away."

The German started. Holmes had mispronounced three words. "Where in Leipzig?" he demanded to know, suddenly very suspicious of them all.

Holmes understood the position. He had failed them. There was little else to do but resort to action. He suddenly drew his pistol, Watson did likewise, pointing his at the driver's head.

"Your gun," Holmes demanded from the surprised officer.

"I'm SS you old fool, kill me and the entire nation will be on your back, I am a war hero."

But Holmes was no longer translating. Cornelia shrank back towards the door to prevent herself being taken hostage.

"Driver, faster, get to the Camp, do not stop," the SS man screamed suddenly, his eyes angry and frightened.

"You will die very quickly if you don't stop immediately," Watson told the driver. Cornelia quickly translating.

The driver ignored them both, preferring to obey his commanding officer, his fear of him greater than the old men with guns. He reckoned without Holmes. He knew how to stop a speeding car and they were getting uncomfortably close to the town of Eberbach ahead.

"Cornelia take my gun, shoot to kill if he makes another sound." She did as she was told, taking the cold gun in hand as Holmes abruptly turned, grabbed Watson's gun and shot the driver in both his legs. The car quickly began to slow, but never swerve, as the driver gripped the wheel in agony, determined not to fail his master by having an accident.

"An unpleasant thing," Holmes remarked, "but necessary, I'm afraid."

The SS man's face was turning white with fear, his eyes filled with a new understanding. "So you are Sherlock Holmes!"

"And you are a great walker," Holmes declared, as the car came to a stop, still some four miles from the town ahead.

"It is a pity about the blood on the driver's trousers," Holmes remarked with disdain, "but perhaps we can leave those on him. Now my SS Colonel sir, you and the driver will remove your clothes. Do not be embarrassed for the young 'boy's' sake, he has enough experience of naked SS officers, who seem prone to removing them."

Watson looked up sharply, not sure what Holmes meant. "Nein," the colonel answered weakly.

Holmes took the gun back from Cornelia saying, "I will shoot and this time it will not be your legs."

Holmes was known throughout the world as a man of his word. In two short minutes the Germans were naked, save for the driver's trousers (he fainted when carried out of the car and proved a heavy burden to place behind the roadside bushes). The colonel, quite pale and sick, himself, was tied up with winter tyre chains, a most satisfactory prison, but Watson, showing compassion placed him alongside the driver, throwing a rug over them both.

Within ten minutes Sherlock Holmes was a gold star SS Colonel, Watson his passenger and young Cornelia Second Lieutenant Hassel, the loyal driver, in her cap and short hair a good substitute.

Holmes looked at the two men shouting at them from the field and nodded.

"Whenever you're faced by two evils, Watson, best to take the one you've never tried before. Now I trust I pass for our friendly colonel?"

"Hardly tell the difference," Watson answered, "save the long hair, Holmes."

"To understand the enemy, one must become the enemy," Holmes declared as they drove away from the exchange area, the colonel's curses hanging like a mist over the receding road. "Perhaps we should cut my hair?"

"Some Coleman's Vita cup would go down well," Watson said, settling back into the warm seat. "We need something to warm us up as we approach the barbarians. Don't worry about the hair, Holmes, I'm only nitpicking."

Holmes smiled at him, adjusting his uniform, feeling a trifle uncomfortable in the newness of it.

"Don't worry about the barbarians, Watson. We will defeat them for we are invisible now. We must all assume the mantle of arrogance, the supreme confidence that becomes the SS. I want you all to remember that. Now Cornelia, at Eberbach, the next town, according to the map, we will take the Neckargerach road along the Neckar river. Cross the river at the Neckarelz and take the Helmstadt route down to Bruchsal on the 292 connecting to the 3. We should have no difficulties until our colonel is discovered missing. I think we should miss out all the major towns."

"I hope you're right, Lord Holmes," Cornelia remarked.

"There is little choice, my dear. The whole of Germany is looking for us. This is our best disguise, our only hope for escape, even if the uniform is a trifle too small for me."

"I say, a bottle of brandy," Watson announced very pleased, opening up a cocktail cabinet.

"After breakfast, I think," Holmes told him sternly. "I have a little money, we can take some time to eat breakfast. They will see only the SS uniform, even old ones will get good service, you mark my words. It would be foolish to attempt to go so far without food, don't you agree Watson?"

"I'm so hungry I could eat a sausage," he replied, much to their astonishment. Cornelia laughed, no small achievement considering the fear in her soul.

***

The valiant SS impersonators soon discovered the pleasures of being in possession of the principal power in the nation. When SS Colonel Holmes wanted breakfast at a roadside inn, breakfast like such a breakfast neither Holmes, nor Watson, had ever seen before was served to them. Not even Kings ate such breakfasts. The very best of everything came out, even champagne was offered, although Holmes refused. All this for the price of a measly breakfast for one at their former hotel, making them realise that there was a price for Germans and a completely different one for foreigners. Petrol, the best service, directions, any and all information was given promptly and accurately. The SS were gods to be treated accordingly and this made their journey towards the border a simple and enjoyable one. A day of comparative ease and relaxation. It seemed no one missed the colonel they had abducted, or that orders for his attackers had not been fully circulated. Either way, they tasted the good life and it was a holiday from the horrors of the past two days.

"We are coming to Karlsruhe," Holmes announced. "We need a plan, for we shall not be able to drive this car over the border to France. We could drive down further and cross from Rastatt to Selz, but it might be more difficult than we assume."

"Why?" Cornelia asked.

"Because France is enemy territory and although the Germans agitate there, congregate there, they do not militate there. Driving an SS vehicle whilst we are in uniform is an act of aggression and we are as likely to get a bullet in our backs from the dismayed Germans as we are the frightened French. It is not the way I should like to end this case, young Cornelia."

"Oh-oh," she said, slowing down as they entered the historic town. "Soldiers checking cars."

They joined traffic flowing in from route 10, the Pforzheim road, every other vehicle an army truck or tank. Signs informed them that there was the Armeemuseum, Scheffel museum, Landemuseum; many more, a cultural town. Holmes' eyes searched the area around them, there were armed soldiers at the windows, at all the strategic places, to escape would be foolish.

"Sound your horn, Cornelia, sound your horn."

She obeyed and quite suddenly there was response. A soldier ran up to the cars immediately ahead of Holmes' and shouted and cursed at them, forcing them to get out of the way. Within minutes Cornelia was able to thread her way through the road block. Holmes was sitting rigid in the back, a very model of a modern SS colonel. Watson shrunk into the shadows beside him.

"Blind obedience our ally, Watson."

But all good allies come to an end.

"I'm being waved down," Cornelia announced as the car turned a corner and passed by a lavish Inn on Kriegs-strasse, a busy, ornate, almost romantic street.

"Better stop," Holmes ordered, making a decision, "remember I have a throat condition and Dr Larstroom here speaks only Norwegian. You are the interpreter Cornelia. Keep calm, stiffen the shoulders."

"Oh God, I hope I remember all this, what if we meet a Norwegian?" Cornelia complained.

Holmes had his answer ready. "Then we declare Watson an imposter and have him shot."

Watson's eyes bulged. "I say, Holmes, that's not the plan..." But you could tell from the smile on Holmes' lips that he was having one of his little jests.

A fellow SS officer walked over to their car, a captain, who saluted and smiled at Cornelia and Holmes.

"This is Colonel Mundt's car, isn't it?" He knelt a little to look inside. Holmes rolled down the window, rolling his tongue for German speech.

"Who enquires after Colonel Mundt?" He asked gruffly, imitating the voice that had formerly occupied his uniform.

"I was with you in Spain, sir. When you were General Mundt. Captain Ansbach, Herr General, my respects sir."

This was a strange experience, Holmes' heart sank.

"Spain?" He asked, knowing that the best way to find out who one is was to repeat questions, turn answers inside out.

"Yes sir. I never understood why you had to take the blame for the defeat of the Madrid assistance. We were given the wrong information and not one of General Hoche's division arrived as promised."

"Well it is kind of you to say so, captain," Cornelia replied for her colonel (in her sharpest Bavarian accent), "but Colonel Mundt has a throat infection, he find himself unable to speak well."

The captain dismissed this with a brave and hearty laugh. "But I hope he can eat well. I have a surprise for you Herr General, you see we do not forget, tonight the Madrid 16 are here in Karlsruhe, we are all SS now and although you are reduced in rank we still call you general sir. This is a celebration, no?"

Holmes was caught in a trap. First Cornelia is mistaken for a chocolate worker, now he for a disgraced general (but not so disgraced he was not still a colonel) "I am old and tired," Holmes whispered hoarsely. "I have a guest, also."

Captain Ansbach was all fired up with enthusiasm by now and would not take no for an answer.

"A reunion of the 16, it is an occasion sir. This town is a dreadful bore once you have seen the museums and the Mausoleum. Your presence is most welcome."

Holmes could see that it would be ungracious to refuse.

"We are to go to France. Doctor Larstroom, the Atom physicist is with us..."

The captain was impressed. "Tonight you shall stay with us, tomorrow I, myself will escort you to France, but not in uniform, I hope, we cannot frighten the enemy a day before it's time."

"Ja, ja, plainclothes, it is a secret mission," Holmes confirmed in a confidant tone. "Himmler himself sent us on this mission."

"Himmler?" He sounded impressed. "So they have not forgotten the hero entirely."

Holmes smiled briefly acknowledging the compliment, thinking that the man, whose uniform he wore had been old, certainly over sixty, shorter than himself and bore little resemblance to himself, but it was, as he had often observed, a familiar case of one seeing what one wants to see.

"Where do we stay the night?" Cornelia asked, being practical. Captain Ansbach accepted the honour himself. "Our base is Der Schloss Hotel itself, a very comfortable hotel. This will be a night to remember."

"My guest," Holmes informed him, "does not speak German, my driver Second Lieutenant Hassel will have to translate, they stay together."

"All are welcome. Any guest of General Mundt is a guest of ours." Captain Ansbach winked at Cornelia and she flushed when she suddenly realised that he did not know she was a woman.

And so it was arranged. The Holmes party was escorted to Der Schloss Hotel and installed as special honoured guests. A banquet was planned and not a man in the Madrid 16 failed to identify their former general, though some muttered (it is true) about how very old he appeared and how poorly Berlin must have treated him. To age so much in four short years, it was a shock and a reminder to them all that one paid a heavy price for being the elite corps of the Third Reich.

Indeed, one of the Madrid 16 was more than curious to see by how much his former general had aged and jestingly asked, "My general, life has been so hard on you, how does it feel to be 92 years old?" The others laughed, but Holmes sought to put the man in his place.

"It is entirely satisfactory when you consider the alternative."

The answer did much to warm their hearts to Holmes and dispel any suspicions.

A banquet is a fine thing when one is hungry, but it can also be a damned uncomfortable occasion indeed if one is impersonating an honoured guest. The banquet hall itself was a fine example of traditional architecture, fine, sturdy, tall ceilings, boars' heads at every available site where there was not a picture of some romantic castle.

On the table there was an incessant supply of beer and the finest sausages in all of Germany. Watson prayed to a merciful God that this really would be their last night in Germany. He dreamed of steak and kidney pies, fish and chips and avoided all questions about Norway, allowing Cornelia to make up replies as best she could, thanking his lucky stars that Atomic physics were outside the realm of ordinary SS officers.

Camaraderie was intoxicating; *Ein Prosit*, the inevitable cry every few minutes. Holmes dug deep into his mental resources for his historic background material. It transpired that General Mundt had been a First World War ace, rivaling the Red Baron himself. Through an enthusiastic Cornelia and his own failing voice he told them of victories against the French and the British, offered comments on the coming war and confessed he was too old to command any longer. The young men must win the glory now, for them all.

It was a tactful suggestion and soon the conversation was diverted to which countries they would take for themselves, much as Caesar's generals might have done. None of it was cheerful news for Holmes, Watson or Cornelia. Not once did anyone query their mission, their German or Watson's atrocious attempts at Norwegian, which sounded remarkably like a list of Norwegian towns and lakes that one might learn by rote at school.

The real trouble came to Cornelia's door. She was accepted as a man, albeit a rather beautiful man, and all through the evening she fended off various lewd suggestions that could end up in some officer's bed. She politely turned them down, in the end turning quite firm and cruel with her refusals, for more than half the gathered company had secretly confessed a strong desire to sleep with her. It was shocking to her, although she thought she handled it well. But that was her error, for one rather fierce officer, who was quite decidedly drunk, made a pass at her, was curtly dismissed but instead of creeping back to his place at the long table, swooped down and plucked her off the bench. He carried her off, ignoring her loud protestations, to the loud snorts and amusement of the assembly, who were not a little irked that they had not thought of it themselves. Cornelia was beside herself with vexation, the brute stank of beer and wine and he was making unprintable suggestions to her, anyone of which was an obscenity and totally new to her ears.

Holmes did not interfere, there was little he could do. Watson buried his head, scared now all would be undone and his Cornelia would be violated most loathsomely.

The drunken brute carried her into the adjoining writing room and threw her down on a small sofa, falling down on top of her, fumbling with her uniform, alternating with his own. She knew what was going to happen. Within a very short time he would discover she was not all she pretended to be. Holmes' impersonation would be discovered and they would be imprisoned within the hour. Her heart beat with this new fright and yet this only made her German fancier all the more impassioned, for he mistook her beating heart for passion. He quickly stood up to remove his jacket, his urgency and the drink making him unsteady on his feet. The leer on his face was quite evil, the fear on her own visage driving him on.

"A virgin," he remarked, getting down on his knees, trying to implant a kiss upon her face, missing entirely as she dodged his head.

"Ah ah, games, you vant games," he laughed, grabbing her forcefully in her private parts, a strange look coming over him as he felt for something that was never going to be there. He looked at her face once again, the drink in him half closing his eyes, he felt around again just to make sure and Cornelia shrugged, her fingers crossed as she hoped he would not grow violent. But violence was not on his mind. He looked down at her shirt, her sudden change to a womanly appearance. A measure of disappointment showed on his face as he slobbered on her neck while Cornelia confessed "I'm not a boy," awaiting for the inevitable explosion.

"Well," he shrugged, "nobody's perfect." He looked at her more carefully, confusion growing in his glazed eyes. And then, the lights went out completely and he collapsed, falling off her onto the floor, unconscious.

Cornelia thanked the god Bacchus for his timely intervention, jumped up off the sofa, straightened her uniform and, with one last look at the sleeping brute snoring on the floor, she went back into the main dining chamber to fetch Sherlock Holmes and Watson for bed.

Great cheers went up as she came out and one man was greatly embarrassed for he had taken bets that the handsome young officer would succumb to the brute. He lost many marks to those she had already refused. Holmes was pleased too, but the assembly would never know how pleased. Of course the charade had to end and Holmes chose this moment to have a coughing fit that had the men's sympathy and much generous help to his room as the party broke up.

"You are not well enough to take the doctor to France," Captain Ansbach told Holmes, greatly concerned for the old man's well being.

"Nonsense," Holmes replied, "sleep works wonders. I shall have him in Lyon by ten o'clock."

But Captain Ansbach doubted his old general was up to it at all and seeking permission to at least assist, a little later he placed a telephone call to SS General Offenbroeder at the Chateau Schwaften – Area Communications Headquarters in Baden-Baden.

General Offenbroeder was surprised Colonel Mundt was in the vicinity, but pleased, especially pleased that the former general was busy on Himmler's behalf and if he was going to France, he himself had something of a sensitive nature he wanted taking there. Former air-ace Mundt was the most reliable man he could think of to take his message. Obviously rehabilitation was possible, not everyone in disgrace was confined to running concentration camps.

"Get him to me, I have a mission for him captain. You take his Norwegian to Lyons, I want to talk to our colonel and send him to Paris."

"Yes, Herr General. I will speak to him immediately."

And thus fate struck a new blow to Sherlock Holmes. Captain Ansbach walked up the wide hotel stairs pleased with his intervention. The re-establishment of his general was an admirable cause, worthy of his time and effort.

Holmes had his own rooms, a connecting one to Cornelia and her's in turn to Watson's. She remained protected this way, her door to the corridor permanently locked, yet even so, events had moved beyond Holmes' control.

Captain Ansbach knocked at his door and within a few short seconds revealed the new orders, stating his part in the business.

"This is the best solution, Herr General. General Offenbroeder is an important man now. You were friends once, you would do well to please him. He has a confidential message that needs to go to Paris. You need not fear of failing Herr Himmler, I will personally see to it that your Norwegian and his interpreter will get to Lyon. I give you my word that you will not be failed in that area. The honour of us all is at stake. They will be here tomorrow morning, I have knowledge of a light plane due to go there early tomorrow morning, at six o'clock."

Holmes had to try. "Herr Himmler expressly ordered me..."

Captain Ansbach shook his head. "We will say nothing to Berlin and a little diversion to see General Offenbroeder can only help. Believe me, mein General, this is the best thing for you. We of the Madrid 16 would all like you reinstated as a full general. You are one of modern Germany's first heroes. It is criminal to ignore you, a man with so much talent. Himmler will never know, for you will still be in France and you can meet up with the Norwegian very soon after. Now it is settled, this is the best solution."

Holmes sighed, at least he was to be sent to Paris. But what if this General knew Colonel Mundt well? This could be a calamitous diversion, its only saving grace being that Watson and Cornelia would get back with all the details from Nürnberg, their safety guaranteed (the irony a small source of amusement) by the Germans themselves. He had to accept, or arouse their suspicions.

"I will leave first thing in the morning," Holmes agreed, offering a Heil Hitler salute. The happy captain returned with his oath to Himmler, Holmes instantly followed suit.

"We shall not meet again for some while, Herr General, on the 18th we go North, perhaps to Norway."

"It is a cold place, I do not envy you."

"My mother makes me mittens and a hat," he joked, his nose twitching as he suppressed a smile.

Holmes was suddenly surprised to think of these young men with mothers. Proud mothers.

"Gute Nacht," Holmes said finally.

"Gute Nacht, Herr General."

Holmes waited a moment then walked to the door locking it, quickly moving to Cornelia's door, knocking and entering. The room was dark, but he could see by the light from his door that she was curled up in bed, already asleep.

"Cornelia?"

She opened her eyes instantly. "Lord Holmes?" Her voice betraying a sudden concern that it might be the brute come for a second try.

"It is I," Holmes told her, walking over to her bed and sitting down with a great sigh, holding the hand she offered to him.

"They are separating us," he told her, filling in all the details, her heart growing fluttery as he outlined the next few days' events.

"Oh no, Lord Holmes. Oh no, this can't be. Oh please refuse, that general could recognize you, anything could happen. We might never see you again!" She began to cry, great sobs that reached Holmes' heart like the fine point of a dagger. Cornelia sat up and near naked as she was, clung to Lord Holmes crying into his shirt, as she had done once before.

"Please, you can't do this, let us steal away in the night, take our chances amongst the wolves."

"No, Cornelia," he ran his hands through her short hair, her tendency towards sentiment and emotional appeals had no effect on him. England first was his motto.

"This town is full of German soldiers, the finest. We might get to the border, but the tiniest suspicion and all three of us would be dead.

"No, my dear, you and Watson are entrusted with the photo-negatives, the chocolate samples and false plans. This way you will be sure to get them to Winston Churchill. Tell him everything, everything you know, about the coming invasion of Norway as well. If you fail, I fail. I am relying on you."

"I won't fail you," Cornelia responded, "but I don't want to lose you."

"I'll be in Paris tomorrow. This general will be like the others, they will never suspect an impersonation. I will be in and out of Chateau Schwaften in Baden-Baden in no time. I will be in Paris before you."

"What are our orders?" she asked, drying her eyes with her duvet.

"Go to Lyon, report to the University, speak to Professor Forché in the Mathematics department. The Professor is an old client. Watson knows him well. He will assist you, for it was a big favour we did for him in '26. But discuss nothing with him, he must not be compromised. I am sure Captain Ansbach will spy on you a while, but I might be wrong, he may simply leave you there, in which case find some way of getting to Paris by the most speedy method, the Express train. In Paris go and see Sir Charles Rottingdean and he will guarantee you a safe flight to London, as already arranged. Explain all this to Watson, but it is you I am relying on to get him to London. Do not fail me."

Cornelia bit her lip and nodded her head, looking up into his dim eyes. "I shall miss you," her voice soft like a child.

"And I you," he confessed, pausing a moment, searching for the right words. "In the beginning I did not want a woman with me, but you have proven your worth. I shall not despair about the fighting spirit of England if there's a few more like you."

"There are, but not all have you as their inspiration and guide."

Holmes smiled, leaning forward, kissing her young bruised forehead, closing his eyes for a moment as he did so, experimenting with emotion but feeling nothing. They stayed that way for longer than a moment and it was difficult for Holmes to make the first move away. At last, he felt Cornelia had had all the comforting she needed.

"We meet in London or Paris, Cornelia. Keep Watson on a tight rein, don't let him forget he's Norwegian."

She smiled. "I won't."

He fumbled in his pocket a moment. "Here, take this. It's the crystal the Irishmen gave us, the ones who patrol France on bicycles. If you are in trouble, find a transmitter, insert this; eight dots, six dashes repeated and they will home in."

She took it, slipped it under her pillow. "I shall not get into trouble. I won't let you down."

"Good girl, I know you won't." He stood up, his legs unusually stiff as he tip-toed to the door.

"I still love you," Cornelia said softly from her pillow, staring at his haunting, spare frame silhouetted in the door frame. Holmes merely gave her a little wave and entered his room, shutting the door behind him.

This sentimental slush was an awkward thing for him – to his mind it was easier to face the Germans anytime.

***

"But he can't have gone," Watson protested, when woken at five by a uniformed Cornelia with a cup of hot chocolate and some cold sausage. He quickly slipped his teeth in and tried to adjust to the news. Cornelia could only affirm that it was so and she had to console Watson for the best part of half an hour. Captain Ansbach arrived ready to take them to the airfield at half-past five. Watson reluctantly resumed his Norwegian scientist impersonation and Cornelia was surprised to find that the Captain had given thought to her uniform, albeit the wrong thoughts.

"I have brought you civilian clothes, our orders are no uniforms shall cross in public."

Cornelia thought back to Christmas at Herr Flohn's and now understood why the German's guests had left in suits on Christmas Day.

"I shall change quickly. I hope they fit."

"They will fit. I described your size to our stores and the manager there is very good at guessing sizes. By the way, Lieutenant Hartheim sends his regards to you and invites you to stay here with him on your return from Lyon. That was the man who carried you off last night. You made quite an impression upon him."

"Lieutenant Hartheim is too kind. I shall certainly bear his invitation in mind." Although she was of the opinion that he had only joined the SS to meet a better class of fellow, she dreaded to think of what he might remember. She had been lucky, that was all, there would be none of this courtesy if the Lieutenant had not been drunk.

The clothes fitted her well, except she did not take to wearing such wide trousers and a tie. The shoes were a little too big, but tissue paper from the hotel closet soon took care of that. She re-emerged fully dressed, smart, hatless, for all the world a handsome lad indeed.

The Captain nodded, liking what he saw. "Lieutenant Hartheim may have to take a position further down the line," he joked, walking up to her stroking her cheek with his gloves. "You are an angel my friend. The SS is no place for you. I see you in ballet, most certainly on the stage. You must meet Herr Von Hipplestar when he comes next week. He will find a place for a face such as your's in one of his films, I'm sure of it."

"Wollen, Malmo, Odenser Borg Borg," Watson spluttered, trying a little Swedish for good luck. "Hur dags gar flyplane till..?"

Captain Ansbach turned to him and shook his head. "I shall not enjoy Norway. I cannot understand a word he says. "Guten Tag, Doktor. We go to Lyon, sofort!"

"We go now," Cornelia explained in her mock Norwegian.

Captain Ansbach picked up Watson's case, but Watson let out such a yelp, the Captain dropped it again allowing the doctor to carry it.

"A sensitive man," he complained. "I was merely trying to help the old bastard."

Reluctantly Watson and Cornelia followed their guide to France out of the hotel room, both of them wishing that Holmes had said goodbye.

"It's lucky there is an aircraft waiting," Captain Ansbach told them in the car. "Mostly everything is moving North this month, this town will be empty by February."

"To join the Soviets against the Finns?" Cornelia asked.

"To take Norway, of course, don't they tell you anything?"

"I don't think I shall tell the doctor that," she said, looking out of the window. The Captain laughed and slapped her on the back. "No, I don't think so."

The car found the route out of town and made its way to the airfield.

"There is a small change," the Captain remembered suddenly. "This aircraft must return immediately we arrive in Lyon. I know I promised General Mundt I would escort you to Lyon itself. It is unfortunate, but I shall have to leave you there."

"We shall survive," Cornelia answered, her heart leaping at the news. "I speak French, I shall get him safely to the University."

"Good, what is it exactly that makes our friend so important?"

"Bombs I think," Cornelia answered, making a guess.

"Bombs," Watson said suddenly feeling he ought to be making a contribution, even though he had not fully woken up as yet, this five o'clock business had him in a tizz.

Captain Ansbach nodded, "that is good. Bombs, that is very good."

***

Holmes had a miserable journey to Baden-Baden. He had been collected at four in the morning and with little time for washing, hurried into a waiting staff car. A Marshall Baumann, impatient, not at all impressed by the legend of General Mundt, was thinking it only an inconvenience to share his car with a discredited General. Consequently the journey was a frigid affair, which did nothing to improve Holmes' apprehension and although he was reasonably sure Watson and Cornelia were safely away, he was increasingly doubtful about his own fate. Sooner or later the real Colonel Mundt would be found and the first place that would discover it would be Communications Headquarters in Baden-Baden. It was just a question of time.

"You think our friend Reinhard Heydrich is to be trusted?" Marshall Baumann asked suddenly, tapping his left hand trying to force the blood to circulate.

Holmes crossed his legs, trying to admire the sunrise, unusually bright and pink for the time of year.

"It is never good to concentrate power in a political man," Holmes replied, thinking out his German carefully. "One must not think 'this is what the Fuhrer wants', our duty in the army is to ask, 'is this what Bismark would want?'"

Holmes was out on a limb here, but he had a reputation to keep up, Colonel Mundt was old school.

Marshall Baumann looked out of the windows, took out a packet of cigarettes and offered Holmes one. He refused on account of his throat but Baumann lit up and relaxed. "If Bismark were here," he said at length, "there would be no Heydrich."

No more words passed between them, but there was a marked reduction in tension for the rest of the journey. Bismark was still a hero in this car.

The Chateau Schwaften, a 15th century pile with belle epoque overlays is situated in the hills above Baden-Baden and is one of the finer examples of the confusion between the identity crisis of Alsace-Lorraine. A cold, whimsical, dominating structure lying in the middle of a man-made forest, serving as protection from the inevitable wind. Holmes was hoping there would be breakfast before he met General Offenbroeder and indeed there was coffee and hot biscuits on hand when they arrived. He stood waiting in the vast draughty entrance hall, distant chandeliers high up on the raftered roof, echoes bouncing back from all directions. However it was nearly seven in the morning and the Chateau was already a hive of activity. General Offenbroeder would see Holmes almost immediately, he was told. Marshall Baumann left after a quick coffee, wishing Holmes luck, something he knew he was going to need.

They left him waiting for almost three-quarters of an hour, a distinctly lonely vigil. He consumed more coffee than he needed to calm his nerves, though to tell the truth they got a little worse with each cup; certainly he ate more hot biscuits than he intended to, more than a tense, taut stomach needed anyway. For Holmes, not master of the situation, it was not the best of times. Possibly it was the worst. He hated uncertainty, his entire life had run in opposition to it. His eyes ignored the vast quantities of antiques that lay in neglected groups all around him, his interest was not captured by mahogany hand-carved lions at the foot of the stairs; he took in only the important details. Doors, number of people in the area, possible hiding places. An escape from such a place would not be easy.

"The general will see you now, Colonel," a voice notified him. Holmes looked down and saw a young man in army uniform. "The General told me to tell you that he is most honoured to have you here and apologises for not seeing you immediately."

"It was no time at all," Holmes announced, following the man up the absurdly ornate stairs.

"The general has a very interesting guest. He is most keen to meet the legendary air-ace, it seems you are spoken of all over the world."

"I only did my duty," Holmes replied, wondering who this interested person could be, another thing to worry about.

"He has been keen to know you since he was a boy. He was to leave last night, but stayed especially to see you. I myself have read of your many achievements, none of us understand what happened in Spain."

"I do not talk of Spain." Holmes snapped.

The young soldier held his silence, thinking that if he had been demoted to Colonel from war hero General, he would not include Spain in his vocabulary either.

It was some considerable distance to General Offenbroeder's quarters. They walked the full length of the upper floor of the Chateau, the views from the narrow windows quite spectacular, the mountain forest swamped in heavy snow, too thick to melt in the weak winter sun.

"The General's quarters sir," the soldier informed him at last, leaving him standing outside a huge oak door with black wrought iron studs embedded into it. He knocked, was told to come in. Heil Hitler's were exchanged, heels snapped together and Holmes was facing a smiling general who held out his hand in greeting, clearly very pleased to see an old friend. Suddenly his guest stepped out from the shadows into the light and was about to say, "Good morning," when he stopped, stared, his eyes opening wide with plain astonishment. He stepped back shaking his head in obvious shock, a slow amused smile crept into his lips and eyes as he looked from the General to Holmes and said; "Good morning, Sherlock Holmes."

Holmes could do nothing, he was undone. "Good morning, Mr Moorehaus, a fine day to sell Heinkels."

"Indeed it is, but even better for impersonating officers of the SS, I see."

"What is this?" asked the General, who did not understand English, "What is going on, you two know each other?"

Holmes took himself to a chair and sat down, experiencing almost a sense of relief, his hands steady, the nervousness gone.

Moorehaus began to laugh, he turned to the General. "Congratulations Herr General, you have caught Germany's most wanted spy. I present Lord Sherlock Holmes."

"But…" the General protested, looking at Holmes' face more carefully, the badly fitting uniform, the flowing white hair under the too small hat. Slowly it began to dawn on him as Holmes' familiar face came into focus from a younger memory and the well known adventures he had read and enjoyed so many years ago. Holmes loosened his tie, something he had wanted to do for a very long time. "I hope you will respect the rights accorded a political prisoner laid down by the Geneva agreement."

Moorehaus was still laughing. It was an unbelievable coup. The General was only just beginning to understand.

"Oh I think we can do better than that, General Offenbroeder," Moorehaus said, clearly an important man in these parts, Holmes' instincts had been right about him. "I think our spy has some explaining to do, but let's have breakfast first. There is no need for torture here. Sherlock Holmes will tell us all we need to know, isn't that so."

Holmes could only agree, he was far too old to be tortured, besides Watson was free, safely away in France already, or very nearly. They could not stop the British Government from discovering the truth. They could take revenge, but that was par for the course.

A show trial, perhaps death was his fate, but they could not defeat him with Watson free.

The General sat down on his desk with a huge sigh, shaking his head at the knowledge of it all, suddenly needing that breakfast. He turned to Holmes once more and confessed, "I never liked General Mundt anyway." He smiled, stabbing two hot sausages, offering one to Holmes who gladly took it. The General's face turned sour again and sternly, he ate half of the sausage, all at once turning back for another, his brain working over some questions in his head. He turned back to Holmes, pulled over a casual chair, sat down close by his prisoner, looking him dead in the eye and said, "I want the truth, you understand, the absolute truth." Holmes nodded, swallowing his sausage, thinking the General very fierce indeed.

"Now Sherlock Holmes," the General continued, looking up at Moorehaus for approval suddenly, "I want you to tell me exactly, how did you escape the Reichenbach Falls?"

14

A Bientot Watson

They landed in thick mist and the pilot was not happy.

"Only two minutes, if this mist gets worse we shall never get off the ground again."

"But where are we?" Cornelia asked, getting up, staring out of the water-streaked windows, pleased to have landed, wherever it was.

"Above five miles outside of Lyon, it's a private strip. Now hurry, this mist looks very bad indeed," Captain Ansbach told her, a worried expression creasing his grey face.

Watson had his case in his hands already and stood by the door.

"Wrong door," the captain yelled out, pointing to the back of the aircraft, cursing his stupid passengers, as he tossed out his packages.

"Quot An Lar Blik." Dr Watson answered.

Captain Ansbach swore at him again. Cornelia went over and took Watson's hand. "Wrong Quot, Dis An Lar Blik."

"Oh," Watson muttered, thanking the gods he did not have to continue with this gibberish any longer.

"Take the road to the right as you leave the airfield. There is a stone cottage with green shutters, ask for Michel, he will drive you to town, he is a friend, you understand?"

Cornelia nodded, she understood, and as soon as the door was opened she hustled Watson out onto the damp grass and pea-soup mist.

"Eine Postkarte," Captain Ansbach said smiling at Cornelia. "Auf wiedersehen," he shouted, slamming the door. The 'plane's engines revved up and almost immediately it began to roll away upfield, disappearing from their view within seconds. The harsh roar of its engines was muted by the mist, but remained in the vicinity for a minute or two becoming a diminishing throb before the sound of it went completely. Cornelia knelt to the soaking grass and laughingly kissed it, bathing her tired face in the heavy dew. "France, Dr Watson, France."

But Watson was not impressed. "I shall not kiss the ground until we reach England."

"Oh don't be a spoil-sport, come on in the water's lovely." She bathed her face again, rubbing her neck and ears as well to waken herself thoroughly. "I wonder what it was they dropped off? It must have been important for them to fly so far with it."

"I can't see anything, I'm not going to look. It is probably French editions of *Mein Kampf,* trying to soften up the natives with it."

She nodded, it was more than likely. She smiled again, happy to be on land and safe. She got up from the ground, instantly regretting her wet knees, linked her left arm through Watson's and marched a tired old man through the wet field, the mist a bad one for an old man with a touchy chest.

"Where is he now?" Watson asked himself, manifestly upset to be without Holmes.

"He'll be in Paris soon," Cornelia said encouragingly, though she herself did not entirely believe that.

Watson sighed, he had never been so far from home without Holmes since Afghanistan. His feet felt heavier than usual, his heart like lead. "It's a terrible mist," he coughed and complained. "Why are we so far from Lyon?"

"Germany is at war, they can't just fly in and land at French airports anymore."

Watson had to accept that, but he was suspicious all the same. Needless to say his suspicions were unfounded. After stumbling around in the mist for the best part of ten minutes, clinging to each other for fear of parting and losing themselves, they found a shed and from this shed a gravel road which in turn led to a tarmac road.

"Right, he said, right," Cornelia mumbled to herself, tugging Watson with her. He was quickly tiring, not up to a long walk, the past few days had taken all his strength. Fortunately Captain Ansbach had not steered them wrong, after fifty metres a stone house with vaguely green shutters stood back from the road, barely visible from where they were. A battered Citroën was to one side amongst the vegetables and clucking chickens; was this the car that would take them to Lyon?

"Cherchez moi?" a man asked, coming out of the gloom with a rifle in his hand.

"Michel?" Cornelia asked, holding Watson's hand, scared suddenly, the man's face indistinct in the mist.

"Oui, je suis Michel, et vous?"

"From Karlsruhe, Lieutenant Hassel, Professor Larstroom on a secret mission," Cornelia switching to a Parisian French.

Michel looked into Watson's face, then Cornelia's, he looked around them as if to check they were alone, but naturally saw no one . "I heard the plane."

"The pilot didn't want to be trapped by the mist," Cornelia explained.

"Yes it has been very bad, I suppose you'll be wanting some breakfast."

Cornelia smiled. "Yes, yes, we left at five with only a cup of coffee."

Michel nodded, then just walked away expecting them to follow him inside. "Coffee's on, but first I want to hear my bulletin," he told them abruptly closing the flimsy kitchen door after them. A child sat at the table, scruffy, dirty fair hair, poor clothes badly patched, a piece of grey bread clutched in a grubby hand, eyes fixed upon them.

"Move, you brat," Michel yelled at the boy, indicating to Cornelia and Watson where to sit.

"I go to town at eleven, if the mist thins out, which it might if the wind comes. You can come with me then."

"Merci," Watson answered, almost ready for a snooze.

"The professor is very tired, that coffee..." Cornelia began.

Michel held up his hand for silence, turning up the volume on his receiver, attending to coffee for them as he listened. It appeared to be a standard news programme from Germany.

"...And the Jew thieves continue to harass German interests in Denmark. An approach to the King has been made to enable the safeguarding of German property..."

Michel seemed to be writing words down, key words from the news broadcast. Slowly Cornelia realised that he was receiving his own messages in code whilst the actual broadcast concerned itself with a riot in Latvia against Stalin's forces, food shortages in many places, supply bottlenecks blamed on scheming Jews, as always. It talked, too, of victorious German achievements in the economy, new ambitious productivity targets. The usual propaganda.

At length Michel set his pen down and looked up with a smile on his face, taking a thin black book down off a shelf and in a silence broken only by Watson slurping on his coffee, the French traitor made sense of his code. Ten minutes later he sat back with some satisfaction reading what he had written out aloud. "Sherlock Holmes has been captured by a General Offenbroeder. They are looking for a Dr Watson and a young girl. Saboteurs to the German economy, spies from England who must be shot on sight. A big reward for their bodies."

Cornelia nearly fainted. Watson sat dumbfounded, there was more news, but neither of them heard another word he said, not even when Michel pushed the red-hot coffee pot under their noses and urged them to try a second cup. They responded like mechanical dolls, all the life was gone out of them. Cornelia's brain struggled to shake off the numbing news of Holmes' disaster. She forced more coffee down her, even though it was bitter and burnt her lips.

"Isn't Sherlock Holmes, the English detective?" Michel asked. Cornelia shrugged, but Watson nodded, saying in appalling French, "I thought he was dead."

"So did I," Michel told him. "An old man and a young girl, what could they do against the Third Reich?"

"Not much," Watson agreed. "Germany is a strong country, one old man could hardly hurt a fly."

"Michel, does your radio transmit?" Cornelia asked breathlessly, an idea bursting through, her eyes fastening on the Frenchman.

"Of course, I report once a week."

"I need to send an urgent message. Will this crystal fit? I have to report immediately.

The man examined the blue glass tube and nodded. "You want to send now?"

"Yes, the mist has delayed us, we must not miss our contacts."

"I understand," he answered, wondering at her clothes, wondering why this Parisian girl was dressed up like a German male student, little realising that all her French was learnt at school.

"Oh I hope I'm not too late," she wailed. Watson saw the crystal and suddenly understood what she wanted to do. Holmes was to have a chance after all, the red-headed bicycle men had promised to come to their aid, but how good was their word?

The Frenchman was extremely helpful, anything to assist his friends of the Third Reich. He understood which way the tide of history was flowing and anticipated the rewards traditionally due a Fifth Columnist. "You can send your message now."

But suddenly Cornelia stopped, she turned to Watson and shook her head, she did not know Morse code. Watson looked at her puzzled expression a moment, then understood. "I will send it lieutenant. Where is our man supposed to be?"

"Chateau Schwaften, Baden-Baden," she answered, hoping the Frenchman was not listening too closely. Luckily he was busy loading wood into the stove. Watson climbed out of his chair, shuffled over to the morse key (hidden inside a box of washing powder) and began a message.

"Holmes captured, Holmes captured. Chateau Schwaften, Baden-Baden, pass the word. Assistance needed." He repeated the message six times and dedicated his luck to the ether.

"Is there any word when we might expect the invasion?" Michel asked keenly, "I have waited these past three years. Herr Hitler promised to scourge the earth of these Jewish Bankers in Paris, will he keep his word?"

Cornelia stood up and shouted, "Heil Hitler," making the little Frenchman jump. "The Fuhrer always keeps his word."

Michel blinked, this young girl was one of the fanatics he had read about. "Heil Hitler," he replied saluting. "I will drive you into the town now fraulein, or is it mademoiselle?"

"Lieutenant," she replied, retrieving the crystal from the radio. "We accept your ride. We are anxious to be in Lyon as soon as possible."

Michel looked outside at the mist, it was not clearing, but he knew this couple did not want to stay in his house. He was thinking it was odd the Third Reich would be despatching such an old man and a young girl dressed as a man, things like this did not inspire confidence.

"There was something left for you in the field," Cornelia remembered to tell him. "But you will never find it in this mist."

"Ah, I wondered," Michel replied, eyeing Cornelia suspiciously, suddenly mindful of the bulletin... an old man and a girl, English. Well they did not look English and the girl spoke French like a native. Nevertheless, shoot on sight, a reward... He walked over to the corner of his kitchen where his rifle lay, the quiet, probably terrified child, watching him closely. It was through the child that Cornelia sensed trouble.

"You must give Michel a reward," she told Watson quickly, standing and walking over to the tense child, discovering his lame leg for the first time. A sad, brutalised child in desperate need of a mother, which this house clearly lacked. "We have some chocolate, German chocolate, the best there is. Only the Fuhrer is allowed this chocolate, and we are delivering some to a special person in France."

"Oh," Michel asked, his hand turning away from the gun. "The Fuhrer's chocolate? I have heard he has it specially made."

"Indeed," Cornelia agreed, "we have just a little of sample of Dr Laubscher's chocolate, we could spare you just a taste, since you have been so kind to allow us to use your transmitter, perhaps the doctor would allow us to part with one bar of the Fuhrer's chocolate?"

"This is Dr Laubscher's chocolate?" The Frenchman asked, walking away from the corner, suddenly very interested. The doctor's fame spread far.

"It is and the Professor can only be in France a very short time," Cornelia explained, "this mist is great annoyance."

"A bar of the Fuhrer's chocolate would be a great honour, wouldn't it Gaston?"

The child nodded vigorously, hoping he would actually get some.

Michel smiled. "My son is dumb, he was born that way, but he likes chocolate. The Fuhrer's chocolate could work miracles, who would have ever dreamed of such an honour."

"But it is a secret," Cornelia emphasised. "The Fuhrer allows no one but him to eat it, no one."

Watson opened his case, he had been following the conversation as best as he could, hoping this little ruse would pacify the Frenchman.

"You will take us to Lyon now?" he asked, extracting a bar of the latest samples given to them by Herr Flohn. A cherry liquor bar, almost eight inches long by two inches wide. A lethal dose.

"You could be arrested if this was found here by other visitors," Cornelia explained, "you'd better eat it now."

Nothing could have stopped them. Michel took it from Watson's hand, divided it three quarters for him and one quarter for the unfortunate and disappointed child. (Though to be sure he was lucky at that).

Watson closed up his case and sat down to finish his coffee. Cornelia helped herself to the bread on the table and ate it with some cheese. They could wait whilst Michel ate chocolate, watching him savour each mouthful, suck the cherry first and thoroughly chew the rest with his brown stained teeth. Watson gave it five minutes.

Cornelia was worried about the child, but he ate only a corner of it and when his father was not looking, he threw it into his treasure tin on the table, for later.

At last Michel was finished, if any suspicions had lurked about his two visitors from Germany they had vanished now, a strange feeling of upliftment was coming over him, a strong desire to break into song. Maurice Chevalier came to mind and before Watson and Cornelia could stop him, the man jumped up onto the kitchen table, broke into a lewd Rhumba and began to kick everything off the table with great precision.

Watson picked up his case, ambled over to the man's jacket hanging over a chair and removed the car key. "Lyon," he said to Cornelia, his usually ever-present amiable smile now absent from his face. The shock of Holmes' arrest was only just beginning to sink in.

Cornelia took off her tie presenting it to the little boy who snatched it from her with great glee. His father was playing the fool, the child could do as he wished for a change.

"Come on," Cornelia said to Watson, taking his arm. "Let's go."

The boy climbed off his chair and limped to the door, opening it for them, following them outside into the mist, thicker than ever. It was going to be very difficult to drive anywhere. The boy was keen to help though and taking Cornelia's sleeve he pulled them through the mist to the old Citroën, opening the back door for Watson to get in.

"Merci, Gaston," Cornelia said, opening her own door, Watson handing the key to her. The child stood back watching them, a new smile on his face that revealed a completely different child.

"Au revoir, Gaston. Your Papa will have a headache soon, avoid him." Cornelia informed him, as she found the ignition and the starter button. She watched the child walk back into the house, strains of bawdy French rugby songs flowing out of the door.

"Can't see a blessed thing," Cornelia exclaimed, glad to be able to speak English again. "If I reach twenty miles an hour I shall be very lucky."

"Are your lights on?" Watson asked.

"Yes."

"Watch the curb, it is just visible, if you can't see it you are on the wrong side of the road, or at a cross roads."

***

By this method of navigation they got on; not at all sure whether they were headed for Lyon or not. Cornelia strained to see and tried her best to keep on the wrong side of the road.

"We can't leave Holmes in the Chateau," Watson grumbled, biting on his knuckles in his anguish. "Oh we should never have let him out of our sight. Impersonating the SS was a very unsound idea."

"We nearly made it," Cornelia asserted, "but remember dear Watson, you have a duty to England. You must go on to Paris, then London. There can be no talk of you going back."

Watson sat in silence, she had voiced his very intentions. Then it occurred to him. "You mentioned only me."

"I will put you on the train to Paris, I will arrange for you to be met, safeguard you anyway I can, but I won't be going with you. I have to go back."

"You? Hey, watch that tree."

She swerved, trying to concentrate better on the nearly invisible road. "I must go back. I am the only one dispensable to this operation. You must get to Winston Churchill, give them Holmes' report on the Jet bomber, the photographs and the chocolate scheme. Lord Holmes will endure his suffering only if he is sure all these items are safely transported to London. How cruel it would be if you failed him by coming back and he discovered that he would die in vain."

"Die? Holmes die?" Watson gasped. "You think they will kill him?"

She negotiated a difficult bend, a farm truck lay in her path and slowing to a crawl, she overtook it, seeing a signpost for the first time indicating 'Lyon – Two Kms.'

"They might kill him, but not without a trial first. Sherlock Holmes is an important man, he has sabotaged their secret factory, impersonated an SS Colonel, serious crimes. Probably excuse enough for an invasion of England."

"They can't kill Holmes, Cornelia, they can't."

"They can. I must get back. Perhaps there is something I can do."

"You?" Watson exclaimed. "How? If Holmes is at the Chateau Schwaften, then there is no hope. That is Communications Headquarters, the best defended site in all Europe, impregnable."

She knew that. It did not make things better. She drove on in silence. She was deep into France already; Holmes was trapped in the Chateau, soon London would know, but their attention would be distracted by developments in Norway. The red-headed Bicycle Brigade might help, but to penetrate a German stronghold when the Germans would be expecting just that very thing...? Impossible.

The mist suddenly began to clear as she approached the city and she picked up some speed.

"I think you should be coming back with me," Watson told her quietly from the back, calmer now, trying to put himself in Holmes' shoes. "Holmes would not want you going off on a wild goose chase, he would have no sympathy for you if you were caught, tortured, thrown into a concentration camp. I know Holmes, Cornelia and I know you love him dearly, as I, but to love him one must think of what would please him most. Going to England with me, explaining to the War Cabinet all we have seen and heard. You were in the Jet bomber, I was not. You saw the distillery, I did not. They have experts there that will listen to you. Believe me nothing could be more calculated to incur the wrath of Sherlock Holmes than disobedience."

Watson spoke the truth, but Cornelia's heart was already back in Germany.

***

The station was crowded, the train almost full. Cornelia and Watson were installed in a cabin along with two nuns, a businessman from Amsterdam and an odious child who was kept quiet only by being bribed with an enormous bag of boiled sweets that Watson hoped would last the boy for the entire journey. Nevertheless, it did serve to remind him that he had not yet consumed any food since the night before and since it was two hours before lunch, a great and urgent hunger came over him. He even began to wish he had eaten the sausage Cornelia had offered him at five in the morning.

"Cornelia, there is a refreshment trolley about one carriage behind us standing on the platform, here are some francs. Please could you get me a sandwich and one for yourself if you like."

She looked at him in surprise, but then realised with shame that she had rather ignored his appetite and something urgent probably was in order. Besides, there was a whole five minutes before the train would leave. She herself felt like something to drink.

"Of course, Dr Watson, now be good, keep your eye on your case. I'll be back in a moment."

(There was no need to worry about the case. It rested on his knees and was tied with rope around his waist for extra security).

She took the money, stepped over the nuns, who possessed very large feet and quickly left the train running for the trolley with its steaming coffee machine. She would have bought coffee and sandwiches too, but for her eyes catching a sudden glimpse of the two tall red-headed men wheeling bicycles from a newly arrived train the opposite side of the station. It could only be them... there were no others.

She abandoned all caution and ran, ran so fast she did not care if she bowled over some fat lady, or young child. She had to go down a tunnel to get to the other side, running, the sound of her rapid feet echoing along ahead of her, her breath running short until she saw steps again and climbing, her heart fit to burst, her chest painful, she surfaced and ran headlong into a bicycle.

Not an ordinary bicycle, a radio-bicycle and the tallest Irishman, Sean was most sorely offended.

"Can you not see where you are going? Can you not see this is a bicycle of the most expensive kind?" His Irish accent jarred in such Gallic surroundings. Not a word of sympathy for Cornelia who lay sprawled over a front wheel. Sean, merely tossed her aside, picked up his bicycle and inspected the trimming, aerials, lamps and valves and all manner of things for damage, telling Cornelia that she was a lucky woman that no damage had been incurred.

"I'm sorry, I'm sorry," she forced out of her throat, struggling to find oxygen, hardly able to speak at all.

"English," the Irishman declared with surprise, almost ready to forgive her, such a pleasure it was to hear a language he nearly understood.

"I'm frightfully sorry," Cornelia repeated, "I was running so fast I couldn't stop."

"Were you trying to catch a train?" The other Irishman enquired, standing patient with his bicycle, his coat flapping in the cool station breeze.

"No, I mean yes, I mean no. I was trying to catch you."

"Us?" Sean asked, instantly reacting, looking about him.

"You got my message, you must have, tell me you did."

"Message?" They tried to look blank about it.

"Yes, oh please tell me you did."

"What message would this be?" Sean asked, suspicious and nervous to be discussing messages on a station platform. "Why would we be getting any messages at all. We are just two Irishmen on holiday in France."

But Cornelia knew better. Sherlock Holmes had described them and their bicycles too well for any mistakes to be made.

"We sent you the message only four hours ago. 'Sherlock Holmes captured, Chateau Schwaften, Baden-Baden, assistance needed.'"

Sean looked at Patrick. Patrick looked at Sean. This was the message they had received all right, but they were surprised to hear it repeated from this girl's lips, if she was a girl, for she was dressed in an odd assortment of clothes.

"And if we received this message?" Sean wanted to know.

"Oh you did, I know you did. Holmes has been captured. He was impersonating an SS colonel and we escaped only because they flew us out, thinking we were someone else."

"And who are you if you are not someone else?"

"I am Cornelia Hainsley and on the train is Sir John Watson whom I know you have met..."

"On the train?"

"Yes..." And as luck would have it, the whistle shrieked at that very moment and the Paris express on the other side of the station began to pull out. "My train," she called out, starting to turn to run for it, but the shorter Irishman with the handsome nose, Patrick, snatched out his hand and held her back. "You'll not catch that train, your John Watson will leave without you."

"Oh no," she wailed, straining to see the train leave. Sean, whose tallness has been recorded could see all.

"An old man, white hair waving a stick. That is Dr Watson of literary fame all right. Young lady, Sherlock Holmes is in trouble, we pledged we'd come in a crisis, you will serve him better by helping us in Germany than holding that old man's hand."

"But he has all the information, the secret of Nürnberg, if he loses it, all is lost..."

"His reputation is sound," Sean announced with authority. "He will deliver the goods. A man is not chosen by Sherlock Holmes by his reputation for failure."

Cornelia knew that was true enough. Watson would fret, he would panic, but short of death, nothing would part him from that case. This was France, he was safe enough, surely. "I must call the Ambassador, he must be told Dr Watson is coming."

Again the Irishmen disapproved. "We shall relay the information Miss Cornelia, it is safer by far. A call from us will have him met by one of our brothers. We will get him to your Ambassador. Patrick, take a ride and let Paris know."

Patrick nodded, passing through the station barrier and was gone from sight in the twinkling of an eye.

"We have a special lorry meeting us," Sean told her, looking at her with a professional stare. "That's a very odd costume you are wearing."

"It can be explained later," she answered, feeling all strange inside.

Watson gone, Holmes locked up, things were certainly in a mess.

"A lorry?" she queried, her voice distant as he walked beside her with his bicycle out of the station.

"We went into action the moment we got the message. A lorry will take us to a place on the border and from there we shall cycle in. We shall fix you up with some warm clothing..." He paused momentarily, looking at her. "Can you prove who you are?"

She could not, Watson had her passport. Inside her fingers closed on the only thing that could prove herself to them satisfactorily, she pulled it out and showed it to him, the blue crystal tube.

He nodded satisfied. "I gave it to Sherlock Holmes myself. This is a sad day for one so great to be locked up by the Bavarian horde."

Cornelia silently agreed and together they moved off through the streets looking for Patrick, her heart near to breaking.

***

Watson sat numb, the train already five miles out of Lyon, the passengers riding with him looking at him oddly, for there was a soft moan upon his lips. Here he was alone, the case firmly upon his lap, but he was alone. Had Cornelia been abducted, or had she abandoned him to go back on a rash, impossible mission to rescue Holmes?

He thought he would get off at the next station, go back to Lyon to look for her... But as the train sped on, the misty fields enclosing the railway, he knew he had a mission, indeed he could hear Holmes' voice coming to him strong, stern, as it always did.

"Watson, ignore the girl. Your duty Watson, remember your duty. The higher calling, a nation in jeopardy. Cornelia is a survivor, but you, you have a sacred mission. Return to London see Churchill.

There is no time for sentiment. I shall not thank you for tears shed on my behalf."

Watson sat staring at nothing for more than an hour; his hands gripping the case handle, a frail reminder of the Watson of former days, but nevertheless, a determined and resolute one.

15

Desperadoes

For three days Sherlock Holmes lay on a sparse lumpy mattress in a damp draughty cell, high up in the lonely tower of the Chateau Schwaften. The wind howled endlessly and when he stood, which was never often, for the beating he had received from the guards on the first day had been severe and had permanently affected his breathing, he suspected a broken rib.

True, General Offenbroeder had been disgusted at the behaviour of the guards. Sherlock Holmes was the enemy to be sure, but a venerated old man. It was surely bad sport to attack an old man so viciously. He banished the guards to night sentry outside the Chateau for six months, a fitting punishment in such a cold and windy place.

However, the General not wanting to seem 'soft', instructed that Holmes would receive no medical attention and little food other than a thin cold gruel, bread and water. He had only the occasional visit from an Intelligence Officer whose name was never revealed. This short little man with beetle eyebrows and a thin, sparrow-like face would sit at the end of Holmes' bed and stare at him, occasionally asking a personal question, always referring to the 'others' in the field.

For some reason he discounted Holmes' ability to have achieved what he did with just the aide of Dr Watson and a young nurse. Holmes got the impression that they were rounding up almost anyone he had contact with.

Herr Flohn, Von Hipplestar, Captain Ansbach, the workers at the chocolate factory. Sabotage and subterfuge was assumed to be widespread. Perhaps it satisfied their egos that way, to have allowed Holmes to have got away with so much, discovering their Jet and jet-fuel plans, abducting an important SS officer, fooling everyone with the impersonation was not something they were prepared to accept he could do without help. Someone was to blame and they would be found and made to confess.

Holmes could only wait. Because of thick snow around Berlin, it had been decided to keep him at the Chateau until a decision could be made about what kind of trial should take place. There was a need, too, for the Third Reich to take maximum advantage of a captured enemy hero. An announcement guaranteed to shatter the will of the English people had to be planned and it was necessary to show the German people that only full obedience to the Reich would be tolerated. Collaborators had to be found, the trial had to be a sensation, not only to strike fear abroad, but at home, redouble the iron-will of the German peoples.

Holmes was the spearhead of enemy aggression, the justification therefore for invasion against those who favoured the total onslaught against the Reich. London would regret the day they sent such a famous man to battle with the supreme commander of the master race, they would grovel at his feet with apologies, repayment would be extracted with the lives of thousands, nothing less would satisfy the German people.

All this Holmes had to sit through and although he was in constant pain, he derived some amusement from this little man's paranoia. He knew the truth, he knew there were no conspirators, but he did not say yay or nay, confusion could only help the allied cause.

He gave no thought to rescue. Each day his health grew worse. It was almost as if he were willing a rapid death upon himself, another way to cheat the enemy. He had won. Watson and Cornelia would be in London. They would have the photographs, the whole story, it was a victory and even if, as the little man had hinted, the jet bomber was abandoned for a jet fighter, it was enough to know the Germans thought the principle of the jet engine worthy of development. England would have to act, they would have to flood Whittle's team with money, get a British fighter up in the sky before the slow, conventional fighters were just flying museum pieces, annoying moths easily plucked out of the sky.

All in all though, it was not satisfactory for him to lay in a lofty prison awaiting the ignominy of a show trial, or the agony of a slow death. Only the comfort of knowing Watson and Cornelia were safe gave him hope. That and three copies of Mr Moorehaus's *Esquire* magazine. The American had left them with him after coming up to say goodbye. He almost seemed to regret having betrayed Holmes, but once done there was no turning back. Besides which, he confessed to have been working for the Nazis for five years and that a total victory was just around the corner for the Fuhrer. History guided him, the future was as plain as day to him and he wanted a slice of the action. Betraying Holmes guaranteed his path was clear, his remorse no help to a prostrate Sherlock Holmes.

Indeed, Holmes saw little value in the man's remorse at all, but he enjoyed some literary smatterings in the magazines and amused himself by looking at the impossible Varga girls.

As new snow fell on this third day he caught a chill and suddenly he knew that here was the beginning of the end.

***

The ridge overlooking Chateau Schwaften was a wonderland. The snow-laden trees sat still, heavy in a permanent mountain of white virgin snow. Three cold windswept figures in white fur coats stood looking down at the fortress-like Chateau, a mixed feeling coming over them as they realised just how hard it would be to penetrate the eighteenth century structure. It had been purpose built to repel intruders.

Sean missed the bicycles and shook his head. It was bad enough he had to traipse thirty miles over rough snow-covered mountain tracks. They had tried lashing the cycles together on the skis, but it had not worked at all and so they had reluctantly abandoned them far back near the French border, a place undefended, the natural forest an inhospitable terrain considered difficult and a safe barrier against the barbarians.

Patrick brushed snow off his skis. Skiing did not come naturally to him. There was rarely much snow to be had in Ireland (last seen in the terrible winter of 1936), but Sean, the more experienced of the two, had once spent a holiday tobogganing in Scotland, thus he knew all about the consistencies of snow, believing it to be all linked with cosmic forces. He was a deep man at heart.

Cornelia was an excellent skier, having spent many happy hours skiing in Wales in winter and three holidays in the French Alps with her Papa. It was the wind and the awful cold she found difficult to contend with, her light body constantly buffeted by gusts of drifting snow.

"I still don't see how we can get him out," Patrick mumbled, "we don't even know where he is!"

"We will find him," Sean told him, "don't be foolish man, Miss Cornelia here has a plan."

"She has a plan," he spat, watching it instantly freeze on his boot. "She has altogether too many plans." Things were not all well between these two.

"Oh don't fight again," Cornelia snapped, her patience running out with the argumentative and sullen Patrick. "And if you say once more, 'it never snows like this in Ireland,' I shall personally push you down the slope in the hopes there is a minefield."

Patrick shut up, he was beginning to suspect the young woman did not like him and him being a popular man with the ladies back in Ireland, this was a new and unnerving experience.

"We could start an avalanche," Sean suggested. "That would tell us all we need to know about mines and their defences."

"But wouldn't they be suspicious?" she asked.

Sean shook his head. "Most normal thing in the world, an avalanche, besides the Chateau is half way up the other side, our efforts would only fill in the bottom."

"Then we'd best do it in darkness."

"Twilight," Patrick said, just for argument's sake, "that way we will see what it achieves."

Cornelia looked at him and sighed, "oh all right."

Sean was looking to the left of him. "I was thinking that they might be expecting a rescue mission, if they are, where would they be expecting it, do you reckon?

"In the Chateau," Patrick answered, thinking it an obvious question.

Sean frowned. "No Patrick, listen to what I'm saying. Sherlock Holmes is in there, naturally they know that, but where out here would they expect us to be?"

"Do you think they expect us?" Cornelia asked. "I'm not so sure London would mount a rescue mission, they'd consider it a hopeless case, cut their losses."

"That's just the kind of thing I'd expect from the English," Patrick said harshly. "No respect, no sense of brotherhood, no..."

"Enough, Patrick," Sean told him, cutting him off. "We are here, we gave our word. A man like Sherlock Holmes would know there's no hope of rescue in times of war, it would be an understanding. It is quite conceivable that the Germans down there expect no rescue attempt at all. We shall have the element of total surprise on our side.

"And secrecy," Cornelia added. "If they don't expect an attack, why attack? We have no guns, we would be a poor match for a fortress. Couldn't we just walk in and take him out?"

"Walk in?" Sean asked.

"Walk out?" Patrick protested.

"Yes, I have my papers that still say I'm Second Lieutenant Hassel. We could be special security sent from Karslruhe to guard Sherlock Holmes. You would have to get me a uniform."

"But our voices, we don't speak a word of German." Cornelia had to think on that. She sat down on her skis and shook her frozen head. There always had to be drawbacks.

"Perhaps if I were to walk in. They mistook me for a man before..."

"You a man?" Patrick laughed, thinking the idea preposterous. "Never girl, never see you as a man in a million years, it's a weird sort of man who makes that sort of mistake."

They both sniggered at that.

"No really, I could. You could knock out the guards just before midnight, take their places, or perhaps steal a car and I will find Lord Holmes, bring him down, pretending that I'm going to take him to Berlin. It's worth a try, don't you think?"

"Impossible, a terrible plan," Patrick told her.

"Suicide," agreed Scan. "I'll be jiggered if we'd do any such thing."

"What about the avalanche?" Patrick reminded them, a gleam in his eye.

"Oh let's do that now," Cornelia said, getting up. "At least it will keep us warm."

***

Holmes sat and stared at the radio they had brought him. It was difficult for him to understand why they had brought it; switching it on and removing the dial so he could not turn it off. They had not brought it for his amusement, for the bread and water remained his staple diet. They had refused his request for a doctor and now there was swelling around his rib cage. His eyes were sore, headaches frequent, only by force of will and habit did he get up from his bed and do the exercises necessary to keep him alive, each hour hastened the moment when he would lose that option. If it was their intention to ruin his health, break him down mentally, this was the way to do it. A man of eighty-three can stand only so much, the radio was a cross he would have preferred not to bear.

He had heard the avalanche, felt it rumble down the slopes. He leapt up off his bed in time to see it crash down into the ravine below the Chateau; trees ripped from their roots, sweeping on down upon the Castle with a terrible roar. A constant thunder of tumbling snow scouring the area immediately before it.

Snow sprayed upwards by the ton and the Chateau reverberated with the shock waves for some time, a pall of icy-snow spray hanging in the air over the decimated forest until well after twilight had stolen the view from his cell.

Holmes had contemplated escape, but there was a hundred feet of sheer rockface below his mountain-facing window. A window fit only for a flying death. The choice between Berlin and that leap was not a pleasant one. The door was locked, but no guard stood outside, it was not necessary. There was but one set of stairs from the next floor down and it led into another heavily locked room. Outside that lay a long exposed terrace connecting the tower to the main Chateau.

An entirely appropriate medieval tower for an historic relic like himself. He felt well pleased it was this and not some dungeon with common thieves for his company. Solitude was something he could tolerate well, a place where he could make amends with his soul. Arrogance had locked him in his room, his own arrogance, it was not a power that worked both ways.

The avalanche was a reminder however, that there were forces more powerful than the Third Reich and it proved to be no end of a consolation to him as he contemplated his daily heavy grey bread and water. Optimism had allies. Baden-Baden water was rich in minerals, they could not remove those, nor its healing properties and the coarse bread was filled with excellent fibre, another positive point. Suffering was all relative, but the radio. That was torture!

Somehow the Holmes doctrine of Nil Desperandum had to be rediscovered.

At seven o'clock having eaten and done his exercises he waited for the daily news on the radio. Instead he received an unexpected visit from his intelligence officer. "Something of interest for you today Lord Holmes," he told him with a leer, tossing Holmes an orange, a double surprise for Holmes had almost forgotten about oranges and this, if he was not mistaken looked like a Moroccan one. His inquisitor's mood was the other surprise, it was a curiously good one, and that meant bad news, Holmes was sure of it. He busied himself with changing the frequency on the radio to a Hamburg station. "I have something of interest for you to hear Sherlock Holmes. Something that will concern you and bring to light certain developments since your arrest. You will be interested to know that an officer of the SS has arrived from Stuttgart, he is with General Offenbroeder now. You are to go to Berlin, the trial will begin the first week of February."

Holmes nodded, wondering whether to eat the orange immediately or save it for later. Such indecision was normally alien to him.

"The avalanche was a distressing annoyance. We have lost both our telephone link and our radio mast. This is the first time we have had such snowfall in January, but bad winter, good summer, I always say."

"Will I be allowed a doctor in Berlin?" Holmes asked tiredly.

"There is one here tonight, he came with the other man. The authorities in Berlin want you fit for the trial, you will eat tomorrow, enjoy many more oranges. They are from Morocco, y'know."

Holmes nodded, a fatted calf to be sacrificed, how childishly simple.

"Now I will go, they will be here presently. You will please listen to the radio."

Holmes sat down on his bed once more and peeled his orange, ignoring the little man who left very pleased with himself, locking the door behind him, his footsteps walking away unheard by a distracted Holmes. Berlin. A show trial. Churchill would be annoyed. The British honour was at stake. To end his life here, now, for the good of England? Yet Holmes had always regarded suicide with distinct distaste. There was always the possibility of escape from Berlin.

The radio started up again startling him. "Germany calling...Germany calling," the fateful words began, "Germany calling..."

Holmes was instantly riveted to the set. That voice, that voice!

"The snivelling spy, Sherlock Holmes is no more. He is a prisoner of the Great Third Reich, accused of leading a pack of Jewish saboteurs in an attack against strategic installations. The English stoop so low to recruit cowards, traitors, scum. The legend of Sherlock Holmes as a great man, is no more. It expires tonight for he is in prison awaiting trial, his accomplices rot with him. A sentence of immediate death would have been too good, too easy. A trial is set; an example to show the world that even in Germany where the strongest reign supreme, we know the meaning of justice. Sherlock Holmes who dares to mock the Fuhrer, dares to sneer at the SS and seeks the destruction, the total destruction of the German nation, was today trapped by hero General Offenbroeder. His instant capitulation typical of the weak, cowardly spirit that permeates the rich, so called upper class of England. England's greatest meddler is finally apprehended and his crimes are unforgivable."

Desperadoes

Holmes stared open-mouthed at the radio, an attack on himself he cared nothing for, the link between him and the Jews merely typical of their deceitful games. No, the actual content did not matter a fig to him, it was the Voice. The voice of evil itself, the voice that had haunted him for nearly fifty years, the man who had the raw nerve of original sin in the palm of his hand, whose very existence was an anathema. Here was the anti-christ, the ultimate heathen and he was working for them! The Nazis had taken the most evil man on earth and set him up on radio. It was an abomination. It hurt deeply, it boiled his very blood, his heart raced, he felt a rage rising up in him, long buried, long submerged by the years of civilised behaviour. But now, the almost animal hatred he felt for that monster welled up inside him.

He stared at the radio. The man's voice was still pouring out filth, lies, corruption, poison. At last he could take no more, he rose up from his bed and with one swift kick he sent the radio flying through the room and out through the window, the dreaded voice dying on the wind, the name of the villain coming rushing out all at once from Holmes' throat.

"Moriarty! Moriarty you beast, you unspeakable swine. A thousand curses, a million, Moriarty." He choked, red-faced, trying to draw breath, his hands shook as he fell to his knees, tangled in his blanket, his hands attempting to shred it in his anguish. He felt wretched, felt as if all his life had been for nought if this monster lived. Holmes was close to a madness that was possibly always there; the chill, his ribs, his hatred for Moriarty, his dizziness from lack of food, all combined to give him a seizure and almost as if his head and heart were set to burst. He cried out, "Oh God. Watson, Cornelia..." He coughed but once and then fell back onto the floor wasted, a man near the door of death itself, a broken heart the cause.

***

Cornelia got up off the ground where she had fallen and brushed herself down. The radio had missed her by an inch only and the sheer force of its explosion on impact with the rocks had thrown her off her feet.

"What in God's name was that?" Patrick asked, white-faced, helping Cornelia pick pieces of wood from her clothes. Sean was removing chipped wood from his shoulders.

"A radio," she answered, "it came from up there in the tower."

Sean and Patrick squinted upward. "Possibly," Sean agreed, "but who would have thrown a radio out of a window?"

Cornelia thought about it a moment. "Sherlock Holmes," she answered firmly, "he dislikes the radio with a passion. It would be a way of letting us know where he is. Perhaps he dropped it to warn us."

Sean looked up at the tower and shook his head. "We might as well go home, you'll not get up there. You're sure he wants rescuing? He might be trying to scare us off."

Cornelia doubted that. They had already been to the front of the Chateau. The avalanche had attracted many soldiers to the surrounding area and posing as an interested boy from the village she had discovered that the communications were destroyed. Patrick's natural instinct for destruction, perfected by the years with the Sinn Fein were a useful skill when it came to starting avalanches. They had started it with the ridge itself, using three hundred snowballs, a little shouting and a helpful boulder. Three hours hard work and one word from Patrick had sent all crashing below. He was wasted in the flatlands of Ireland.

She had also discovered that Holmes was to be moved that very night. Although he was not mentioned by name, their talk about the 'famous prisoner' could not have been anyone else. If they were to succeed at all, their moment was immediate, they had only to wait until after suppertime and the soldiers settled down for the evening. Now it was nearly seven o'clock, dark enough to begin Operation Rescue.

"They'll take him in a car most probably," Sean said, starting down the slope for the Chateau gates, the only exit for cars.

"But which car?" Cornelia asked, following suit.

"The one they brought him in," Patrick declared. For once Patrick had said something that made sense. Sean continued on down the slope, indicating to Patrick and Cornelia to stay back. They sat beside a boulder and drew breath, watching Sean shrink into the night below them.

"We shouldn't be in white down here," Cornelia remarked, concerned. "There isn't so much snow about the gate they might mistake us for a bear."

"A bear?" Patrick queried with great surprise. "They have bears in Germany?"

"Yes, I have seen many pictures of German bears on the beer mugs. But they mostly have brown coats and sleep in the winter."

"So we would be white bears, wide awake," Patrick pointed out. "I would not like to be thought of as a great bear, white or brown, but it gives me an idea."

"Well make sure they don't see your red hair, Patrick, you would frighten them to death if they thought you were a great white bear with red hair. And mind no falling radio takes you unawares."

266

This was a challenge to Patrick. He untied his hood and brazenly shook his head, allowing his plentiful wild hair to spring back into place. "Just let them try," he told her with a big grin.

They could see Sean had reached the towering gates and was lying quite close to the guards, talking in low mutters down there. They must have been very slow guards for they did not once notice Sean sliding up to the gates, but then he did look very much like a large blob of snow, or bear. An arm went up twice. It was the signal.

Patrick darted from Cornelia's side and began his descent to the gates, Cornelia following at a safe distance behind, unsure of what the Irishmen might do. She worried she might set off a fall of snow and rock, accidentally alerting the guards. One avalanche was enough, she thought.

She was no more than half way down when there was a shout and two snarling Irish bears leapt upon the inattentive guards and brought them down with a great clout onto the road. The surprise was all their's, the guards never pulled a trigger, nor said another word. The two red-heads quickly took off their white coats and quickly adopted the guards' uniforms (but being sensible fellows, they put the white coats back on for they did not intend to freeze to death for any Englishman). The naked, unconscious guards were tipped into a nearby snow drift, an unfortunate way to go, but well deserved, for all that.

Cornelia arrived at the scene and congratulated them. "I thought you really were bears for a moment," she said, straightening out Patrick's hood. "Your snarl, Patrick was so evil."

"So did they," he grinned, very pleased with himself and wonderfully warm in all his clothing. "I think we're safe from radios here."

"Shall I sneak in and see if there are any cars from outside the area?" Cornelia asked.

Sean looked through the grille in the great wooden doors and spied an illuminated courtyard filled with all manner of transportation. There were more guards stationed further in and probably more after that. He did not think it a good idea to go on, they were fine where they were. No one could go in or out without passing through this exit.

"If Sherlock Holmes is coming out tonight, we shall find him soon enough." He declared.

Cornelia looked into his face and accepted his word. "I shall hide over by the tree. When the car comes, make the driver get out, I will take his place."

Sean nodded. Patrick stamped his cold feet, cursing the heavy rifles, worried about how little spare ammunition they had.

Nothing happened for the next two cold hours and it was near to ten o'clock before even the sound of a human or dog, or anything at all was heard, the snow acting as a great sound insulator. However, it was dogs that signalled something was afoot. Three men on foot patrol came along the road with two enormous, snarling alsations, struggling at the end of their leashes. They came to the gate, the dogs immensely curious about the two Irishmen. They sniffed with more than their usual interest at the guards.

Sean did not know what he had just been asked exactly, but he guessed it was something to do with the gates. A snag developed almost immediately. Neither he, nor Patrick knew how to open the gates.

Both men grew quite afraid suddenly. Sean muttered a few "Hail Marys".

The foot patrol waited impatiently for a moment whilst Sean searched the gate for some kind of knob. There was nothing and the game would have been up if Patrick had not, in sheer desperation, pulled on the old fashioned bell pull set into the stone wall. Instantly a generator clicked and with no further ado, the gates swung inwards and the foot patrol, offering a few well-chosen curses aimed at incompetant guards, passed through, dragging the snarling dogs with them. Patrick pulled the bell wire again and the doors closed. German ingenuity impressed him no end.

"Be Jesus, modern inventions, what's wrong with a door knob?" Sean complained, unsettled after all that tension. He wiped perspiration from his brow. "That was lucky, Patrick, my son. Those dogs were a mean and nasty lot. I have seen dogs and dogs, and those were the meanest."

They would have discussed dogs more, but there was a sudden hooting of a car horn behind them in the Chateau yard and looking through the grille, Sean could see a car wanted to come out. This was the moment!

"Pull the wire," he ordered Patrick. "Miss Cornelia," he whispered as loud as he dared.

Cornelia was there in a flash, she had seen the dogs and nearly had a heart attack when they had not been able to open the door. All could have been lost right there.

"If it's him," Sean said, "I'll just raise my rifle. You tell the driver to get out. He may not understand a simple Irish request."

Cornelia nodded her head as the great wooden gates swung wide open.

A small DKW motored out first, with four soldiers inside, a large black Mercedes behind.

Two cars! This they had not bargained for.

"Oh glory be," Patrick swore as the DKW motored out. He purposely dropped his rifle on the ground in front of the Mercedes which jerked to a halt, the driver instantly letting down his window, hurling curses at the stupid guard. "Scheisser, get out of the way." Sean opened the driver's passenger door and aimed a rifle at his head, instantly silencing him. Cornelia stepped out from the shadows and looked inside the car. Two men she had not seen before sat either side of a pale old man. This was the right car.

The DKW had stopped fifty metres ahead, the men inside obviously an escort, worried, suspicious of the hold up, fortunately too far away to see all the details.

"Get out," Cornelia ordered the driver, "Schnell, schnell."

"Nein, nein," he began to protest, but with the odds the way they were. Sean couldn't afford any arguments. He shot the driver stone dead. Patrick wrenched open the door and pulled the dead driver out, pleased that the window had been open, allowing the man's brains to leave the car without making a mess, there was little blood in the car at all. Cornelia quickly stepped into the driver's seat ignoring the wet stains as best she could, shaking with shock, trying to blot out the image of the violent death.

"Shut the gates, Patrick," Sean ordered, climbing into the back seat, his rifle aimed at the head of one of the Germans. "You wouldn't think of using your guns, would you?"

Patrick pulled the bell wire, the doors began to react and Cornelia drove out of their way, Patrick running, scrambling into the seat beside her. Sean found to his surprise the Germans had no weapons. They sat in silence unsure of their position, perhaps confused anyone would be so foolhardy to kidnap them and their prisoner with four armed soldiers up ahead in the DKW. Indeed, one soldier was out of the car looking back at them, but Cornelia flashed her lights as she picked up speed and he got back in, obviously satisfied that things had been rectified.

Holmes was drugged, there was no doubt about it. His head dropped, he failed to recognise anyone or anything, he looked close to death, it was a pitiful sight.

"This is far from over," Sean said, noting that the DKW was moving again ahead of them. "We have to lose that escort, or we shall not escape alive."

"I know," Cornelia answered, "what shall we do with the Germans?"

"You will let us go," one of the Germans answered in good English. "No need to be foolish about this – you are completely outnumbered. I am Doktor Hoffnung, it is very admirable that you attempt to rescue Sherlock Holmes, but I must warn you that he just suffered a massive heart attack, he is being transferred to the Hospital in Karlsruhe. You would be making a great mistake to attempt this rescue, it would only kill him."

"It is a bluff," Sean told Cornelia, who knew about bluffs.

"No, it is not a bluff," the doctor answered, cool and calm. He knew he was dealing with serious, desperate people. One did not kill a man so quickly unless you were prepared to kill others. The other man, a political intelligence officer in SS uniform was indifferent to either the slain driver or Sherlock Holmes. He was concerned for his own life, no old man not likely to survive the journey to Berlin was going to deprive him of it.

"Holmes, Lord Holmes," Cornelia shouted back, "Lord Holmes it is me, Cornelia."

She negotiated a bend and they entered a village, the DKW immediately in front of them now, a man looking back at them through the rear window. Did they suspect anything was wrong? Her headlights flooded the little car.

"Holmes," she repeated, "Lord Holmes, can you hear me?"

Holmes lifted his head, his eyes in a fog, his mind slipping on a wet surface. The injection! A huge needle. He remembered them finding him prostrate on the floor...

"Lord Holmes, it's me Cornelia, can you hear me?" Her voice was more desperate now. He must know her, he must!

"Cornelia," he muttered. It was impossible, she was in London. What games did they play with him now?

"We are rescuing you. You will get back to England. Watson is there already, you hear? Watson is home."

He heard Watson's name, the words filtered through the cobwebs in his mind, which pounded with a dreadful pain. His throat was desperately dry.

"Watson in London?" he rasped.

"Yes," Sean called out, "you're safe Sherlock Holmes, this is the Irish Red-Headed Brigade who've come for you. Remember?"

"Irish?" Suddenly something came to him, an expression, a name that haunted him. His lips opened, he stared out at the illuminated road ahead, the dancing headlights making him dizzy. At last something broke through, he cried out, "Moriarty." Then he fell back in a faint again, the drugs too strong to overcome.

"Moriarty?" Sean asked, wondering if he had heard right. "My God, by the hair splitting saints, did he say Moriarty, Patrick?"

"It was the word I heard," he replied, tense and much disturbed, crossing himself.

"This is most amazing, an astonishing turn of events." Sean added.

"Why?" Cornelia asked, who only knew Moriarty as a name from Holmes' past.

270

"One of the greatest criminal minds that ever left Ireland, Miss Cornelia. He could have been another Shaw, another Shakespeare or even a Shackleton, but he became..."

"Moriarty," Patrick said.

"In a word, yes," Sean confirmed. "The arch villain, the reaper of souls, the seller of tickets to America in ships with holed bottoms. If he is here, if he is in Germany, we must hunt him down, we must find him, there's no greater enemy to the Irish people than one of their own turned against them."

"Oh dear," Cornelia whispered. "I suppose that means you won't help me take Lord Holmes back."

"We undertook a pledge," Patrick declared, "we shall keep to the bargain. But not unless you drive with more concern for the condition of the road."

"It's slippery," she complained.

"Moriarty," Sean muttered, the word itself utter dread in his heart. He had to speak to Holmes as soon as possible, these German villains had obviously drugged the man to move him. They would pay for that, all Germany would.

The Germans seemed unperturbed however. Neither of them knew this Moriarty, but it obviously had a great affect on the people around them. But it was no concern of their's, all this would be over in a matter of minutes, there was a road block outside Rastatt which would take care of their abductors.

Sean's eyes opened in surprise as they approached a bend. He made a quick decision, this stretch of road was ideal, he knew it.

"Stop here," he yelled, cocking his rifle, "stop, turn around."

Cornelia piled on the brakes, skidding to the side of the road, Sean and Patrick already had their doors open and they rolled out onto the narrow road watching and waiting for a reaction from the DKW ahead. They were on a sharp, narrow bend with a steep drop to one side, lined by granite boulders just visible with the headlights. The wind whipped through the gaps rocking the car, blowing loose snow into their faces.

Cornelia busied herself with turning the car, Patrick watching from the road for trouble from their passengers. Sure enough, the political officer bounced right out of the car making a run for it. Patrick took aim, fired once and brought the man down clean, the rifle crack echoing away on the wind. Cornelia scrambled out of the car and ran to roll the body off the road.

"That will bring them," Sean said with satisfaction in his voice, looking for a confrontation to get things solved (though he was worried about the wind blinding him at an awkward moment). "Keep your heads down."

Back in the car, Cornelia looked into her mirror, headlights were approaching fast, the DKW was coming back. It would be coming around the bend any second.

"Scheisser," a voice muttered softly. "I'm not moving," the doctor told her. "I'm not going anywhere."

But Cornelia was not listening. She was just looking at the odds. Four armed professional soldiers against two Irishmen with two rifles and hardly any ammunition.

She need not have worried, the Sinn Fein trained their men well. Patrick's eyes were on the coming glow of the headlights, his rifle firm in his hand as he lay on the cold road. Sean already had the car in his sights and as the car came around the bend at speed, both Irishmen fired. A tyre burst, the windscreen shattered, the driver lost control and the car abruptly lurched left into a boulder, ricocheting off it violently. It abruptly turned over onto its roof and continued on, sailing with a grace it never had on four wheels over the jagged cliff, sinking from view, its occupants either dead or dazed. Not one of them had had time to get off a shot.

"Fine work, O'Reilly," Sean remarked.

"Yourself, McCully."

They ran over to the waiting car, jumping in the back, both guns focused on the doctor.

"I'm not going to resist, your man is ill. He needs to get to a hospital." But they could tell, he just wanted to save his own skin.

Cornelia moved off, Sean looking at her in the driving mirror.

"There's a country road to the right, about a mile back, Miss Cornelia, take that and keep going till we get to that village we passed at noon.

Cornelia complied, hoping the car was not too heavy for that steep climb.

"The road's blocked with snow," the doctor pointed out, trying to be helpful.

"Not any more," Sean told him, "they put a snow plough through it this afternoon trying to fix up the telegraph. Now tell me doctor, what was it exactly that you put into our friend Sherlock Holmes here? And don't tell me about his heart. This was a fit man no more than a few days ago. That Chateau was not good for him, I can see that, torture can ruin a man's heart."

"And we don't want to hear about taking two aspirins and getting a good night's rest either," announced Patrick. "The truth man before I split your nose in two."

The doctor didn't want to argue, he sat silent, staring into nothing.

Sean didn't like his attitude. "Don't play games with me, doctor, where I come from a doctor is no more important than the last child he failed to cure of the colic. I've seen doctors and I've seen doctors, sending out the bill is the only thing you think about. Now what is in Lord Holmes?"

"It is just a sedative, that is all. He wouldn't leave his cell, he was hysterical, shouting out curses, names, I had to calm him. It will wear off in time."

"So there's nothing wrong with his heart?" Cornelia asked. She was pleased to hear it as she put the heavy car into a slide around a blind, slippery bend. The wheels spun on a hump of loose snow, then gripping, propelled them forward again, the back of the car snaking all over the road, tossing the rear seat occupants all over the place.

"Careful now," Patrick shouted nervously, never one to favour a car over a trusty bicycle. He was thinking that those Germans in the DKW would not have died so easily if they had been on bicycles. It would have been a different kettle of fish then, to be sure. The modern soldier could learn a thing or two in Ireland and that was a fact.

The car sped on up the narrow snow-covered road, Holmes unconscious, the Irishmen silent, keeping a wary eye on the doctor, whilst Cornelia was just relieved that she had Sherlock Holmes back in English (and Irish) hands.

"The village is coming up," she told them, "what now?"

Sean knew the answer to that one.

"We sleep the night here at that holiday house, Herr Doktor too. We can hide the car in the cow shed under the house. We took care of all the business down there, by the time they realise both cars are missing in Karlsruhe, it will be another hour from now, then they will have to search. The snow will hold them up. I should be very surprised if they look for us so near the Chateau."

It seemed reasonable, though the doctor was disappointed. He had thought they would try and distance themselves from the Chateau, the net would be cast wide to find Sherlock Holmes, but most probably not in the immediate vicinity. "Whose problem am I?" he asked, turning to Sean, who had removed his hood and was busy shaking out his wild crop of red hair.

"You're no problem, doctor," Sean replied. "You just get our friend cured here, get him back on his feet and we will let you free. We aren't cruel men. Killing a doctor would be an unlikely thing indeed, unless he did something stupid, and something stupid would annoy my friend Patrick very much indeed. He isn't a patient man."

"I'll second that," Patrick declared in the absence of others to do it. Cornelia smiled, switching off the car's engine, turning off the lights.

The cowshed was narrow, but large enough for a car. Patrick jumped out and closed the shed doors, which groaned loudly, unused to such activity.

"Lucky thing we noticed this place," Sean remarked. "Now what we need is a lamp. Miss Cornelia, turn on your lights again, it's as dark as a politician's mind in here."

Cornelia switched on the lights and Patrick ran to the back to find the stairs up into the house. Holmes began to come around, his eyes opened and one could tell by the way he focused upon Cornelia's smiling face, by the utter surprise he registered upon seeing the large red-headed Irish man, that he was going to be all right, even though he could not speak and was clearly having trouble with body coordination. The drug administered must have been a very strong, mind-crushing one.

"Let's get him upstairs," Sean said, making the doctor take one arm and drape it around his shoulders, Sean taking the other. "Cornelia, the moment we disappear, get these lights off and go outside, get rid of our tyre tracks coming in here."

"Yes." She watched them go, struggling with an awkwardly heavy Holmes, a man who had never been so low in all his life. It was a sad sight.

She did her cold duty outside, even covered up the car engine with a rotting horse blanket, for it was a fearfully cold night. Eventually made her way upstairs, where the only sounds were the incessant wind howling from every corner and the creaking house.

The hours passed slowly. Only once did they grow concerned. A car drove by and stopped almost directly outside the house, but it was with great relief that they realised that Cornelia had filled in the tyre tracks, even as far as the nearest corner, trusting to the snow and wind to cover the rest. It seemed that the car was just having trouble with the cold, for it moved on after several attempts to restart it, continuing down the hill, the engine spluttering into spasmodic fire as the driver wrestled with the cold, damp, spark plugs.

Sometime soon after that Cornelia went to sleep and remained oblivious to the next development until it was already far too late.

***

It was morning, the quiet of it was so intense one might have been in church, but even church is never so totally quiet. The thick snow deadened all sound as effectively as if one had stuck one's head into a basin of porridge; so utterly silent one dared not move for shattering some God-preserved moment. Cornelia lay in a heap, a coarse blanket was slung over her and she was aware of two things. She was freezing cold, stiff from having curled up with her knees almost touching her chin, and she was entirely alone.

She stood up, uncertain about her legs, her shoulder aching from lying on a hard floor; the thick, unpleasant taste of an unwashed mouth. She advanced to a window, brushed aside the thick frost on the glass and stared out over the distant hills to a remote and menacing Chateau below. Its towers shimmered with a new overlay of snow. She looked at the heavy-burdened trees all around the house and shivered some more. Her snow-suit was not enough to keep her warm when she herself was cool. The sky was milk white, no sun visible at all.

There was no smell of breakfast, they had nothing and now, nearly thirty hours had passed since she had eaten anything. She felt weak. The utter silence did not help much. What had happened, where was everyone? She walked to the stairs and began to descend to the cowshed.

It was empty. The car had gone, not a soul around. Had they abandoned her? She ran to the old hay bales, piled to one side of the wall and pulled away at them, sighing a huge sigh when she saw that the skis were still there. Then she walked out into the snow, another eight inches had fallen in the night, at least, or the wind had shifted it, it was hard to tell. Everything looked most beautiful, almost alien. There was no colour other than white anywhere, even the house walls were covered by snow drifts, the tree trunks smothered by ice and snow in the perpetual wind. She noticed the Mercedes car tracks led off up the hill towards the village further on. What could they be doing there?

She had to wash her mouth so she chose the mountain method; scooping up snow, cramming it into her mouth and chewing it until all had gone, spitting out the resulting water. It was not perfect, but it was refreshing.

Suddenly she became aware of the sound of an engine approaching, struggling in the snow, the noise of it shattering the serene silence. Quickly pulling herself together, she ran to the trees, hiding under the first one, zipping up her suit, fastening her hood to make herself as invisible as possible. The black Mercedes came into view, snow-covered, a smashed fender on the right side, Holmes was driving! This was an extraordinary recovery.

She waited until the car had stopped and then, as Patrick and Sean got out of the car, she broke from cover and ran with a joyous heart to Holmes.

"Lord Holmes," she shouted, waving happily.

He stopped, turned and with a face that showed a flicker of pleasure he smiled and stepped forward to meet her. "Cornelia," he whispered, the exhaustion written into his face. "I'm so happy," Cornelia said excitedly into his chest, "I'm so happy you're all right. I thought the doctor had poisoned you, I..."

He shook his head and wagged his finger. "You were a very foolish girl, my dear. You ignored my request to accompany Watson to London."

"But..."

Holmes' eyes stared at her and he broke into a smile. "But it is what I myself would have done if your life was endangered. I thank you from the bottom of my heart." His eyes searched her own, the honesty in their exchanged looks was revealing, it was the look equals give one another, a mutual respect and unspoken admiration.

Holmes would never be the one to waste time on pleasantries. It was enough that both of them were alive, to know that if she had been captured it would have been her thank you, he would have had to endure.

"You are well?" she asked with concern. "Where's the doctor?"

"I am very well, fired with enthusiasm for the chase and the doctor is on a long journey across the snowfields to help deliver a child. Something altogether more rewarding spiritually than trying to soften me up for the Berlin torturers."

"Breakfast," Patrick called from within the house, "one egg or two, Miss Cornelia?"

"Eggs?" she laughed happily, stepping back into the snow to look at Sherlock Holmes. He really did look quite well again, it was remarkable.

"They are a donation from a Watson fan. Seems a farmer in this village has read everyone of Watson's adventures. He donated breakfast and provision for yourself and Patrick. We shall get our food the normal way from Inns and market stalls."

Cornelia frowned. "Patrick and I?" Her voice sounded distant, small. There was a real fear in her voice, her happiness dissolved.

"Do not be afraid," Holmes told her, stretching out his hand. "I cannot shrink from danger, I'm no stranger to it now and nor are you. The rules have changed my dear, something has come up that cannot be ignored."

She frowned, remaining silent.

"Come on. I shall explain over breakfast."

She followed reluctantly, knowing that the real heart that would break would be Watson's. She herself felt quite sick at the thought of Holmes staying in Germany.

"It is an odd thing," Holmes remarked, as he sat down to plate of fried eggs and bacon on rye bread piled high in chunks underneath it, the coffee on the boil atop of a hastily made fire at the back of the cowshed. "I feel more rested than I have felt in many months, even with my cracked rib."

"Cracked rib?" Cornelia asked, most concerned.

"It is nothing, the doctor has bound my rib cage and I'm in no immediate danger. No, what is worrying me is far more dangerous than cracked ribs or chocolate factories with Jets in them. I could not return to London and receive a handshake from Winston, a 'well done old boy' and be forgotten for evermore. Not now I know that through your help I was spared for another purpose, a higher calling."

Cornelia ate her eggs, staring at the silent faces of Sean and Patrick, wondering what higher calling? Had they converted him to Catholicism between midnight and breakfast? Was this some sinister move by the Pope and the cohorts of Mussolini's fascists to abduct Sherlock Holmes by spiritual intervention? She sat quiet as a mouse, searching Holmes' radiant face. His new mission providing him with an internal vigour, the benign fusion of purpose and challenge had spread a glow over his ageing face, swept away the years that had resolutely sat there the day before.

"In a word," Holmes continued, accepting a good cup of coffee from the camp fire chef, Patrick O'Reilly. "The word is, Moriarty."

"Moriarty," the two Irishmen intoned, leaving only Cornelia with it unsaid upon her lips.

"Moriarty?" she asked, at last, knowing Sean hated the man, whoever he was.

"This very morning Sean here and myself will be taking ourselves to Hamburg. This is where these terrible evil broadcasts emanate and if it is the last thing we do, we shall remove this scourge from upon the earth forever. There shall be no more broadcasts by traitors, no more talk of a Free Europe whilst Adolf Hitler lives. Moriarty will regret his decision to throw his lot in with the Nazis."

"We go together," Sean emphasised. "It is my duty as well as my intention to kill this traitor, this double traitor. Moriarty will speak no more after we have had a word with him. I'm willing to bet a thousand bicycles that this will be so."

Cornelia could tell by the look on Holmes' face that this was so, that nothing she could say would change his mind.

"We shall obtain some bicycles in Rastatt," Holmes told her, "and then we shall move stealthily, dressed as common workers, heading north to Hamburg."

"But Lord Holmes, you are not well enough..."

He nodded, he understood her concern. "The main part of the journey will be made by train, our bicycles on board."

She nodded, this made sense, but Lord Holmes was terribly fragile for that sort of thing. "Your health, your eyes, I worry so."

Holmes held up his hand. "Don't try to oppose this, young Cornelia. At home in England I would be useless, decorated, a stuffed peacock, but useless, they will not risk me again. Already they think me captured. Moriarty's lies continue, they still advertise my forthcoming trial, so confident are they of finding me. All England will know I have been captured, but Watson will be there, you and he will set them right as to what we have achieved. To go back now would make me a hero, but I should not be at peace with myself until Moriarty has perished for once and for all.

"When I left Franken-Höhe and the Reichenbach Falls, I was content to believe Moriarty dead, but I see now he merely stayed in Germany, fertile ground indeed for his kind of evil poison. His students are no doubt the elite of the SS by now. Perhaps he had a hand in the forming of the Reich's Fuhrer as well. Everything is possible with Moriarty. Evil is drawn to evil!"

Cornelia realised she would have to accept this situation, she had little choice. Sad, and wondering how Watson would take all this, she ate her breakfast, drank her coffee in quiet contemplation.

"You will be looked after by Patrick, who has to get back to his bicycles in any case. He'll be glad of your help in the riding of one to a place of safety." Sean told her, standing up, stretching his stiff body.

Cornelia nodded, she could not say anything, she knew she would cry if another thing was said to her. Luckily they turned to making plans and talking about money and winter clothes, leaving her to tend to the breakfast things and waxing the skis for the long journey back to France.

At ten o'clock that very morning, Sherlock Holmes, attired in the warmest clothes and an enormous fur hat was sat in the Mercedes with Sean McCully at the wheel.

"We shall drive to the fork and head for the cross country roads around to Rastatt, wish us luck Cornelia."

She nodded her head. "God speed," she whispered, putting her head through the car window and kissing Holmes on the cheek.

Holmes looked at her with a bashful expression, then took out a letter from his jacket pocket. "For Watson," he said, "it explains everything."

Sean started up the engine, which soon filled the cowshed with noxious fumes. Holmes took something else out of his pocket and pressed it into

Cornelia's hands; his eyes stern, ungiving, trying hard to will away all emotion. He disliked parting and from Cornelia he disliked parting most of all. "Goodbye," he said, turning away from her, "Goodbye".

That was it. Sean let in the clutch and they were away. Holmes did not even look back once to watch a painfully distraught Cornelia standing alone in the snow, staring after the car long after it had disappeared from view. The throb of the engine had diminished to nothing.

Patrick appeared at her side of the house with skis and an old kit bag – filled with provisions for their journey.

"Why did they go during the day?" she asked, puzzled by their sudden departure.

"Radio up at the next farmhouse said a storm expected tonight. We have to get over the mountain. They want to get to town and find some disguises. There's some logic to driving about in a German staff car during the day – no one notices the expected, that's what his Lordship said anyway. They'd expect them to skulk about at night, but to go out brazenly in daylight, there's a greater chance of success."

She nodded, it sounded like Holmes' logic to her and she walked over to her skis sticking up in the snow. She remembered the gift he had given her and she looked into her hand, finding a small gold locket there with the inscription Sherlock Holmes engraved upon it.

She opened it and inside was a lock of her hair entwined with a lock of his own white hair. Her own and Holmes' together. It was the most perfect of gifts, she would treasure it forever. Brushing a lone tear from her cheek, she asked, "If there's a storm?"

"We'll be ahead of it once we are over the mountain. I'm more worried about the bicycles. Too long in this sort of weather and the vital parts will rust."

It was typical, Cornelia thought, that an Irishman should worry about his rusty vital parts before giving thought to a woman, but she put up with it. Holmes had gone, she had a letter to deliver to Watson, a war ahead of her, the battle had only just begun. Perhaps Churchill would have something else for her to do when they got back. Surely they would not expect her to go back to Wales and tend her father's rose garden. The Hainsleys had always served their nation in time of trouble, this Hainsley was no exception.

"Ready?" Patrick asked with a grin. "It's a climb, but there'll be some champion stuff the other side."

"Then be prepared to give up the crown, Patrick, I'll out ski you any day."

"Never," he swore, "never." Then he laughed, setting up off the slopes before her. "Come along, we haven't got all day."

16

Valediction

Watson read the letter again with shaking hands. Winston Churchill took his cigar out of his mouth and frowned, staring at the young Cornelia, her lips peeling from frostbite, her skin wonderfully tanned from the sunny slopes of France. It was the First Lord's personal office; a confusion of maps, leather armchairs and cigar smoke. He looked exhausted, worn out like some hallway carpet. Things were clearly not going well for him, assorted messages shouted in large type the latest shipping tonnage sunk by the Germans.

"And Holmes went to Hamburg?" Churchill asked for the third time. "After this Moriarty?"

Cornelia nodded. She had told the story ten times already and was as surprised as Watson to find London not in the least receptive to their revelations. The amazingly high resolution photographs that Watson had brought back and had quickly processed were merely glanced at. That was all. England had apparently discounted that any such thing as a Messerschmitt Jet bomber could fly, refused to consider molasses as a fuel source, but found the chocolate scheme of interest, if only from a counter propaganda point of view, but overall, the War Cabinet had been lukewarm.

The news of Holmes' capture had been headlines in all the papers and effectively denied. A carefully and cleverly arranged telegram from Bermuda telling the Daily Express that he was on holiday there and was not likely to visit Germany; a good countermeasure to the newly released picture of him, Dr Watson and Cornelia attending the Wagner evening in Nürnberg. It was clearly German black propaganda. No Englishman would visit Germany in a time of war. The popular press showed far more interest than the War Cabinet, but it was hardly satisfactory and Watson was mightily disappointed, even if they had been promised decorations in the next Honours list.

Watson and Churchill were disappointed Holmes had elected to remain in Germany to chase Moriarty. British Intelligence had no record of this individual being in Hamburg running an anti-British campaign, but then, they had no record of Herr Flohn, or his factories. Things were sadly much amiss. The War Cabinet was, in short, not impressed, though Churchill was very pleased with the results on a personal level.

London as a whole was far more interested in London, ration plans, bureaucracy, new secrets, something about a new method of seeing in the dark, to be worried about chocolates or jets; neither of which seemed strategically important in late January 1940. In fact, the Prime Minister was heard to have said that, "Sherlock Holmes had missed the bus, it was time he retired, let someone else have a go."

Mr Churchill could fume and rant, but he could not sway them, gaining satisfaction only from the sure knowledge that his time would come.

Meanwhile, it was a bitter pill for Watson and Cornelia to swallow. Just 'thanks for the effort' and a decoration. The DFC was all very nice, but the lack of enthusiasm from all sides detracted from the lustre of it.

Churchill was embarrassed, anyone could see that and knowing he looked a little foolish, if not downright rude, he tried for an explanation.

"I've had my confidence in you both all along. Of course, it is a tragedy that Holmes isn't here. It would make things so much easier if he was, but damn the others, their ignorance will be their folly. I'm damn proud of you both. If it had been anyone else we'd have had half the British armed forces in South America by now. You saved the day Dr Watson, Cornelia. You wait, maybe not immediately, but when my turn comes, as it must, I'll see that you get recognition, everything you deserve. I'm hamstrung now y'see, but those dunderheads in Number 10 and 11 will soon see what's what. The Germans will come to us – and soon."

He beamed at them, shrugging a little as he relit his cold cigar. "Don't let Holmes disappear forever Miss Cornelia. Britain needs him here, we can't win this war without him. We are like the country of the blind, only our one-eyed king is away on business. Get him back before the gates shut on Europe forever, Dr Watson."

Cornelia set Churchill's rather fat cat Nelson down and sighed, momentarily thinking of another cat in Germany that had saved her life. She went around to Watson' bathchair, a welcome old friend and said, "Mr Churchill, thank you for seeing us. Dr Watson here was hurt you'd not wanted to see him when he returned. Two weeks is quite a time to wait, but I'm glad you've heard our story now. I'm sure when Lord Holmes returns he will tell you more, he is in good hands."

"Oh, I'm sure, I'm sure, Miss Hainsley. I shall be thinking of something for you to do, soon as I can my dear. How would Washington suit you?" He held up his huge pink hands. "I make no promises, but there is a crying need for an intelligent woman like yourself over there trying to persuade the Americans to come in on our side. You could be quite an asset."

"Rather," Watson enthused, his voice a slur. He had not quite recovered from the removal of Sherlock Holmes from his life. 221b was fast becoming a shrine, for he had let nothing be disturbed or dusted. Holmes might come back any moment, he was convinced of it.

Churchill saw them to his door, his manner grave, his problems immense. He took Watson's hand again. "You can be sure that when the time comes for our answer to Germany, your chocolate factories will be bombed first, Dr Watson, that is a promise. Between you and me, the situation must change, stronger men must take charge."

Watson nodded. "Thank you, thank you. You are most kind. Sherlock Holmes will be back Winston, don't you worry."

Churchill nodded. "Soon I hope, but do not be disappointed by your response here, your information will bear fruit in time. I promise you that. The curse of the Iron Cross will defeat them in the end. We shall crush our enemies, of that I'm certain. We succeeded before."

Cornelia looked at the First Lord, she saw that he meant every word.

She pushed Watson out into the corridor and looked back only briefly. Churchill stood at the door relighting his cigar, staring after them, sending out a wave to her before going back to his desk, calling out for his secretary. John Colville came in promptly, hovering nervously beside the desk.

"I want all the information we have on Moriarty, Colville, and send two letters of thank you from me, one to Sir John Watson and one to Miss Cornelia Hainsley. Then get these photographs of their's over to Naval Intelligence. I don't care what the Cabinet says, we need someone working on Jet engines, and soon. Find that Whittle chap Dr Watson mentioned, I believe he's with the RAF. The Boché can't get away with this. Mrs Hall? Where is the woman. I want to write a letter."

Moribund and despondent, Watson and Cornelia sat down in a cold St James Park, the trees bare, the wind cold. There was no snow, but they would have preferred it if there was, it might have lightened their spirits. It was no use, they felt hard done by indeed. London just had not welcomed them with any enthusiasm. Indeed, poor Watson had been left digging his heels for those two weeks before being invited to report in along with Cornelia, who had returned only the day before, anxious to hear the results. She had been astonished and bitterly disappointed to find they had been totally ignored. Their offering had been studied by 'experts' but not a question asked of them, not a piffeling word. No way to win a war.

Watson sat silent in his bathchair staring at a man reading *The Times*. Cornelia sat reading Holmes' letter.

My dear Watson,
I entrust this letter to you with the only person I know who would have the guts to deliver it intact. If Cornelia were a man, Watson, she would outshine us all, as it is, she has redeemed the weaker sex in my eyes and now I can at last perceive of an age when they will be considered equals. Look after her well, Watson, see to it she is recognised for her heroics and her loyalty to us both.
For your records, for I know you are keen to know what happened. I now relate the events following the night of the Karlsruhe dinner...

"Cornelia?" Watson asked suddenly, staring hard at the two men reading *The Times* opposite them now. Two identically dressed men, same shabby raincoat, the paper an odd coincidence, or not?

"Watch these two," Watson muttered, "instincts tell me there's something afoot..."

Cornelia watched keenly. Everyone knew London was awash with spies, fifth columnists and the like. No eyes were more perfectly trained to spot them than their own, unless it was Holmes himself and she expected no word from him for a while, it was not his habit to communicate regularly.

Watson observed the men swop newspapers, the one who had waited longest leaving immediately, going west, the other sitting a moment longer, lighting a cigarette before abandoning his newspaper to a litter bin and walking off towards Birdcage Walk.

"Quickly, Cornelia," Watson urged, "get that paper out of the bin and let's follow the fellow. Something is going on, I'm sure of it."

She had the discarded paper in a trice. Watson was busy wheeling himself along already and she had to hurry to catch up and push with quite an effort to catch the man up ahead in his grey raincoat. "I think we are headed for woods," Watson told her, "don't lose track of him. Push harder, we're losing him."

They just managed to keep the man in sight. Cornelia strained to the limit.

She could see they were in the lonely part of the park now.

"Slow down," Watson urged, as the man stopped and waited for them to pass, ignoring such an old man and his plainly dressed assistant with the funny short hair. He stepped off the pathway and walked into a thicket of bushes and trees, emerging quickly and walking back the way he had come, without his newspaper. They waited at a distance, observing closely.

"Now we must search," Watson declared, "before anyone comes to claim that paper."

Cornelia spun him around and together they left the pathway, plunging into the trees and bushes just where the man had left them.

It took as long as five minutes, but Cornelia, standing at the very top of the bathchair poked her head into a squirrel hole and there she discovered the copy of *The Times*.

"I'm sorry Mr Squirrel, but there has been some kind of mistake, you were supposed to get the *Daily Mail*."

Watson smiled at her as she came down with the paper. "Here put the other in its place," he told her and she did just that, thinking it an excellent idea.

"Now let's away to some hiding place to see who comes to fetch this. I'll watch, you call up Mr Churchill immediately, tell him what has transpired, we need help if we are to follow the spies."

Cornelia had him hidden in some bushes across from the path where he could get a good view of who came and went. "What is it they are hiding?" she asked.

Watson was busy unwrapping the paper and there on page four lay a document headed TOP SECRET – FOR BSC EYES ONLY. It was a photographic reproduction of two typed sheets with diagrams. RADIO DETECTION AND RANGING – RADAR. A blueprint, no less.

Cornelia knew it must be very important. It looked as though Holmes had been right all along, there was a mole, a spy working in the War Office!

"I'll call Mr Churchill right away," she said, "stay here Dr Watson. Do not attempt to follow anyone on your own. I will have help here in no time."

Watson was left in the bushes looking at the blueprint, then at *The Times* which looked infinitely more interesting to him.

Suddenly something moved in the bushes causing his heart to leap.

It was only a dog, but it alerted him to the danger of his position and soon the blueprint and newspaper were safely installed in a secret compartment in his bathchair, (where he used to hide Holmes' tobacco). He moved the bath-chair as best he could towards a park bench with a good view of the tree. He could wait, waiting was something he knew a great deal about, but slowly and surely he began to nod off.

The next thing he remembered was hearing Cornelia's feet running down the path, arriving out of breath, exhausted by a long run, shaking him awake.

It was five o'clock already and darkness had descended. It was terribly cold, every joint in his body was stiff and unworkable.

"I'm sorry Dr Watson, I'm sorry," Cornelia said, her voice downcast, her cheeks tearstained. "I tried everyone I could think of, but it's Friday, everyone went home at four o'clock. There's nothing we can do."

Watson felt a rising anger, it was nonsense, why in his day... "Did anyone come?" Cornelia asked, knowing full well Watson had been soundly asleep when she had returned. His silence betrayed his guilt. She felt she must see for herself and quickly she wheeled him over the path back into the bushes and once again she stood on the bath-chair reaching a hand down into the squirrel hole. She was astonished to discover nothing there.

"It's gone. The paper has gone, Dr Watson."

"Oh curse these tired eyes, this weak body. Cornelia please forgive me. I saw nothing, heard nothing. Holmes would disown me. I am as useless as I feel."

She climbed down and kissed Watson's head. "You're forgiven, of course you're forgiven. We have the blueprints, they do not. We will return them Monday. There has been no harm done, Dr Watson, and what could we have done with the villain? We could not give chase, your engine wouldn't keep up with any getaway car. Be happy we foiled them at the very start."

"Yes," Watson agreed, taking heart from her stirring words, "We have tried our best. Come my dear, let us return to Baker Street. Mrs Hudson will be moaning we are late for tea."

In silence Cornelia pulled Watson out of the bushes once more, both of them feeling very sad, though pleased they had achieved something. Cornelia was wondering how important this RADAR was, whether it really would make any difference if the Wehrmacht got hold of it. Whitehall certainly did not seem to keep a strong hold of their secrets. It also seemed to her that radio played a big part in modern warfare.

"If only Holmes were here," Watson muttered as they emerged onto Piccadilly.

"He'll come back, I'm sure he will, he won't abandon you. Once he has sorted out Moriarty..."

Watson sighed, pulling the engine cord on his re-tuned velocette, coaxing it into life as it hesitated at first, then with a loud explosion burst into life, saved by quick action from Cornelia who throttled it down.

"You don't understand," Watson called out to her. "Once he's got Moriarty into his system, he'll stick to it for days. He's obsessed with the man. It's a calamity, Cornelia. England needs him now. How could he desert us at a time like this?"

"He hasn't deserted us," she told him, climbing on the back of the bath-chair. "I'm sure we will hear from him soon." Though she did not believe her own words.

"Oh I hope so. Churchill is a good man, but the rest of 'em, they need Holmes to give them a good talking too. Churchill believed us about Norway, but no one understands the seriousness of the situation. It's just like the First World War, Cornelia. Kitchener squandered millions of lives, felt nothing for the pain and suffering in his foul trenches. The same could happen again unless men of action take over."

"I'm sure that kind of slaughter couldn't happen again," Cornelia remarked. "No one would allow that."

Watson turned to look at her. "That's just the problem, my dear. At the beginning of a war everyone is so optimistic. Just wait until the Boché fly their Jet planes over London, it will soon change their tune. Now, let's hope there's jelly for tea."

Without further ado, Watson let in the clutch and the bath-chair roared away towards Hyde Park Corner, Cornelia clinging on for dear life, her coat streaming away in the wind behind her.

Twenty minutes later, a carefully negotiated bath-chair was parked outside 221b Baker Street and one exhausted Dr Watson, knight of the realm, entertained Miss Cornelia to a tea of haddock and poached eggs accompanied by an excellent bottle of French wine from L'Aude country.

"Are we safe?" Cornelia asked, "might not people be looking for us and these blueprints? We might have been followed, we could be in danger ourselves."

Watson considered the problem, but dismissed it with a wave of his hand. "We are safe, I'm sure of it. I feel ashamed we cannot pursue this investigation further. Holmes would be working on it, he would be half way to solving it by now. He's the centre forward you see. I've always just been a goalkeeper."

Cornelia could see Watson was not going to survive well without Holmes. The entire room was filled with Holmes memorabilia, awaiting the detective's return. They had lived together too long. Watson did not really exist without Holmes. "Goalkeepers are vital too Dr Watson. They keep the other side from scoring goals."

She got up from the table and wandered over to the windows, peeking through the curtains at the dark street below. She felt so sorry for Watson, but would Holmes return? All of Germany sought him. Could he pursue Moriarty to the end of his days? Watson would not last long in this isolation.

Suddenly she saw a shadow, a bicycle pulled over in the street outside the house. She looked back at Watson pouring himself another glass of wine. Who could this be? Had they been followed? Were the plans safely hidden?

Mrs Hudson's bell rang and in a moment they could hear voices below.

"Who could that be?" Watson asked, a certain familiar optimism in his voice.

"It won't be Lord Holmes, Dr Watson. He wouldn't need to ring the doorbell, nor come on a bicycle."

"Oh," he answered crestfallen, "quite, of course, of course."

But soon the creaking bones of an aged Mrs Hudson were heard on the stairs and Cornelia quickly made her way to the door, meeting Mrs Hudson half way, the old woman straining at every step.

"Thank you for tea, Mrs Hudson. Who was at the door?"

"A telegram for Dr Watson, Miss Cornelia. Did he eat all his supper? He's been off his food of late."

"Every bit, here let me take the telegram, thank you for bringing it up."

Happy to relinquish it, Mrs Hudson gave up the telegram and Cornelia quickly made her way back to Watson, handing it over to him.

"You open it," he told her, "I can't find my glasses."

She tore open the envelope and unfolded the message inside. "It's from Paris. It's in French. I shall translate it."

MORIARTY IN BERLIN OUT OF REACH STOP BRITISH SECRETS ON SALE HAMBURG STOP WE MUST STOP LEAK STOP ARRIVE 09.20 VICTORIA SATURDAY STOP BOTH MEET ME STOP INFORM W.C
STOP HOLMES STOP

Watson was almost in tears he was so happy. "Cornelia he is coming back, he's not lost." And then a more serious expression came over him. "Send a telegram to the Admiralty, to Winston…"

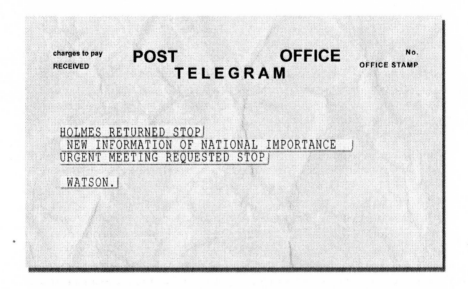

"By crikey, Cornelia. We'll get this war organised yet. I think this calls for a brandy, what? We're not finished by a long chalk, my gel. We will show them what's what, eh?"

Cornelia just frowned, as she wrote out the telegram, suddenly thinking about the precarious cross channel ferry and the U-boats on the lookout for easy prey. She would pray this night, pray hard for Holmes' return.

Postscript

Winston Churchill became Prime Minister on 12th May 1940 and only hours after the event wrote this personal note in his diary.

It could be said that one war is already won, another begins, even though we still await the first test in the ring. But all thanks to Lord Sherlock Holmes, Sir John Watson and the courageous Miss Cornelia Hainsley, England's most secret device has been preserved for the home shores. Better still, the rumours of an invincible German army marching on some wonder drug that the Nazis' propaganda would have us believe in, was proven, by Holmes, to be absolutely untrue. Remarkably real evidence of Adolf Hitler's addictions have now proved to be absolutely true, further proof for me that the enemy we seek to destroy, no matter how long it might take, is a weak and vulnerable one. No matter how hard things will undoubtedly become, the decay has set in within the German High Command and if we can withstand their early victories, time and patience will see their self-confidence and follies with stimulants destroy them.

To my mind, without Holmes and his consorts, the war would have been over well before I came to office. By their extraordinary personal heroism, their sacrifices, the British nation remains a free nation yet. We all owe them a profound and lasting debt.

W

Authors note 1981: *Dr Laubscher changed his name to protect his identity. It is believed that he is still alive and his sons work in the chocolate industry in Brazil.*

Previous titles by Sam North

Diamonds – The Rush of '72
Lulu Press 2004. USA – ISBN 1-4116-1088-1

"This is a terrific piece of storytelling... highly recommended for lovers of the Old West and, more importantly, for all those who enjoy a good adventure story well told."

The Historical Novel Society Review

Going Indigo
Citron Press, UK

"Treading really new ground in its off-beat child's-eye black comedy."

The Independent.

Ramapo
Sphere Books, UK

"A gripping, tension filled thriller."

Mail, Hartlepool.

209 Thriller Road
St. Martin's Press, New York.

"A fine British mystery paced with whimsy and suspense."

Statesman Journal Salem Oregon.

———

Written as Marcel d'Agneau:
Eeny, Meeny, Miny, Mole
Arrow Books, UK

"Imitation of such quality zaniness is the sincerest form of flattery"

Christopher Wordsworth – *The Observer*

Also available from Lulu Press by Sam North

Diamonds – The Rush of '72 – ISBN 1-4116-1088-1

Diamonds – The Rush of '72 is the true adventure set in the American West history. It is about greed, treachery and bravado. Two prospectors John Slack and Philip Arnold arrive penniless and near starving in San Francisco to deposit raw 'American' diamonds in the Bank of California, it causes quite a stir. As rumours fly about fabulous riches to be made they try to hang on to the biggest diamond find since Kimberley and keep the claim secret. They attract the attention of California's biggest banker William Ralston and New York finest investors, including Horace Greeley, only to discover that these fine gentlemen intend to cheat them. But Slack and Arnold are wily men, hardened by years on the mountains. They won't be taken easily. What begins as a trickle in the Colorado mountains would grow into the great rush of 1872.

> 'This historical mining is an elegant and convincing novel, a novel of comic moments and dark overtones.'
>
> George Olden – *Falmouth Review*

> 'This is a terrific piece of storytelling highly recommended for lovers of the Old West and, more importantly, for all those who enjoy a good adventure story well told'.
>
> Chris Lean – *Historical Novel Society Review*

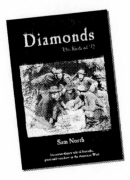

Sample and buy *Diamonds – The Rush of '72* now
go to:
www.books.lulu.com/content/68464

Acknowledgements

A special thanks to Carine 'Kit' Thomas for all her patience and sterling efforts in designing this book, also to Dominic Robson whose advice and help was invaluable. Thanks to all those who encouraged me to bring back Holmes – in particular Beverly & Geoff Howard, Sara Towe, Jane Robson, Stuart Olesker, Dominic Symonds, George Burrows, Gemma 'Roxy' Williams, Christine Taylor and not least to Koko for all those long theraputic walks in Kitsilano, B.C.